"*Defy the Thunder* ... s your interest from ... ..., adventure, intrigue, and romance. Kay gets better with each book! I love her flowing and descriptive style. Christian is a wonderful hero! (He's strong, mature, sensitive, and intelligent.) It is a fast, easy, and very enjoyable read. A marvelous coming-of-age for the heroine."

—*New York Times* bestselling author
Janelle Taylor

A THREAT . . . OR A PROMISE?

"I don't intend to kill you, Miss Pembrooke," he whispered as he slid one arm around her waist and slowly pulled her delicate form against his body. "All I want is to finish what we started back there in my room at the inn."

Alexandra could feel every inch of his powerful frame molded against her, how the steely strength of his arm held her imprisoned, and wherever her body touched his, it seemed a thousand tiny needles pierced her flesh. She also sensed by the way he was lowering his head that he was about to kiss her, and that if she let him, he wouldn't stop there . . . she summoned the courage to scream just as his warm breath fell against her lips.

"But not now," he murmured, a coldness frosting the edges of his words and turning the paleness of his eyes a dark, flinty blue. "Not here . . ."

DEFY THE THUNDER

KAY McMAHON

JOVE BOOKS, NEW YORK

DEFY THE THUNDER

A Jove Book / published by arrangement with
the author

PRINTING HISTORY
Jove edition / January 1991

ISBN: 0-515-10489-2

Jove Books are published by The Berkley Publishing Group,
200 Madison Avenue, New York, New York 10016.
The name "JOVE" and the "J" logo
are trademarks belonging to Jove Publications, Inc.

PRINTED IN THE UNITED STATES OF AMERICA

10 9 8 7 6 5 4 3 2 1

To my wonderful new friend in Sydney, Australia,
Val Sherriff

··⊰[Chapter One]⊱··

September 30, 1825, Cornwall County, England

THE FURY OF THE TEMPEST HAD DIED, BUT THE DISTANT RUMble of thunder echoed in the clouds and an occasional flash of white light still pierced the black sky beyond the treetops in the east. The fresh aroma of sweet rain filled the air and gave proof to the violence of the storm. Yet with its passing, a quiet peacefulness had settled over the countryside while the twilight hours of another day dispassionately claimed the land.

Along the muddied road that wound its way to the coast, a single carriage passed through the night, its high wheels slinging droplets of brown water in their wake as the rig hurried toward its destination. Inside, the couple, who rode facing each other on opposite seats, appeared to be unaware of each other's presence as they watched the scenery pass by through different windows.

A deep, troubled frown scored Hardin Wittemore's pale brow. He cared a great deal for Alexandra Pembrooke, the beautiful brunette with strikingly unusual green eyes who shared the carriage with him, but he loved life more. His gambling and taste for danger had pulled him into a whirlpool of debt, and the only solution he could find was to do exactly as he'd been told. He had been promised that Alexandra would not be harmed and that she would never learn the real reason he had brought her along with him, but the underlying knowledge that he had made a trade with a ruthless criminal did little to ease his worry. Garrett Ambrose stole, cheated, and lied every day of his life. Why would the man make an exception in his case? Hardin wondered. Squirming uneasily on the thick leather seat, he wished there had been some way for him to

1

hide a pistol under his frock coat. He and Alexandra would be outnumbered, but a gun would buy her enough time to get safely away should something go wrong, which, he feared, was a distinct possibility.

A soft smile curved Alexandra's mouth and an excited glow warmed her jade-green eyes. They were nearing the inn where Hardin had guaranteed her they would meet the famed Garrett Ambrose, smuggler, pirate, and outlaw. Tales of the man's adventures had been a topic of conversation at every social function she had ever attended, and at the numerous meetings held by her father behind closed study doors as well. The wealthy of Plymouth and the surrounding area feared him. Alexandra fantasized about him.

Being the daughter of a very rich and influential man, Alexandra had never wanted for anything and had long ago grown tired of her uneventful life-style. She thrived on the excitement of defying her father at every turn and, what's more, of keeping her adventures a secret from him. Tonight would be the supreme accomplishment for her, as she would be doing something her father could only dream about: standing face to face with the most wanted criminal in all of England. As a representative of the king, her father had been trying for years to build enough solid evidence against Garrett Ambrose to have him brought to trial, and he hadn't even come close. Only recently had he resorted to an experimental method: the infiltration of some of his own men into Ambrose's gang as spies. But even that had failed, as Ambrose suspected everyone.

The smile on Alexandra's lips grew wider. No doubt Garrett Ambrose would be suspicious of her, too. Especially since she was the daughter of Sir Wallis Pembrooke, the head of a newly formed organization designed to bring about his end. But that was a part of the thrill for Alexandra. She invited the danger. She longed for it. She welcomed it, and Hardin Wittemore, in his stumbling way, had supplied the means for her to experience the most stimulating moment of her life.

Lowering her gaze from the window, she covertly peeked over at the young man with whom she fashioned herself in love. Hardin was only a couple of years older than she, came from a well-known, aristocratic family, loved to gamble, and to take chances no other man his age ever dared. That alone was what drew her to him. Tall, handsome, and refined, he complemented Alexandra's remarkable beauty whenever the two of them were seen together at one of society's more prominent functions. Every available young woman envied Alexandra, and she knew it. They assumed she had everything. What they weren't aware of, however, was how lonely she was.

"Hardin," she said upon seeing his troubled expression, "is something bothering you?"

Hardin stiffened and stared out the window, as though something on the horizon outside had caught his interest. He hadn't meant for her to notice his uneasiness. "No," he replied simply, hoping she'd be satisfied. He had never been very good at lying . . . especially to Alexandra.

"Then why are you frowning?" she baited with a vague, playful smile.

His scowl deepened. "I wasn't aware that I was," he answered, his eyes still trained on an imaginary object in the distance. Her soft laughter jerked his attention to her before he could catch himself.

"You're not nervous, are you?" she asked.

Hardin shook his head and stared outside again. "Why should I be? I've told you that this isn't the first time I've met with the man." He squared his shoulders and raised his jaw slightly. "Where did you think I got the silk for that gown you're wearing? You won't find anything like it in the shops at Plymouth or even in London."

Unconsciously, Alexandra ran her fingertips along the smooth fabric covering her thigh. Hardin had told her that he had chosen its color because it had reminded him of her eyes, and indeed it did. The jade-green, Grecian-style gown with its short puffed sleeves and low square neckline accentuated her bosom and made her feel deliciously scandalous. Above-the-elbow-length white gloves, clocked stockings, and pumps with low heels in the same shade of green completed her attire. She had swept her hair on top of her head, secured the heavy mass with pearl-tipped pins, then covered it all with a huge scoop bonnet adorned with green plumes and satin ribbons. Only a swirl of dark brown curls showed from beneath the brim, lying provocatively against her smooth brow. A slight blush colored her cheeks and a touch of rouge accentuated her mouth. Around her throat she wore an emerald necklace that had belonged to her mother, and on the seat next to her lay her cashmere shawl.

"Then why are you nervous?" she asked again, certain that he was. "You told Mr. Ambrose that all I wanted was first choice of the fabrics he'd brought in from France, didn't you? He believed you, didn't he?" She laughed lightly and looked out the window again. "He certainly can't think I've come to spy on him. I'd be the last person he'd have to worry about."

Hardin closed his eyes and gave an inward sigh. If it were up to Alexandra, she'd discard her fancy clothes for a pair of men's trousers and a shirt, and join Ambrose's band of roughnecks out of pure spite for her father. Hardin knew she was no threat to the outlaw, but he also knew Ambrose had no reason to believe such a claim. If Hardin had as much at stake as Ambrose, he'd be doubtful too. Deciding to make a second effort at cautioning his careless companion, he drew in a deep breath and exhaled quietly.

"Garrett Ambrose isn't someone to take lightly, Alexandra. You know that, don't you?" he asked, continuing to stare outside. "Your being a woman makes no difference to him. He treats everyone equally. Should you anger him, I don't believe he'd hesitate even a second before striking you, and I'd be powerless to stop him. He's never alone. So, please, don't say anything foolish. And for God's sake don't flirt with him."

"Flirting is half the fun, Hardin," she playfully objected, her green eyes sparkling with devilment as she studied his profile and waited for his reaction, which wasn't long in coming.

"I mean it, Alexandra," he growled, his jaw tight as he turned his head to look her squarely in the eye. "Garrett Ambrose is no gentleman. He'll take your sweet words and fluttering lashes as encouragement to do whatever he pleases . . . with your approval. Then when you protest and cry foul, he'll only laugh and have his way with you, while *I'm* forced to stand back and watch . . . at gunpoint." He scowled at her and looked out the window again. "This isn't a parlor game, Alexandra. These men are heartless. I think it fair to say they'd murder their own mothers to have what they wanted."

Hardin always preached at her whenever they were about to do something daring. Alexandra had grown to expect it. But there was something in his lecture just now that hinted of fear, and she couldn't quite pin down what it was. The smile disappeared from her lips, and she settled back in the plush leather seat to study the strong line of Hardin's brow and to contemplate what was causing his unease. The first thought that came to mind was jealousy, and a dark, softly arched brow lifted in speculation.

Although the gossip about Garrett Ambrose centered mostly around his cruelty toward his victims, Alexandra's female friends chose to ignore that aspect of the man's character. They preferred discussing his physical attributes. Alexandra guessed it was because the fine ladies of society foolishly thought they would never have to come face to face with Garrett Ambrose and his gang, and therefore didn't have to concern themselves with his villainous side. Instead they talked about the rumors they'd heard in regard to his handsomeness. Tall, lean, and dark, he was assumed to be of French ancestry. They ignored the manner in which he acquired his wealth and commented only on his style of dress and how they were sure he set the trend in men's fashion. Alexandra, for the most part, had listened to their commentary without offering her opinion, since she knew all she had to do to learn the truth was to ask Hardin. Yet despite her attempts not to be swayed by her friends' gossip, their influence had led her to daydream about the infamous smuggler. Of course, the idea that her own father spent every waking hour plotting ways to catch the man only added to his mystique and made her crave meeting him.

Recalling Hardin's attitude of a moment ago, she remembered her enthusiasm when pleading with him to take her to meet Garrett Ambrose and how she had unwittingly admitted she wanted to see if he truly was as handsome as everyone said he was. Hardin's reaction had been less than amused, and although she hadn't given it much thought at the time, she wondered now if he hadn't been jealous. It flattered her to believe Hardin might actually feel threatened by her interest in another man—an emotion he'd never shown before—while at the same time it had a suffocating effect on her. The most important reason she and Hardin got along so well, she felt, was simply because neither of them made any demands on the other. They were free to say or do whatever they pleased without first having to ask permission. Now, it seemed, all that might be changing.

The bright yellow orb slipping beyond the horizon stretched out long golden fingers toward the black clouds lingering in the sky overhead, as if fighting for one last hold on the earth. Alexandra viewed the struggle between night and day with cool indifference. By the time darkness prevailed, the carriage in which she rode would roll to a stop outside an inn on a bluff overlooking the sea. From there, they would be taken on foot to a secluded spot along the shoreline where they would meet a member of Ambrose's gang waiting for them in a rowboat. Their eyes would be covered to mask the direction they would take, and once they stepped on shore again, they would be put in a wagon and driven to the place where Ambrose awaited their arrival. That feature of their escapade alone promised to stir her blood and make her heart pound, but the closer she got to experiencing it, the less exciting it became. She could not dismiss the sudden change she saw in Hardin. Everything between them had been fine up until now. But if he was about to turn into the kind of man who watched her every move, she wanted nothing more to do with him. She liked her freedom and there was a strong indication he was about to compromise it.

The air in the main room of the tavern, already filled with thick cigar smoke and the pungent odor of ale, was charged with tension. The gaiety of the men who crowded the commons had quieted over the past hour, and although no one commented on a reason, Christian Page sensed something important was about to happen. Instinct also warned him that he would be in the middle of it, but that thought didn't surprise him. The truth of the matter was that he expected it, since he had been forewarned about his initiation into Garrett Ambrose's elite band of hoodlums. The uncertainty stemmed around the method the man would use and how Christian would have to prove himself.

"You'll be risking your life, Christian," Lewis Rhomberg had declared the last time they spoke, "every minute you're with him. He's still a free man because he trusts no one. If he had a brother, I doubt he'd trust *him*. Remember that. He'll always be testing you, so expect the worst . . . and expect it when it's least expected. It's what will keep you alive."

Christian had smiled at his friend's intensity but said nothing. He'd been taught that lesson long ago by a very wise old man.

"And if you can figure out how to sleep with one eye open, I suggest you do it," Rhomberg had advised. "No one has penetrated his group, Christian. No one! Not with any success, anyway. And it's my contention someone's feeding him information. That's why I've decided not to tell anyone else what you're up to. I'll be your only contact. If you get in too deep, get word to me. But, for God's sake, don't let it come to that, you hear?"

Christian hadn't answered right away, and from the grim look on his face, Rhomberg had suspected why.

"Getting yourself killed won't solve anything, my friend," Rhomberg had cautioned. "He'll never let you close enough to even pull a gun on him, let alone fire it."

"Every man has a weakness," Christian had argued. "All I have to do is find his."

A shadow fell across the table where he sat, drawing his attention to the present and reminding him that he'd gotten careless. Sang Soo had taught him that to lose one's self in thought could be deadly. Lifting his gaze, he discovered, much to his relief, that the shadow belonged to the young barmaid who had returned with the mug of ale he'd asked her to refill. Wisely electing not to voice his gratitude, he gave her a slight nod instead and covertly watched her walk away. The fifteen-year-old French girl belonged to Ambrose, or so Christian had been warned, and he didn't want the bandit to misinterpret his appreciation for interest in the child. Dominique was indeed very pretty, but far too young for Christian's taste. And he wasn't looking to satisfy his male needs. He was here to pay a debt.

Alexandra wasn't sure just when her intuition took over, but the closer they came to their destination, the more she sensed something was wrong. Perhaps it had to do with Hardin's odd behavior or the failure of the man in the rowboat to insist they wear a blindfold. In fact he hadn't even mentioned it, and that concerned Alexandra. If Garrett Ambrose wanted to keep his hideout a secret, why had his men overlooked such an important detail? Indeed, the driver of the wagon, too, had not bothered with a blindfold, and even though it was dark now, Alexandra was sure she could find her way here again if she really wanted to pay Ambrose a second visit . . . or to send an armed party to arrest him. Growing more uneasy by the moment, she glanced up at the driver, then over at Hardin as they sat on the straw-covered floor of the wagon.

"Hardin," she whispered, hoping the rattle of the wheels and the pounding hooves against the hard ground would blot out the sound of her voice from their companion. "Hardin, something's not right."

Ribbons of black and silver crossed his face as the moon fought to shine down through the trees under which they passed. "It's called an adventure, Alexandra. Danger. It's what you wanted," he replied a bit sarcastically. "You didn't really think it could be likened to a leisurely Sunday-afternoon ride around the country, did you? You wouldn't have come, otherwise."

Fearing their escort would hear them, she awkwardly moved to sit next to Hardin, oblivious of how dirty her lovely green dress was getting. "This is different," she countered. "No precautions have been taken to make sure we can't find our way here again."

Hardin shrugged one shoulder and continued to watch the road up ahead of them. "Ambrose never stays in the same place for very long. So I guess it really doesn't matter, does it?" He gave her a quick look, then glanced away again. "Besides, even if he were captured, no one would testify against him. He has too many friends. He's quite the rogue. You'd be surprised how many of your acquaintances know him personally . . . *lady* acquaintances, I mean."

"So *that's* it," she concluded with a sigh. "You're worried I might be added to his list. Really, Hardin. I never would have guessed you thought so little of me."

Taken aback by her bold assumption, he twisted around to face her. Several seconds passed while he stuttered and fumed and fought for the right answer. "That's ridiculous!" he finally exploded.

"Oh?" She raised one brow at him. "Then why haven't you been yourself tonight? All you've done since we left the house is preach about how I should behave when I'm in Garrett Ambrose's company. He won't be the first scoundrel I've met. What makes you think I'll react any differently to him?" She tugged her bonnet back into place and added, "You're not jealous, are you?"

"Jealous?" he rasped. "Most certainly not! I care a great deal for you, Alexandra. You know that. But you also know part of the reason why we enjoy each other's company is because we give each other plenty of room. Jealousy—on either side— would ruin it."

Remembering the driver, she threw a warning glance at the back of the man's head, then at Hardin as she pressed a finger to her lips. "Then perhaps you'll explain why you're so . . . unstrung," she whispered, bending close. "I've never seen you like this before. You're worrying me, Hardin, and that takes all the fun out of being scared."

"Scared," he rebuked with a sarcastic grunt. "You've never been scared a day in your life, Alexandra Pembrooke. You don't know what fear is. If you did, you wouldn't be here right now."

Alexandra wanted to agree, but she couldn't, not when the vision of her mother's bruised and broken body lying at the bottom of a cliff came to mind. Alexandra had been scared then. She had been scared she would lose her father, too. Not wishing for Hardin to see the expression on her face, she turned her head just enough to shade her eyes from the moonlight with the wide brim of her bonnet.

"And if I hadn't wanted to come, you and I wouldn't be having this conversation," she predicted, that ever-present, willful smile returning to her mouth. "You'd be sitting here with someone else."

No, he thought, regretting the weakness that had allowed him to involve her, *I wouldn't be here either. And once this is over, I'll be doing you the biggest favor I could possibly give to anyone. You and I, my fair Alexandra, will be parting company.*

The wagon lumbered around a curve and started down a steep incline, jostling Alexandra against her friend. Catching her in the crook of his arm, Hardin held her close while the two of them focused their attention on the building they could see outlined in the distance. Ashen light bathed the two-story structure, the stone face and red-tiled roof, and a yellow glow from nearly every window cut through the darkness and heralded the end of their travel and the beginning of a quest Alexandra had dreamed about for a long while. Yet deep inside her a gnawing restlessness stirred, and she shivered at its cryptic message.

"Remember, Alexandra," Hardin cautioned her quietly as he helped her to the ground and brushed pieces of straw from her skirt, "he thinks you've come to look at fabrics and for no other reason. So don't go changing his mind. He doesn't even know your name. If he did . . . " Hardin paused, stared into her beautiful green eyes for a moment, then reached up to straighten the satin bow on her bonnet she had tied under her left ear. "Well, I'm sure you can guess what he'd think if he knew who your father was."

The door to the tavern swung open behind them and light spilled out across the steps, silhouetting the man who stood in the opening. Nervous, Hardin pulled his gaze away from him, smiled weakly at Alexandra, then took her elbow to lead her inside. What he really wanted to do was to apologize to her. He wanted to assure her that if there had been some other way of squaring his debts with Garrett Ambrose, he wouldn't have agreed to bring her here. The only thing that stopped him was his confidence in Alexandra's unshakable nature. He truly believed she'd find the whole affair quite amusing once it was over, and especially after she learned her father had been duped by the very man he had vowed to see brought to trial. Yes, Alexandra would laugh about tonight, and with any kind of luck, she'd be thanking *him* for the fond memories.

"We're here to see Mr. Ambrose," Hardin announced when it appeared the man in the doorway had no intention of stepping aside. "He's expecting us. I'm Hardin Wittemore, and if you'd be so kind as to—"

The huge man suddenly turned his back on them without saying a word and retraced his steps, leaving Hardin and Alexandra alone at the door.

"I guess that means we may go in," Hardin observed in a hushed tone.

A thick gray haze hovered near the low ceiling in the commons. Through it, Alexandra could see the bright flames in the fireplace opposite her, but it gave her little feeling of warmth once she noticed the sea of faces staring back at her and Hardin. A quick glance took in some two dozen men waiting for someone to say something, and she wondered if she would hear a single word over the pounding of her heart. This had been what she wanted: the ultimate thrill, something more daring and exciting than all of her other little escapades put together, a contest that would live in her memory forever. But now as she stood at its threshold, she questioned the wisdom of her recklessness as she became acutely aware of her femininity and the numerous eyes devouring every inch of her.

"Hardin," she said without moving her lips, "is this what a fox feels like when it's cornered by the hounds?"

Before he could respond, a movement on the staircase to their left drew their eyes to the couple descending the steps. Alexandra hardly noticed the pretty young girl who preceded her partner or the somewhat cool look the child gave her, as her attention was immediately pulled to the handsome stranger following two paces behind her. Thick hair the color of a raven's wing was combed back off his dark brow and was tied with a plum-colored ribbon. A white ruffled shirt covered the expanse of his shoulders and fell open at the throat. Black trousers hugged his muscular thighs and shiny black shoes with gold buckles graced his feet. Dark brown eyes stared back into hers and a wry half smile parted his lips. If this was Garrett Ambrose, and Alexandra was fairly certain it was, he more than lived up to his reputation as being an extraordinarily striking man.

"Wittemore," she heard him call out, and she forced herself to look at Hardin. If she'd learned one thing about the art of flirtation, it was to keep the opponent guessing. Pretend disinterest, then give the man a bold look, a soft smile, or a come-hither glance. Hardin would admit her ploy had worked on him, and he held more interest in gambling than in women.

"Mr. Ambrose," he replied, and Alexandra noticed an edge to his voice. She shifted her gaze back to the man who stood before them now, and a chill touched the hair at her nape when she found Ambrose's eyes brazenly studying her.

"I trust your journey wasn't too uncomfortable, my dear," he said, ignoring Hardin as he took her hand and curled it over the bend in his arm.

With gentle insistence, Ambrose turned with her toward the large trestle table in the center of the room. The men already seated there scrambled from their chairs without instruction, but they lingered close by, and Alexandra wasn't sure if it was because they sought to protect their leader or to stare at her.

"Would you care for a glass of wine?" he asked, pulling out a chair for her.

Alexandra bobbed her head slightly as she sat down and untied the ribbon on her bonnet. A murmur raced through the crowd once she had pulled the hat from her head and a torrent of dark brown curls cascaded from beneath it. Ordinarily she would have appreciated the silent compliment, but not tonight. She wasn't exactly in the presence of kings and lords who knew how to behave themselves. Thinking that perhaps she should conduct her business and be on her way before things got out of hand, she removed her gloves, draped them over her lap, and laid the bonnet on the chair seat next to her before glancing up at Ambrose who had taken his place at the head of the table.

"Hardin tells me you have some fine silks from the Orient," she remarked as she took the goblet he held out to her.

"Oh?" he answered before sipping his wine.

She nodded. "And furs from Russia. I'd be interested in seeing them."

A strange smile curled Ambrose's mouth as he nonchalantly

inspected the glass he held up in front of him. "Is that all you're interested in seeing?" Only his dark eyes moved to look at her. "Miss Pembrooke," he finished, his voice cold and challenging.

Alexandra's heart skipped a beat, but she managed not to show her surprise. She sampled her drink, set down the glass, and casually glanced over at Hardin where he stood surrounded by four of Ambrose's men. The fear in his eyes as he stared back at her made her suspect that her introduction to Garrett Ambrose hadn't been solely her idea. It also explained why he hadn't been himself all evening.

"Yes, Mr. Ambrose," she replied quite calmly, her gaze meeting his again, "that's all I'm interested in seeing. What other reason would I have for coming here in the middle of the night, in secret and without adequate protection? I won't pretend that you don't know who my father is, but I will tell you this: his business affairs don't concern me. We never discuss them, and I can assure you that I would never willingly aid him in his endeavor to see justice done." She picked up her glass and added, "To be quite truthful, Mr. Ambrose, I find the idea of everyone living within the limits of law rather boring."

"Yes, so I've been told," he confessed, smiling and shifting his gaze momentarily on Hardin. "And it's fortunate for me that you do. You've saved me a lot of trouble."

"Trouble?" she repeated, curious. "What kind of trouble?"

He finished his drink, then set the glass on the table in front of him and leaned back comfortably in his chair. "I had already decided to use you to send a message to your father, only I wasn't quite sure how to do it. Then Hardin gave me the answer." He laughed when he saw her eyes darken, certain she had misunderstood his meaning. She had spunk, this Alexandra Pembrooke, and he liked that. What a shame it was that he'd never have the opportunity to get to know her better.

"And what answer is that?" she questioned, casually returning her glass to the table. "I'm sure it must involve money. Everything Hardin does involves money."

Ambrose smiled appreciatively. "Very astute, my dear," he said. Rising, he pulled a cheroot from the pocket of one of his men and strolled to the fireplace, where he lit the cigar with a taper he had touched to the flames. White smoke curled about his head and he squinted when some of it drifted into his eyes. "Originally, yes, it did involve money. You see, your friend here owes me a great deal of it, I'm afraid. After tonight, we'll be even."

Pulling her shawl off her shoulders, she carefully folded it and laid it on the chair beside her bonnet. "I hope you're not planning to hold me for ransom," she advised with a smile. "My father won't pay. Actually, I think he'll be glad to be rid of me."

"I doubt that, Miss Pembrooke," Ambrose denied, resting an elbow on the stone mantel. "But that's something neither of us will ever find out."

A slight frown creased her brow, and she unwittingly glanced at the row of men lining the path between her and Garrett Ambrose. They were a grubby lot with unshaven faces, wrinkled clothes, and leering grins. She quickly looked away. "I have no money of my own, sir. And I certainly wouldn't carry it with me if I did." She lifted her eyes to his again. "I'm afraid I—"

"It's quite simple," he explained. "No money will change hands. The mere fact that Wittemore brought you to me will clear his debt." He shifted his attention to one of his men and motioned toward the door with a jerk of his head.

"No!" Hardin exclaimed, yanking free of the hands that suddenly gripped his arms. "I won't leave without Alexandra. You promised that I could stay with her—"

"There's only one reason why I make promises, Mr. Wittemore," he replied, puffing on the cheroot. "To have what I want. I seldom keep them," he added, flicking an ash in the hearth. "In my line of work, it's too risky." He began to roam around the room, talking as he went. "Everything about what I do is risky. I can't trust anyone. I don't have any real friends. I'm always on the defensive, watching, listening, making sure I'm not about to get stabbed in the back. It's not a pleasant way to live, I assure you, but it's the life I've chosen. I like the danger." He paused near the bar and looked back at Alexandra. "The same as you do, my dear." He smiled and returned to his place at the head of the table. "And of course I enjoy all the luxuries I can buy." He chuckled as he refilled his wineglass. "Or should I say 'steal'?"

Alexandra glanced over at Hardin, sensing for the first time how very helpless she was. "And where do I fit into all this?"

"You're here for two reasons," Ambrose announced. "The first I've already stated: I want to send a very clear message to your father not to interfere in my business." The pleasantness disappeared from his face. "The second is to prove someone's loyalty." He fell back in his chair, his legs stretched out in front of him and one arm resting on the tabletop. "Mr. Page," he beckoned.

A murmur of voices rippled through the room as all eyes turned away from Alexandra and focused on the man sitting alone at a far table. A path opened up that gave her a clear view of him, and although he sat with his face away from her and had yet to turn his head, his profile stirred a strange sensation in her. Thick, sun-lightened blond hair emphasized the coppery tone of his complexion, his bronzed skin dark against the stark whiteness of his shirt with its billowing sleeves rolled up to his elbows. Tight-fitting brown trousers curved along his thighs and disappeared in the knee-high leather boots he wore, and he didn't have to stand up for her to know he was a man of tall, well-proportioned stature. One hand cradled a pewter mug, the other held a cheroot that he leaned forward to snuff out in a dish on the table, and as he did, she noticed the pistol lying there. Then, as though reluctant or possibly even annoyed, he turned his head to look at the man who had called his name.

Alexandra's heart seemed to stop beating when the most incredible pale blue eyes briefly touched her face then looked away. They were the color of a robin's egg, framed by long dark lashes, and for a second she wondered if she would ever grow tired of looking at them. They had a hypnotic power that left her paralyzed and unaware of how she was staring at him, at his full mouth, strong chin, perfect nose, and the frown that drew his brows together and shadowed those startling eyes. No one else in her entire life had impressed her the way this man did, and she marveled at the hot flush that seared her face and at how difficult it was for her to breathe.

"I think the time has come, Mr. Page," she heard Ambrose state, "for you to prove your worth." He nodded at Alexandra. "Kill her."

·ᐁ[Chapter Two]ᐃ·

THE COMMAND CHILLED ALEXANDRA TO THE BONE AND ALL the warm sensations that had spread through every limb turned to numb terror. She didn't want to die, not now, not like this. She hadn't lived yet. Or loved. Or *anything*! Perhaps if she reasoned with her executioner or promised him anything he wanted, he would let her live. But which of the two men should she try first? The one who gave the command or the one who would carry it out? Round, fearful eyes moved from the man called Page, who had silently risen from his chair, picked up his pistol, and started toward her, to Garrett Ambrose. There was no compassion on either face, and since Page was nothing more than Ambrose's puppet, she decided to plead with the one who pulled the strings.

"I'm afraid, Mr. Ambrose," she courageously declared, "that you've misjudged my father." She sensed how close Page was getting to her and glanced over at him, then back at Ambrose. "Killing me won't stop him." She looked at Page again, saw that he was only a few steps away, and clumsily left her chair, putting it between her and her assailant. "He'll have more reason than ever for wanting you caught and brought to trial. He'll hunt you down. Both of you," she warned, her stare locked on the cold blue eyes watching her.

"And if he doesn't, I will!" Hardin shouted, struggling to break the hold two of the men had on him. "You bastard! You swore to me she wouldn't be hurt. I never would have agreed if I'd known what you had planned."

"Of course you wouldn't have agreed, Wittemore," Ambrose lazily replied. "Don't you suppose that's why I didn't tell you

17

the truth?" He waved a hand. "Take him out of here."

"No!" Hardin cried. "Alexandra! Oh, God. I'm so sorry. Alexandra, forgive me!"

The terror in his voice only added to hers. The slamming of the door behind him as he was roughly ushered from the room made her jump. Trembling, she unwittingly looked down at the black bore of Page's gun pointed at her stomach. How could anyone be so cold-blooded? Could he actually pull the trigger? Was he really so inhuman as to do anything Ambrose told him, no matter how terrible? Feeling the tears welling up in her eyes, she lifted her gaze to him. Hardin was wrong. She'd been scared plenty of times. Her fear was what fed her excitement. But tonight . . . tonight there were no words to describe how she felt.

"I gave you an order, Page," Ambrose challenged as he sat forward in his chair and laid his folded arms on the table. "What are you waiting for?"

Alexandra closed her eyes. She couldn't bring herself to watch, to see his finger curl around the trigger and then tighten.

The eyes are the window to one's soul. The old Chinaman's words filled Christian's head. *Your enemy will know what is in your heart, your mind, by the look in your eyes. Hide your feelings, Christian. Let no one know what moves your spirit.*

It had been a hard lesson for him to learn, and Sang Soo had said it would take years to master. But Christian didn't have that long. Steeling his emotions as he stared back at Wallis Pembrooke's daughter, he realized Alexandra didn't have that long either.

"Kill her, Page," Ambrose ordered again. "Either you do it or someone else will. And you'll die right along with her."

A slow smile lifted the corners of Christian's mouth as he continued to stare at the beautiful woman trembling before him. She was courageous; he had to give her credit for that, but she was damn stupid, too. Well, perhaps her bravery would see her through this. He released the hammer with a dull click and bent his wrist, raising the muzzle of his pistol toward the ceiling. "I'm sure you had a quicker method in mind, but I'd rather take my time." He shifted his cold, hard look on Ambrose.

"With your permission, of course."

Ambrose's dark brows rose with suspicion.

"I'm assuming you don't care when she dies," Christian answered. "Only that she does."

Ambrose nodded slowly, not fully trusting the newest member to join his group.

"Then I'd like to have a little fun beforehand," Christian replied.

He smiled crookedly, cocked an eyebrow, and waited for his meaning to sink in. When he saw comprehension dawn on Ambrose's face, he took a step closer to Alexandra, who had opened her eyes to stare confusedly at him, and shot out a hand. His fingers caught the low neckline of her gown and curled deep, the tips buried in the valley between her soft breasts. She let out an ear-piercing shriek that brought a howl from the group of men and a broad, approving smile from Ambrose. Bending his elbow, Page rested the barrel of his gun on his shoulder, nodded at Ambrose, then moved toward the stairs, dragging his unwilling captive with him.

Alexandra had never been treated in such a humiliating manner in all of her young life. She forgot where she was, who filled the room, or that only a second ago she faced death at the hand of a stranger, the same man who was treating her like some harlot he'd found in a brothel. Appalled by his brazen, undignified behavior, she gritted her teeth, grabbed his wrist, and sank her nails into his flesh. He flinched, stopped, and scowled back at her as a hush came over the crowded room. A long moment passed in which Alexandra could not read a single emotion in the pale blueness of his eyes, and she soon wondered if he could feel anything at all. Then without warning he released her, but only long enough to jam the barrel of his gun in his waistband, seize her arm, and yank her toward him as he leaned forward slightly and caught her over his shoulder. She screamed as the onlookers burst into encouraging shouts and uproarious laughter as he stood and headed for the staircase again.

Christian mounted the steps two at a time, keenly aware that every person in the commons was watching and enjoying the entertainment he was providing, everyone, that was, except

Garrett Ambrose. He might have liked the barbaric fashion in which Christian made his claim on the woman, but he was far from convinced he could trust him. If Ambrose didn't order someone stationed in the room with them, Christian was sure the man would have a guard posted outside . . . to listen, if for nothing else.

At the top of the stairs, he turned and started down the hall, sensing the small party of men who followed. At the end of the corridor, he stopped outside his door and looked back at the group.

"This is as far as you go," he commanded. "The lady and I would like some privacy."

Their disappointment showed on their faces, but none of them had the mettle to argue with him. There was a quiet, stealthy ambivalence about Christian Page that had everyone wary. One moment he seemed friendly and relaxed, and the next he could give a man the kind of look that struck pure terror in his heart. No one was willing to test him, yet everyone wanted his loyalty, and if doing what he asked brought them one step closer to winning his approval, they would do it, especially since many of the men were predicting how soon it would be before Christian Page took over and Garrett Ambrose was following orders.

Christian watched the group slowly disband, all except for one: a man by the name of Benton Wall. Lewis Rhomberg had told Christian that Wall was Ambrose's closest companion and that he could be as dangerous as the leader himself. He was Ambrose's eyes and ears whenever Ambrose wasn't around, and there was never any discussion with Wall. He stood close to six and a half feet tall. He was all muscle, of little intelligence, and had a mean disposition that sent nearly everyone running. He could kill a man—and usually did—without warning and by using any method available to him: his gun, a knife, or even his bare hands. Christian had already heard the rumor that Wall had torn out a man's tongue just for lying to him, and whether any of it was fact or not, Christian knew he would have to get past Wall first before dealing with Ambrose. From the second they met, he had realized that sooner or later he and Wall would face each other. But the idea of taking on a

man of his strength, size, and temperament didn't really alarm
Christian, for he'd been taught by a master and knew how to
deal with that kind of foe, whether it required the simple strat-
egy of a physical contest or the subtlety of mental games. Right
now it would be the latter. Wall was silently telling Christian
that he intended to establish himself outside the door and then
report back to Ambrose. It was what Christian had expected
and what he wanted. Benton Wall was about to help secure
Christian's place in Ambrose's gang.

Alexandra had ceased her struggles when she heard her
captor order the men away and sensed one had defied him.
She was foolishly thinking that the man who remained would
become her savior, and as she hung draped over Page's shoulder, she pressed her hands to the small of his wide, hard back
and twisted around enough to see the one who was silently
challenging him. What she saw made her gasp. He was tall and
huge and ugly with a thick, unkempt dark beard and brooding
eyes. Hardly the sort of man she would describe as an ally.
But then, what had she honestly expected? She was dealing
with criminals. To escape one meant falling into the hands of
another. Her view of the titan changed when Page turned to
open the door, and although she couldn't be absolutely positive
about Page, she guessed his opponent was of the nature to
share. Once he finished with her, he would probably pass her
around to the other drooling simpletons downstairs. Christian
Page struck her as being selfish.

Foolish assumption made Alexandra grab for the doorjamb
as she was hauled into the room. The result was a sharp tug,
burning fingertips, and silence from the man who carried her.
The slamming of the door, followed by the key turning in the
lock, echoed in her ears and fear seized her heart. She knew
what all of it meant. And she knew she had only her own
resources to draw on if she was to survive. Yet when she felt
herself being dropped on her back in the middle of the bed,
tears sprang to her eyes. There had been a few times in her
past when she had had to fend off a man's advances, but they
had usually wanted nothing more than a kiss. Christian Page
was after more than just a kiss, if he planned to kiss her at
all.

"I-I meant what I said earlier," she declared as she twisted around and started to crawl off the bed. "My father will hunt you down!"

She screamed when she felt his fingers wrap around her ankle and yank her back, bringing a quick end to her exodus. She kicked out with her other foot but found it entrapped by a steely hold as well, and she sat up as she brought around her clenched fist, hoping to connect it with his jaw. The man seemed to have more than his share of hands when he easily thwarted her offensive by snaring her wrist and squeezing. The pain he inflicted crippled any further attack she might have had in mind, and a long while passed as they stared into each other's eyes.

Christian could see the overriding fear behind the brave front Alexandra tried to present him. He also suspected that buried deep inside her zealous nature was a more reserved persona, one that was berating her stupidity in having willfully allowed herself to walk into such a situation. By now, he guessed, she strongly regretted her foolhardy decision and would do just about anything to change its results. The price she was about to pay would be a high one, and he could only hope it would have a bearing on how she behaved in the future.

The vision of another young and beautiful face stirred his memory, and he recalled the fear he had seen in her dark brown eyes and the feeling of hopelessness he had fought to control, the sorrow that had nearly destroyed him. Min Le had been his life, his love, and she had died because of him. He would not be responsible for the death of another young woman when it was in his power to stop it.

"Do not fear me, Miss Pembrooke," he whispered, conscious of the ears listening at the door. "Hate me. Your hate is what will give you the strength to survive."

The meaning of his words was lost to her, for in that same moment he slowly pulled her to her feet. His free arm swooped around her waist, yanked her forward, and crushed her delicate body against the rock-hard leanness of his own. The shock of his actions barely registered on her brain before she felt quick fingers tugging at the fastenings on her gown, and the fear that had paralyzed her only seconds before vanished.

"No!" she hissed through clenched teeth, a tiny fist striking his shoulder. She fought with every ounce of fury she had in her. She pushed against his powerful chest, twisted within his viselike hold, and kicked his shins, none of which seemed to have any affect on him. His heart as well as his body was made of granite, and her desperate pleas for mercy fell on deaf ears.

During her struggles, the pins fell from her hair and sent a deluge of long dark brown curls cascading down her back. She didn't seem to notice or care, as her strength was quickly fading and he had already unhooked the top three buttons on her dress. The masculine scent of him, his power, and the heartless way in which he was forcing her to submit smothered the breath from her. Her mind raced, her muscles ached, but underneath it all a strange, inexplicable sensation welled up inside her. Drained, she momentarily ceased fighting and glared up into his pale blue eyes, her own shooting sparks of rage and unbridled hatred.

"You're no better than Garrett Ambrose," she spat. "In fact you're worse. *He* intended I not suffer."

Christian only smiled, then tightened his grip when a second effort by the scrappy young woman nearly won her her freedom.

"You heathen!" she rallied, pushing against his chest. "Quick and painless, that's what Ambrose wanted. But you . . . you'd rather drag it out. You're hoping for tears." She bravely raised her chin. "Well, you won't have them. I shall not cry."

"I'm glad," he answered softly, his eyes dipping to her pink mouth. "I really hate tears. They're so meaningless and of such little use."

"As are women," she countered.

His blue eyes found hers and he looked at her questioningly.

"Women are meaningless and of little use. Isn't that how you view us?" She didn't wait for him to answer. "If you thought otherwise, you and I wouldn't be here right now." She strained against his imprisoning hold. "You wouldn't be trying to prove what a big man you are."

"Don't flatter yourself, Miss Pembrooke," he replied coldly. "I have nothing to prove to you." The muscle in his jaw flexed and his nostrils flared. "Except, perhaps, to show you how foolish you've been. You shouldn't have come here. You should have stayed at home with your servants and maids, sipping lemonade and complaining about the weather. You have no place among men, except to bear their children and please their carnal needs. You played with fire, Alexandra Pembrooke, and you're about to get burned."

Alexandra opened her mouth to suck in an angry breath of denial and to hurl at him every degrading remark she could think of, when suddenly she felt his hand trap the back of her head and she knew he was about to kiss her. Everything inside her rebelled, and she lashed out at him with her elbows, fists, and feet as she tried to turn her face from his. The painful entanglement of her hair around his fingers and the unrelenting, cruel manner in which he held her prevented a retreat lest she sacrifice a few tendrils to have her way. Unwilling, she succumbed, but only halfheartedly. Instead, she clamped her teeth together, pressed her lips tightly shut, and wouldn't close her eyes. If he wanted to kiss her, it would be like kissing a stone statue. He would find no fiery vixen eagerly awaiting his embrace. *She would not give in!*

The instant his lips touched hers and his body curved along the full length of her own some of her will to fight him diminished. He kissed her hard, pressing his mouth across hers while he teased her lips with his tongue. One hand trailed down her spine while the other held her head immobile. But when the bold caress moved across her waist to her ribs then up to cup one breast, she gasped in outrage, a mistake that cost her dearly. His hot, demanding kiss grew bolder as his tongue explored the sweet crevice of her mouth and ignited a strange fire deep in the core of her being. It began as a tiny flame, a warmth foreign to her, that grew as quickly as the rising sun spreading light across the darkened land at dawn. It coursed through every limb. It made her heart beat faster and numbed her consciousness, and she wondered at its mystery as she unknowingly relaxed in his arms and breathed in the scent of him. There was a gentleness beneath his forceful insistence, a truth that belied his intent, and while she surrendered to the kiss, she questioned the revelation, its meaning. Who was this Christian Page?

Unaware, she draped her arms around his neck as he slowly lowered her to the bed. But once the soft cushion of down stopped her descent, a voice inside her head bade a warning. It spoke of falsehoods and a time of shame to come, of anger and regret. It charged she think again and reconsider, that this moment of passion would haunt her all her days. It beckoned her to remember that this man, this stranger had been instructed to kill her and that he had agreed . . . but first, he had declared, he'd have a little fun.

Fun!

The word exploded in her brain. He thought of her as a pleasant, amusing distraction, and that once he was finished with her, he'd put his gun to her temple and pull the trigger! The heat of desire that had scorched her soul took on a different force, channeling its energy to one purpose. She would show this arrogant rogue that she was not a plaything. He would learn through bitter experience that not *all* women were impassive cowards . . . especially not Alexandra Pembrooke! With a throaty growl she tore her lips from his.

"If you think me the fool," she gasped, "then know you are a bigger one, Christian Page, for I am not the kind of woman you assume I am."

His hand was bold upon her knee and burned the flesh beneath her white mesh stockings, and Alexandra shrieked as it moved under her skirt and traveled to her thigh. She strained to push him from her, which seemed to excite him all the more, and out of desperation she freed one arm. She tried to rake her nails across his handsome face, but he caught her wrist and twisted it beneath her where their weight held it captive and useless. She screeched again when his knee forced her legs apart and his hand slid beneath the lace edge of her chemise.

"No!" she wailed. "Stop!"

Tears rose in her eyes again and she cursed them. To cry would make him laugh. He would taunt her for her weakness and subtly claim a victory, and she would not, *could* not give him even that.

Alexandra felt her skirts being pushed up past her hips and the lean fingers of his hands touching her in private places. A tight rush of fear knotted her stomach, forcing her to choke back a sob and to find new strength to fight him. Then, as if to aid her in her quest, he lifted slightly from her, and she wasted little time in seizing the opportunity he gave her. Rage fueled her need and blind desire drove her on as she sat up, pushed with all her might against his shoulders, and drew up her knees. Braced against her elbows for leverage, she kicked out with both feet before he could regain his balance. The heel of one shoe hit his thigh and the other struck him low in the abdomen, lower than she realized. His reaction puzzled her, for she had thought him immune to any pain she might inflict. Instead of laughing at her attempt or showing even a glimmer of disapproval, his tan face whitened slightly, his brows dipped sharply together, and he stood hunched over, one hand on his knee, the other pressed against his side. He didn't utter a sound or look her way, but Alexandra could see by the expression on his face that she had hurt him . . . greatly. She couldn't understand why; she had hit him several times before and he had merely shrugged it off.

Does it really matter? she silently asked herself as she pushed down her skirts and hurriedly slid off the bed. *He was planning to kill you, remember?*

Her jade-green eyes quickly scanned the room, and when they fell upon the pistol he had laid on the dresser, she mentally shook off the idea of shooting him, as the noise would bring the man in the hall. Then she spied the large pitcher sitting in the washbasin on the table near where Christian stood bent over. She rushed to it, and seizing it in both hands, she raised it high above his head and brought it down as hard and as fast as she could. The piece of porcelain shattered into a hundred tiny shards once it struck its unsuspecting victim, but its destruction didn't concern her. All Alexandra cared about was rendering her attacker unconscious, and she held her breath while she watched him stagger, stumble, and then fall. He landed facedown with his head turned away from her, and although he didn't move, Alexandra worried he was only pretending. Then she saw the dot of blood darken his blond hair and she deduced even Christian Page could not shake off a blow as hard as the one she'd given him. Glancing nervously at the door, she realized her next feat was to escape the inn without being seen, which obviously meant she wouldn't be able to make an exit the conventional way. That left using the window, and she had very little time to succeed. Drawing on what courage she had left, she crossed to the curtained aperture and looked out, her heart lurching in her chest when she saw the distance to the ground.

"Do you have a choice?" she whispered, unhooking the lock and pulling up the sash. "Sure you do. Stay here and die or climb out on the roof, lose your footing, and land on your head." She glanced back at the inert figure on the floor. "Some choice," she muttered bitterly. Twisting around, she perched a hip on the sill and brought up her legs. But before she stepped out onto the steep roof surrounding the dormer, she paused to look at Christian again.

"If God grants me this chance to redeem myself for all my past transgressions," she pledged aloud, "you, Mr. Page, will be the first to feel the result. My stupidity will become yours."

Her green eyes darkened with the heat of revenge, while hidden in their depths gleamed a spark of emotion that challenged her vow.

⋯❂❘ *Chapter Three* ❘❂⋯

A FLAWLESS BLUE SKY GREETED THE MORNING AND BRIGHT sunshine glistened in the dewy grasses. The distant sound of the crashing surf as it hit the bluffs filled the air and a gentle breeze stirred the majestic, low-sweeping branches of the willows on the front lawn. Alexandra viewed the splendor from the bedchamber's window, but she could find little beauty in what she saw. From the moment she had opened her eyes, her thoughts had centered around the adventure of the night before, how she'd been so very lucky to have come across an old man in a two-wheeled cart on the road who simply gave her a ride and didn't ask questions, and how very close she had come to dying. She thought of Garrett Ambrose and his shocking, heartless decree that her execution would serve as a warning to her father, that her life meant nothing, that she wasn't of any real value except as an example of what Ambrose was capable of doing.

Dark, finely arched brows came together at the realization that Hardin had had a part in it. She wanted to believe that he had been ignorant of Ambrose's true intentions, but the fact remained that he had used her to settle his affairs. He had put money ahead of her. She knew she should hate him for it, but she couldn't. Hardin had never lied about his feelings for her or that his interests lay more in gambling than in her. She also realized she didn't love him and never had. He had merely been the key that unlocked the door of her restraint, a guide who took her to places about which, before, she could only dream.

Suddenly the image of Christian Page came to mind. Now, *there* was a man she could hate with very little effort. Indeed, he had asked to be hated. He was a cold-blooded killer who thought nothing of his victim's fear. He showed no mercy or any kind of emotion whatsoever. He simply took what he wanted. Of course, she mused, that was until he met her. Alexandra had taught him never to let down his guard unless he was willing to pay the price. A half smile pulled at the corners of her mouth as she stared out across the gardens at the golden sun climbing higher in the eastern sky. As far as she was concerned, his lesson wasn't over yet. A headache—and having to explain to Ambrose how he had let her escape—did not equal what he had put her through or erase the truth that he would have shot her. No, they were far from being even. And she knew a perfect way to settle the score.

A light rap on the door startled Alexandra. Certain that Aimee had come to check up on her, Alexandra didn't bother to call out. Instead, she pulled the sash of her robe tightly around her waist and crossed the room to let her in.

Aimee Welu, a pretty, blond-haired, petite young woman, was probably the only real friend Alexandra had. They had grown up as neighbors and whenever one of them needed someone to listen to her problems, she knew where to go. Aimee didn't really approve of Alexandra's reckless side, but she seemed to understand the reason for it: it was the release Alexandra needed to deal with her mother's suicide . . . or at least to help her forget for a while. Thus when Aimee's maid awoke her in the middle of the night to inform her that Alexandra was waiting outside for her, alone and on foot, Aimee had ushered her friend upstairs to one of the guest bedrooms before the rest of the household learned of the young woman's unacceptable behavior. Aimee had seen how visibly shaken her friend was, that she was missing a bonnet and shawl, and that her dress was soiled and torn, but she had learned over the years that if Alexandra wanted to talk, she would. If not, there was no use pressing her. All Alexandra had told her was that she was worried Hardin hadn't made it home safely and would Aimee find out for her. The girl had assured her she would send one of the stable boys to inquire and at the same time he would take a message to Alexandra's father telling him that his daughter would be spending the night at the Welu estate.

"Feeling better?" Aimee asked as she stepped into the room and closed the door behind her.

"Much," Alexandra replied, sitting down on the edge of the bed. "Is Hardin all right?"

"I guess so," Aimee told her with a shrug. "I mean, he's home, but Webster didn't talk to him. One of the servants said he came home late and went straight to his room." Her pale brows drew together. "Lexie, he didn't . . . well, try to . . ." She heaved a sigh and sat down beside her friend. "I don't know how else to say it except by being blunt. Did he force himself on you?"

"What?" The question rang with laughter. "Of course not. He knows better." Remembering who had, the smile faded from Alexandra's lips. "Oh, he's a big part of the reason I'm sitting here right now, but no, he was a perfect gentleman . . . as always." She frowned and left Aimee's side to stand at the window again. "And even though he doesn't deserve it, I suppose I should send him a note telling him I'm all right." She gritted her teeth and added, "No thanks to him."

Aimee surmised there was more to Alexandra's anger than whatever Hardin had done, and she wanted to ask what it was, even though she knew her friend wouldn't tell her unless she wanted her to know. Biting her lip, Aimee decided silence would be the best form of prodding: Alexandra hated it when Aimee just sat and stared at her.

Only a few moments passed before Alexandra sensed the brown eyes watching her. A second or two more elapsed before Aimee's ploy grated on Alexandra's nerves.

"All right," she moaned, facing the girl. "I'll tell you everything, but you've got to swear to me that you won't breathe a word of it to anyone. Especially your mother. I love her dearly, but you know she'll run right to my father with it, and he's the last person I ever want to find out. Do you swear?"

Aimee quickly bobbed her head. "But you really needn't

ask, Lexie. I've never told Mother anything we discuss."

Alexandra raised a dubious brow and cocked her head to one side.

"Only once," Aimee admitted, a bit peeved that Alexandra wouldn't let her forget it. "And if I'd known she would tell your father, I wouldn't have confided in her. I'm not a hard learner. It won't ever happen again."

Alexandra knew her friend was being totally honest with her, and she really didn't blame Aimee for telling her mother that her best friend was thinking about getting married. It was the kind of news a girl *should* share with her mother. The mistake came from Alexandra's minor oversight: she forgot to wait with the announcement until *after* Hardin had asked her. Then there was the matter of dealing with her father once he'd heard about the impending nuptials. He truly despised the entire Wittemore family and had never tried to hide the fact. Learning that his daughter intended to marry into the clan had sent him into a rage, and Alexandra had delighted in waiting a whole week before correcting the rumor. His threats about sending her to a boarding school in France hadn't worried her either; she knew he'd never follow through with it once she had recanted the tale. But the story she was about to tell her friend couldn't be so easily explained away if Wallis Pembrooke ever learned of it. Nor would he simply dismiss it if he thought for one minute that his daughter had been compromised. He would arrange a marriage to the first man of whom he approved and Alexandra would be powerless to stop it.

"Well?" Aimee's voice cut into her thoughts. "Are you going to tell me or not? I think I have a right to know since you've inadvertently made me an accomplice."

Alexandra smiled ruefully. "Yes, I guess I have. And yes, I'm going to tell you. But the reason is twofold."

Aimee couldn't help but cringe. Whenever Alexandra used that tone with her, it meant trouble, and as far as Aimee was concerned, her friend was in enough trouble already. Aside from that, however, it sounded as though she intended to pull Aimee in with her. Shaking her head, her shoulders drooping wearily, she muttered, "Sometimes, Lexie, you expect too much out of our friendship. So tell me what it is I have to agree to before I'm to hear even a single detail of what happened last night."

Her green eyes sparkling, Alexandra replied, "A promise that you'll help me deliver a message to my father."

"What kind of a message?" Aimee asked worriedly.

Grinning, Alexandra proclaimed, "A note that will tell him where he can find a man named Christian Page."

Angry voices buzzed near Christian's head, and he wasn't sure if he was imagining them or if they were real. Struggling to open his eyes, he could feel the ropes tied around his wrists and the pain that tortured his body. He was hovering close to unconsciousness and would have welcomed its relief, if it didn't mean he'd become easy prey for the men who surrounded him.

"I say we kill him," someone raged. "He hasn't proven anything . . . except how careless he is."

"I agree," a second man spoke up. "And who's to say he didn't just let her go?"

"And then hit himself over the head?" a third pointed out, obviously not as convinced as the first two. "I'm not saying I fully trust him either, but every man deserves the chance to speak in his own defense."

"All right," the second relented. "Let him talk. Then we'll kill him."

A mad rush of voices filled the room, growing in volume and intensity until no one's single declaration could be heard. Suddenly a gunshot rent the air, stilling the arguments and cooling the rising threat of violence among the men. All eyes turned to look upon the one who fired the pistol.

"You're forgetting, gentlemen," Garrett Ambrose coolly stated as he tossed his gun down on the tabletop and relaxed back in his chair, "that *I'm* the one who makes the decisions here." He glanced at Benton Wall, then jerked his head Christian's way, silently giving his instructions to rouse the man to wakefulness.

A pitcher of water was roughly thrown in the bound man's face, startling him upright in his chair as he fought to open his eyes and focus his gaze on those standing near him. Silence choked the room while only one man seemed at ease. Yet once the accused had gathered his wits and had settled his attention on the one who would determine his fate, his gaze held no fear, no defiance or rage, only cool indifference.

"If I let them," Ambrose claimed, "they would kill you." He smiled confidently and waited for a reaction. When none came, he laughed, impressed with Page's pointless but undeniable courage. "You surprise me, Mr. Page," he said, reaching for the mug in front of him. "I know very few men who, in your situation, wouldn't be begging for their lives. Yet you sit there calmly staring at me as if we're discussing the food this wretched place serves." He made a careless gesture with his hand, indicating the tavern. "Why is that, Christian Page? Have you no fear of dying?"

The question had never been put before him until now nor was it one he had ever considered. It was true he hated death—when it touched someone close to him, when a life was taken unnecessarily, but as for his own. . . .

A flood of memories filled his head, visions of Min Le and the tiny infant in her arms. He saw the flames, smelled the smoke, and heard the screams. He felt her pain and his own, then the rage and the overpowering need for revenge, a force that would have brought about his own end if the words of her grandfather hadn't come in time.

"Grieve for her, Christian," Sang Soo had proclaimed, "for your son, but do not dishonor them. Your death will not bring them back. They must live in your spirit, in your wisdom, in the morning sun and the pale light of dusk. Listen to their voices in the songbird, see them in the tiny flower bud, the stars. Hold them close to your heart, my son. Then they will live forever."

Even now Christian could feel the razor-sharp emptiness that had filled his days and nights, and with Sang Soo's help, he had learned to forgive. He had turned the other cheek as it was taught in the Holy Bible, took his enemy as a friend and looked deep into that man's soul to understand that he, too, had loved Min Le. But Li-Chen's attack upon Christian's family hadn't happened out of greed. He hadn't meant to kill Min Le and the baby. It had been an accident. The death of Christian's uncle, however, had been a cold-blooded act, and this time Christian would have his revenge.

"We all have to die one day," he said in answer to Ambrose's query.

"True," his opponent replied as he set his mug on the table again and lit a cheroot. "But if you had the chance to postpone it, wouldn't you try?"

Christian knew what Ambrose wanted him to say, and even if he were of a mind to beg, he wouldn't. Not to Garrett Ambrose. "Words have never gotten me very far," he admitted, "if that's what you're proposing."

"Actions have," Ambrose concluded. With Christian's affirmative nod, he lazily pointed the tip of his cigar at the ropes entwined around Christian's wrists and elbows. "I'd say that's a little difficult to achieve right now, wouldn't you?"

One side of Christian's mouth moved. "An inconvenience, but not impossible," he declared.

Throwing back his head, Ambrose laughed loud and long. "I like your grit, Christian Page. You remind me of myself. Even in the face of death we look at all the options." He waved at Benton Wall. "Cut him loose."

"No!" one of the three men standing beside Christian shouted. "He's put us all in danger by letting that bitch get away! He should pay with his life!"

The look in Ambrose's brown eyes hardened and the smile left his face. "What kind of danger is that, Barrows?"

Short and heavyset, the man posed no real threat except for his mouth. He seldom kept his opinions to himself, and it appeared he would speak his mind again as he puffed out his chest and lifted his chin. "Are you forgetting who her father is?"

Ambrose slowly raised the cigar to his mouth and clamped it between his teeth as he replied, "No, Barrows, I haven't. Why do you ask?"

"Why?" he rallied, his eyes bulging in their sockets. "Because she'll go straight to her father and tell him where to find us. You know he'd do just about anything to catch the famed Garrett Ambrose. And if they find you, they find all of us. At least send someone after her."

Ambrose quickly raised his hand when Benton Wall took a breath to speak. "Why, that's a very good idea, Barrows. So good, in fact, that I think you should have the honor." He took a puff on his cigar, watched the smoke drift toward the ceiling, and added lightly, "And take whomever you wish with you." His çold gaze fell on the man to Barrows's left. "Edwards, perhaps." He looked at the third of the group. "And Clark, since the three of you seem to find this situation the most uncomfortable."

Failing to recognize the true meaning of Ambrose's suggestion, Barrows eagerly accepted the duty. "We'll leave right away."

"You do that," Ambrose returned, drawing on the cheroot again. Flicking the ash on the floor, he casually studied the brown tobacco leaves rolled into a tight, round length as he listened to the three men hurry from the tavern. Once the door had closed behind them, he looked up at Wall. "Take care of it," he ordered quietly.

An understanding glowed in Benton Wall's eyes, and without hesitation, he left the room.

"They're such fools," Ambrose proclaimed as he stood and walked over to Christian. Pulling a knife from his belt, he slid the blade beneath the ropes around Christian's wrists and arms and easily cut him free. "You're not a fool, are you, Mr. Page?" he asked, reaching for the bottle of rum sitting near him on the table and handing it to Christian. "You know the instant Wall found you lying unconscious that I would have sent someone after the woman, don't you? I mean, that's what you'd have done, if you were in my place."

Christian nodded rather than reply as he raised the bottle to his lips and took a drink. It stung the cut on the inside of his mouth and burned going down, but it helped sharpen his senses and revive his memories of the period after Alexandra had hit him over the head. He wasn't sure just how long he'd been out, but once Wall had broken down the door, Christian had been dragged to the commons and tied to a chair. He could remember the anger of everyone in the room and the relentless beating he'd taken once he'd come fully awake. He did not enjoy taking the kicks and punches, but the punishment meant his plan had worked, that Alexandra Pembrooke had gotten away. The pale light shining in through the window told him it was morning and that there was a strong possibility she was already back home, safe in her father's protection. And if she were any other woman walking the face of this earth right now, he concluded that at this very moment she would be telling her father everything that had happened, but in this case he doubted it. Lewis Rhomberg had told him a few of the stories he'd heard about Alexandra Pembrooke and how she defied her father every chance she had. Rumor had it that the young woman blamed her father for Jocelyn's suicide and that she had taken on some sort of death wish of her own by playing with danger. Yet underneath it all, Alexandra Pembrooke was still a lady, and the events that led to her escape were something she would never tell her father. All Christian could hope for was that she'd learned her lesson, and that she'd think twice before doing something as stupid again. As far as he was concerned, he'd seen the last of the foolish woman.

"Good morning, Sir Wallis," William Jones said from behind his desk, as he looked up from his work and saw his employer coming through the door.

"Good morning, William," Pembrooke replied as he headed toward his office. His days always seemed to start off in the same manner—the usual friendly exchange, the smiles, the comments about the weather—and ordinarily Pembrooke would graciously comply with the custom. But not today. He hadn't slept well the night before, and the never-ending search for Garrett Ambrose and his gang was taking its toll. The committee had been working on the case for over a month and they weren't any closer to finding Ambrose now than they were when they had started. Pembrooke had known it would be a difficult task, but the lack of progress upset him nonetheless. Nor did it help to have Sir Robert Peel, head of the committee of law enforcers, inquiring as to their progress at least once a week. Pembrooke hated having to admit to Sir Robert that he wasn't fulfilling the man's expectations almost as much as he hated admitting it to himself. He wanted to apprehend the outlaw more than he wanted anything else in his life.

A frown creased his brow as he entered the small office and hung his hat on the rack. Perhaps catching Ambrose wasn't *the* most important thing in his life, but it seemed the most feasible. If he had a choice, he'd work on repairing his relationship with Alexandra, although he'd come to the conclusion that winning her love and respect was impossible. No matter how hard he tried to make things right between them, he failed. With each effort he seemed to drive her further away. Last night was a prime example.

Rounding his desk, he sat down in the chair behind it and absently leafed through the stack of papers lying there. He'd caught Alexandra on her way out for the evening and even though he suspected with whom she planned to spend her time, he had asked anyway. Her answer had made him grit his teeth rather than restate his obvious dislike of Hardin Wittemore, and just when he was about to tell her that he preferred she stay home, she cut him off by turning her back and walking out the door without comment. Jocelyn had always been the disciplinarian of the family, and because he had no idea how his wife had handled the girl, Pembrooke had been at a loss in deciding which course to take. Instead, he had merely let her go, vowing that as soon as this assignment concerning Ambrose was over, he'd dedicate more time to his daughter. But would it be that simple? he wondered, remembering the exact moment when his charming, carefree daughter turned against him. It had been the same moment his world had fallen apart.

He'd worked late that night as always and had skipped having dinner with his wife and daughter. He'd come home somewhere around midnight and had gone straight to his bedchambers, expecting to find Jocelyn already asleep in their bed. They had been arguing of late, and when he discovered that not only hadn't she retired but she wasn't in the house, he had sensed the reason why long before he had found her letter on the nightstand. In a panic he had awakened Spencer, his valet and trusted employee, and bade the man to take three others and search until they found her.

Morning had come much sooner than anyone would have hoped. Pembrooke, after hours of combing the countryside and hoarse from calling his wife's name, had gone back to his study to think. A few minutes later, Spencer and a stableman appeared at the doorway.

"We found her, sir," Spencer had solemnly reported, his eyes red-rimmed and tired-looking. "I'm sorry to have to tell you this, but there's been an accident. She's dead, sir."

Even though it had been what he had expected to hear, a tightness had seized his heart and he had had to lean against the window frame for support. "Where?" he had managed to ask, his back to the pair.

"About a league from here, at the bottom of a cliff. It will take some time to get to her, I'm afraid. It was a long way down. The constable is there . . . and a surgeon, although I doubt—Well, no one could have survived a fall like that."

Pembrooke had closed his eyes, willing himself the strength not to break down. "Thank you," he had said after a moment. "You may go now."

He had waited until he heard their footsteps fade in the hallway before he turned for his desk and sank down in the wing chair behind it. He knew she hadn't fallen. It was no accident. She had done this on purpose and he had no one to blame but himself. Remembering the note he had found on her nightstand, he had pulled it from his pocket to reread. Why hadn't he seen it coming? Why hadn't he made amends before it went this far? Because he was too busy, that's why. He was always too busy. His work came first. Now she was dead and it was his fault.

Tears had choked him then as they threatened to do so now. They always did whenever he let himself remember that night and how he had tried—and failed—to console his fourteen-year-old daughter. Her accusations had cut deep, and he didn't try to defend himself. They both retreated into their own private worlds to grieve and lay blame where it didn't belong. They had drifted apart after that, seldom talking to each other and never communicating. Now, it seemed, he had waited too long to explain to his daughter and to beg her forgiveness.

"Sir?"

Jones's voice startled him. Glancing up at his employee, Pembrooke raised questioning brows.

"A messenger just delivered this, sir," Jones told him, holding up a sealed letter.

Pembrooke extended his hand, silently asking Jones to bring it to him. "Who sent it?"

"The messenger didn't know for sure. Said a young boy passed it to him and that he'd had it given to him by another boy. Jones shrugged. "It appears that whoever wrote it wishes to keep his identity a secret."

Pembrooke grunted as he broke the wax seal and unfolded the paper.

If you really want to find Garrett Ambrose, it read, *ask your daughter's lover. He not only knows where Ambrose is, but he can take you there.*

A mixture of emotions knotted Pembrooke's stomach. The implication that his daughter and Wittemore were intimate made him sick inside, while at the same time the idea of finally having a possible clue to the outlaw's whereabouts sent his blood racing. Refolding the letter, he stuffed it in his breast pocket with the intention of burning the document in the fireplace at home as soon as he could.

"Find Collins," he instructed, rising from his chair, "and have him meet me at the livery."

"Trouble?" Jones asked anxiously as he watched Pembrooke reach for his hat.

"For Garrett Ambrose," Pembrooke declared, then added as he patted the pocket where he'd put the letter, "providing this information is correct."

"But you will take others on your mission, I trust. Ambrose runs with some very bad men, sir, and from all accounts, it's a *large* group of men."

"I appreciate the warning, William," Pembrooke replied, reaching out to squeeze the man's shoulder. "And yes, we'll be taking all the men we can find. But right now I have to verify what's written in this note. It could be a trick and I'd rather not be running all over the countryside chasing shadows." He walked out of the office ahead of Jones, muttering, "Ambrose would love seeing me make a fool of myself, and I'll be damned if I'll give him the satisfaction."

Hidden within the dark interior of the closed carriage, Alexandra watched the two men alight from their coach on the opposite side of the street, a pleased and cunning smile on her lovely face.

"Lexie, this is insane!" Aimee exclaimed in a loud whisper. "What if we're seen? Don't you suppose your father would march right over here and demand to know what reason we have for sitting outside Hardin's house in the middle of the day?"

"Let him," Alexandra replied, unafraid. "I'll simply tell him we've come to pay Hardin a visit." She giggled and corrected, "That I've come to visit my lover."

Aimee's pale cheeks flamed and she groaned as she fell back against the seat. "You realize, don't you, that by suggesting you and Hardin have . . . have . . . have done more than just hold hands while you've danced . . . well, it could have some very chilling results. If he doesn't kill Hardin because of your lies, he'll marry you off to the first man he thinks can control you."

Alexandra's mischievous grin widened as she struggled to hold back her laughter. "Do you honestly think there is such a man?" she teased, her green eyes sparkling.

"No," Aimee replied tightly. "Or should I say there isn't a man stupid enough to accept the challenge." Miffed, she smoothed the wrinkles in her skirts. "And you had better pray you never give birth to a daughter. She could turn out to be just like you."

"Aimee!" Alexandra scolded with a smile. "What a dreadful thing to say. Of course I want to have a daughter." The spark of humor disappeared from her eyes as she turned back to watch her father and Donald Collins walk up the cobblestone path to the Wittemores' front door. When she spoke again, there was a sadness in her voice. "She'll have no reason to behave the way I do because she'll never have to doubt how much her parents love her."

Aimee started to speak, but she changed her mind. She and Alexandra had discussed the subject hundreds of times, and no amount of arguing on Aimee's behalf could convince her friend that Wallis and Jocelyn had both loved their daughter more than they had loved each other.

·⊰❘ *Chapter Four* ❘⊱·

PEOPLE BEGAN TO GATHER ON THE COURTHOUSE STEPS SHORT-
ly before dawn. By ten o'clock the crowd had grown so large
it spilled out onto the sidewalk and clogged the street. Everyone in Plymouth and for miles around had come for the trial of Garrett Ambrose and to get a peek at Sir Robert Peel,
home secretary to Parliament and founder of the London police
force. He and Sir Wallis Pembrooke would be long remembered as the men responsible for ending Garrett Ambrose's life
of crime, and the town would celebrate this day with wine,
food, dancing, and laughter well into the night.

"Lexie," Aimee said as the two girls sat studying the crowd
from within the safety of their carriage, "I really don't think
this is such a good idea. We're likely to get crushed just trying
to get inside."

"Then wait in the coach if you're scared," Alexandra replied
sternly, a bit short-tempered with her friend. "I've waited over
a week and went to a lot of trouble to see this brought about,
and I will be there to hear the judge pass down his guilty verdict."

"But you're not even really sure he was caught along with
Ambrose and the rest," Aimee argued. "What if he managed
to escape before your father's men arrived? Or later? Or what
if his trial is scheduled for another day? You could be pinched
and poked and stepped on for no reason."

"Oh, he's there," Alexandra guaranteed, her green eyes nar-
rowing and her mouth curling in a vindictive smile.

Alexandra might not have seen Christian Page caged up with
Ambrose and the rest of his men, but she knew he was there.

43

She had positive proof he was there. He had been captured the first night along with his cohorts, and she had been in her father's office to witness the excitement when the deputies came bursting in to make their announcement. She'd also been there when the gaoler asked to speak with her father, and when Mr. Jones had told him he'd have to wait. The mere fact that he'd made an uncustomary visit to her father's headquarters and so soon after the arrests had set off an alarm in her head, and when she was sure her father was too busy to notice, she'd taken Newell Quimby aside under the pretext that she would forward his message for him rather than make him wait.

"It's about one of the prisoners," he had advised her, blinking anxiously as he dug in his pocket and retrieved a gold ring. "He said I could keep this if I'd get a message to Lewis Rhomberg."

"Lewis Rhomberg?" she had repeated, at first surprised that any of Ambrose's men had even heard of one of her father's deputies, then not surprised at all since Rhomberg was one of the best and very well known. "What kind of message?" she had asked as she took the ring from Quimby's palm to examine. "And which prisoner?"

"The man called Page," he had replied, missing the startled look on her face when he briefly glanced toward the sound of laughter coming from the inner office. "And no message, really. Just that I was to tell Mr. Rhomberg that Page was in gaol." He paused for a moment. "I only took it 'cause I didn't know what else to do. He made it sound like he and Mr. Rhomberg are friends or something, and I . . . " He had clamped his mouth shut as if he had hated the words he had nearly spoken.

"You what?" Alexandra had pressed, seeing the anguish on the man's face. "You can tell me, Mr. Quimby. It's the same as telling my father."

He thought about it a moment longer, then replied, "Money is a terrible temptation, Miss Pembrooke. It can poison a man's honor. I'm not saying Mr. Rhomberg has switched his loyalty, mind you—I ain't got no proof of that—but it bothers me that a member of Ambrose's gang would ask for him."

It had bothered Alexandra too. But not in the same way.

"And I'm glad it did, Mr. Quimby. My father will be glad, too, once I tell him, but not for the same reason as you're thinking. Lewis Rhomberg is a good man. Father trusts him completely, and I'm sure he'd tell you the same thing I'm going to tell you," she said as she curled her fingers around the ring and covertly slid it into the pocket of her skirt. "This Page is grasping at his last hope of living out his life as a free man. He intended either to bribe Mr. Rhomberg or to tell him some false tale that would win him a pardon. Whichever it is, it's something that doesn't have to concern you."

Alexandra remembered Quimby's hesitation and how she had had to assure him before he reluctantly left the office that Christian had probably picked the first name that had come to mind, that Lewis Rhomberg, more than likely, had never met Christian Page, and that she would tell all of their conversation to her father. Even now she thanked her good fortune at having been there to intercept the man's visit, for if she hadn't—

"Lexie?"

She jumped at the sound of Aimee's voice and tried to mask her woolgathering by fidgeting with the satin ribbon on her bonnet as she said, "Hardin swore to me that Christian Page was hauled off in chains like all the rest. And the magistrate likes to save expense. They'll all be tried for the same crimes and all at the same time. He'll be there."

"Hardin," Aimee scoffed. "I'm surprised you can even say his name after what he did to you." She plopped back in the seat, primly folded her hands in her lap, and raised her chin. "If you ask me, Hardin Wittemore should be sitting beside Mr. Page rather than testifying against him. He's guilty of a far worse crime than anything Christian Page may have done to you."

"Aimee!" Alexandra gasped, jerking her head around to gape at the girl. "How can you even think that? Christian Page tried to . . . to . . . " She blushed furiously and couldn't bring herself to say the word. Angry at the memory of the incident, she looked back outside. "There's a big difference between what *he* planned for me and what Hardin thought would happen. I'm not pleased with Hardin, but he's never behaved improperly toward me."

Aimee's brown eyes lightened a bit as she looked askance at her companion. "It seems to me, Lexie—if you'd be fair in your thinking—that Hardin endangered your life and Christian saved it."

"Saved it?" Alexandra echoed, shocked that her friend could ever consider such a notion. "Apparently you weren't listening to everything I said about that night. After he had had his way with me, he intended to *kill* me!"

"I know," Aimee relented, "and maybe he would have if you hadn't clobbered him over the head. But think about it for a minute. He was ordered to kill you right there in front of everyone and he refused . . . sort of. Instead, he took you upstairs to his room—"

"Where he proceeded to force himself on me," Alexandra sharply reminded her.

"*Where,*" Aimee insisted, "he allowed you the chance to escape . . . whether on purpose or by accident. I guess you'll never know for sure now. But in a way he saved your life." She tossed her head and looked out the window. "That's all I'm saying."

"*I* saved my life, Aimee," Alexandra rallied. "Me! All by myself. *I'm* the one who fought and clawed. *I'm* the one who had enough wit about me to hit him and knock him out. *I'm* the one who climbed along the roof to a tree and nearly broke my neck trying to reach the ground. No one gave me a ride in a comfortable carriage to your house, Aimee. I rode in the back of a cart! I survived because *I* made it happen. So, please . . . give credit where credit is due, and stop looking at Christian Page as some kind of hero." A burning warmth suddenly seared her flesh in all the places where Christian had touched her, and she shivered. "Believe me, he isn't," she finished, looking outside again. "I just wish Sir Robert Peel hadn't changed the laws. Mr. Page deserves to hang for what he did."

"Then tell your father the truth," Aimee snapped, tired of their conversation. "If he isn't hanged for it, your father will undoubtedly shoot him."

Her companion's remark surprised and puzzled Alexandra. Frowning, she turned her head to look at her. Aimee knew she couldn't tell her father about that night *and* she knew why.

Hardin had understood, and he hadn't blamed Alexandra for sending that note to her father implying his association with Ambrose. He would have preferred not getting involved—Garrett Ambrose's remaining friends, those who had not been arrested, would most assuredly try to silence him before the trial—but Hardin had recognized a debt and knew he was honor-bound to pay it. He owed Alexandra. He cared about her reputation, and subtle though it might be, he would avenge the wrong done her. Aimee, however, was making it sound as if she thought Alexandra had overstepped her limits, and because Alexandra valued their friendship, she had to ask why.

"I'm not saying Christian Page shouldn't be held responsible," Aimee amended, her young face troubled. "Lord knows he's probably guilty of all sorts of heinous acts. What upsets me is your contribution to this mess, the fact that you allowed yourself to be threatened *and* very nearly killed. If you'd have behaved like a young lady should, you wouldn't even know Christian Page existed."

Alexandra's spine stiffened. "So this is all *my* fault?" she railed.

Aimee gave her a tired look. "Whose is it, then? Your father's? Is it his fault his daughter can't put the past to rest and get on with her life? Do you think the man is any less angry over his wife's suicide, any less hurt and remorseful than his unforgiving daughter?"

The reprimand stung. It had struck too close to the truth. Furious, she twisted around, grabbed the door handle, and made a hurried exit. With her feet solidly on the ground, she took a moment to fluff out her skirts and straighten her bonnet. She had to look confident and in full control once Christian Page spotted her for the first time, for until that very second he would be wondering why Lewis Rhomberg hadn't come, and she wanted him to know the truth. She wanted him to see the look in her eyes, to feel her hatred, to sense the satisfaction she was getting by witnessing his downfall.

"Miss Pembrooke!"

The deep voice of Donald Collins rose above the roar of the crowd and drew Alexandra's appreciative smile as she watched him elbow his way over to her. Even though he was ten years her senior, Collins had the freckle-faced appearance of youth and the nature to match. It was his bulk as much as the authoritative tone of his voice that made men respect him, and both were the reasons why her father had taken him along when they set out to arrest Garrett Ambrose and his gang. Collins loved to laugh and always looked on the bright side of things, but he could be very serious when his job called for it. Alexandra felt safe with him and she was glad he had appeared just then.

"Your father didn't tell me you'd be here," he admitted, taking her elbow and pulling her closer to the protection of his massive size where crushing bodies couldn't harm her.

"I didn't tell him," she replied, wincing when someone stepped on her toe despite Collins's efforts. "If I had, he'd have forbidden it, and I—"

"And you would have come anyway," he finished with a chuckle.

His mood was infectious, and she couldn't help smiling. "Yes," she confessed. "I guess you know me pretty well."

"I know your father," Collins replied. "And it only stands to reason that if he's stubborn beyond comparison, then his offspring would be the same." He laughed, then pulled her in front of him to shield her with his arms as he aimed them toward the side of the courthouse. "And having declared that, I assume nothing I can say will change your mind. Therefore, I will escort you through this throng of bloodthirsty justice-seekers to a safe entrance."

His description of the others, who had come for the same purpose as she, disturbed Alexandra, and once they had slipped inside through the doorway used by the magistrate and other officials, she drew him aside to ask what he meant.

"Those out there on the steps aren't here to see a man receive a fair trial, but to hear the sentencing. And most, I'm sure, hope the accused get the full extent of the law." He squared his broad shoulders and glanced at the door. "And I don't think I'd be wrong in saying the majority are hoping for the gallows."

For a brief second Alexandra felt ashamed that, although innocently stated, she deserved to be included in his portrayal. In defense of her own feelings she replied, "But some of these

men are murderers, Mr. Collins. Don't you agree that if someone takes the life of another, he should pay for it with his
own?"

"Very much so," he concurred, touching her elbow to guide
her down the long corridor to the courtroom. "But, you see,
Mr. Wittemore is the only witness to their crimes, and murder
is not one of them. The new laws Sir Robert has established
have done away with such severe punishments, except in the
case of murder, of course, which means the most these men can
get is ten to twenty years, not the gallows. It won't please the
crowd waiting outside, since most of them have been affected
by Ambrose's rampages in some way or another, and there's
likely to be a bit of a riot once they hear he isn't going to
hang."

"What about attempted murder?" she asked before she realized she had.

Pausing in front of the closed door ahead of them, Collins
shrugged as he faced her. "If there's someone who can swear
to it, I suppose it would carry the same punishment as having
actually succeeded at the act." He paused. "Why do you ask?
Has Mr. Wittemore told you more than he's told us?"

Realizing her mistake in having brought up the subject, she
forced a laugh. "I was just curious. I know how much everyone
would like to see Garrett Ambrose get what's coming to him,
and I thought . . . well, I was thinking that maybe Hardin had
overheard something that might be helpful."

She was getting herself in deeper the more she talked, and
she knew that Collins wouldn't let it rest if he suspected
something. His ability to second-guess someone was one of
his best qualities, a talent that made him of unequaled value to
her father. He could almost solve a case before it happened,
and if she didn't change the direction of their conversation in
the next few seconds, he'd be on his way to talk to Hardin.
Alexandra doubted Hardin would tell him anything that might
give her away, but she couldn't chance it. Nor could she rely on
Hardin's determination to stand firm. Donald Collins had a way
of making a man talk even if he didn't have anything to say.

"Gracious me," she purred in her most flirtatious manner.
"I've gone off and left Aimee in the carriage." She smiled

sweetly at him, lowered her chin, and looked up through thick, black lashes. "Would you mind terribly? She's such a frightened little goose I'm sure she'd sit there all day if someone didn't come for her." She could see the doubtful, somewhat guarded look in his eyes and knew she hadn't completely tricked him. "Please?" she added with a flutter of her lids. "She won't speak to me for a week if she thought I left her there on purpose."

Donald hesitated a moment longer, then replied, "Of course. But you're to promise me that you won't go in that courtroom until we come back. The crowd is just as angry in there as they are out on the steps. Promise?"

Alexandra gave him her most convincing smile. "I promise." But the smile quickly faded, replaced by a look of desperation once he had turned his back on her. She had to warn Hardin to choose his words carefully lest the truth come out, and that meant finding him before the trial started.

Christian Page watched the four-legged intruder scurry along the wall, then sniff the air, the stone floor, and the scattering of straw before it squinted up at the narrow stream of light peering in through the barred window of the cell as if it, too, sought a way out. The wounds Christian had suffered during his arrest had healed in the past week, but they had never concerned him. For the cost of the gold ring he had worn, he had paid the turnkey to take a message to Lewis Rhomberg. But that had been on the first night of his stay in this godforsaken travesty of a prison. Six more had passed since then, and he had yet to have a visitor or even word that his friend was working on his release. The gaoler, conveniently, hadn't shown his face again since that night, and Christian was already wondering if the ring had merely served to buy the man a tankard of ale, a woman for the night, and a bed to sleep in.

Resting back against the wall, Christian drew in his feet and wrapped his arms around his knees. Loud snoring suddenly filled the dank, dark cubicle, and he turned his attention to the man who shared the cell with him. Christian hadn't bothered to ask the stranger's name or anything about him, since in his mind knowing wouldn't make a difference. The only time they'd had any kind of a conversation at all was when the man informed his new roommate that the cot belonged to him and that Christian would have to sleep on the floor since he wasn't of a mind to share. Christian hadn't argued. He preferred the floor with a thin cushion of straw. That had always been the way he slept when he and Min Le—

The vision of his young wife filled his thoughts and the pain of his loss tore at his heart again. They had been married less than a year, and she had been dead five times that. Yet the emptiness and the hurt were still just as fresh and vivid as if her death had occurred only yesterday. He had shared his grief with her grandfather and together they had tried to help each other heal. Sang Soo had dealt with his sorrow much more quickly than had Christian, which Christian could understand. But what hadn't made any sense to him was Sang Soo's insistence that Christian return to England, to the life he'd had before setting out to conquer the world.

"Your pain is here, Christian Page. In your homeland, with your own people, you will lose sight of your tragedy with other things to occupy your mind and your heart. You will never forget Min Le and your infant son, but you will walk again in the sunshine if you leave the past behind."

Christian could remember how angry he'd gotten and how he'd told the old man that running away wouldn't help.

"Staying will not help either," the Chinaman had argued. "Too many memories. Too much hurt. You cannot change what has happened, but you are the master of your own fate, the builder of your dreams. Reach out, Christian Page. Take what is yours. Fill your heart with joy again. If you do not, you will wither and die like the flower in the winter's snow."

Christian's anguish had deafened him to the deeper meaning of Sang Soo's words and it hadn't been until he saw the fear in Alexandra Pembrooke's eyes that he had truly understood. Sang Soo had been trying to tell him that the love Christian had given Min Le should not be wasted because of her death, that in time Christian would and *could* love again, that what he had felt for his wife had enriched his very existence, made him one, complete. Until he found that again, he would be adrift in an ocean of self-pity, never to know happiness again.

He shook his head ruefully as he recalled the way in which Alexandra Pembrooke had gained her freedom, and he guessed Sang Soo would laugh if Christian ever retold the tale to him. The old man had repeatedly warned his young protege that his one weakness was a lack of concentration, and Christian— along with Miss Pembrooke's help—had proven him right. Christian had intended she escape, but how hadn't crossed his mind. The young woman, however, hadn't been at a loss for ideas and had easily solved the problem on her own. For that he was grateful. What he would have appreciated, however, would have been a means less painful.

Christian hadn't realized until now that since Min Le's death he hadn't given himself the pleasure of a woman's company. It hadn't been something he'd done deliberately. He'd simply been too busy with other things to give a woman notice, and he probably wouldn't have noticed Alexandra Pembrooke if she hadn't been thrust at him. The others had guessed her companion was the one who had summoned the authorities, since Wittemore had been called to testify, but Christian knew differently. The frightened, foolhardy girl had found the courage *and* the way to have her revenge without exposing herself, and he admired her cunning. And now that he thought about her, he admired her beauty as well.

For the first time in a long, long while the ice-blue color of his eyes softened as he drew a mental portrait of the dark-haired, fiery-tempered woman responsible for his being in prison, and despite the stench of the cell, he recalled the sweet scent of her perfume. She was much taller than Min Le and their eyes weren't the same color, but the thickness of her hair and the silky smoothness of her skin reminded him of his wife. Their natures, however, were on opposite ends of the scope: Min Le never seemed able to do enough for him, while Alexandra Pembrooke couldn't do enough *to* him. Otherwise he wouldn't be in gaol right now. Their upbringings were totally different, and even their style of dress differed greatly. In truth it was hard for him to imagine how one man could be attracted to two women who had so very little in common. Yet he was . . . and he wondered why.

The sound of voices in the corridor distracted him, and he came to his feet and crossed to the barred window in the cell door. He hadn't quite given up hope that somehow Lewis Rhomberg would hear about his imprisonment and the impending trial, but he really wasn't expecting to see the man's face among the crowd of people heading his way. If Lewis wanted to talk to him, he'd come alone, and certainly not with a group of women. Chances were this party was nothing else than more of the curious elite of Plymouth wanting a private showing of the famed Ambrose gang, and if the diversion didn't promise a brief escape from the monotony of being locked up, he'd settle himself back down on the floor and ignore them.

"How many of them are there?" he heard one woman ask.

"Countin' Ambrose, eighteen altogether," the guard proudly answered. "There were twenty-one, but three of them were shot tryin' to get away from the posse."

"Are they all in the same cell?" another foolishly questioned.

"No, m'lady," the man replied. "We had to divide 'em up. Especially Mr. Ambrose from this one."

The voices had grown louder as the group neared Christian's cell, and following the last comment, a thumb was nearly thrust in his face when the guard swung it in his direction. The gesture surprised him, but he didn't flinch or back away. He merely stared at the gawking faces that crowded around to get a look at him.

"Why?" a young woman in a huge pink bonnet inquired.

"Because Mr. Ambrose is blamin' him for their gettin' caught. Says he'll kill him if he ever has the chance."

A collective gasp followed the statement, and although it was the first Christian had heard of it, the probability didn't come as any real shock. If *he'd* figured out Miss Pembrooke was behind the arrival of an armed posse, then Ambrose would have too. And if Miss Pembrooke was the reason they were in prison, then of course Ambrose wanted to kill him. Christian had let her escape.

"Then why not put them all in the same cell?" a heavyset, older woman proposed. "Maybe they'd kill each other off and save the expense of a trial." She laughed at her own suggestion and the others quickly joined in . . . all except for one, a tall, shapely woman near the back.

"Why, Martha, if they did that, we'd miss out on all our fun," her companion giggled.

"Not really. The gaoler could let us watch," the other replied.

Their idea of fun sickened Christian. He agreed Ambrose deserved to hang and he wanted to be there to witness the execution, but even a murderer had the right to die with some kind of dignity. What these ladies preferred was just as ruthless and callous as anything Garrett Ambrose had done. For all their fine silks and diamonds, he thought, they seemed as bloodthirsty as any criminal.

"So where is he?" the girl in the pink bonnet demanded. "We haven't come here to look at his men. We want to see Garrett Ambrose."

"Yes!" the rest chorused. "Show us Garrett Ambrose."

The gathering moved away and Christian idly watched them depart. Then, just as he was about to return to his spot on the floor, he sensed that one of the women had lingered behind, and he shifted his weight and craned his neck to peer out at her. The fleeting thought that for some reason Lewis Rhomberg had sent a messenger in his stead crossed Christian's mind, vanishing just as quickly when he realized there was no need to be secretive anymore. So what did she want?

The pale light of the sconces on the wall shadowed her face, and for a moment he wondered if she was intentionally hiding her identity from him, for she seemed reluctant to lift her head so that he might see beneath the wide brim of her hat. Curiosity bade him to speak, but Sang Soo's teachings reminded him that safety came with caution. Thus he waited, his gaze pulling in every detail of her slender figure, the rich cloth of her gown, her gloved hands, the tight-fitting high waistline adorned with a satin ribbon beneath her bosom, and the tips of her slippered feet peeking out from under her hemline.

Alexandra could almost feel his eyes upon her, how they traced her profile and strained to see her face. She could guess his wonderment and fought the cynical laughter teasing her mouth as she imagined his shock once she favored him with a look. It hadn't been her plan to come to the cells where the prisoners were kept. She had been searching for Hardin when she came upon the women begging the guard to give them a tour, and her first reaction had been disapproval. Who'd want to look at thieves and murderers and rapists? But then, remembering Christian Page, she had quickly joined the group starting down the long, dimly lit corridor, thinking that there would never be a more perfect opportunity than this to prove to him that women weren't as stupid as he assumed they were. Pulling open the strings on her purse, she dug inside for the object that would bring Christian Page to his knees.

"I have something I think you might be interested in seeing," she murmured before lifting her eyes to look at him, and the instant she had, a white-hot surge of emotion charged through her, stealing her breath and causing every muscle in her body to tremble. She had forgotten how handsome he was with his sun-streaked blond hair, tanned skin, and those extraordinary blue eyes framed by dark lashes. Just looking at him stirred the vivid memory of the kiss they had shared and the sparks he had ignited deep within her. She quickly dropped her gaze and focused on the party of women down the hall, as if worried one of them might see or hear her.

In his wildest imaginings Christian had never thought they would meet again. He hadn't even expected her to come to the trial, let alone to his cell. But there she was, standing before him in the foul-smelling, darkened bowels of the prison, and for a moment he thought of her as the first ray of bright sunshine breaking through a cloud-choked sky after a storm. He caught himself smiling at her. Could it be, he wondered, that she had guessed the reason behind his actions that day, and she'd come to thank him for it? Or had Lewis gone directly to her father with the truth about him, and he in turn told Alexandra? Was she here to tell him he was free?

"Never assume anything, Christian Page," Sang Soo's voice rang out. "Your friends can be your enemies. Just as the sparkling surface of a pool hides the depths beneath it, so can the sweet promises spoken by a friend mask true feelings."

But for what other reason has she come? he silently asked his mentor as if he expected Sang Soo to answer.

A frown replaced the smile as the lessons he had learned

flared up to warn him. Though he knew little of the real Alexandra Pembrooke, he knew enough of women and their order of things to guess she would not so easily forgive him— even knowing the truth about him—and he settled back to wait. It was *her* wish they speak, not his.

The silence that surrounded her, the smell of the place, and the nearness of Christian Page despite the heavy door that separated them made Alexandra shiver. The urge to turn on her heel and run was great, but the desire to scorn him held her steady. She drew in a breath, gritted her teeth, and forced herself to remember that at a time not so very long ago he would have killed her without any remorse.

"Mr. Quimby came to see my father," she announced, her confidence restored as she raised her chin and met his stare. "He was worried, but I set him straight. You see, he feared one of my father's agents had chosen an easy way of life, and you rather confirmed it when you gave him this." She held out her hand and uncurled the fingers. There, cushioned on the white cloth of her glove, lay the gold band he had given to the gaoler. "Lewis Rhomberg won't be coming, Mr. Page. He doesn't even know you're here." Her green eyes snapped with spiteful pleasure. "And I know why you sent for him. You thought he would win your freedom," she surmised as she dropped the ring back in her purse. "Well, you shan't have it, my scheming rogue. You will spend the rest of your life rotting in this hole cursing the day you met me. And I"—she smiled vindictively as she closed the silk bag and held it up for him to see—"I shall have this to remind me of what fools men are, a trophy of a game well played and won." She narrowed her eyes and added, "You should have done as you were ordered to do, Mr. Page, instead of giving in to that itch in your trousers." The sound of the others returning warned her to hurry. Catching the strings of her purse in one hand, she raised the hem of her skirts with the other, preparing to make her exit. But before she turned away, she added one last biting remark. "Someone gave me a very wise piece of advice one time, and I think I should pass it on to you. Hate me, Christian Page. Your hate is what will give you the strength to survive."

She had traveled only a few steps away from his cell when

his threatening voice loomed loudly all around her, his words chilling her to the bone and the promise he made striking terror in her heart.

"Then listen well to the advice, Miss Pembrooke, for someday I'll no longer be imprisoned behind thick metal doors and barred windows. And when that time comes, you can wager all your fine silks and jewels that the first person I plan to visit will be you."

··❧ Chapter Five ❧··

"WHICH ONE IS HE?" AIMEE WHISPERED EXCITEDLY AS THE prisoners filed into the room and were directed to the box where they were to stay during the trial. "No, no, don't tell me," she quickly amended, her eyes sparkling. "I've already figured it out." She raised a gloved hand and pointed. "The third one in. Am I right? I have to be. Oh, Lexie, he is handsome!"

"He isn't handsome," Alexandra corrected, her tone sharp, as she forced herself to look at the place where Hardin sat to the left of the judge's bench, instead of at the one man who had caused her so much grief in the last seven days. "Hardin is handsome, and there's simply no comparison."

As she stole a peek at the group of men, it seemed as if the golden streams of midmorning sunlight spilling in through the tall, diamond-paned windows in back of the courtroom had deliberately singled out the very man about whom they talked. He hadn't seen her yet, but Alexandra was sure that once he did, he'd bore holes in her with his angry stare. That idea irked her: for what reason did *he* have to be angry? *He* was the criminal, the murderer, the rapist. *He* was the one who had broken the law, got caught, and now had to stand trial for his actions. It certainly wasn't Alexandra's fault! Remembering the promise he'd made her a few minutes ago in the corridor outside his cell, she unwittingly clutched her purse and prayed the magistrate would sentence him to death. Christian Page didn't seem to be the forgiving sort or a man who forgot a threat. As long as he was alive, she would fear the day of his release from prison. Perhaps she should learn how to fire a gun and then sleep with it under her pillow.

"What a shame," she heard her friend declare with a woeful sigh, and she looked up to find Aimee still staring across the room at Christian.

"What's a shame?" she asked suspiciously.

Aimee's cheeks flushed as if she'd spoken without realizing it and the discovery embarrassed her. She shifted uneasily in her chair and dropped her gaze to her lap. "Nothing."

"Nothing?" Alexandra repeated. "I doubt that. I saw the look in your eyes, Aimee Welu, and I can guess what you were thinking."

"Oh?" the girl challenged haughtily. "And what's that?"

"You find Christian Page fascinating, and you think it's awful that he's going to be locked up for a very, *very* long time," Alexandra predicted as she removed her gloves and fought the rising heat that moved up her neck and stung her face. Hoping to sound dispassionate toward him and his situation, she added coolly, "If he isn't hanged."

"Hanged?" the girl echoed. "Good gracious, they won't hang him, will they? I mean . . . well, he hasn't done anything so terrible that he should hang for it." The statement had barely escaped her lips when she realized how it would sound to her friend, and her face flamed all the more. "I'm sorry," she mumbled apologetically. "I shouldn't have said that. What he did to you was deplorable and he should be punished. I just wasn't thinking."

Aimee gave Alexandra a brief glance, then settled her gaze once more upon Christian Page. What he'd done *was* deplorable, she supposed, and he *should* be held responsible, but since Lexie hadn't truly been harmed . . . well, he was just too handsome to be hanged. She lowered her eyes again and covertly peeked over at Alexandra. Her friend certainly wouldn't agree, but in a way this man had actually done Lexie a favor. That little incident at the inn that night had changed Lexie. Aimee wasn't sure just how it had affected her, but some of Lexie's wildness had ebbed, and that could only be for the good. The young woman's escapades had been growing bolder and much more dangerous over the past few months, and Christian Page had shown her just how foolish she was being. In Aimee's opinion, he shouldn't hang for it. In fact, he should be toasted and set free.

And if it comes down to it, Aimee silently declared, *I'll make sure he doesn't hang. I'll tell Sir Wallis the truth. I'll tell him that because of Christian Page, his daughter is still alive and behaving a lot more sensibly these days.*

Feeling much better about the man's situation, Aimee raised her chin, squared her shoulders, and settled back to listen to the proceedings, unaware that sometime during the last few minutes, Christian had surveyed the crowded courtroom and would have willingly given just about anything in exchange for a few moments alone with one person seated there.

The darkness of the corridor outside his cell as well as the dimly lit commons where they first met had hampered Christian's ability to appreciate fully the young woman he had been ordered to kill. But here, in the warm glow of sunlight, he saw for the first time how truly beautiful she was. He assumed many men had fallen victim to her sensuality and charm, while only he knew what lay beneath the guarded surface. She had a cold, vindictive heart, if she had a heart at all. She was obviously spoiled, reckless, and uncaring, selfish to a fault, and it had been his misfortune to become the object of her scorn.

The only shred of luck that had fallen his way was her fear of retribution should her father learn of her visit to the inn and the resulting predicament in which she had found herself, for if the truth were told, Christian was sure Alexandra would be walking down the aisle on her father's arm to meet her new husband and Christian wouldn't have been given the luxury of a trial. Sir Wallis Pembrooke, more than likely, would have ordered one of his men to take Christian to a secluded spot and put a bullet in his head before Christian had the chance to explain. For that, he was thankful . . . or he should be, anyway. He wasn't dead, but from the look of things, he might as well be. If Lewis Rhomberg didn't make an appearance pretty soon, Christian would be sentenced to several years in prison. That aspect didn't bother him, since he knew that sooner or later Lewis would hear about it and go to Pembrooke with the truth. What concerned Christian was Garrett Ambrose and the possibility that he would have to share a cell with him and a few of his faithful followers. Outnumbered, Christian wouldn't last the night. Yes, thanks to Alexandra Pembrooke's interference, Christian was caught in a very awkward dilemma. If he told the truth here in court, no one would believe him, and Ambrose would have all the more reason to want to kill him. If he remained silent and let himself be sentenced along with the rest, he just might be able to trick Ambrose into believing Christian *was* one of them. After all, what man in his right mind would allow himself to go to prison for a crime he hadn't committed? Then all Christian would have to do would be to sit back and wait. It seemed simple enough. Yet from experience and through Sang Soo's teachings, Christian had learned things were never quite how they appeared. Something could always go wrong, and if it did, he'd have no one to thank but Alexandra Pembrooke. Surprised by the anger he felt toward her, he gritted his teeth and unknowingly pulled against the shackles locked around his wrists.

The crack of the judge's gavel stilled the crowded courtroom, and all eyes centered on the man seated behind the bench. His Honor William Blakesley had presided over the court of Plymouth for the past twenty years and had the reputation of being a fair but stern judge. If a man was found guilty in his court, he was sentenced to the maximum. Few were ever vindicated, however, for it was His Lord Chief Justice Blakesley's belief that an honest man would never get himself into such a predicament that he'd be arrested for it. Thus, those who jammed the limited viewing space assumed they were there to hear the sentencing and nothing more.

"Hear ye! Hear ye!" the bailiff chorused. "This court is called to order. All complaints and charges against the accused shall be herewith declared and judgment of defense shall be witnessed. His Honor Lord William Blakesley officiating."

Again the crowd of spectators shifted their attention back to the man clothed in a black robe and white peruke as he took several minutes to read over the documents before him, and only the rustle of ladies' fans stirring up a refreshing breeze in the close confines of the room was heard. It was a ritual that had to be observed, but most of those who waited felt it was unnecessary. Garrett Ambrose and his gang were guilty. There was no need for formality.

"Mr. Attorney General?" the magistrate beckoned as he laid aside his papers and took the gold-rimmed spectacles from his nose. "Present your case."

"Thank you, Your Honor," Horace Wittney replied as he left his chair and stood in front of the jury box, his long black robe flowing about his legs. "The eighteen prisoners you see there"—he motioned toward the box where Christian stood along with the others—"are all accused of the same crimes and therefore shall be tried as one. They have caused this fair city of Plymouth and its people enough expense, most of which we shall never redeem, and—"

"Mr. Attorney General," the magistrate warned, "the facts, please. They have not yet been found guilty."

"Yes, Your Honor," Wittney yielded with a slight nod of his head.

This had been the trial Horace Wittney had waited for all of his professional life. To be the one responsible for convicting a criminal of Garrett Ambrose's magnitude would most assuredly place him in high standing with the people of Plymouth— and more importantly with King George. His name would long be remembered after the sentencing was passed down. He only hoped he could convince Blakesley that the gallows and nothing less was what Garrett Ambrose deserved. Raising his thin nose in the air, he turned back to address the jury.

"These men are here today to hear the charges brought against them. It is my duty to prove to you, the honored jurors, that the charges are correct, and that these men did, indeed, commit a crime against the Crown. Once I have done that, it will be your responsibility to agree on a guilty verdict. To do anything less will be a travesty against the Crown and against yourselves." With a regal air, Wittney returned to his desk and the paper lying there. He glanced briefly at it, then scanned the crowded room for the witness he wished to question first. "I call Sir Wallis Pembrooke to state the facts as he saw them."

A buzz of voices shot across the room as the one requested rose from his chair. Alexandra knew this was a proud day for her father, and she wished she could share in his joy. She wished only *his* name would be spoken when stories were repeated about Garrett Ambrose's capture, but once her father told of the events leading up to the outlaw's arrest, everyone would wonder who had sent the unsigned letter naming Hardin Wittemore as a gambler and a man who could find the gang's hideout. Feeling even more ashamed of her part in this business, she lowered her gaze to the blue satin of her gown billowing out around her legs.

"What's the matter, Lexie?" Aimee whispered behind her fan, her tone edged with sarcasm. "Have you just now realized how damning your little note could be?"

Alexandra's head came up, and her expression reflected her worry. "What?"

"Your note. The message you sent to your father. The one that said his daughter's lover could lead him to Ambrose." A frown knitted Aimee's brow with the discovery that her friend hadn't given it any consideration. "Good heavens, Lexie. I thought you were smarter than that."

A hard knot formed in Alexandra's stomach. No, she hadn't realized that that vague message written on a scrap of parchment could and in all probability would become a very important piece of evidence. Dear Lord! If her father were asked to explain how he knew where to find the famed outlaw—

"Tell the jury, if you will, Sir Wallis, how you came to know where to find Garrett Ambrose and his men," the attorney general instructed.

The knot moved to Alexandra's throat and she quickly dropped her gaze to her hands. But instead of finding any comfort there, the sight of her purse resting in her lap reminded her of what she had hidden inside and how it had gotten there. That, in turn, reminded her of Christian, and thinking of him raised the possibility that if given the chance, he would announce to everyone in the courtroom the name of the person he guessed had written the letter and how he had come to that conclusion. He had debts to pay. He'd said so. And he could begin by exposing her, by ruining her reputation, by shaming her father. Her heart sank. Good God, what had she done?

"I was sent a message telling me to question Mr. Hardin Wittemore in regard to the smuggler's whereabouts," her father announced, his voice steady and confident.

Alexandra didn't have to look up to know he was staring at her. She could almost feel his eyes upon her. Or was it Christian she felt staring at her?

"A message," the attorney general repeated. "And who sent the message, Sir Wallis?"

"I don't know," he answered. "It wasn't signed."

"And do you have this message on your person?"

"No, sir."

"Can you get it?"

"No, sir."

"Why not, Sir Wallis?"

"I've mislaid it."

A murmur of voices filled the room, followed by the crack of the magistrate's gavel which silenced the crowd. It was the contention of all those who listened that without that vital document, the case would be lost. For Alexandra it meant her father was protecting her, and her shame mounted.

"But you must have realized at the time how important it was."

"Not really," Pembrooke answered. "I was more interested in proving its validity."

"By questioning Mr. Wittemore," the attorney general finished.

"Yes, sir."

Horace Wittney, thoughtfully stroking his chin as if contemplating the answer, turned his back on the witness. A moment passed in which not a soul breathed, everyone awaiting the next question and Pembrooke's reply.

"Since the court will not have the privilege of viewing the letter, we will have to trust your memory, Sir Wallis," Wittney said. "Tell us, if you will and to the best of your recollection, what was written in the note."

For the first time since the questioning began, Alexandra was able to look at her father. He had chosen to wear buff-colored trousers, a gold brocade waistcoat, and a frock coat of brown broadcloth with a high collar. His dark hair was combed back neatly off his brow, and a frown shadowed the intense green color of his eyes. He was tall and thin, and very handsome, so handsome in fact that all the available women for miles around had, at some time or another, brazenly shown their interest in him. But Sir Wallis Pembrooke wasn't looking for a wife. The only woman he had ever loved had died five years ago, and he would never love another woman as much as he had loved his Jocelyn.

"It said that if I really wanted to find Garrett Ambrose, I was to ask Hardin Wittemore, that he not only knew where Ambrose was, but that he could take me to him," Pembrooke recited, carefully omitting the reference to his daughter being the man's lover.

"And you have no idea who might have written the note," the attorney general restated as he paced slowly back and forth in front of the jury box.

"No, sir, I do not."

"All right," Wittney continued, "then tell the jury what you did after you received the note."

While her father held everyone's attention for the moment, Alexandra stole a peek at Hardin. He seemed calm enough, yet from the way he was continually tugging at his silk cravat, she knew he really wasn't. And he had a right not to be. Even if Ambrose was found guilty and sentenced to life in prison, he still had friends on the outside, friends who would settle the score for Ambrose, and Hardin knew it. The young man's only hope of living a full life was for him to leave England and change his name. After the trial, Hardin Wittemore would be a marked man.

"Hardin must really care a lot for you, Lexie," Aimee reasoned, hiding her words behind her fan so that only her companion would hear what she had to say.

"What makes you think that?" Alexandra questioned.

"Well, even I can figure it out," Aimee scoffed. "The man has signed his own death warrant by testifying against Ambrose. There won't be a place in all of England for him to hide. I hope you're happy."

Alexandra's curiosity turned to anger. "Happy?" she echoed. "I'm far from happy, Aimee Welu. This whole mess has been quite upsetting."

"And all your doing, I might point out," her friend snapped in return. "You simply had to make Hardin take you to meet

Ambrose, and then when things didn't turn out the way you had planned, you used *him* to get back at Christian Page."

"Wait just a minute, Aimee," Alexandra argued. "You're forgetting something. If I hadn't come up with the idea first, Hardin would have suggested it anyway. He was using me, Aimee. Now I'm using him. So don't go trying to make a martyr out of him."

"I won't have to," Aimee jeered, her nose in the air. "If he's killed, the people of England will make him a martyr."

Alexandra opened her mouth to correct her friend's assumption and decided against it. There was no use in arguing the point. Aimee's mind was set and nothing Alexandra could say would change it. Slumping back in her chair, she focused her attention on the attorney general.

"Thank you, Sir Wallis," he was saying as he returned to his desk and sat down. "That will be all."

"Mr. Solicitor General?" the judge called. "Have you any questions for the witness?"

"No, Your Honor," George Broughton declared. "But I reserve the right to reexamine if the need arises later."

Taking the quill from its well, the Lord Chief Justice jotted down the request on the paper in front of him. "So noted," he replied as he glanced over at Alexandra's father. "Thank you, Sir Wallis. You are excused." His gaze shifted to Horace Wittney. "Call your next witness."

All eyes turned on the young man sitting alone in the box next to the judge, certain Hardin Wittemore would be that witness.

"I call Hardin Wittemore," the attorney general announced.

An excited murmur raced through the courtroom, and before the magistrate could raise his gavel a third time, it stilled. There wasn't a person there who wanted to miss a single word of Mr. Wittemore's testimony.

"You've heard Sir Wallis Pembrooke's claim, haven't you, Mr. Wittemore?" Wittney asked as he left his chair and slowly walked back and forth in front of the witness.

"Yes, sir," Hardin replied.

"And how say you? True or false?"

"True," Hardin answered without hesitation. "I had, on several occasions, dealt with Garrett Ambrose, and I knew where to find him."

"What kind of dealings, Mr. Wittemore?"

Hardin took a deep breath and forced himself not to look at Alexandra. "I purchased many of the goods he and his men had smuggled into England."

"What kind of goods? Can you be more specific?"

"Silks from the Orient, spices, Persian rugs, and a fur or two from Russia."

"And what did you do with these items?"

Alexandra's heart started a trip-hammer beat, certain Hardin wouldn't name her as one of the recipients of his lavish gifts but anxious nonetheless. She bit her lower lip and waited for his reply.

"I gave them to various lady friends of mine. I never sold them, sir, if that's what you mean. I wasn't out to make a profit. I'm wealthy enough already." His gaze never wavered from the attorney general's face.

"I see," Wittney replied. "But Garrett Ambrose was."

"Yes, sir," Hardin answered. "I would say it was fair to state that he made his living at it."

"And where did he get his merchandise to sell? I mean, how do you know he was the one who did the actual smuggling?"

"He openly admitted it to me. I guess you could say he bragged about it. I had no reason to doubt him."

The attorney general's robe flew out around his ankles when he suddenly and unexpectedly turned on Hardin, his frown deep and his hands clasped tightly on the balustrade that separated him from the witness. "And isn't it true, Mr. Wittemore, that there were several times when you *hired* Garrett Ambrose to secure certain items for you, items that had to be smuggled into England?"

An explosion of startled exclamations mixed with disbelieving remarks filled the room, and before the judge could bring everyone to order again, Wittney rushed on.

"Isn't that how the two of you met? You wanted to give one of your lady friends a trinket, a bottle of French perfume, and saw no way to do it without smuggling the gift into the country. And since you, yourself, are not a smuggler, Mr. Wittemore, you commissioned someone who was. Is that not correct?"

Alexandra noticed that Hardin's face had paled a little, but aside from that, he maintained his composure. She had known for many months that he purchased stolen goods from Garrett Ambrose and men like him, but she had never dreamed Hardin had hired the man to obtain the goods he wanted to buy. Feeling sick inside, she decided she couldn't listen to any more of it and started to rise.

"Where do you think you're going?" Aimee demanded, catching her friend's wrist and pulling her back down. "You brought all of this on. It's only fair you stay to hear it out. You owe it to Hardin." She waved her fan beneath her chin and added, "Besides, if you walk out now, everyone will know you're one of the lady friends he was talking about."

Alexandra reluctantly had to admit Aimee was right. The minute she stood up, everyone in Plymouth would know, and many of them would probably even suspect her of writing the note her father had received. She'd stay where she was, but only until the judge announced the guilty verdict. Then she'd slip out before the sentencing and before the crowd could miss her. There were bound to be some very pointed questions directed her way, and right now she wasn't up to answering them.

The rest of the trial passed in a blur for Alexandra. Hardin admitted his association with Garrett Ambrose, and the solicitor general, upon cross-examination, tried to convince the jury that *Hardin* was the mastermind behind the smuggling ring, and that Garrett and his crew had only followed orders and weren't aware that what they were doing was illegal. The crowd had roared with laughter over such a suggestion and had to be reminded several times that if they refused to remain quiet, they would be ushered from the courtroom.

After an hour of testimony and arguments by both sides of court, the jury was led to private quarters where they could decide on a verdict. Even Aimee had noticed the weak defense offered by George Broughton on behalf of Ambrose and his men, and that none of those charged were given the opportunity to speak in their own behalf. The trial had been a technicality. A guilty verdict was inevitable. The memory of the whole affair would be long-lasting and a topic of conversation for months to come. For Alexandra it would mark the beginning of a change in her. From this point on, she wouldn't be as reckless.

During the entire course of the trial, Christian had watched the dark-haired beauty sitting across the room from him. He had expected to see a smile on her face from the moment he and the others were led in, until the magistrate announced sentencing and the prisoners were dragged off again. This had been what she had worked so hard to achieve. So why did she appear to be upset? Wittemore had protected her. He had never mentioned a woman being in his presence whenever he met with Ambrose, and he had even been careful to speak in generalities when referring to his lady friends. And within the next few minutes the jury's decision would be announced, and he'd be carted off to prison with the rest of the men. She'd have accomplished what she'd set out to achieve. Then why the look of dismay? The conniving little vamp had won!

"You had your chance, Page," a deep voice in back of him declared, "and you let it slip through your fingers."

Feeling those around him move aside to make room for Garrett Ambrose, Christian decided to keep still while he waited for the man to finish whatever it was he had to say.

"I'd like to believe the little bitch simply caught you off guard, that you hadn't expected her to do anything more than cry and whimper and beg you not to hurt her. I'd like to believe that, Mr. Page, and maybe I should, since you're standing here with the rest of us with a look on your face that tells me you'd love to put a gun to her head. We'd all like that chance. But the fact remains, you *had* the chance and you messed it up. As a result, I'm going to have to pull in a lot of favors owed me so that I won't have to spend any more time behind bars than necessary, and that will put *you* in my debt. Think about that, Christian Page, while you pace the floor of your cell. On the day of your release, I'll be waiting outside to collect."

Christian had expected as much. Garrett Ambrose needed to blame someone, and since Christian was the newest member to join the gang, it only made sense to push the responsibility on him. The irony of the matter was that he truly was responsible. However, for his own protection he needed to put doubt in the minds of the rest of the men . . . at least until Rhomberg showed.

"And I'd like to believe letting Hardin Wittemore go wasn't a mistake," Christian countered over his shoulder without turning around. "I'd like to believe he didn't send the message to Pembrooke about himself as a cover, that he wasn't bent on revenge for what you did to him and his woman. I'd like to believe that," he mimicked, "but I can't. Hardin Wittemore was more of a threat to you than Miss Pembrooke could ever be. She had her reputation to protect. Wittemore had his honor to defend." The silence that followed brought a vague smile to his lips, knowing his point of view hadn't been considered by any of the men. For Ambrose's sake, he added mockingly, "Think about it, Ambrose, while *you* pace the floor of your cell waiting for favors to be repaid. On the day of my release, *I'll* come looking for *you*. There's a debt to be collected, all right. But I'll be the one doing the collecting." He could almost feel the look of hatred Ambrose gave him and how the man's body had probably stiffened in rage. Christian had made an enemy for life, but the idea didn't worry him. If all else failed, Christian planned to call the man out rather than let the law deal with him. It was what he should have done in the first place.

The door opened to the anteroom where the jury had gone only a short five minutes before. The crowd's attention was total, as was their silence, as everyone watched the group of six men file out and reclaim their seats near the judge's bench. Their decision had taken longer than the gathering of onlookers had expected.

"Have you reached a verdict?" His Lord Chief Justice asked.

The foreman, a short, rotund little man whose wig sat crookedly on his head, stood up, his hands clasped in front of him. "We have, Your Honor."

"And how do you find the defendants? Guilty or innocent?"

"Guilty, Your Honor," the man replied, and the courtroom burst into loud cheers and noisy applause.

"Order! Order!" the magistrate bellowed with a sharp rap of his wooden gavel. "This court is still in session. Quiet! All of you!"

"Well, Lexie, you got what you wanted," Aimee said disgustedly while the judge fought to control the joyous crowd. "Christian Page is going to prison and Hardin Wittemore will have to run for his life. How does it feel to know that you alone are respon—" Her question was cut short when her companion suddenly bolted to her feet and began to push through the mob on her way out of the courtroom. "Where are you going?" Aimee demanded. "Don't you want to hear how long they'll be locked away? Isn't that what all of this was about? Lexie!" But her friend wasn't listening, or at least she wasn't interested in hearing the judge's declaration, and Aimee begrudgingly left her place to follow after the hurriedly departing young woman.

"Bailiff!" His Lord Chief Justice shouted. "If order is not restored immediately, you are to clear this courtroom!"

Since the spectators had come for only one purpose, the cheering stopped almost instantly, and within a few moments everyone was again seated, quietly awaiting the judgment to be handed down. While some watched the expressions on the faces of the prisoners, others studied the man seated behind the bench. Only a few looked at Pembrooke and Sir Robert Peel, who sat beside him. One or two glanced at Hardin Wittemore, wondering what would become of him after the trial. No one noticed Alexandra's absence . . . except Christian.

"It is the decision of this court and its jurors that the accused are guilty of the charges brought against them," the magistrate declared once he had entered the findings on the document before him. "It is therefore ordered and adjudged by this court that Garrett Ambrose and his associates be transported upon the seas, beyond the seas, to such a place as His Majesty, by the advice of His Privy Council, shall think fit to direct and appoint for the term in years of a score and three." Seizing his gavel, His Honor Lord Blakesley smacked it hard against its cradle. "Court dismissed."

·❦] *Chapter Six* [❦·

NEWELL QUIMBY SELDOM ALLOWED THE FATE OF ONE OF HIS prisoners to affect him, since every convict had a story to tell and each seemed more pathetic than the last, most of which he was sure had been the result of an overactive imagination. The head gaoler, as the convicted saw him, was their only hope of escaping their sentence, if they could somehow convince him that they had been wrongly accused. Quimby had, therefore, learned to ignore their pleas. Those who said nothing, he concluded, were guilty and had accepted their lot. The newest group to join the ranks fell in the latter category—with the exception of one. There was something different about Christian Page, something that bothered Quimby. He neither protested nor hurled oaths at the guard who brought his meals the way every other prisoner did. Christian Page seemed content with his situation, as if he were waiting for something—or someone—to come along. And he had drawn the attention of Quimby's men as well.

"He's a strange one, sir," Stanley Nelson declared, entering Quimby's office after completing the dinner rounds with the prisoners.

"Who?" the gaoler asked, looking up from the letter he was writing.

"Page," Nelson replied. "Christian Page."

Quimby returned to his work. "I know," he mumbled.

"I'm more afraid of him than all of the Garrett Ambroses thrown in together," the guard admitted as he dropped down in a chair. "I don't mean I fear for my life—I don't honestly believe Page would kill me if he had the chance—

I mean his attitude scares me."

Quimby stuck the quill in its well and fell back in his chair with a heavy, troubled sigh. "Yes, I know what you mean. I've never met anyone like him."

"And that stuff he's doing," Nelson went on to say. "What is it? He acts like he's lost his mind with all that struttin' and posin' and swingin' his arms. I had to look twice to make sure he was alone in his cell. Why, he acts like he's fightin'—or dancin' with a ghost." Nelson stiffened his frame as he shook off the shiver that raced up his spine. "One minute he's movin' around, and the next he's sittin' cross-legged and barefoot on the floor with his eyes shut. It's almost like he's prayin'. But I ain't never seen nobody pray like that. Do you suppose he's snapped?"

With his elbows resting on the arms of his chair and his fingers entwined, Quimby tapped his chin with the knuckles of both thumbs. "No," he confessed after a moment, "I don't."

"Then what's he doin'? Tryin' to drive the rest of us crazy?"

"I believe he's doing whatever it will take for him *not* to go insane in a place like this. While an innocent man cries for his release and the guilty hopelessly plot ways to escape, Christian Page is dealing with the inevitable. If he can survive the prison, the hulk, and the voyage to Australia, he'll have the strength and the sanity to survive whatever his future brings."

"Why bother?" Nelson scoffed. "Ain't no kind of a life he's goin' to over there. He's got the best part of his good years to serve out as a slave to some rich man, with very little hope of returnin' to England when he's free again. Don't make no sense to me."

"Oh, but it does," Quimby argued. "I believe Mr. Page is innocent."

"What?" Nelson shot back. "How can you think that, sir? He was captured right alongside Garrett Ambrose. He was given a fair trial and accused by Mr. Wittemore of smuggling. And he never spoke up denyin' he was. The jury found him guilty, so he is."

"Maybe," Quimby said slowly. "And maybe not."

"Well, I guess everybody's got a right to their own opinion," the guard admitted as he pushed himself up from the chair and headed for the door. "But as I see it, you ain't got no reason to think that."

"Yes, I do," Quimby muttered to himself as the door closed behind Nelson. There was the ring Page had given him as payment to fetch Lewis Rhomberg. The gaoler had misunderstood the prisoner's reason for wanting to see Rhomberg, and because of it, his request had been denied. There was even the possibility that Page had been found guilty of a crime he hadn't committed because of Quimby's hesitation. Well, he was about to rectify that. Leaning, he withdrew the quill again and signed his name to the letter he'd written. As soon as he'd eaten his supper, he'd take the letter to a friend who in turn would see it delivered to Lewis Rhomberg. They'd talk in private first, and once Quimby was satisfied that his suspicions were correct, he'd help Rhomberg any way he could to free Christian Page.

"You must be one with yourself," Sang Soo had always told his pupil. "Concentrate. Find the center of your existence. See it as the sun burning inside of you. Let its warmth spread throughout your body. Find your peace. Nothing of the earthly world can touch you then."

In silence Christian repeated the words as he sat on the cold, hard floor of his cell, his ankles crossed, knees spread apart, and his eyes shut. He focused on an imaginary spot just below his breastbone, while he closed out all of the sounds of the prison, its people, and the twilight hours marking the end of his fourth week locked inside the dark, dank walls.

Let nothing distract you.

The bright light began to grow.

Feel it. Surrender to it.

A hot sensation curled his belly and relaxed the muscles in his chest. His limbs began to tingle. His breathing slowed.

Concentrate.

A frown defiantly creased his brow.

Concentrate, Christian Page!

He tried harder, fighting the vague image stealing in through his subconscious, the sweet aroma of perfume, green satin, and the long, shining locks of dark brown hair. Suddenly, victori-

ously, the vision of Alexandra Pembrooke shattered his meditation. His eyes flew open, his nostrils flared, and the muscle
in his jaw flexed.

"Damn!" he snarled, springing to his feet in one effortless
leap.

In the corner of the small room, he leaned with his palms
pressed against the stones, his head lowered between his outstretched arms, and his feet wide apart. It had become increas-
ingly difficult for him of late to get the green-eyed beauty out
of his mind, and until he did, he'd have no control over his
future. The stench of the place alone would drive a man mad,
not to mention the offal the guard passed off as food. Being
locked up by himself held no threat—Christian preferred it—
but the agony of knowing it might last his lifetime had already
begun to work on his nerves. He needed to achieve a deep inner
peace, an immersion within himself, to survive. And by God,
he would survive! He must! As long as Garrett Ambrose still
had a breath of life in him, Christian's work wasn't finished.
His imprisonment might have moved his goal a little out of
reach and delayed it a bit, but it didn't mean he'd just give
up. He owed it to Marion Troy.

Jerking upright, he caught sight of the tiny square opening
near the ceiling above him. Its only purpose was to let in fresh
air, a ray of sunlight, and to act as a subtle torment for the prisoner who couldn't reach it. The aperture wasn't large enough
for even a child to squeeze through, providing the youngster
had a way of scaling the wall, and each time Christian looked
at it, he found himself wishing he was a bird, a hawk, if he
had the choice.

His anger lessened as he envisioned the winged flight of the
majestic creature, its gold eyes, and brown and beige plumage.
He remembered the first time he had watched a hawk stretch
out its wings and take to the sky, how it had soared higher
and higher until it was all but lost among the clouds. He could
hear the shrill whistle that altered its course and brought the
powerful bird swooping earthward again. He could feel the
excitement and the touch of fear that had seized the young
boy of twelve as he watched his uncle boldly hold up his jack-
eted arm on which the hawk would land, and he remembered

thinking that Marion Troy was the bravest man he had ever known.

"And the most stubborn," Christian mumbled as he fell against the wall and slid to the floor, one knee bent and his elbow draped over it. "If only he'd seen what I was trying—"

A pain stabbed at his heart and stilled his recital. If anyone was to blame for his uncle's death, it was Christian. He might not have pulled the trigger, but his actions years ago had brought on the events that led to the man's cold-blooded murder. And until he avenged Marion Troy's death, Christian would never be at peace with himself.

"Christian, I can understand your rage," he remembered Rhomberg telling him after Christian had gone to his friend for help. "But Ambrose didn't actually kill your uncle . . . or your cousin. Russel was killed by a deputy when he tried to run. Burnell Wagner shot your uncle, and *he* was killed over a year ago. The court won't convict Ambrose on either charge."

"Maybe not. But as I see it, Ambrose is responsible for both my cousin's and uncle's deaths," Christian had argued, barely able to hold his anger in check. "If there's no other way to make him pay, then I'll kill him myself."

"And wind up dancing on the gibbet?" Lewis had countered.

"*If I must!*"

Christian recalled how they had argued well into the night, and that several times he had picked up his gun and powder bag and had started for the door, only to have Lewis throw himself in the way.

"There's more to this than what you've already told me, Chris. Your anger comes from deep inside you," Lewis had finally observed. "It's almost as if you're blaming yourself. I can't let you leave feeling that way. Tell me everything. Let me understand so that I can help you."

Even now Christian could remember how difficult it had been for him to relive his past, the arguments he'd had with his uncle and how blind he'd been not to realize that his cousin, a young boy of nine, would be affected as he stood by listening in silence. He also recalled how, once he'd finished with the story, Lewis had made him understand that what had happened hadn't truly been his fault. Christian had no control over what others thought and did. Yet he still blamed himself to some degree.

Marion Troy, a widower with an infant son, had taken in his orphaned nephew when Christian was only eight years old. He'd loved him, cared for him, and taught him right from wrong. He kept him warm and fed, and treated him as an equal to his own son. Life was simple and fulfilling until Christian reached the age of young manhood, a time for dreams and the desire to have more than the basic needs his uncle's carpentry shop could provide. The aristocrats of England had, for some time then, been using their courts to weed out the "less respectable class" of people by finding them guilty of trumped-up charges and shipping them to the penal colony of Australia, and Christian had begun to fear for his uncle's safety. He'd heard about the riches to be had in America, and because he saw it as a way to escape the injustices at home, he fervently suggested that his uncle sell the business and that the three of them settle in America. Marion wouldn't hear of it, and so the arguments began, bitter disagreements that grew so out of proportion that one day, without warning, Christian left.

He had signed on as a deck hand to a merchant ship in order to pay for his passage to America. Then, once they had dropped anchor in Boston, Christian looked for work as a carpenter's apprentice, planning to save all he earned until he had enough money to start his own shop and send for his uncle and cousin. Being only eighteen at the time, he had been full of great hopes. But jobs weren't that easy to find, and the first year there he had nearly starved to death. Out of desperation he had turned to the only kind of work available to him, and the following year found him in China, where the merchant ship on which he worked had sailed with its cargo hold full of tobacco and cotton for trade. He'd become very ill on the last leg of the voyage, and when the ship was ready to return home, he'd been left behind. Sang Soo had taken him in, and with Min Le's help, they had nursed him back to health. By then Christian had fallen in love with the land, its people, and, most of all, Min Le.

What Christian hadn't known during those years was that Russel had come to blame his father for Christian's abandoning them. He, too, argued that they should sell the business and go to America looking for Christian. When Marion refused, Russel rebelled and ran away. Somehow his path crossed Ambrose's, and pulled in by the lure of riches, Russel, at thirteen, had joined the band of thieves. Less than a year later he was shot and killed by a deputy who had come to arrest him.

Marion's rage had been expected when the constable informed him how his son had died. The actions he took in revenge hadn't been. Blaming Garrett Ambrose for the tragedy, Marion had contacted a business acquaintance of his who Marion knew traded with Ambrose. Told when the smuggler was supposed to make his next delivery, Marion had loaded his musket and had waited in the shadows.

"I came home to find that not only had Russel been killed, but my uncle as well. Maybe Wagner did the actual shooting, but he did it to protect Garrett Ambrose, and Russel died doing the man's bidding," Christian had seethed once his story was finished. "And by God, Ambrose will pay!"

"How? By knowing that his death will be yours too?" Lewis had shouted. "Yes, he will pay, Chris. But not the way you have planned. *My way!*"

A soft smile curled Christian's mouth as he sat on the floor of his cell remembering Lewis's enthusiasm as he laid out his scheme to connect his friend with Garrett Ambrose. It had worked, and everything was going as planned until Alexandra Pembrooke walked through the door of the inn. Christian had known he would have to prove himself sooner or later, but he had never expected it would require he take the life of the daughter of the very man who could help Christian in his quest. Not that it mattered who sired the woman—Christian would never kill any woman—but the irony of the situation had come as a sign, a warning that his mission wouldn't be as easy to complete as he had thought it would. The idea had been to join the gang, observe, and collect facts, information that would bring Ambrose to trial for murder and treason.

Christian wanted the death penalty for Garrett Ambrose: he
wanted to witness his execution. He wanted to stand at the
base of the gallows and just as the rope was slipped around
the man's neck, he would call up the names of Russel and
Marion Troy. Ambrose's last thoughts on earth would be how
he'd been tricked and by whom. It would still happen, Christian
silently pledged. It would just take a little longer.

A small shaft of morning light fell in through the tiny window of the cell and found its inhabitant already awake and
executing his self-imposed routine of rigid discipline. Christian knew that in order to keep his body fit, he would have
to adhere to a daily regimen of strenuous activity, and since
there was little else to do, he spent most of the day employing
the Chinese art of kung fu. The rest of the time he meditated,
and only rarely did he allow himself to think about his confinement. Hardly a day passed, however, that he didn't question
the guard, who brought his foul meal and a fresh cup of water,
about Garrett Ambrose's captivity. If the man actually managed to manipulate his way out of prison ahead of Christian, it
would mean that Christian would have to start all over again,
only this time it would be doubly hard for him to win his way
back into the gang, if he succeeded at all. As a last resort,
he would sacrifice his own life in exchange for the taking of
Ambrose's. Thus, when he heard the sound of footsteps in the
corridor, he quit his training and moved near the door.

"So who found him, Nelson? You?" Christian heard one of
the guards ask his companion.

"Me and Fischer. Found him slumped over his desk. The
surgeon says it was his heart, that it just gave out."

"When did he die, do you suppose?" the first asked.

"From the look of it, just after he ate his supper last night,"
Nelson surmised. "His plates were still there, but they were
empty." He laughed harshly as he held up the bowl he carried.
"Probably wasn't his heart, though. Ol' Quimby probably died
from eatin' this swill."

The panel in the metal door slid sideways and Christian
stepped back to accept his breakfast of mush and the tin of
water.

"Here ya go, Page," Nelson jeered, peering in through the bars. "Eat hearty. If you're lucky, it'll kill ya like it did the gaoler. It'd save us the extra work and end your miserable existence."

Christian gave the man a cold stare. Was life so meaningless that someone like Nelson could make a joke of it? If their roles were reversed, Christian doubted the man would find anything humorous about it, but explaining it to him would be a waste of energy.

"Ya know something, Page?" the man continued. "Me and Quimby were talkin' about you last night. The old fool said he thought you were innocent. 'Course, I told him he was crazy. Actually, I told him I thought *you* were crazy. Ya are, aren't ya?" He laughed again. "And before ya ask, Ambrose is still here, but not for long. The whole lot of ya is gettin' moved today . . . to the hulk." He slammed the panel shut. "So enjoy your lodgings while they last. Where you're goin' ain't half as nice as this."

The man's callous laughter echoed down the corridor as he and his companion moved to the next cell. Nelson enjoyed tormenting the prisoners any way he could. With the one called Christian Page, Nelson had come to the conclusion that nothing would upset him. If he'd stayed by the man's door for a moment longer just then, he would have realized he'd been wrong.

Christian's first sight of the half-burned, pitiful-looking remains of a once mighty warship moored at the docks of Plymouth came as a surprise. He'd heard the deplorable stories of how the convicts were treated while they awaited transport to Australia, but it was worse than he expected. The foul odor emanating from the wreckage reached Christian's nostrils long before the prison wagon in which he rode had rolled to a stop near its gangplank. Huge, gaping holes in its sides and decks assured him of no dry place to hide during a storm, and no one had to tell him of the crowded conditions in which he'd be forced to eat and sleep. Stanley Nelson's claim had been correct. The prison cell left a lot to be desired, but in comparison to this, the six-by-eight-foot room had been a piece of heaven.

An armed guard approached and ordered everyone to get out of the wagon, a feat that proved difficult because of the heavy leg irons clamped around the prisoners' ankles. Christian was the second man to leave the rig and while he waited for the rest to join him, he surveyed the other prison wagons that had arrived ahead of him, hoping to catch sight of Ambrose. If Nelson hadn't lied to him earlier, the outlaw had to be somewhere close by, and Christian wanted to know where. By now, he realized, Garrett Ambrose wouldn't look the same as he had— even Christian had a month's growth of beard and needed a ribbon to hold back his hair—but even so, he felt sure he would recognize him. Ambrose had an aura about him that even a blind man could sense.

"Move along!" the guard rasped with a jab of his musket in Christian's back.

Caught unawares, Christian nearly stumbled, but he managed to regain his balance with the help of the man beside him, then shuffled off behind the group of prisoners heading toward the gangplank. There were close to fifty men, making the wait to board the hulk long and slow. But the single file of men clumsily walking up the wooden ramp enabled Christian to see each man clearly, and once he spotted Benton Wall's huge bulk, he knew the man behind him had to be Ambrose. In that same moment, as if the heat of his stare had singed Ambrose's flesh, dark eyes turned to glare back at Christian. A long while passed as the two men sent silent messages to each other, and only the shout of a guard broke the trance. War had been declared.

That night as Christian prepared to lie down and sleep as best he could in the cramped quarters, he wondered which smelled worse: the overall stench of the place or the man next to him. He'd get used to it, he supposed, given time, the same as he'd grown accustomed to the solitude of his prison cell. What he did wonder, however, was if he'd ever get used to not being allowed to bathe whenever he needed it. One of the first things he'd learned about the Chinese people was their belief in a clean body as well as a clean spirit. He had liked the custom, and doing without it was a strain.

His job that afternoon had been repairing a cobblestone

street. He and five other men, under the supervision of a guard armed with both a musket and pistol, and sporting a cat-o'-nine-tails, had used pickaxes to break up the old paving. While two of them shoveled the stones into a pushcart and hauled it away, the other four started on the next section. It was tedious, slow, and back-breaking work, complicated by the heavy leg irons they wore, the heat of the late-afternoon sun, and the guard's refusal to allow the men a short break for even a few sips of water. Of those in his group, Christian was the only one who had withstood the strenuous labor, but he knew that in time even he might collapse from exhaustion. All that would keep him going would be the thought of Garrett Ambrose, how he would suffer, too, and the promise Christian had made to himself and to his uncle. But now, as he stretched out on his pallet of dirty straw and stared up at the stars in the sky through the hole in the deck, someone else came to mind.

At first the vision of Alexandra Pembrooke pleased him. She was the most beautiful woman he had seen in a long while, with luxuriant dark hair, alabaster skin, delicate features, and the most incredible green eyes one could imagine. Kissing her had been a delight. The scent of her had intoxicated him. The feel of her supple body pressed against him had awakened a long-forgotten passion in him, and he knew that if she hadn't come to her senses when she had, he would have made love to her. And it wouldn't have been forced as he had originally thought it would have to be. In a way he was wishing she hadn't realized her weakness so soon. He would have enjoyed exploring every curve of her young body, the blending of their souls, and the fulfillment such a time together could have given them. But it hadn't happened. She had gone from a soft and willing partner to a she-devil, fighting and clawing and . . . He winced at the memory of how she had gotten free of him, and how her method had destroyed the moment. Whether she had known what she was doing or not, the effect was the same, and while he had struggled with his pain, she had finished off her attack and fled.

The warmth those memories stirred cooled rather quickly when he recalled the next time they had met and why she had come to his cell. If God would have granted him the ability, he would have reached through the metal door that protected her from him and wrapped his fingers around her long, lovely neck. Instead of being grateful that she had escaped with her life *and* with her virtue intact, she had set out to satisfy her need for revenge, and in the process condemned him to this. He closed his eyes, wishing he could block out not just the sight of the place, but the smell and the sounds as well. His only comfort came from knowing that Garrett Ambrose was probably wishing for the same thing.

By the end of his second week in the hulk, Christian had abandoned any hope that Lewis Rhomberg would be able to find him. While he was in a prison cell, the guards knew him by name. Here among two hundred other convicted men, Christian had become just another body awaiting transport. If Lewis had been notified, it would take weeks for him to find out where Christian had been taken, and by then the chances were strong that he would already be on a ship sailing for Australia. That realization would have taken its toll on an ordinary man, but with Christian, he focused his thoughts on the fact that wherever *he* went, Garrett Ambrose would be coming with him.

His jobs varied from day to day. Sometimes he'd be assigned to simple tasks such as cleaning out the stables, unloading supply wagons, or carrying crates from the merchant ships anchored at the wharf near the prison vessel. A few times he was put on the burial detail for those convicts who hadn't been able to endure the hardships of their incarceration or for those who had succumbed to illness. The more strenuous work involved dredging silt or mud in the harbors. Christian actually preferred the latter as it gave him the opportunity to wash the filth from his body while he stood in waist-deep water. The sacrifice he had to make in exchange, however, was that he had to sleep in his wet clothes. There were many nights when he lay awake shivering, but knowing he was cleaner than he had been before eased a little of the discomfort.

Hardly a day passed without his seeing Garrett Ambrose. Benton Wall was always at his side, and Christian noticed that whenever the guards weren't watching, Wall did his companion's work for him. He also shared his ration of food and water with Ambrose, and Christian wondered if the giant realized his loyalty was being wasted. Ambrose cared only about himself, and if it came down to choosing, the man would save his own life without giving his friend's safety a second thought. There were plenty of other men like Benton Wall waiting to take his place, and Ambrose knew it. The promise of wealth and riches could buy a hundred men like Wall. Ambrose's greed, however, had bought him something else he'd never bargained for: Christian's hatred and the promise of death.

It always amazed Christian to see the wide range in ages of the newest group of convicts to join the prison wreck. Some were crippled old men while others were hardly more than children, and he soon began to doubt the wisdom of the English courts. Perhaps their crimes were such that the penalty warranted imprisonment, but old men and babies didn't belong in the company of the likes of his fellow inmates. The old were abused and the young were tormented.

Christian had sworn an oath to himself on the day of his arrival not to get involved with anyone's problems, and perhaps it was because of who he saw persecuting the young, dark-haired youth that he stepped in, but something inside him stirred that night when he saw Ambrose yank the bowl of porridge from the youth's hands. The boy, not more than twelve, Christian guessed, objected until Wall raised a large fist and struck him across the temple. The blow sent the boy crashing to the floor, bloody and dazed, and when no one moved to aid the child, Christian found himself leaving his pallet before he'd taken a moment to think about the results.

The irons around his ankles slowed his approach, but before Wall could bend to grab the boy by the hair and deal him a second round, Christian moved between them. Every muscle in his body grew rigid as he curled the fingers of both hands to the middle knuckles, tucked in his elbows, raised his left half-closed fist even with his jaw, and pulled his right hand in close to his waist. The shackles hampered perfect balance, since he couldn't spread his feet more than the length of chain allowed, but he counted on the element of surprise to make up for it as he prepared to defend not only the child but himself from the threatening giant.

Although none of the other inmates moved, all of them paused in the sampling of their fare to watch the contest between their own David and Goliath. If any had possessed the necessary coins, wagers would have been made, for even though the majority knew the outcome of the Biblical match, only a few thought the smaller of these two men would win this time. David, at least, had had a sling and a rock.

"Come now, Mr. Page," Garrett Ambrose said with a broad grin as he sat on an overturned barrel, the stolen bowl of boiled cereal and milk held in his left hand. "You're not thinking to fight with Mr. Wall, are you? He could crush your skull with one blow. And for what? A child? A bowl of slop? Why, Mr. Page? What makes you so careless?"

Christian's eyes never left those of his opponent. "Principle, Ambrose," he replied, his voice deathly calm and composed.

Ambrose's laughter rang throughout the semidarkened, foul-smelling cavity. "Principle, you say. You're defending children because of principle? In case you've forgotten, my good man, the only way any of us will survive down here—or anywhere else for that matter—is to abandon our principles and hang on to life any way we can. If the weak perish, so be it. Only the strong will live to see tomorrow." He jammed his fingers in the bowl and scooped up a helping of mush. "I plan to see many tomorrows. You've seen your last." He nodded at Wall, then settled his attention on eating.

Those who were closest shielded their supper dishes with folded arms as they moved out of the way. Everyone wanted to witness the confrontation, but no one could afford to sacrifice his meal to do it. At the moment filling their bellies was more important. Yet if given a choice, many of them might willingly give up one meal if it meant bringing an end to Ambrose's tyranny; since the man's arrival, their humble existence had grown even worse. They knew there would always be someone like him to take up where he left off, but right now it appeared that the one who challenged the titan was their only hope of easing some of the atrocities heaped on them. They wanted to cheer him on; they wanted him to win; they even wished they could help somehow. But everyone realized the impossibility of such a hope. Christian Page was simply outclassed.

"Watch your opponent's eyes," Sang Soo had preached while sparring with his pupil. "Concentrate. Never take your eyes from his. He will tell you when he will strike. You will see it. You will sense it."

The words flashed through Christian's mind and all the while he stared. He never blinked. His breathing was measured and shallow, enabling him to keep the muscles in his chest and belly rigid. He kept his spine stiff, his hands tight, and he waited. Benton Wall had to make the first move. Christian's success would come from his defense and the surprise of his reaction to Wall's attack.

Standing only a few feet away from his foe, Wall assumed that all he would have to do would be to reach out and grab the man around the neck. Within a few seconds he would have squeezed the life from him and the fight would be over. Page would be out of the way, Wall would be satisfied, and Mr. Ambrose would have proven again that he had what it took to be a leader. Confident, the bulky man lowered his chin slightly and smiled an evil, victorious smile as he took a step closer and raised his hands. He harbored no resentment against Christian Page, but his presence had become a nuisance. It would be a shame to have to kill him.

Had any of those who observed stood back and judged whose face showed the most surprise, it would have been difficult if not impossible. Long before Wall's outstretched hands had made their claim on his opponent's throat, Christian had counterattacked. With a quick, powerful thrust of his left arm, Christian's open hand—the fingers straight and the thumb extended—shot out and struck Wall sharply across the Adam's apple. The result was immediate and exactly what Christian had planned. Wall, unable to draw a breath, threw back his head and gasped for air. Immediately Christian struck again, this time with the knuckles of his right hand to Wall's sternum. The carefully placed blow knocked the wind out of his adversary and dropped Wall to his knees almost instantly, and while everyone else stared in shocked disbelief, Christian turned to the man who had ordered the contest.

Garrett Ambrose had witnessed innumerable fights over the years, but he'd never seen one quite like this, and never one involving Benton Wall's defeat. Nor had he seen the style of defense Christian Page had used. Mystified, Ambrose simply stared. When Christian held out his hand, silently demanding the return of the boy's porridge, Ambrose gave it to him without a protest of any kind.

"Mister, I ain't never seen nothin' like it," an old man confessed enthusiastically as he helped Christian pull the youth to his feet and guide him to Christian's straw bed. "And if somebody had asked me beforehand, I would have said you'd never have stood a chance against that huge bloke. Where'd ya learn to fight like that?"

"A friend taught me," Christian quietly replied, preferring not to be any more specific than that. The less people knew about him, the better he liked it, for their sake as well as his own.

"Well, thank your friend for me," the old man instructed as he moved away. "I know I'll sleep better."

The cut on the boy's head had already stopped bleeding, and other than a slight headache and dark bruise, Christian assumed the youngster would be all right by morning. Handing the child his dinner bowl, Christian twisted around and sat down cross-legged beside him.

"What's your name?" he asked as he retrieved his own food and began to eat.

"T. J.," the boy replied, greedily scooping the mush into his mouth as though he hadn't tasted such a delicacy in a long while.

"T. J.," Christian repeated. "What's it stand for?"

"Don't stand for nothin'. It's just plain T. J."

Christian suspected that wasn't true, but he decided not to press. "Do you have a last name, T. J.?" he asked, very much aware of the youth's hunger and mildly surprised that anyone could eat slop like this with so much relish. Perhaps the child was used to nothing better.

"Savage," the boy answered between mouthfuls.

Christian tested its sound. "T. J. Savage. A nice, strong name. How old are you, T. J.?"

The boy's right shoulder bobbed up and down. "Don't know exactly. My ma died when I was little, and my pa left 'fore I was born."

The vision of a young child fending for himself brought a frown to Christian's brow. "You're not telling me you've lived in the streets since then, are you?"

The eating stopped long enough for the youngster to give his companion a sarcastic look. "Hell, no. I went to live with my pal, King George."

Christian had known it was a stupid question even before he'd asked it. If Marion Troy hadn't taken *him* in, he'd have probably wound up like T. J. With an embarrassed smile, he gazed down at the bowl he held and said, "I take it you two didn't get along very well."

Realizing that the stranger wasn't as dumb as he'd first assumed, T. J. paused a moment to evaluate his companion. The life he'd been forced to lead had taught him not to trust, and even though this man had saved him from a beating *and* had won him back his supper, he was reluctant to change his ways. "You could say that," he replied before turning back to finish up the last droplet in his bowl.

Christian could sense the reason for the boy's hesitation. If he'd been thrown out into the streets at such a tender age, he wouldn't be too quick to make friends either. He understood, but it didn't mean he'd let the youngster go on thinking no one was worth his trouble. Noticing how T. J. was staring at his empty bowl as if he were contemplating its flavor, Christian reached over and took it from him.

"Here," he said, offering the boy his own half-eaten portion. "Have mine. I'm not really hungry anyway."

T. J. seemed close to refusing Christian's generosity, when his hunger won over his independent streak and he made a grab for the food. "Thanks," he said through a hint of a smile.

"You're welcome," Christian replied easily as he stretched out his legs behind the boy and lay down with his arms folded under his head for a pillow. "You're more than welcome, actually. You're doing me a favor."

"Oh, yeah?" T. J. questioned, lowering the dish from his mouth. "What kind of favor?"

"I hate to see food go to waste," Christian admitted, "even if it really isn't fit to be called food. If you hadn't wanted it, it probably would have been thrown out."

The insinuation that what he ate wasn't palatable made T. J. pause with his hand in the bowl. It was mush, just old cereal and milk boiled together until it had no flavor. Sure it wasn't roasted boar and gravy, but it filled his belly. What more could he ask for? A silver dish and spoon? A napkin? A white tablecloth?

"You ain't been in a place like this before, have you?" he guessed with a sour look as he began to shovel in the remainder of his meal.

"And you have," Christian remarked as he stole a peek at Garrett Ambrose and Benton Wall. The two men were both settling down on their pallets for the night. He knew it wasn't finished between him and the giant, but at least Wall wouldn't be so quick to grant Ambrose's wishes next time.

Feeling much better now that he'd had his fill, T. J. set the bowl aside and licked the sticky residue from his fingers. "Yeah, I have. And it won't take you long to learn not to be givin' away your food. Ya don't get second helpin's, ya know. Why, in a couple more days, you'll be stealing somebody else's . . . just like him." He jerked his head in Ambrose's direction. "The bastard. He only picks on them he's sure he can bully." Remembering that he had recently been a victim, he touched his fingertips to the gash on his head. "I guess I should thank you for what you did, but you shouldn't have done it."

"Why not?" Christian asked, closing his eyes. The work he'd done that day was beginning to weigh him down, and as soon as the sun came up in the morning, the guards would be there to rouse everyone from their beds. He could do without a full meal tonight, but he needed his rest.

" 'Cause I don't think Ambrose is the forgivin' type."

A slow smile worked the edges of Christian's mouth. "Neither am I, son. Neither am I."

··❦⟨ *Chapter Seven* ⟩❦··

THE WINSOME AROMA OF JASMINE AND THE EUPHONIC MELO-
dy of the wind as it swayed the majestic willows against the
backdrop of a cloudless blue sky filled Christian's dream. The
shimmering gold of a sunset reflecting off the smooth surface
of a pond and the sight of a young woman in the distance
moving gracefully toward him in small measured steps lifted
his spirit and soothed the torment of his soul. He became lost
in the fantasy of his inner thoughts. He willingly allowed the
illusion of his imaginings to blur reality. He lived once more
in the past as the vision of his wife took shape and filled his
mind with joy.

"Min Le?" he heard himself call out to her. "Min Le."

"Yes, Christian," came the soft reply. "I'm here . . . with
you."

A gossamer veil of mist enveloped her and swirled about
her shapely figure as she moved closer to him. From within the
silver cloak a delicate hand reached out for his, and he eagerly
accepted it, pulling his wife's tiny body into the tender fold of
his arms. Hungry for her, he kissed her mouth impatiently and
with an urgency that sparked the fires in his loins and set his
heart hammering in his chest. His marrow ached to have her,
to sample once again the splendor they had shared, the love,
the laughter and the promise of oneness through all eternity.

Suddenly a black cloud scored the sun-bathed horizon. It
stole the golden light, the fragrance in the air, the soft breeze
playing lightly all around them. Within its bowels thunder
cracked and lightning split it asunder, but no rain spilled
upon the earth. Instead an evil red flame grew up amid the

rolling blackness, staining the cerulean sky with its threat of destruction. Acrid smoke billowed forth and stung his eyes. It choked the breath from him. Its denseness thickened and long dark fingers reached out from it and tore his beloved wife from his arms.

"No!" he screamed. "Damn you, no! You won't take her from me. She is my wife and she belongs with me!"

Shrouded by an ebony curtain that seemed to mock him, to dare him to find her, he groped and pawed his way forward. His hand brushed against something soft and alive and warm, then moved away before he could claim it. He tried again and failed. He called out his wife's name, but only silence crackled back at him. Each breath he took burned his lungs; panic tightened the muscles in his body; exhaustion threatened to overcome him. Then, up ahead, a bright light shone through the inky shadows and he stumbled toward it. The closer he got, the clearer an image in its midst became, the image of a woman. Even though he prayed it would be that of his dearest Min Le, he knew it wasn't. She was tall and slender with flowing dark brown hair and skin the color of a pearl, and the air with which she held herself erect hinted of an independent nature, unlike that of his wife's. Drawn by some force, he unwillingly came to her, squinting in the swirling mist in an effort to see her face. Then Min Le's voice whispered sweetly in his ears.

"I will always love you, Christian. We will share a life eternal. But you are of the flesh and I am of the spirit. Love again, my husband. Know the joy it can bring. Forget the pain. And when your soul takes flight and soars high above your mortal being, we will once again be together."

"No!" he shouted to the heavens. "I will never love again. God blessed me once when He sent you to me. How can I be twice blessed? Why would I seek it?"

Silence came as his only answer, and just as he was about to call out again, the swirling fog lifted and the image of a green-eyed beauty appeared before him. Surprise, confusion, then rage filled him as he stared back at the alluring face of Alexandra Pembrooke. Surely Min Le didn't mean this conniving, spoiled, irresponsible siren could bring him peace and happiness! There was nothing about her to love. He doubted he even liked her. In fact, should he ever again have the chance, he would show her what a mistake it was to have ever thought she could challenge him and win. And he would have that chance . . . as long as Lewis Rhomberg was still alive, there was hope.

Suddenly a warm hand touched the cool clamminess of his arm, piloting him upward from the dark abyss of his dreams, and he came fully awake with a start when his subconscious cautioned danger.

"Hey!" T. J. Savage objected, jumping back out of the way when his companion's curled fingers came close to smashing his nose. "I didn't do nothin'. Ya was talkin' in your sleep and I thought ya'd probably not want anyone ta hear. But if ya're gonna hit me—"

"I apologize," Christian quickly assured the boy as he sat up and wiped the perspiration from his forehead, the dizziness of his dreams still swirling around inside his head. "What did I say?"

T. J., reluctant to accept the man's regrets, scowled angrily back at Christian. "Didn't really make no sense, but I figured ya wouldn't want to take the chance. Ya said a lady's name— anyway, I think it was a lady's."

"Min Le?" Christian supplied, glancing up at the dark sky above him through the gaping hole in the ship's main deck.

"Yeah. That was it. Funny name."

"It's Chinese," Christian explained. "Min Le was my wife."

The boy's eyebrows shot upward. "Oh, yeah? I ain't never met nobody married to a Chinese person before. She know ya're here?"

"Not really," Christian replied softly. "My wife died five years ago."

"Oh," T. J. whispered, sorry he'd been so short with the man. "Ya miss her, huh?"

"Yes, T. J., I miss her," Christian admitted as he swung his legs around to make room for the boy to sit beside him.

"You two have any children?"

"We had an infant son, but he died with his mother."

T. J.'s face wrinkled. "That's awful, Mr. Page. How'd they die?"

Christian would have preferred not discussing it, but the question was a simple one and T. J. wasn't really being nosy. Besides, Christian figured it might help if he talked about his tragedy to someone who really wanted to hear about it, someone like this dirty-faced scalawag who would understand pain. T. J., no doubt, was a scholar in that field. Suddenly remembering where they were and how many others might hear if they were only pretending to be asleep, Christian answered, "In a fire. It was . . . an accident." He glanced at the boy, nodded toward the mass of dozing bodies all around them, and added, "I'll tell you all about it sometime, when there aren't so many eavesdroppers."

T. J. nodded understandingly. "Where'd ya meet?"

"In China."

"Really?" The boy's excited tone conveyed how impressed he was. "I ain't never been nowhere 'cept England." Recalling the reason he and Christian Page had met, T. J.'s upper lip curled. " 'Course, now I'll be goin' ta Aus . . . Aus . . . "

"Australia," Christian finished for him.

"Yeah, Australia," T. J. jeered. "I hear it's hot over there, *real* hot. *And* I heard it'll take months to sail that far, three or four months. I don't like the water, Mr. Page." He leaned closer and admitted, "If I get the chance, I'm gonna escape 'fore they can put me on the next ship."

Christian smiled warmly. "We'd all like to do that, T. J. Every single man, woman, and child sentenced into exile for some laughable crime. So don't be surprised if you're not alone when the chance comes."

"That include you?"

Christian's blue eyes shifted their gaze on the two unmoving forms some distance away from him as Wall and Garrett Ambrose slept soundly on their pallets. "It depends," he answered.

"On who our company is?" T. J. guessed, for he'd seen where his companion's attention had gone. "You and Ambrose hate each other, don't ya?"

"Well, let's just say we're not fond of one another," Christian remarked, chuckling. "And if you know what's good for you, you'll stay as far away from him as you possibly can."

"I ain't a hard learner, Mr. Page," T. J. confessed with a touch of sarcasm. "I don't have ta get hit twice ta know who my enemies are."

"And what about your friends?" Christian posed. "Do you know who your friends are?"

"Ain't got none," came the sharp retort.

"Oh, but you do, son," Christian corrected, his knees drawn up and his arms draped loosely around them. "You have me." He waited for the youth to amend the declaration, since he guessed T. J. Savage liked not having any ties, and then raised a brow when the boy didn't respond or move a muscle. The youngster had obviously been mistreated his whole life and more than likely the perpetrator had always been a grown man. It wasn't easy for him to change his attitude that quickly, but at least he was considering the possibility that perhaps one grown-up was different from all the rest.

"You'd better get back to bed, T J.," he instructed. "It will be morning soon enough."

"Yes, sir," the child replied, scooting off the pallet and onto his own straw bed. "Good night, Mr. Page."

"Good night, T. J.," Christian answered as he lay back down. "And the next time I talk in my sleep, just nudge me. But be sure to duck right away."

The boy's laughter seemed to mock the utter dreariness of the place and brought a soft smile to Christian's lips. A moment later he lay staring up at the velvety black sky and twinkling stars overhead as he fought to unravel the meaning of his dream.

The docking of the *Adventure,* the infamous convict transport, came as a surprise to everyone. Even the guards hadn't been expecting it. Nearly two months had passed since the last transport had collected the prisoners from the hulk at Plymouth, and many were foolishly praying they had been overlooked or, better still, forgotten. For Christian it meant his last hope of Lewis Rhomberg finding him in time had vanished, for talk among the guards had centered on the finality of a man's life once he was shipped to that faraway land. No one ever returned.

During the past month Christian and young T. J. had formed a solid friendship. They had shared secrets, watched out for each other, and helped nurse each other when their difficult labor had resulted in blistered hands, sore feet, and pulled muscles. They had made the best of their bleak existence, and while no one else had ever seemed to find anything to laugh about, Christian and T. J. had.

Ambrose and his disciple had kept their distance, but with a very watchful eye that had weighed heavily on Christian. He knew Ambrose would jump at the opportunity of provoking him any way he could and the easiest method would be to hurt T. J., possibly even to kill him and make it look like an accident. Since then, Christian had slept lightly.

Protecting the boy these last weeks had been hard enough, but on board the transport, Christian worried it would be next to impossible. Once they anchored in Botany Bay, he had no idea of what might become of his young friend. It was entirely possible they'd be separated permanently. Therefore, while the two of them waited their turn to descend the gangplank, he reaffirmed his decision that T. J. Savage wouldn't be coming along.

"T. J.," he whispered as they were ushered off the ship and toward the end of the pier. "Do you know how to swim?"

"Well, I won't drown, but I'd never win a race," the boy admitted. "Why? Ya got a plan?"

"For you," Christian said as he carefully studied the guards and the procedure awaiting them.

The line of convicts was being led to a small shack where their irons were removed before they went inside. Upon emerging, each man was wearing a new shirt, canvas trousers, gray jacket and shoes, but without the restrictive leg irons, and from that point they were directed another hundred yards down the pier to the wooden ramp of the *Adventure*. At the top they were shackled in groups of four and taken belowdecks. Christian's idea would work, but for a young boy like T. J., it would be dangerous.

"Whaddaya mean ya got a plan for me?" the youth demanded in a loud whisper. "Ain't you comin' too."

"I can't," Christian told him. "I have to cause a diversion

so you'll be able to get away safely. Besides, where Ambrose goes, so do I."

"Yeah?" T. J. sneered. "And if I'm not with you, who'll protect your back? Ya can't deal with him and his moron alone, ya know."

"I was doing just fine before you came along," Christian advised, suppressing a smile.

The boy snorted derisively. "Yeah, sure ya were. Ya did so good that's why ya're standing in this here line. Don't try feeding me that crap, Mr. Page. You need me as much as I—" T. J. hadn't realized the truth until he had nearly said the words aloud, and with the discovery came a sadness he hadn't felt in a very long while. "Mr. Page," he continued, his eyes lowered, "I . . . I want to stay with you."

Knowing how hard it must have been for the boy to admit his feelings, Christian gently laid his hand on the youngster's shoulder and squeezed. "And I'd really like to have you stay. But this isn't a fit place for a man, let alone a boy. I truly believe you'd never survive the voyage, and I'd never be able to live with the knowledge that I'd let you die because of my selfishness. Besides, you'd be doing me a great favor by staying behind."

"How?" T. J. questioned testily.

"Remember the name of the friend I told you about?"

"Lewis Rhomberg."

Christian nodded. "I want you to find him and tell him what happened to me. He'll take care of you then, and he'll see to it that my name is cleared."

"How will he do that?"

"By paying a visit to Sir Wallis Pembrooke."

"It's a fine idea, Mr. Page, but what good will it do ya?" T. J. scoffed. "You'll be in Aus . . . Australia by then."

"That doesn't mean I have to stay there," Christian answered confidently. "If I'm acquitted, I'd be free to work my way back to England." He gave the boy a gentle shake. "And you'd better be here waiting for me."

T. J. stared at his friend for a long while. He wanted to believe it would be as simple as Christian Page had said it would be, that all T. J. had to do was find Rhomberg and then wait, but the miseries he'd had to endure in his short life reminded him that hope and promises weren't something on which he could count. His mother had sworn she would take care of him and that she'd never leave him, and she'd done just the opposite. Now this man, the first real friend T. J. had ever had, was making him the same kind of oath.

"I'll do it," he suddenly announced. "But only 'cause I owe ya." His small chin came up and his brown eyes flashed. "I'll find Lewis Rhomberg and tell him where ya are and why, but don't go expectin' me ta hang around for long once I have. I like livin' on my own."

Christian could only guess the reason behind the boy's sharp words, and he silently accepted it. T. J. had no reason to believe him. Even Christian wasn't sure he'd ever be allowed to leave the penal colony. Yet if there were some way of doing it, he would. He'd prove to this scrappy young boy that Christian Page always meant what he said.

The plan was that once both he and T. J. were free of their leg irons, Christian would pick a fight—with Benton Wall. Since their confrontation, they had been the talk of every man in the hulk, many assuming they would do battle again. This time, however, those who had missed the first contest swore they would have a front seat at the next skirmish, and that aspect was what Christian prayed would come true. By drawing a crowd, he'd make it possible for T. J. to slip off the pier and into the water below. From there he was to swim beneath the wooden dock until he reached a safe place some distance away. If all went as hoped for, the boy would be on his way to London by nightfall.

"What if the guards just shoot you instead of tryin' ta break up the fight?" T. J. nervously proposed once they had changed into the clean clothes they'd been given and were starting their walk toward the *Adventure*.

"They won't," Christian assured him, ruffling the boy's dark hair.

"How do ya know?"

"Well, think about it, T. J.," Christian instructed as he covertly glanced over his shoulder to see that Wall and Ambrose weren't far behind him. "What other entertainment have the guards had all the while they've been doing their jobs? They're bored. They'll welcome the distraction. Besides"—he smiled mischievously—"I plan to give them quite a show."

"Yeah, well, I don't like it," T. J. responded. "I think we oughta forget the whole thing."

"Do you?" Christian asked as he carefully judged the right location to begin his demonstration. When he was through with Benton Wall, even the guards wouldn't feel safe hiding behind their muskets. "Then I guess I'll just have to toss you off the pier in full view of everyone. How much of a chance do you suppose you'd have then?"

T. J.'s shoulders dropped. "About as much as you," he muttered, realizing the uselessness in arguing. "So when does the curtain go up?"

Calculating that they were equidistant from the last armed guard and the next, Christian stopped and bent down to roll up his trouser legs. "Now," he said, slipping out of the oversize shoes he'd been issued.

"Christian," T. J. beckoned, his tone masking the terror he felt. "Don't forget your promise. I won't wait forever."

Warm blue eyes glanced up and the smile that flashed across the handsome face of his friend gave T. J. the courage he needed to challenge the murky, swirling depths of the water below the pier. Christian Page had given his word, and for the first time since his mother's death, T. J. let go of his carefully guarded emotions and smiled back.

The clamor of feet as they moved out and around Christian marked the moments before the exhibition would begin. From out of the corner of his eye, he watched his intended adversary move closer, certain Wall was just as conscious of his presence as Christian was of Wall's. However, his plan was to make it appear to everyone around them that Christian had gotten careless where the man was concerned. Just as Wall was about to step around the crouched figure, Christian stood abruptly and with deliberate purpose scored the first blow as his head came up beneath Wall's chin. A loud *clop* followed when the man's mouth snapped shut, and before Wall's mind registered what had occurred, an elbow jabbed him in the stomach. To those who witnessed the incident it seemed to have been nothing

more than a clumsy accident, until those same realized who
was involved.

For a moment Benton Wall questioned his own wisdom as
he stood staring at the red smear on his fingertips where he
had touched them to his tongue. He'd seen Page stooped down
in front of him. He'd spent the last weeks carefully eyeing
the man, expecting at any moment to have to face him again.
Yet when that time came, he'd walked right into it. His only
excuse, Wall surmised, was that he hadn't guessed Page would
be the aggressor. Now that he'd made his position known, Wall
intended to settle the score. Without looking to Ambrose for
permission, he straightened his wide frame, wiped the blood
on his shirt front, and motioned for Page to make the next blow
worthwhile, silently promising he'd regret it if it wasn't.

Sang Soo had always told Christian that the size of his
opponent never mattered. Every man was built the same in the
respect that certain parts of the body were always vulnerable:
the throat, heart, eyes, stomach, kidneys, and of course the
area that distinguished men from boys. These, however, were
only used when nothing short of death would stop the foe, and
since Christian didn't want to kill Wall—especially in front
of witnesses—he had already decided on a crippling form
of attack. The kneecaps were the best choice, particularly
in Wall's case. If Christian didn't break the joint, he would
surely dislocate it, and that would pretty much be the end of
Benton Wall. Moving back a step, he curled his fingers and
held his arms in close as he braced his feet and bent his knees
slightly.

"Watch his hands!" Garrett Ambrose warned as he joined the
rest of the crowd in getting out of the way and giving the two
men plenty of room. Ambrose, more than any of the others,
wanted to make sure he wasn't hit by a misplaced fist or elbow.
"You know what happened last time."

Wall didn't have to be reminded. He'd had a dark bruise on
his chest for nearly a week, and it had taken longer than that for
him to talk clearly again. He planned to protect both spots this
time *and* keep his eyes on Page's hands. As soon as he moved
in the slightest, Wall would know how to block the punch.
Then in a split second he'd have him where he wanted him.

Christian could read every thought going through Wall's mind. His eyes reflected not only his determination to win, but his reluctance to make the first move. Obviously, the memory of what had happened last time was still very clear, and his hesitation would play right into Christian's plan.

A lot of the art of kung fu came with the ability to predict the foe's intentions and to lure the opponent into making a mistake. Quick reflexes and clear thinking assured the advantage. Balance and speed, and a perfectly placed jab could finish off the adversary in one blow if done correctly, but ending the match in a hurry wasn't what Christian wanted. T J. needed all the time Christian could give him.

"So hit him, Page," Ambrose heckled. "Or are you afraid now that he knows what to expect?"

Christian's gaze never wavered from the face of the large man standing before him, but his senses told him that the crowd around them had grown immense, and that the guards had yet to decide if they should intervene.

"Yeah, Mr. Page, hit him," someone within the throng encouraged. "Put the bloke on his back."

"Hit him 'fore he hits you!" a second man called out.

"It'll never happen," a third declared. "Wall won't never lay a hand on him. Page is too quick."

"Like a snake," another decreed.

"And his bite's just as deadly," a deep voice proclaimed.

"Maybe ya oughta hit *him* first, Wall," someone else advised. "It'll probably be the only chance ya get."

A howl of laughter followed, which worked in Christian's favor, for Wall wasn't a man to be laughed at. A red hue began to creep up his neck, starting just above his shirt collar, until it reached the lobes of both ears. By the time it had spread to his face, Benton Wall was out of control. Throwing back his head, he let out a roar that vibrated off each plank on the wharf and widened the eyes of nearly everyone who heard it. Then in much the same manner of a grizzly bear, he raised his hands above his head with the fingers curled like giant claws and lumbered forward to attack.

The entire group of onlookers cringed in expectation of Page's first blow, certain it would fell the huge man. Instead they gave a collective gasp of surprise when Christian merely ducked beneath the widespread arms and came up to stand facing him from behind. No true brawler would avoid a fight even when the opponent was twice his size, and many of the witnesses wondered if their champion wasn't a coward after all.

"Hit him, Mr. Page!" one of them begged. "Show him ya got the grit it takes ta be a man!"

"Ah, leave him alone," his companion said with irritation. "He knows what he's doin'."

Apparently Wall had drawn much the same conclusion as those who watched with gaping mouths, and his second mistake came in thinking his fearlessness had given him the advantage. Facing Christian again, his lips curled in a mocking sneer, he doubled up his fist and launched his next assault. The roundhouse blow was meant to land against Christian's ear, but he simply leaned back out of the way. The hard knuckles whizzed by and the force behind them swung Wall in a full circle when they failed to connect. The confident smirk disappeared. Awkwardly regaining his balance, he spun back, ready to strike again. This time he curled his left hand and brought it round with the intention of hitting Page with the back of his closed fist. This, too, failed when Christian raised his arm and blocked the punch, then followed the defensive with a quick, sharp jab of his knuckles to the side of Wall's rib cage. The snap of bones cracking made everyone wince involuntarily, but Wall didn't appear to feel the pain as much as he felt the surprise of the counterattack.

"Sweet Mother of God," Ambrose barked. "I thought you knew how to fight, Wall. Are you going to let a man half your strength beat you?"

Wall glanced angrily at Ambrose as if contemplating a change of foe. A second later his eyes shifted to a pile of lumber stacked on the wharf.

Christian immediately saw where Wall's gaze had fallen and he just as quickly guessed the man planned to arm himself. But before he could block Wall's path to the rough-cut boards, the giant had crossed there and had selected a thick, heavy piece. Clutching it with both hands, he turned, raised it high, and let out a loud bellow as he rushed forward.

A deathly quiet came over the crowd as all who viewed the contest feared a quick end to the man they had adopted as their protector. Christian, however, was worried about a premature finale to the smoke screen he had created for T. J.'s sake. He had seen the boy slip over the edge of the dock the instant everyone's attention had fallen on him and Wall, but he had hoped to give the youngster ample time to get away. Now, it seemed, T. J. was on his own. Shifting back on one foot, he carefully scrutinized his attacker and the weapon he held.

Benton Wall neither saw nor expected the punishing kick that jarred his body when his opponent hopped from one foot to the other, leaned back, and brought up his leg to strike Wall horizontally across the belly. His breath left him in a rush and the board slipped from his fingers to thud noisily on the pier, leaving him vulnerable for the next assault. Without mercy, Page struck again. Bending his arm, he jabbed his elbow to the back of Wall's neck while the man leaned forward gasping for air. The blow dropped Wall to the deck facedown, and before anyone could help him—if any truly felt the desire—Page caught the man's ankle, twisted him onto his hip, and dealt a staggering blow to the side of Wall's leg with the same elbow jab as before. A loud snap followed, then a cry of anguish as the huge man, reduced to a harmless mass, writhed and cried out in agony.

Cold blue eyes lifted to glare at the man who had been the cause of so many others' pain. Christian knew Wall's defeat meant little if anything at all to Garrett Ambrose. There were a hundred other men like this poor wretch eagerly awaiting the chance to serve him. Ambrose would merely commission another, and Wall would be forgotten as quickly and as easily as Ambrose had forgotten Russel Troy. Perhaps the youth hadn't made a lasting impression on the outlaw, but Christian had vowed long ago that Garrett Ambrose would curse the day he had let a young boy die.

·∾❧▌ *Chapter Eight* ▐❦∾·

A SINGLE CLOUD ON THE HORIZON, STAINED PINK BY THE RIS-
ing sun, had drifted aimlessly across the pale blue sky as if to
herald the coming of dawn. Long amber fingers of morning
light stretched out beyond the surface of the sea to claim the
sandstone cliffs. Cabbage-tree palms, ferns, mosses, yellow
sprays of mimosa, and pink-, white-, and rose-colored everlast-
ings greeted the new day. Earlier, amid the breathtaking pano-
rama, a huge ship had slipped into the Sydney harbor under the
cover of darkness. Its sails had been furled, its anchor dropped,
and its passengers awakened before the arrival of the *Adventure*
had been discovered by the throng of people awaiting word
from home.

"Australia!" The name burst from Alexandra's lips as she
stared out the window of her hotel room and absently studied the sight of the latest convict transport to drop anchor in
Botany Bay. Her reaction to her father's plan of moving to this
distant land had been a mixture of disbelief and shock. Wallis
Pembrooke had lived his entire life in England. His wife, his
parents, all of his ancestors were buried there. His friends,
his job, and his home were there. He had wealth, high rank,
and security living in England. He had to be insane to leave it
all behind, she thought. Yet on the day they had packed their
trunks and boarded the ship that would take them to Sydney,
Alexandra hadn't said a word. Somewhere in her befuddled
state, she had assumed she would awake to find that it had
all been a horrible dream. But that had been the better part
of a year ago, and this room had been her sanctuary for two
months now. It was no dream. They had sold the house and

property in Plymouth and there was no turning back. She knew that now. But she was still determined to try.

"Australia," she muttered again, her gaze shifting to the crowded streets below her. Although she couldn't see him, she knew her father was among the throng inching their way to the pier *and* she knew his reason for going. It had been the root of their argument over breakfast that morning in the hotel dining room and the excuse he needed to leave while he still had his temper under control. His success in the next few hours would mean this land with its enormous variety of flowers and trees, kangaroos, snakes, birds, lizards, and fierce crocodiles would become her new home. She had to admit that this oversize island was beautiful—at least what she'd seen so far had been fascinating—but she by no means wanted to spend the rest of her life here. She missed Aimee's companionship, the house where she had grown up, the social life she'd left behind, and the freedom to come and go as she pleased. But more than that, she knew there would come a time in the not too distant future when she'd want to settle down and get married, even raise a brood of children. But she couldn't very well do it here. The only available men for miles around were convicts, and she certainly didn't want one of them to be the father of her children. Of course there was always Wayne Pleasanton. Alexander frowned. If that weak-kneed, homely milksop was her only choice, she would die a spinster. With a disgusted sigh she turned away from the window and crossed to her bed, where she threw herself across it, her pink satin skirts billowing out around her ankles.

The Pleasantons had been among the first people of any high standing in Sydney she and her father had met. They had traveled to the city to await the arrival of their new neighbors, once they'd heard that the property next to theirs had been purchased by a titled Englishman, one who was well respected by the king. Davis and Phoebe Pleasanton had left their homeland some thirty years earlier, and even though they had grown to accept Australia as the place where they would be laid to rest, they missed the elegance of London and its society. They were also hoping to find a suitable wife for their son, Wayne. Although Alexandra had honestly liked Phoebe, a petite, dark-haired, blue-eyed woman of about fifty, she despised the bony, pale, timid creature Phoebe introduced as her only child the instant his soft clammy hand took hers and pressed a dry kiss to the backs of her fingers. Her disapproval had grown by leaps and bounds once Wayne let it be known that he was a step above the immigrants, which included Alexandra and her father, for the simple reason that he was of the first generation born in Australia. Alexander truly didn't see the importance, but apparently it meant a lot to Wayne, since every chance he got, he reminded her of the fact.

Alexandra wasn't sure just how her father felt about the Pleasantons since, as always, they rarely talked about much of anything. But by the end of their first week in the Sydney hotel and the constant attention heaped on them by Davis and Phoebe, her father suddenly announced one morning over breakfast that he would be leaving that day to ride out to his property. Alexandra, he added, would be staying behind with her maid, since Pembrooke had no way of knowing what to expect once he got there, and although she would have preferred returning to England, Alexandra was at least thankful her father had allowed her the luxury and conveniences of living in a hotel for a while longer.

She had spent the next three weeks touring Sydney, making new friends, visiting the shops, and listening to the gossip about the penal colony and why, socially speaking, it wouldn't be a very good place to live. That bit of knowledge, and the hope that her father had been disappointed with the tract of land he'd acquired, would give her the ammunition she needed to convince him to return home. Despite all her efforts, however, the moment she rushed into the hotel dining room to meet him for dinner on his first evening back, she knew her work had been for nothing. Instead of the quiet, scowling man she had always known as her father, she saw a happy, suntanned, radiant face smiling back at her.

The property, he explained, had been everything he hoped it would be. There was plenty of thick, rich grassland, a stream, and even a house in which they could live while he had a bigger one built that was more to his taste. The scenery, fresh air, and promise of a bright future would, he guaranteed, delight even Alexandra. Stunned by his enthusiasm, she had remained silent, until in passing he had remarked about his plans to purchase twenty sheep that afternoon and twenty more by the end of the week.

"Sheep?" she had questioned, leery. "You're going to buy sheep?"

"Of course," he had laughed, his eyes sparkling. "What did you think we'd be raising? Crocodiles?"

As Alexandra lay on her bed remembering that conversation, she also remembered thinking that crocodiles couldn't possibly smell as bad. After all, they spent most of their time in the water . . . or so she'd been told.

Angry again, she shot off the bed and marched back to the window to stare outside at the mass of people pushing toward the pier. How could her father ever think she'd be happy living in such a place? The only excitement these people enjoyed was rushing to the dock to stare at the newest shipment of criminals. By God, she wasn't going to turn into one of those mindless twits who lived from one ship's arrival to the next. She was going home. But how? With each day that passed, her father had settled more comfortably into his new life, which meant she'd have to sail back to England alone, if he would allow it. And after this morning's argument, she was sure he'd shackle her in leg irons like the men working the chain gangs before he'd put her on a ship and wave to her from the dock.

For the two months they'd been in Australia, she had stayed at the hotel while her father traveled back and forth from the property. Work there hadn't gone as quickly as he had thought it would; he'd been short of competent help. That pleased Alexandra. It had given her extra time to circumvent his plans—at least she had thought she was gaining ground—but this morning's discussion hadn't gone at all the way she had hoped.

She had donned a new pink satin dress with puffy sleeves and demure neckline, then arranged her long dark hair on top of her head and adorned it with tiny pink bows. Around her neck she had worn her mother's diamond and ruby necklace, the one her father had given his wife on the first anniversary of their marriage, and something Alexandra hadn't worn since her mother's death. That alone would get his attention, she had surmised. She had been terribly wrong.

He was already seated at their usual table in the dining room when she arrived, and other than the brief glance he gave her as he stood and pulled out her chair, he hardly seemed to notice her. Whatever was written on the paper he was reading was of more interest to him than the arrival of his daughter.

"Papa," she had said for the third time, her fingertips tapping impatiently on the heavy linen tablecloth. It seemed he'd gone deaf as well as being distracted. "Papa, I don't see why we can't just live here in Sydney instead of traipsing off across some treacherous mountain range to Lord-only-knows where." If he thought she had grown to like Australia or, more specifically, Sydney, he might meet her halfway and relent. Then she'd start on the second part of her scheme—making him homesick. "It's too dangerous living out that far with all the bush bandits roaming the hills."

"Bushrangers," her father corrected, not bothering to look up.

"What?"

"The escaped criminals who hide out in the hills are called bushrangers."

Alexandra flipped a hand. "It doesn't matter what they're called. The point is, we'll be easy prey living out so far. And why, for God's sake, do you want to raise sheep?" She wrinkled her nose when an imaginary odor assailed her. "Sheep," she muttered. "You don't know the first thing about raising them. We'll be totally penniless before the year is out. Why don't you write to Sir Robert and ask him to give you a government job?"

"We've been through all of this before, daughter," Pembrooke replied tiredly as he looked up from his notes. "I resigned my commission because I no longer wish to work for the government. I'm through taking orders." Annoyed with her constant badgering, he returned his attention to the paper he held in his left hand. "Besides, I decided it was time for me to be a father."

His answer caught her completely by surprise. She stared at him for several seconds, speechless, mouth agape, the warm blush of her cheeks fading, before the memory of why her mother had died stirred the errant nature in her. "Your time for that ran out years ago. I'm not a child anymore, in case you haven't noticed. I'm a grown woman. It's a little late to be giving me fatherly advice."

The elder Pembrooke's shoulders straightened. "Oh, really?" he asked, his green eyes moving to look sternly at her. "Then perhaps you could explain to me why a grown woman would consort with the likes of Hardin Wittemore." He quickly raised a hand to forestall her answer when she took a sharp breath to reply. "If you're thinking of telling me that he comes from a fine family, I'll have to agree. His ancestry can be traced back hundreds of years to the most prestigious names in all of England. But *that,* my dear daughter, does not make *him* a gentleman, and I'll not have an offspring of mine ruining her reputation by associating with him."

Alexandra's chest heaved with indignation. "Is that the only reason you dragged me all the way to this wretched country? To keep me from seeing Hardin?" She laughed derisively and raised her chin in the air. "I'd say that's a little extreme, Papa, especially since Hardin left England right after the trial. No one knows for sure where he went, but his future certainly doesn't include England. *You* made sure of that."

Pembrooke sat back and looked hard at his daughter. "*I* made sure of it? My dear Alexandra, I had nothing to do with it. You know the old saying: if you lie down with dogs, you'll get up with fleas. Hardin knew what he was doing, and he's smart enough to have known that sooner or later he was bound to get caught. If it hadn't been me and my men, it would have been someone else. So don't go blaming the wrong person, Alexandra. The responsibility lies solely on Hardin's shoulders." As he spoke, he folded his papers into a neat stack and slipped them into his vest pocket. "Now, if you'll excuse me, I have to be at the gaol yard before the prisoners are taken off the ship. I need to make sure I'm assigned a carpenter, a good one."

His lecture had stung as he had intended it to, and although she was still smarting from the truth of his words, Alexandra couldn't let him leave without one more attempt at persuading him to change his mind. "A convict, you mean. You wish to surround yourself with thieves and murderers and pretend they're nothing more than hired help. You flee England on the pretense of saving your daughter's reputation and then turn around and subject her to the same sort of element. I see no difference except that we're living somewhere else."

Pembrooke's dark brows came sharply together. His nostrils flared and the muscle in his jaw twitched as he leaned closer to his daughter and kept his voice low so that the other patrons of the dining room would not hear his answer. "There is an unquestionable difference, Alexandra. None of the men assigned to us will come from noble families. Therefore, I doubt any of them will catch your eye." Not wishing to hear her reply, if indeed she had one, he roughly left his chair, plucked his top hat from the corner of the table where he had laid it, and headed for the exit.

The oblique meaning behind his remark had brought an instant rush of hot blood to Alexandra's face. Her heart had thumped against her bosom, and tears, unusual to her character, had risen to burn her eyes. Fearing everyone in the place could guess their exchange, she had clumsily unfolded her fan and fluttered it beneath her chin while she nervously looked about to see who was staring at her. A moment later she had slipped from the dining room without having eaten a bite of breakfast to hide away in her room and think about what her father had said.

With a tired, forlorn sigh she leaned her cheek against the cool pane of glass in the window, her heart aching and her thoughts rushing around inside her head in a desperate attempt to excuse herself for what she had done. She had failed miserably. She knew she'd acted rashly and without forethought and had only herself to blame. Even Aimee had tried to warn her.

Her young friend had predicted the consequences of the anonymous note to her father, but Alexandra hadn't listened. She had wanted only to hurt her father, and instead had enraged him enough to cause him to give up everything and whisk his daughter off to a faraway country where her shameless behavior, in his mind, couldn't catch up with her. The embarrassment she felt came from the realization that not only had he believed the story, but that he thought her capable of continuing such conduct. That, in turn, had hurt her. Deeply. She wasn't a harlot. She didn't seek out men with whom to have affairs. The notion of stripping off her clothes and crawling into bed with a man without the benefit of marriage or a promise of commitment disgusted her. It was unthinkable!

Suddenly the image of a blond-haired, blue-eyed brigand flared up in her mind, and she jerked upright with a gasp. She could remember the blistering sensation of his kiss, the excitement that had stirred deep inside her when he pressed his hard length against her own fragile frame. She squirmed at the memory of his fingers trailing a burning path up the inside of her thigh, and how in that moment she hadn't tried to stop him. More than six months had passed since that time and the emotions she had felt that night were still just as fresh and vivid and titillating as if she'd experienced them only last night.

"Damn you, Christian Page," she hissed under her breath.

The only good that had come out of all this was the pleasure she took in knowing she would never, ever see him again. He was locked up in a cold, dark cell thousands of miles away on the other side of the world.

You're paying for your foolishness, Mr. Page, she thought bitterly. Then in an ironic change of heart she added, *And so am I*.

The docking of a convict transport in Botany Bay, no matter the time of day or night, was always greeted with excitement by the townsfolk of Sydney. Its arrival meant the hope of seeing a familiar face among its solemn passengers or the delivery of a letter from home. Some came to the pier simply to relieve the boredom of a tedious existence. Hence the streets, their sidewalks, and all other possible avenues to the wharf were filled to overflowing, hampering Wallis Pembrooke's journey to the gaol yard and shortening his temper.

He wanted to have first pick of the newly arriving convicts, and to do that he had to be there ahead of all the other landowners wanting the same thing. In his case, however, Pembrooke wasn't just looking for strength in one of his workers, but skill, something the British government had failed to take into account when assigning the prisoners to their "masters." Of the ten workers he already had, none of them had ever seen a hammer, much less knew how to draw up a sketch and then turn the diagram into a building. Lynn Boone was the only man among them all who had any common sense and a willingness to try, but other than that, he didn't know the first thing about carpentry, having spent the greater part of his adult life in the service of His Majesty's Royal Navy. Instead of the farmer, cook, blacksmith, and carpenter he needed, Pembrooke had acquired two candlemakers, one accountant, one jeweler, one not-so-holy man of the cloth, a locksmith, a cobbler, and two others who had never done an honest day's work in their lives. If he was to succeed, he had to have knowledgeable men, those experienced in the kind of work it would take to build his empire, and that meant talking to David Catton as soon as possible.

"Allen!" Pembrooke called up to the driver of his rig when it seemed his carriage hadn't traveled an inch in the last ten minutes. "Allen!" he repeated with a rap of his knuckles on the roof. "I'm getting out here."

"Here, sir?" the man questioned, hurriedly setting the brake when he heard his passenger open the rig's door. "It's still another two blocks to the gaol yard, sir."

"I'm aware of that," Pembrooke stated. "It will be faster on foot." Stepping down onto the bustling sidewalk, he momentarily doubted the wisdom of his choice, for the crush of bodies before him appeared not to be making any better progress than his carriage had made. Annoyed and impatient, he changed directions.

"Sir? Sir!" Allen beckoned worriedly as he watched the man round the end of the rig and move into the street. "Where are you going, sir?"

"I'll take my chances with the horses," Pembrooke called back. "I doubt they'll step on my toes. At least not deliberately."

A short while later Pembrooke arrived, top hat in hand, at the closed metal gate to the gaol yard. The crowd was much smaller here, giving Pembrooke the opportunity to speak with the man in charge, David Catton, before the list of assignments had been made out. Eager to have his say, Pembrooke edged closer to the gate in the seven-foot-tall brick fence and rang the bell. A second later the panel covering the peephole slid to one side and Catton's face appeared framed in the small opening.

"Sir Wallis," he exclaimed, obviously surprised by the man's presence. "You're out rather early this morning, aren't you?"

"Yes, Mr. Catton, I am," Pembrooke confessed. "I'm here on business. The assignments for the new prisoners haven't been made yet, have they?"

"No, sir."

"Good. Then I'd like to make a request."

"What kind of a request, Sir Wallis?" Catton asked.

Preferring not to air his personal matters in front of the others standing close by, Pembrooke nodded at the lock on the gate. "Privately, if you don't mind."

Catton thought about it for only a second or two, nodded his head, and then opened the gate. Sir Wallis Pembrooke's reputation and word of his plans to live in Sydney with his beautiful daughter had long preceded his actual arrival. Nearly everyone assumed he'd been commissioned by the king to take over the displacement proceedings of the convicts, and even after he had purchased land on the other side of the Blue Mountain range—therefore discrediting the idea—many still refused to believe he had honestly given up his former life to raise sheep. Catton was one of those who doubted. He was also hoping for a promotion, and if doing a favor for the eminent gentleman would assure him of that, he'd do whatever the man asked of him.

"Is there a problem, Sir Wallis?" Catton asked once he had secured the gate behind his visitor and the two of them stood alone away from eavesdroppers.

Plopping his hat back on his head, Pembrooke retrieved his notes from the inside pocket of his frock coat. "I'm in need of a carpenter, Mr. Catton, a good one. I was hoping you'd allow me to have a look at the list of new prisoners before they—"

"Say no more, Sir Wallis," Catton cut in with a smile. He

was assuming there was a secret project going on, one that required a skilled craftsman, and he didn't want anyone accusing him of standing in the way of its execution. He would have liked knowing the details of the mission, but he was smart enough to realize that misplaced curiosity could and often did lead to one's expulsion from a comfortable job. "Let's go in my office, Sir Wallis," he suggested.

Inside, Catton offered Pembrooke the chair in front of his desk, then sat down to pull open a top drawer. All sorts of ideas were racing through his head about Sir Wallis Pembrooke's covert assignment, but the one that seemed most likely was the task of rounding up bushrangers.

"Here we are," he announced, pulling out a stack of papers and laying them on the desk top. After a quick glance, he shrugged. "Not as large a group as before, I'm afraid. But I'm sure we'll find someone suitable." He looked up and smiled at the man sitting across from him. "I suppose you'd prefer a young man?"

"If that's possible," Pembrooke admitted. "But right now his skill is more important than how much he can lift."

Several minutes passed while Catton ran a finger down the long list of names, the crimes each had committed, and whatever trade he or she had employed. When he neared the bottom, he began to squirm. There wasn't a carpenter among them, and even though that fact was not of his making, Catton felt sure Pembrooke would blame him anyway. Then he remembered the second list, a group of names already claimed by the superintendent of convicts, made long before the one Catton held in his hands. It was the practice of the local board to skim off the most desirable of prisoners to work for the government in public labors, and to leave those who were lazy and unskilled for distribution among the landowners. Ordinarily Catton would pretend he didn't know about the existence of the list, but in this case he knew he must make an exception.

"Just a minute, sir," he begged, awkwardly scooping up the pile of papers and shoving them haphazardly back into the drawer. Rising, he crossed to the door leading to the room adjacent to his office, opened it, and made a hurried exit. A moment later he reappeared with a new stack of papers in his grip and was already shuffling through them before he sat down again. "Ah-ha!" he burst out joyfully. "I was sure I could help you out. Yes, sir. In fact there's two carpenters available. Do you want them both?"

"No," Pembrooke replied. "Just one, the younger, if that's acceptable."

"Anything for you, sir. Anything at all." Catton scanned the list again. "How about a map maker? Or a gunsmith? You want one of them, too? Or both?" He laughed nervously when he saw the odd look Pembrooke gave him and decided it wasn't his business to ask. If the gentleman wanted someone else to help in his cause, *he'd* be the one making the request, and he'd do it in such a way that no one would get suspicious. After all, this was meant to be a secret.

Pembrooke's usually stern expression took on a look of vague bewilderment. The man's eagerness to comply with his wishes—and then some—was out of place. He'd heard about the government's practice of keeping the best choice of convicts for its own purposes and knew there was nothing he or any of the other landowners could do about it. So why had David Catton offered him not only a prime candidate, but extras as well? And what would he want with a map maker or gunsmith? He could use a farmer better, one who'd raised sheep for a living and knew what crops to plant and how. He also knew that he'd get only one worker from this group of prisoners, since his allotment had reached its limit. Thus he declined Catton's offer simply because he needed a carpenter more than a farmer right then. However, he would remember the man's generosity and use it later once the barn, house, pens, and shearing shed were finished.

Of the five hundred and twenty-three convicts shipped to Australia on board the *Adventure,* only three men, one woman, and a nine-year-old boy had perished during the voyage, and they had been ill before they embarked on the journey. The doctor assigned to travel with the convict transport had done everything he could to save them, but their poor health, the rough seas, and the depression that had befallen them all had proven stronger than his medicinal remedies.

Christian had adapted quite well to the confinement, the shackles, and the rolling of the huge ship better than any of the others. His past experience as a sailor made him resistant to seasickness, and his practice of kung fu helped him ignore the other discomfort. Still, he was just as thankful to leave the ship as those who crowded the gangplank with him, since all the concentration in the world couldn't eliminate the fact that it had taken the *Adventure* four months to reach Botany Bay.

As always Christian knew exactly where to find Garrett Ambrose and his partner and just how much distance he should keep between himself and the pair. During the voyage the group had been closely guarded, and the leg irons they wore hampered any chance of a confrontation they might have taken, but since Christian had no idea of what lay ahead, he knew he'd have to keep a close eye on the duo. The injury to Wall's leg had healed months ago, but the slight limp that impaired his walk was a constant reminder of who was to blame, and Christian was sure Wall would like to even the score. More than that, however, Christian watched the two because he wanted to know where Ambrose would be assigned. He wasn't through with the man yet, and even if it took him the full extent of his sentence to win his freedom, he wouldn't forget the reason why he was here and who had caused it.

Every prisoner had been given a bath, haircut, shave, and new set of clothes before leaving the ship, but the irons remained. They had been gathered in groups of some sort, though Christian couldn't quite figure out why, unless it had to do with the crime the individual had committed or the length of their sentences. Next they had been ushered down the gangplank, told to stay in a single line and to follow the first guard to the gaol yard. Once there they would have their clothes stenciled with broad arrows in red or black paint, and then they would be dispatched to the prisoners' barracks to await distribution by the local board to farms or public work.

Christian only half listened to the instructions. He was more concerned with the prospect that he might be given out ahead of Ambrose and taken away before he could hear where the man had been assigned. Australia was a big country, and Christian didn't like the idea that he might have to waste good time trying

to locate Ambrose all over again. All Christian could hope for
was that since the man was in the line ahead of him, *his* name
would be called first.

An hour later the convicts were still resting in their barracks while they awaited the displacement proceedings. Christian had already heard the gossip among the other prisoners
concerning the "chain gangs," the stiffest form of sentence a
man could receive, and although he felt Ambrose deserved to
be chained, guarded around the clock, and forced to clear land,
dig ditches, and build roads from sunup to sundown, he didn't
want the man to die by someone else's hand. That pleasure
was reserved for him.

When the first group of convicts was called up, Christian
hurriedly left the cot on which he lay to peer out the window
above the head of his bed. Ambrose was in that bunch. Yet
once he had a clear view of the yard and the throng of people
crowding in to have a look, his concentration faltered for a
moment. It appeared as though every man, woman, and child
in the whole of Australia had come to witness the event, and
their interest surprised him. The crowd, however, wasn't the
only thing he noticed. Wondering if perhaps the long voyage
had somehow had more of an effect on him than he'd realized,
he awkwardly pulled himself up onto the cot with his hands
wrapped around the bars in the window. There, standing off
to the side of the huge gathering was a man, a tall, dark-haired,
finely dressed, important-looking man. Christian blinked and
shook his head as if to disengage the cobwebs he was sure
altered his vision. He looked again.

It can't be, he silently declared. *It just can't be.*

A guard appeared in the barracks' doorway calling out orders
for the second group to step forward. That included Christian.
He hesitated for an instant, glanced again at the tall, distinguished gentleman with the top hat, and then jumped down
from the cot to follow the rest of his party outside.

In the full light of the midmorning sun and from a different
angle, there was no mistaking the identity of the man. Christian
couldn't even begin to guess how Pembrooke had arrived ahead
of him, or why he had decided to come himself, but if Sir
Wallis Pembrooke was here, it had to mean he'd been in con-

tact with Lewis Rhomberg. Did it also mean T. J. was safe? He hoped so. Feeling as if a heavy burden had suddenly been lifted from his shoulders, he smiled secretively and shifted his gaze to Ambrose. He, Wall, and two others were being assigned to work for a man named Abbott; that was all the information Christian could learn. Of course, it didn't really matter since Pembrooke had access to any and all government documents and could have the answers he needed within moments. But first things first. Right now Pembrooke had to use his authority to free Christian.

Christian's smile slowly began to fade once he realized that instead of being led to the raised platform in the middle of the yard, his group had been rerouted and was now heading toward a different building on the other side of the compound, away from Pembrooke. Glancing back, he saw that Pembrooke wasn't moving or even looking Christian's way, and serious doubts began to arise.

"All right," the guard commanded. "Hold up right here and when your name's called, you're to go inside and pick one of the cots as your own. As soon as everyone's settled, we'll be directing you to your work place. Anderson, James."

Now that he'd had the time to think and the shock of seeing Wallis Pembrooke had passed, Christian realized how wrong he'd been. If Rhomberg had gotten to Pembrooke with the truth, he would have pulled Christian off the hulk right away. If he'd been too late, he would have sent a written order for Christian's release rather than setting out on a four-month voyage to give the order in person.

"Michaelson, Stuart."

And even if he'd missed catching him before the *Adventure* set sail, there was no way Pembrooke could have gotten to Australia ahead of him!

"Stevens, Harold."

Turning, Christian frowned back at the figure dressed in elegant clothes. No, Pembrooke was here for a different reason altogether. The startling truth of the matter was that Sir Wallis Pembrooke probably didn't even know Christian was in Australia.

"You there!"

The explosive demand jerked Christian back around to find that he stood alone outside the barracks and that two guards were glaring at him.

"I said, what's your name?" the taller and meaner-looking of the pair repeated.

"Page. Christian Page," he quickly obliged.

The second guard hurriedly scanned the sheet of paper he held. "Ain't no Christian Page on the list."

"You sure?" the first challenged.

The other checked again. "I'm sure. Must be a mistake. So what do we do with him?"

"It's no mistake," a voice from behind Christian guaranteed. "His name shouldn't have been included in the first place. And I'll take care of him."

The two guards gave a quick, unpolished salute. "Whatever you say, Mr. Catton," they said before turning away.

Christian's curiosity began tickling his senses again, though he didn't know why. It very possibly *could* have been an oversight and this Catton fellow had caught it in time. He glanced briefly at the man and wondered at his odd smile.

"Consider yourself very lucky, Page," Catton was saying as he turned his companion back in the direction of the crowd. "Working as a government man can be very strenuous. Of course, the job Sir Wallis Pembrooke has in store for you might even be harder."

·❧⟨ Chapter Nine ⟩❧·

AS FELICE HELPED HER MISTRESS DRESS FOR DINNER THAT night, the young woman noticed a heaviness in Alexandra's movements. It was almost as if Sir Wallis's daughter wasn't looking forward to dining with Governor and Lady Darling and a host of other important, titled Englishmen and their wives. Perhaps, she decided, it had something to do with the announcement Mistress Alexandra's father had made that morning after his visit to the gaol yard. Whether his daughter liked it or not, they would be leaving for their new home in the morning.

Felice's mother, Amelia, had been employed by the Pembrookes shortly before their marriage. When Amelia had died, her daughter had taken her place as Alexandra's companion and maid. But even after eleven years of serving Alexandra in her mother's place, Felice still could not figure out the root of her mistress's many and varied moods. The suicide of Alexandra's mother had to have scarred the young girl, possibly even placed an unjustified guilt in her heart, but it didn't explain why Alexandra should blame her father for the tragedy. However, Felice was not of the nature to insist her mistress talk about it. Her mother had always taught her daughter to serve, not interfere, and Felice would never go against her mother's teachings.

"Felice," she heard Alexandra beckon, and she shifted her attention from the pile of thick, shining hair she was styling to the green eyes reflected in the mirror.

"Yes, mum?"

"What do you think of living in Australia?"

Felice's gray-blue eyes dropped back to the strand of miniature pearls she was artfully arranging among the satiny curls of her mistress's hair. "Don't rightly know, mum. 'Aven't been 'ere long enough."

"But you never complained or objected or threatened to quit my father's employ when you were told we were leaving. Why not?"

A vague smile flickered across Felice's mouth and disappeared before Alexandra saw it. "I didn't 'ave no reason ta stay, mum, and ye 'ave always treated me fair."

"But to leave your home and sail halfway around the world?" Alexandra just couldn't believe anyone would be so ambivalent about such a decision. "I never would have done it if I'd been given a choice."

"Of course ye would 'ave. Ye wouldn't 'ave stayed behind and watched yer father sail off, not knowin' if ye'd ever see 'im again," Felice quickly declared. A second later she was sorry she had voiced her opinion. It wasn't her place to criticize. Grabbing more hairpins from the box, she stuck them in her mouth and concentrated on finishing up her work.

It had occurred to Alexandra of late that despite the fact that Felice had been her maid for over ten years now, the two of them had never really talked . . . not the way two friends would share secrets. Perhaps she was just missing the heartfelt tête-à-têtes she had always had with Aimee, but whatever the reason, she found suddenly that she wanted to learn more about her maid.

"Felice," she began, watching the woman's reflection in the dressing table mirror. "I might have been only a child when your mother died, but I remember her quite well. I also remember how she refused to talk about your father. Do you know why?"

"Yes, mum," Felice admitted through a mouthful of pins. "She wasn't too proud of 'im."

"What do you mean?"

"That me father never married me mother." Her brow lifted in surprise. "Your mother was aware of the situation. Ye mean she never said nothin' to ye about it?"

Alexandra could feel a warm blush sting her cheeks. "No, Felice, she didn't . . . probably because I was too young to understand." She softened her words. "I'm sorry I pressed."

"Why?" the other replied with a bright smile as she secured the last pin and laid the rest aside. "I'm not ashamed of it, if that's what ye're sayin'. I'm sure me father would have asked her if he'd 'ad the chance."

"Why didn't he?" Alexandra couldn't help inquiring. Her curiosity had gotten the better of her.

Turning her back on her mistress, Felice replied as she went for Alexandra's shawl lying on the bed, "He was arrested and shipped off 'fore he could, that's why."

Alexandra twisted around on the stool. "Arrested?"

"Aye, mum. He took a chicken that didn't belong to 'im."

"And he was shipped off for that? Where?"

The somewhat impish smile Alexandra saw on her maid's lips when Felice faced her again said more than if she'd spoken out loud. "You're not serious! Here? He was sentenced to Australia?"

Felice bobbed her head and toyed sheepishly with the fringe on the cashmere wrap she held.

"Well, it's no wonder you weren't opposed to coming with us," Alexandra observed, smiling. Then in a more solemn vein she asked, "But surely he wouldn't still be here, would he?"

"Aye, mum. He was sentenced to seven years, but once a man has served 'is time, he's too poor ta buy 'is way 'ome. He's still 'ere."

"Have you found him yet?"

"No, mum. But I will."

The glow Alexandra saw in the woman's eyes and the excitement she heard in Felice's words made her suddenly feel ashamed. While *she* was scheming to return home to England with or without her father, Felice had traveled across an ocean to find hers. The hope had to be thin, but apparently it didn't concern her. Nor was she bothered by the fact that her parents had never married. Felice had forgiven him as if it hadn't been his fault, while Alexandra blamed *her* father for not loving Jocelyn enough to keep her from killing herself. But then their situation wasn't the same as that of Felice's mother and father. No longer wanting to think about it, she stood and held out her hand.

"I guess I'd better go downstairs," she said, the good feeling she had had only moments before gone. "Papa's probably waiting for me."

"Aye, mum."

The drive leading to the governor's home was already teeming with carriages by the time the Pembrookes arrived. To an unknowing eye, one might mistakenly think the elaborate manse and its elegant grounds were located just outside London. Alexandra knew differently, and that knowledge, along with the dread of leaving Sydney in the morning to take up residence on a piece of land where sheep wandered freely about the place, ruined the excitement of the lavish evening ahead of her. Unless she could somehow change her father's mind in the next few hours, she was doomed to live out her life there.

Once they had stepped into the spacious foyer, a maid received their cloaks, then directed them to a wide doorway at the right of the winding staircase. The moment their presence was noticed, they were ushered into the oversize parlor, reintroduced to each and every guest, and offered a glass of wine. The men discussed politics, the current controversy over changing the convict system, and the increase of new settlers and the need for more land, while the ladies talked about fashion, bringing the theater to Sydney, and more adequate ways of keeping their children separated from the offspring of the city's second-class citizens. Alexandra took it all in without offering her opinion, since she was wondering if these women would view the grandchildren of a man who raised sheep as noble or second class.

The conversation turned to less specific topics then, and before a second glass of wine could be offered, the butler announced that dinner was being served. Escorted by her father, Alexandra followed the others into the huge dining room and took a seat next to him at the long, fully bedecked table. Forty guests in all lined both sides, and to Alexandra it seemed that nearly that many servants filed in with armloads of delicious food.

While they ate, the subject of the latest convict transport was brought up. Alexandra would have ignored the discussion if someone hadn't asked her father how he felt about living in a penal colony, especially since some of the convicts were men Wallis Pembrooke had helped send to prison. His answer was exactly what she expected him to say, that if he had feared reprisals from criminals for doing his job, he never would have agreed to work for Sir Robert Peel.

"I'm sure of that," Governor Darling replied. "But you must admit, Sir Wallis, that Garrett Ambrose is no ordinary criminal. He's ruthless, insensitive, and from what I've heard, he's unforgiving. If he learns you're here in Australia, he very well may try to find a way to get to you."

Alexandra knew it was rude to laugh, but it slipped out before she could stop it. "My apologies, sir, but that would be rather difficult, since Mr. Ambrose is in a London prison."

"Oh, haven't you heard, my dear?" Olive Morrison, the wife of a huge landowner—and the town gossip—said. "Mr. Ambrose arrived this morning on the convict transport." She looked away from Alexandra to her husband while she added, "He was sentenced for a score and three, I believe. Isn't that right, dear?"

"Yes, Olive," William Morrison replied. "But most everyone feels it isn't long enough. Ambrose, as I hear it, was responsible for a good number of deaths. He should have been hanged." He turned his attention on Pembrooke. "I was also told you had men working in his gang. Weren't any of them able to testify?"

Pembrooke wiped his mouth with a white linen napkin, glanced briefly at his silent daughter, and then leaned back in his chair. "At the time of his arrest, no, I had no one who had infiltrated the gang. The last agent to accomplish it met with a questionable and fatal accident. We're reasonably sure Ambrose ordered it, but without proof, we had to settle for the smuggling charges. I agree he should have hanged, but we'll have to be content with knowing he'll be an old man before he's set free again." He reached for his wineglass and took a sip. "I would imagine by then he'd find other things more enjoyable . . . such as sitting in a rocker waiting for the sun to go down so he can go to bed."

Nearly everyone at the table laughed, since none of those present felt any threat from the famed outlaw. Alexandra, however, had lost what little appetite she'd had. In her opinion Governor Darling had struck upon the truth. The moment Garrett Ambrose learned her father was living here in Australia, he'd do everything in his power to have his revenge. Hadn't he already proven his capabilities and the extent to which he'd go when he tricked Hardin into bringing Alexandra to him? If she hadn't escaped and then sent the message to her father about Hardin, Ambrose would still be free and the celebrated lawman, Sir Wallis Pembrooke, would be mourning his child's death. Her father was no match for him. And the longer they stayed in Australia, the higher the risk would become for Ambrose to have the chance to demonstrate it. Feeling weak and physically trembling, Alexandra raised a hand to her forehead and closed her eyes. This was all her doing. Her carelessness and spite had endangered her father's life, forced them to leave England, and all but destroyed Hardin's future. It was time she confessed. She had to make her father understand how insane it would be for them to stay.

"Alexandra?"

The deep resonance of her father's voice pulled her out of her thoughts abruptly. She dropped her hand away, looked up at him, and was about to admit to the whole sordid mess when she sensed everyone at the table was staring at her. Her face flushed instantly, and deciding their conversation was meant to be private, she picked up her wineglass and took a drink to help settle her nerves.

"Aren't you feeling well, Alexandra?" Pembrooke asked, his concern genuine and very obvious as he leaned closer and peered into her face.

"Just a little shaken, Papa," she replied. "I wasn't aware Mr. Ambrose would be sentenced here. Otherwise—" *Otherwise, what?* she asked herself. *You wouldn't have sent the note? Even if you'd have known ahead of time; it wouldn't have made a difference. You weren't after Garrett Ambrose. And how could you have guessed that your father would decide to take up residence here?*

"I'm sorry, child," she heard her father saying. "I should have told you, I suppose, but I really didn't see the need. He doesn't frighten me, and his presence here in the colony shouldn't concern you. His actions will be closely guarded at all times. I promise. Besides, once we leave in the morning, he'll be miles away. Too many for him to walk with his feet shackled. We'll be perfectly safe." He glanced up at the governor and gave the man a quick, covert nod, silently asking his help in reassuring Alexandra.

"Your father is right, you know," Darling spoke up the second he understood. "Ambrose will never be able to get to you living out so far, especially since his gang has been disbanded. Men like this Ambrose are brave only when they're surrounded by their friends. I'm sorry I brought it up, Alexandra. It was thoughtless of me."

A fluttering began deep in her belly and kinked its way to every nerve in her body. She hadn't given a moment's thought to Ambrose's gang or, more specifically, to Christian Page. Suddenly stormy blue eyes in a handsome face, a chiseled jaw, a mouth twisted in an angry grimace flashed to mind, and she shivered. Governor Darling wasn't saying the gang had been separated once they got off the transport, was he? He meant each man had been sent to different prisons in England, didn't he? And only Ambrose was shipped here. That's what he was trying to tell her, wasn't he? Desperate for the knowledge, she opened her mouth to ask, changed her mind once she saw the curious look on her father's face, and grabbed her wineglass instead.

"Alexandra?" Pembrooke queried. "You were going to say something. What was it?"

She shook her head. "Nothing, Papa. Please . . . I didn't mean to ruin the evening."

"Nonsense, child," Lady Darling cut in. "If you're worried about something, tell us what it is and maybe we can soothe your fears. You haven't ruined anything."

"Yes, Alexandra," her father pressed. "What is it?"

Glancing nervously around the long table to find everyone waiting to hear her reply, Alexandra knew nothing short of a lie would bail her out of this one. "It's not really that important," she began, hoping the comment would be enough to convince her father into dropping the subject.

"Are you worried about Ambrose's men?" he guessed.

The look on her face must have given her away, for her father laughed softly as he reached to pat her hand.

"Well, don't be," he assured her.

The answer wasn't what she wanted to hear. It didn't tell her anything, yet it had served to end the conversation when someone else at the table asked her father if he intended to continue his work for the English government. His response was negative—as Alexandra already knew it would be—and while Morrison offered his opinion on how her father could get the most work out of his assigned convicts, she picked up her fork and forced herself to eat the rich dessert she'd been given. She didn't want anyone to think she hadn't dismissed the topic as easily as everyone else had, since to them it seemed unimportant. Alexandra felt differently, however. It was *very* important, and just as soon as she got back to her hotel room, she'd figure out a subtle way of tricking Felice into finding out for her.

Perplexity, fear, anger, and disappointment took turns on Alexandra's face the next morning as she sat gripping the edge of the wagon seat with one hand and her parasol with the other. She had assumed the Blue Mountains had gotten their name because of the illusion the blue-green density of the trees and shrubs covering their peaks created. What spread out before her now was very different from what she had imagined while she and Felice had packed their things and supervised the loading of their baggage. For the most part some sort of foliage blanketed the ground. Tiny violets crowded by insect-eating sundews, ferns, and heaths added color to the landscape, while eucalyptuses ranging in variety from tall blue gum, peppermint, scribbly gum, black ash and white ash to stunted mallees lined both sides of the narrow, crude road on which her father directed their caravan. Alexandra didn't know anything about raising sheep, but even she realized that the four-legged, woolly little jumbucks had to have grass to eat, and she therefore assumed that further on ahead the scenery would change.

She hadn't expected the sheer sandstone and shale cliffs, however.

"Papa . . . " she began with a quick glance over her shoulder at the second wagon following behind them. "Papa, how—"

"I know what you're thinking, girl," Pembrooke cut in as he snapped the reins to hurry the horses along. "I had the same doubt the first time I saw the bluffs too. But believe me, we will get across them. This road cuts all the way through to the other side."

"And then what?" She was hoping he'd tell her that they would be able to see their property from there, but she knew better. This was all a part of her punishment.

"And then we'll camp."

Alexandra's green eyes widened and her delicate chin dropped. "We'll *what*?"

Laughter rumbled in his chest. "It won't be that horrible," he promised. "We've brought along a tent for you and Felice. You'll have your privacy."

She didn't try to hide her concern. "Only one tent? Where will you sleep?"

"Here . . . in the wagon."

She gave a slight nod of her head in the direction of the second supply wagon where Felice had been instructed to ride with Thomas, a recently pardoned convict Pembrooke had hired as a cook, and another man her father referred to as their carpenter. "But what about them?"

"Who?"

"The hired help," she explained, her tone laced with a mixture of sarcasm and worry. "Where will they sleep? You surely can't trust them to be there in the morning. Or that we won't get our throats cut the second we close our eyes. Good Lord, Papa, they're convicts!"

"Thomas chose to come with us. He's a free man now, so it wouldn't make any sense for him to run off and even less for him to murder us. As for the carpenter . . . well, he's nothing more than a thief. Besides," Pembrooke casually admitted, "I don't plan on taking off his shackles until I'm sure he can be trusted. That's why Thomas has the reins instead of him."

Alexandra's heart pounded with the thought of having to live anywhere near criminals. Heaving a nervous sigh, she forced herself to consider a different subject. "Doesn't he have a name?"

"Who?"

"The carpenter," she supplied, exasperated.

"Of course he has a name," her father scoffed, sounding as if this had been another one of his daughter's less than intelligent questions.

The sharp retort piqued her temper. "Well, I've never heard you refer to him as anything but 'the carpenter.' What's his name?"

From the icy bite of her words, Pembrooke realized she had misunderstood him. But rather than explain, he clamped his mouth shut. Yes, the convict he'd just been assigned was important, probably more important than any of the other men. And yes, the man deserved their respect. The problem was, Pembrooke couldn't remember the carpenter's name.

Alexandra assumed by the angry expression on her father's face that the discussion was over. Not that she cared one way or the other. She could certainly go on living without knowing the convict's name. Besides, she was tired. They'd been traveling since early morning and the ride on the unupholstered wagon seat had made her bone weary. All she really cared about right now was stopping sometime soon to rest.

The summer heat back home in England hardly ever made Alexandra break out in a sweat; the temperature in Cornwall was usually moderate and the numerous rainy days prevented much of a chance for the sun to show its bright face. When it did, there were always the cooling sea breezes to remedy the problem. Oftentimes in winter it snowed, but never enough to make her uncomfortably cold as long as she had a fur cloak to wear outside and a roaring blaze in the hearth waiting for her in the parlor. But Australia was different. She'd been told that its summers were unbearably hot and humid, while the winter months were cool in the daytime and slightly chilly at night. The only threat of snow might be in the peaks of a mountain range—like the one Alexandra's father was leading them across. The higher they climbed, the more certain she was that within a few weeks a blizzard would make the journey back to Sydney impossible.

Boredom set in when she eventually lost her curiosity with the landscape and its trees, flowers, and plants. Before long she found herself thinking about Hardin, Aimee, and the other friends she'd had to leave behind. Although she'd made new friends in Sydney, she doubted she'd ever have someone like the sharp-tongued confidante who had lived next door to her all the while she was growing up. Aimee was special. No one could ever replace her, and the realization made Alexandra sad.

The discovery that Felice actually had a voice *and* an opinion of her own now and then had helped Alexandra cope with her depression. Alexandra wasn't anywhere close to confiding in her, but there was a subtle assurance about the maid's loyalty that made Alexandra think there was hope they'd become more than just mistress and servant. Felice had shown that side last night while she helped her mistress dress for bed. She had appeared to sense her mistress's nervousness and although she didn't ask what caused it, she had lingered longer than necessary after Alexandra had slipped into bed. Seizing the opportunity, Alexandra told Felice about the conversation around the dinner table and how she was worried for her father's safety, hoping her maid would take the initiative to get the answers Alexandra wanted to hear. Felice had reacted immediately by volunteering to talk with an acquaintance of hers about the Ambrose gang. Her friend, she had admitted, worked for Norman Heritage, one of the members of the Board of Enquiry, and if anyone could find out, Felice's friend could.

The next morning while they packed their luggage and had one of the hotel's footmen carry the bags to the wagon, Felice sadly confessed that her news wasn't as encouraging as she had hoped it would be. Ambrose and one of his gang had been assigned to the same "master," while five others from the group had been sent to the prison barracks on Norfolk Island. The sixth and remaining cohort shipped to Australia was working for the government, a job that kept the prisoner too busy and too tired to think of anything devious. It settled Alexandra's mind to some extent to know that Ambrose and one other were the only possible threats, but it didn't tell her where Christian was. Felice's friend hadn't mentioned the men by name and Alexandra knew she mustn't even ask.

Perhaps I can ask later, she silently decided, *once I'm convinced Felice would rather die than breathe a word of it to Papa. Of course, by then the waiting may have driven me mad.*

Wondering how her maid was faring riding in a bumpy wagon over an even bumpier road, she absently glanced back over her shoulder at her. Felice smiled instantly, which Alexandra took to mean that either Felice would never complain or that she had more padding where it counted than Alexandra had. Whatever the reason, her lightheartedness affected Alexandra and she smiled in return before she knew she had.

Maybe, she thought, *things won't be so bad as long as I have Felice with me.*

She was about to turn back around when the man riding in the back of Felice's wagon shifted positions and caught her eye. The seat on which her maid and Thomas sat, along with Felice's full skirts and the cook's legs in the way, made it difficult for her to see much more of him than his head and shoulders and the wide-brimmed straw hat he had pulled down over his face. He was leaning back against the side of the wagon as if he might be trying to sleep, and until that moment Alexandra hadn't realized she had yet to look closely at him.

At the hotel that morning, everything had been rather chaotic while the supplies, their personal belongings, and a few pieces of furniture had been loaded into the wagons. Her father had overseen the task while she said good-bye to the friends who had come to see her off. Only once had Alexandra noticed the convict carpenter and that had been when she heard his leg irons rattle. Even then she hadn't looked at his face while he awkwardly climbed into the back of the second wagon. The shackles that hobbled his step had been more important at the time, since she couldn't imagine how anyone was able to tolerate them. They had to cut into the man's ankles and even though the carpenter appeared to be young and healthy, the extra weight and the inability to move freely had to take its toll. But then he'd obviously deserved what had befallen him, and she had no reason to feel sorry for him.

She had easily dismissed the man, and until now hadn't been

at all curious about him. She had ridden beside her father with her eyes straight ahead for nearly the whole time, never once thinking how uncomfortable the convict must be sitting in the back of the crowded wagon. What confused her was why, all of a sudden, she couldn't turn away. He was just a man. A prisoner, actually. A thief, her father had said. So—

Despite the warm rays of sunlight beating down through the heavy foliage of palms canopying the road, Alexandra felt a sharp chill grab her spine. As it ever so slowly began to creep upward, she deliberately jerked back around on the seat, suddenly sensing the reason why she was having difficulty breathing and why the hair on her nape and across her arms was standing out. Yet the longer she thought about it, the crazier the notion became. Of all the places in the world or just in Australia alone, how could he . . . they . . . her father. . . Knowing the absurdity of it, she drew herself up, raised her chin, and bravely took a second look to confirm it. Pale blue eyes, their centers darkened with rage, were already staring back at her, and her world suddenly careened dizzily on its axis. Everything around her began to spin. She felt cold and hot at the same time. Her stomach was doing a dance, and her lungs ached for the sweet breath of fresh air she couldn't seem to inhale. In the next second the pounding in her temples grew distant, and without being aware that she had dropped her parasol or that her father was hurriedly bringing the wagon to a stop, she unwittingly closed her eyes and surrendered to the serenity of unconsciousness.

No one could see the cold, flinty smile on Christian's face as he settled back in the wagon and lowered his hat down over his brow again. From beneath the shade of its brim, he listened to the clatter of wheels, horses' hooves, and the brake being set as Thomas reined the rig to a halt behind Pembrooke's wagon. He didn't have to look to know Felice had probably scampered from the seat and was rushing to aid her mistress or that Pembrooke, certain something grave had happened to his daughter, had gone pale. Nor did he have any desire to comfort the green-eyed, mean-spirited shrew. He'd already done his share.

There had been several times in his life when Christian had considered himself blessed. The instant he saw Alexandra coming from the hotel he guessed he'd used up his ration of good luck for a while. And what made this particular event so much more special than any of the others was the mere knowledge that since she had obviously not told her father about that night, she was powerless in obstructing Christian's revenge, whether it was simple, complex, swift, or endless. If she threatened him in any way, he'd remind her that all it would take was one word from him to her father and she'd have twice the trouble she already had. In his mind, it would almost be worth the sacrifice.

He had nearly dozed off again when a sharp slap on his arm brought him around. Peering out from under the straw hat, he saw Thomas glaring at him.

"Sir Wallis wants to stop here for a while," the cook explained. "Says he wants me to fix everyone something to eat. You're to find some firewood."

The idea appealed to Christian since he had eaten nothing so far that day. Sitting up, he shoved his hat securely down on his head and swung his feet to the ground. Besides, he'd enjoy the exercise, even if it was somewhat limited.

"And here," Thomas instructed before Christian had moved away. "Take this to Sir Wallis first." He dug through one of the trunks in the wagon and retrieved a silvered flask. "Brandy," he explained, when he saw the frown on his companion's face. "For Miss Pembrooke. The poor thing swooned. Too much heat, I suppose."

You could say that, Christian silently agreed as he took the flask and rounded the end of the wagon.

Luckily for Alexandra, her father had been quick-thinking enough to grab her before she had toppled to the ground. Then, once he'd pulled the rig to a complete stop, he had gotten out, lifted her in his arms, and carried her to a shady spot at the side of the road where he gently laid her down on a bed of grass and dried leaves. Several minutes had passed before her eyelids fluttered open, and even though she had assured him that she was all right, he could see something terrible had frightened her, though he couldn't understand what it could have been. The jangling of chains coming up behind him distracted his thoughts for a moment, and without looking around, he assumed the carpenter had brought the brandy he'd asked Thomas to fetch. Knowing how his daughter felt about convicts, he motioned for Felice to take the flask from the man, while he helped Alexandra sit up.

Christian lingered just long enough for Alexandra to notice him. Her green eyes lifted for only a brief second, looked into his, then fell away from him as if he were a stranger to her and his presence held no interest. If he weren't aware that she had fainted because of him, he might have wondered if she'd forgotten who he was and how they had come to know each other. But that was not the case, and now he was more certain than ever of how important it was to her to keep it all a secret from her father. After handing over the flask and the parasol he had picked up from the ground as he passed by, he turned away from the trio in search of firewood.

The sun was beginning to disappear over the horizon by the time the small caravan had reached the plateau at the top of the mountain range and they'd chosen a place to make camp for the night. Christian's first assignment was to collect wood for Thomas, and while the cook prepared something for them to eat, Pembrooke enlisted Christian's help in setting up the tent. Even though he was working as quickly as he could, his movements were slow and awkward because of the leg irons he still wore, and when he tripped and nearly fell, he cursed his disability under his breath without realizing who might be listening. The second time it happened, however, he could feel Pembrooke's scowl aimed his way, and he glanced up to confirm it as he resumed his task. He wasn't about to explain or to apologize, since he figured the man was smart enough to know he wasn't deliberately trying to be difficult, but just as he reached for the rope he had been preparing to tie off on a tree branch, Pembrooke called to him.

"I've always believed in giving a man a second chance to prove himself," he declared, unaware that his daughter was watching every move his companion made. "I know nothing about your particular case, only that you were sent here in chains because you stole something. There are many reasons why someone steals from another. It could have been greed, revenge, or simply that you were hungry. There's even the possibility that you're an innocent man. That, however, is no concern of mine, since I can't do anything to change it. But I can make your life here comfortable or a living hell. It's up to you." Reaching for the valise he had laid on the wagon seat, he rummaged through it until he found what he was looking for, and turned back to face his laborer. "I was going to wait to do this until I'd had time to study you. Unforeseen circumstances have forced me to change my mind." He held up the key he had taken from the bag. "I'm going to remove your leg irons, but not before I tell you that if you even *think* about running off, I won't hesitate to shoot you. Do I make myself perfectly clear?"

More than you know, Christian thought as he nodded his head. While laying down the rules, Wallis Pembrooke had unknowingly validated his ignorance of Christian's situation. He wasn't aware that Christian had been one of his agents, that he and Lewis Rhomberg were friends, or that Christian had been brought to trial as one of Garrett Ambrose's gang. Pembrooke had also unwittingly contradicted Catton's claim that Christian was a part of Pembrooke's greater plan for some kind of secret mission. To Sir Wallis Pembrooke, Christian was nothing more than the carpenter he needed to help build his new house.

"What is he doing?" Alexandra breathed more to herself than to the woman at her side as she watched her father hand Christian the key to his shackles. *Has he gone mad? Doesn't he know Christian will kill me the first chance he gets? He mustn't turn him loose.* Quite shaken, she turned and grabbed her maid's hands. "Oh, Felice, you've got to tell my father not to unshackle Christian. You must!"

"I will, mum," Felice promised as she gently guided her mistress to the rocker Thomas had taken from the wagon and placed near the campfire. "But I'm sure your father knows what he's doin'. 'E needs the man's help, 'e does. Ye can understand that, can't ye, Miss Alexandra?" Once she had seen the young woman resting comfortably in the rocker, Felice quickly poured her mistress a cup of fresh, hot tea and handed it to her. "I'm sure he'll put the shackles back on the bloke once the two of 'em are finished with the tent, so don't ye worry, ye 'ear?"

Whether it was the tea or her pledge that calmed her mistress, Felice wasn't quite sure, nor did it really matter. What concerned her was Alexandra's reaction to the carpenter and the fact that she had called him by his given name. Felice, too, had blamed Alexandra's swooning on the heat, even though she had noticed that her mistress's gaze had settled on the convict right before she'd fainted. Just a coincidence, Felice had decided. Now she wasn't sure at all. Shifting her attention to the two men stringing up the canvas tent, Felice frowned.

··꘎】 Chapter Ten 【꘎··

ALEXANDRA COULD HEAR HER HEART POUNDING OVER THE crack of thunder in the distance as she lay on her cot inside the tent. She hadn't slept much during the night, and although the sun wasn't visible through the dense storm clouds, she was sure it had to be morning. She'd spent the entire night listening and waiting for Christian to come. Whimpering, she rolled over onto her side and stared at the closed canvas flap, her blanket pulled up snugly under her chin. She'd given up trying to figure out how he had finagled his way into her father's employ or to explain why God had let this happen. She wondered fleetingly if He would rescue her in exchange for an apology to Christian.

"Never!" she stubbornly refused. "I will *never* apologize to that wretched man."

Jade-green eyes flashing with renewed determination and spirit, she thought about the man she guessed was sleeping soundly outside near the fire. What did she have to apologize for? She hadn't done anything. *He* was the one who put his hands on her and assumed he could get away with it. *He* was the one who would have killed her if she hadn't stopped him. All *she* had done was make sure he went to prison for it. He had no right to be angry. It wasn't *his* virtue, *his* life that had been threatened. And she'd tell him that the first chance she got.

Feeling a little better, she lay back again and closed her eyes. Besides, he wouldn't try anything as long as her father was around. Even Christian Page wasn't *that* stupid . . . was he?

She stared worriedly up at the ceiling of the tent again. Of course, he could always make it look like an accident or shift the blame entirely. Anyone crafty enough to get this close when all the odds were against him could easily figure out a simple solution like that. Well, she'd just have to be more cunning. *And* she'd have to keep a close eye on him. She mustn't ever allow him to catch her alone.

Thunder rumbled again, this time much louder, and Alexandra smiled to herself as she watched the flashes of lightning illuminate the canvas roof of her quarters. She'd like nothing better than to have the sky open up and saturate the spot where Christian lay. Maybe luck would be on her side and he'd drown. She giggled at the vision it conjured forth and how she'd just stand there watching rather than help save him.

"Please, Alexandra, do something," she mimicked his words in a whisper.

She determinedly shook her head. "Never, Christian. Never in a million years. You deserve to die."

"But why?" she answered for him. "What did I do that was so horrible?"

"What did you do?" she replied, envisioning the innocent façade of his expression. "You know very well what you did. You . . . you touched me."

"Touched you?" her male counterpart exclaimed.

"Yes!" she hissed quietly so as not to awaken Felice as the maid slept peacefully in her cot a few feet away. "And you kissed me."

"Of course I kissed you. You wanted me to."

"I did not."

"Then why did you kiss me back?"

"I never—"

"You did."

"I did not. If I had kissed you back, you would have fainted from the sheer bliss of it. I don't recall seeing you swoon."

"How could I? You hit me over the head before I had the chance."

"I don't care. If I'd kissed you, you'd have swooned immediately and I wouldn't have needed to hit you over the head."

"Prove it."

"What?"

"I said, prove it. Now. Fish me out of the water and kiss

me. Then stand back and see what happens."

Alexandra liked where her imagination was leading her. . . .
Pulling her pillow out from under her head, she held it up
before her as if the feathered mound were flesh and blood.

"All right," she graciously yielded. "But don't expect me
to catch you when you fall."

Closing her eyes, she pulled the imaginary Christian to her.
But instead of experiencing the rough texture of the pillow, her
memory supplied the feel of warm, moist lips upon her own.
The shock of her own mind betraying her made her gasp, and
thinking that somehow Christian had practiced sorcery and had
switched himself for the down cushion, she sat up and flung it
away. A cold sweat dampened her brow. Her rage fought to
overpower all her other stronger emotions. Yet while she sat
trembling on the cot and staring at the shadowed lump on the
floor as if she expected it to move, something stirred inside
her. Feeling suffocated and hot, and wanting to clear her mind,
she scooted off her bed, threw the blanket over her shoulders,
and headed outside, unaware that most of her drama had been
witnessed by her maid.

The cool, early-morning air felt good against her fevered
brow as she closed her eyes, raised her chin, and inhaled a
long, deep breath to calm her jittery nerves. Lightning flashed
close by, and the earth vibrated with the thunder that followed
a second later, drawing her attention to the muted gray light of
morning struggling to pierce the black clouds overhead. Off to
her left she could hear the roaring water of the cataract as it
fell from one sandstone ledge to another, an inviting sound
that offered a moment of peace for her tormented mind. She
glanced in its direction but didn't move, lured by the soothing
rush of water yet hesitant to walk that far from camp.

Last night after they had eaten and her father had engaged
Christian's full attention with his plans for the construction
of the house and outbuildings, she and Felice had gone for a
stroll and had found the noisy waterfall. Soft-leafed shrubs and
herbs lined both sides while a forest of eucalyptus protected it
from intruders. Large, flat rocks lay as stepping-stones across
its shallow width, and a chorus of lorikeets sang their melody
from high atop their lofty perches. It had been Alexandra's

idea of paradise the moment she saw it, and she was tempted to visit it again and lose herself in the serenity of it. She needed *something* to ease her troubled state.

So, who's stopping you? she silently asked. Her gaze shifted to the sleeping forms lying near the dying campfire. *Certainly not Christian. Felice said Papa would chain him again after the work was done.*

Craning her neck to get a better look without having to move closer to him, she was almost sure she could see the shackles around his legs. With a pleased smile, she turned and headed into the woods.

Cool grasses and dried leaves cushioned her bare feet as she made her way forward. A light breeze stirred up the sweet bouquet of orange banksia and mottlecah and the scent of rain. Lightning guided her journey and within minutes she stood at the edge of the rippling water. She wanted to hate this wild, untamed land, and she wanted her father to hate it too. She wanted him to take her back home . . . to England, to her friends, to a society that amused itself with fashion, food, balls, the theater, and with seeing who could do the least amount of work for the most amount of money. She doubted Sydney would ever become such a place, that it would ever match London or even come close. Yet while she listened to the hypnotizing splash of the cascade in front of her, she realized it didn't matter. Australia was meant to be different. It was beautiful and exciting on its own. It didn't need kings and queens, elaborate mansions, the gaiety of a crowded dance floor, or beautiful women clothed in furs and satin to make it special. It was rich in other ways.

"Careful, Alexandra," she bade herself as she hugged the blanket around her and lifted the hem of her nightgown to sit down on a large rock beside the steady flow of water. "You're beginning to sound like you might actually enjoy living here. Remember, you haven't seen the worst of it yet. You haven't shared the same space with a bunch of smelly old sheep. You could change your mind, you know."

That thought brought the vision of her father, and it, in turn, reminded her of Christian. Sighing, she wondered what he had in store for her. Would it be sudden? Or painful? Or would he go on pretending she wasn't even there just as he'd done so far? He'd shown no concern for her when she'd fainted nor had he gloated. He'd hardly even looked at her. All the while he and her father had set up camp, he had concentrated on his work, not where she might be at the moment. After he'd filled his dinner plate, he had moved away from the rest of them to eat alone. She was sure her father wouldn't think so, but she had the feeling it was his subtle way of telling them that if he had a choice, he'd have nothing to do with them. She couldn't really blame him. Before either of them had entered his life, he'd been free to do whatever pleased him . . . even if it was unlawful.

The snapping of a twig behind her jolted Alexandra to her feet. She was certain Christian had somehow broken his shackles and had followed her. Spinning around to face him squarely and courageously, she held her breath, positive he had decided that now would be the best opportunity for him to kill her. The crash of water behind her deafened her to any further hint of his whereabouts, and the shadowed spaces in the trees enshrouded his tall, muscular frame. The seconds dragged by. Fear knotted her belly and made her ache. She wanted to scream and doubted she could. She wanted it over with, but she didn't want to die. Then suddenly, as if God had given her a reprieve, a bolt of lightning seared the sky and lit up the forest before her, singling out the slender figure of her maid standing twenty feet away.

"Felice!" Alexandra gasped. "You nearly scared me to death! What are you doing here?"

"I'm sorry, mum," the woman shouted through the boom of thunder that shook the ground and every bone in her body. "I didn't mean to. But when I woke up and found ye gone, I worried for yer safety. Don't ye think ye oughta go back inside the tent?" She pointed a trembling finger at the sky. "It's goin' ta rain real soon."

As if Felice's declaration had been a signal to some greater power, cold, biting droplets began to pelt the earth. With a squeal, Alexandra ducked her head and ran toward her companion, waving at Felice to lead the way. Running back to camp, with their eyes trained on the hazards ahead of them,

neither of the women saw the tall, broad-shouldered figure
watching their departure from a safe distance away. Once
they had disappeared within the thick growth of the forest,
Christian turned and headed back the way he'd come.

Riding next to her father on the wagon seat, Alexandra wondered at his mood. He seemed happy, almost ecstatic now that
they were on their way again, judging by the smile on his face.
The storm had passed with nothing more than a lot of noise and
a little rain. They'd eaten a light breakfast, packed everything
up, and had climbed into the wagons before the sun had a
chance to chase away the last of the night shadows. And, as
before, Christian acted as though there were one less person
in their party. Alexandra honestly didn't mind being invisible.
She actually preferred it, since one look from him had already
stripped her of her dignity. But Christian's behavior wasn't
what gnawed at her. It was her father's joyfulness that disturbed her, for as hard as she tried, she couldn't imagine the
reason for it. Finally, she decided to voice her curiosity.

"I pray I don't sound beyond myself, daughter," he sighed,
the smile still clinging to his lips, "but in the past I've seldom
been wrong about a person."

Alexandra thought of Donald Collins, her father's assistant,
William Jones, Clyde Pearson, and Manning Robertson, all
devoted agents of his, and how her father had personally selected each man. In that regard, yes, he'd been wise in choosing
them. They'd never been anything but loyal to him. Yet . . .

"Perhaps it's just the excitement I'm feeling or my desperate
want to succeed," he went on without his daughter's encouragement, "but I must confess I have a good feeling about Christian."

"Christian?" The name exploded from her lips.

Pembrooke chuckled, believing his offspring had no idea of
whom he was speaking. "The carpenter. His name is Christian
Page."

I know what his name is, Alexandra mentally seethed. *What
I don't know is how you can feel good about him!* Curling her
fingers in the thick layers of cloth draped over her lap, she gritted her teeth and drew in a deep breath, praying she wouldn't

reveal her apprehension when she spoke. "What about him, Papa?"

"I haven't asked him yet what it was he'd done to get himself thrown in prison, but I sense he had good reason. I don't feel he's the usual kind of criminal one expects to find in chains."

A mixture of feelings flooded over Alexandra, and one question more than any other rose to her lips. Hadn't her father recognized him from the trial? Didn't he know who Christian was? Apparently not or he wouldn't feel good about him! And unless she was mistaken, it sounded to her as if her father actually *liked* Christian. Alexandra's nervousness increased. "Oh?" she asked, inwardly cringing at the sound of her voice cracking.

"He's smart," her father explained. "Book smart, I mean, as well as having common sense." Pembrooke's smile disappeared as he snapped the reins and continued with his evaluation of the man in a more serious vein. "In the short while we talked last night, he showed me the error in my thinking about the shearing shed and why it would be wise to build the house on a knoll away from the barn. He told me how I must chalk the belly of the ram in bright red before turning him loose with the ewes—"

"Whatever for?" Alexandra cut in. She mistrusted people who seemed to know everything, and in Christian's case she felt he warranted close scrutiny. If he hated her, he surely hated her father, and that meant he might utilize their ignorance for his own benefit.

Pembrooke cleared his throat, obviously uncomfortable with the question.

"Papa, please," Alexandra sighed, for she'd noticed his reluctance and assumed he thought his daughter too dumb to understand. "As much as I dislike the idea of living with sheep, and pray that someday soon you'll miss the excitement of the city, I'd prefer you not exclude me from learning all I can about raising them. I'll have too few friends with whom to chat as it is, and if you keep me in the dark about your work, I'll have absolutely nothing to say."

Pembrooke's green eyes glowed. When he'd made his decision to pack up his daughter and everything they could take with them, he'd done it in the hope of saving his only child from herself and her reckless behavior. He'd never imagined it might bring the two of them closer. So, if she was willing to learn the details in producing a large flock of sheep, he'd be more than willing to supply the knowledge.

"Once the ram mates with a ewe, the red chalk will rub off on her hindquarters, letting us know there's a chance she'll have a lamb in the spring," he replied as discreetly as possible.

Alexandra's face flamed instantly as she envisioned not only a pasture full of red-bottomed ewes, but Christian standing there with a leering grin on his face and the container of scarlet chalk in his hands as though he planned to use it to mark her. Unaware that she had blushed, she stiffened her spine and started to glance back over her shoulder at him, when she heard her father laugh.

"I asked Christian the necessity of it and he said it would help us decide how many rams we'd need," Pembrooke continued, failing to realize how his explanation had disturbed the young woman at his side while he concentrated on the narrow road ahead of them. "Says even rams can lose interest now and then."

I'll wager he never does, Alexandra silently surmised, her eyes closed as she gulped down the lump in her throat. What a perfect job for him: overseeing the breeding of her father's stock! She shivered as she wondered if that might include her.

"Are you cold, child?" Pembrooke asked once he'd seen her tremble and noted the way she was hugging her arms to her slender frame.

"No, Papa, I'm fine," she quickly assured him.

"Then what's wrong? You seem . . . upset."

"I am," she replied. She couldn't let her father go on thinking Christian was something he wasn't. She had to warn him. "It's this . . . Page fellow," she began, twisting around to look him squarely in the eye. "I don't think you should be so quick to assume everything he tells you is gospel. You don't know anything about him. Why, he might be lying to you just so he can have a good laugh over it later."

Pembrooke shook his head. "Nonsense, child. He has no reason to lie." His dark brows came together in a frown as he studied the road again. "I'm right about this man. I can feel it. Christian Page will do a lot to help our place be a success and one day you'll realize it too."

"But, Papa—"

"No, Alexandra," he warned. "Until you've had a chance to talk to him and to judge for yourself, there's no sense in arguing about it."

Clamping her teeth together, Alexandra fought against the turbulent fear rising inside her. If Christian won his way into her father's confidence, she'd be forced to deal with him on her own. It was already too late for her to tell her father who actually wrote the note he'd received concerning Hardin. He'd never believe her. He'd assume she was making it up just to spite him . . . or for the sake of arguing . . . or out of her dislike for convicts. And if he asked Christian about it, *that* one would lie to protect his own hide!

Suddenly she shivered again, and without a care as to how her father might react, she jerked around on the wagon seat to look back at the roué she was positive was staring at her. A moment passed before hard, cold eyes peered up at her from under the wide brim of the straw hat. A tense jaw and firm set to his mouth marked his disapproval, and just as she was about to show her own disdain by lifting her nose haughtily in the air and turning back around, Christian easily trumped her effort when he looked away first as though the birds winging overhead held more interest to him. Singed by the affront and unable to do anything about it, she gnashed her teeth, sucked air into her lungs, and faced the road again, thinking that if it be in the life hereafter, she would win this battle that raged between them.

Along the western base of the Blue Mountains, late-afternoon sunshine splashed broad strokes of yellow-gold bands across a lush green plain that seemed to spill out beyond the horizon. Patches of petrophile, orange banksia, and isopogon formosus dotted the edges of a stand of blue gum eucalyptus. Scrubs grew in sparse clusters over the rolling terrain, and the squawk of a parrot pierced the otherwise peaceful tranquility of the land.

Had she been asked, Alexandra would have denied the warm sensation that came over her the moment her father swung the wagon off the main road and down a winding avenue to the south, giving her an unobstructed view of the place they would soon call home. Although nothing about the scenery could be compared to what she had left behind in England, the quiet composure of the grassy landscape promised a satisfying reward if she was willing to take it.

"Isn't it grand?" Pembrooke asked, smiling proudly, his green eyes glowing.

"Yes, Papa," Alexandra quietly admitted. "It's very beautiful."

"You'll learn to like it here," he rushed on, when he expected her to list the bad points. "The Pleasantons live on the other side of the knoll." He motioned off to their right. "About an hour's ride, and Phoebe told me last week that her niece will be paying them a visit soon. She's about your age, I'm told, so you'll have someone to talk to. Her father, Phoebe's brother, is a military man, and they've been living in Parramatta for the past ten years. I'm sure you'll enjoy her company."

Alexandra smiled lamely. She had serious doubts about the niece for the simple reason that she was related to Wayne.

Once the small caravan had rounded a bend in the road and passed over the last hill, Alexandra was able to see a cluster of buildings not far ahead. Her father didn't have to tell her that they belonged to him or that the largest one was where he expected them to take up residence. At least that was what she surmised since it was the only structure that even slightly resembled a house. The single-story, wood-framed building sat near what she guessed was the kitchen, a barn, tool shed, and livery, and close to the convicts' quarters—*too* close for her liking. It needed a fresh coat of paint, new shutters, and repairs done on the roof. A large veranda ran the entire length of its perimeter and near the opened front door she saw one straight-backed wooden chair, a spot, she guessed, where one could escape the heat of the house in the late afternoon. She could only imagine what awaited her inside.

"It isn't much right now," her father admitted as if reading her thoughts. "But it will be. Christian will see to that. As

soon as you've rested, the three of us will sit down and discuss
plans for a new house. You can tell him what you want, and
he'll draw up a sketch." He failed to see how pale her face
had become when he turned to point over his left shoulder.
"Christian said we'd be wise to build the house away from
all the other buildings. Right there would be a good spot. I
think it's far enough away. Don't you?"

Alexandra glanced in the direction he indicated, smiled
halfheartedly, and gave a slight nod of her head rather than
voice her opinion that even Capetown, South Africa, wouldn't
be far enough away.

"Of course, it will be a while before it's done," he went on
as he snapped the reins and headed them toward the group
of men who had started to gather in the yard. "The shearing
shed and repairs on the barn come first. We have to earn some
money before we can spend any of it."

A hint of a frown wrinkled her brow for a brief second when
she realized he had probably spent all they had on the purchase
of this land, supplies—and those wretched sheep!

"Good evening, Sir Pembrooke!" one of the men called out,
drawing Alexandra's attention to their welcoming party.

The one who spoke was tall and thickly muscled, almost to
a fault, as his shirt strained at the seams each time he moved.
He had taken the straw hat from his head in a polite display
of manners, and by doing so he revealed thinning brown hair
and a very high forehead. Warm deep brown eyes sparkled in
the dying sunlight and his cheeks held a rosy hue as though
he'd worked outside too long that day. He walked and held
his broad frame with a certain amount of pride, and seemed
genuinely pleased that his master had returned.

"Good evening, Lynn," Pembrooke greeted him cheerfully as he pulled the wagon to a stop and set the brake. "Has
everything gone well in my absence?"

"Yes, sir," the man replied as he motioned for one of his
companions to step forward and take the horse's bridle. "And
I trust your reason for going was rewarding."

Pembrooke smiled with a short nod of his head. "Better than
I could have hoped." With the agility of a man twenty years
younger, Pembrooke jumped to the ground, then turned to help

his daughter. "Lynn, I'd like you to meet Alexandra."

The man's smile widened as he feasted his eyes on the lovely lady at Pembrooke's side. "I'm honored, Miss Pembrooke," he said, bowing at the waist and sweeping his hat with a flourish.

When he stood erect again, he winked playfully at her. "But I would have known who you are without being told. Your father talks of no one else."

Uncomfortable with the knowledge, Alexandra forced a smile and prayed no one noticed the blush to her cheeks.

"Alexandra, this is Lynn Boone, my . . . ah . . . foreman, of sorts," Pembrooke explained. "He's also a man you should watch very closely. Until his temper got the better of him, he was a lieutenant in His Majesty's Royal Navy . . . a sailor. He knows exactly how to flatter a woman until she forgets herself. So beware."

Their easy banter surprised Alexandra. She had never seen her father so relaxed or looking so young as he did in that moment. She could only attribute it to an absence of the pressures associated with his work in England. What puzzled her was his familiarity with this convict, Lynn Boone. They were behaving as though they'd been friends for years, and that out here, in the vast grassland miles from pomp and circumstance, they were equals rather than master and servant. Confused, she glanced at the others standing several yards away. Did her father treat all of them in the same manner? In the future, would that include Christian?

"I'm not the rogue he makes me out to be, Miss Pembrooke," Boone asserted, breaking into her thoughts. "I assure you I will always remember my place around you."

"You'd better," her father warned, while the smile on his face contradicted any serious concern that the man would be anything other than a gentleman at all times. Or at least Pembrooke had assumed as much until he saw the way Boone's expression changed from jovial to absolute distraction when something behind him caught the other's eye. Frowning, Pembrooke glanced around and had to stifle a laugh once he spotted the cause of Boone's distress. "Perhaps I bade a warning to the wrong woman," he joked, noticing how Alexandra's maid was staring back at Boone as though no one else existed in the world but the two of them. "Felice, this is Lynn Boone. Lynn, Felice. She's my daughter's maid."

The young woman's face flushed the second she realized everyone was looking at her, and out of desperation she focused her eyes on Thomas as he helped her to the ground.

"And the gentleman with her is Thomas," Pembrooke advised. "Our new cook."

The idea of having something palatable to eat for a change brought Boone out of his trance in an instant. "New cook?" he exclaimed excitedly.

"Yes, my good man, our cook," Pembrooke said, laughing. "So I suggest you take special care of him. He's a free man— which means he can leave anytime he so desires." He raised a hand to indicate the third member to descend the wagon. "And this is Christian Page. He, Mr. Boone, unlike you, knows how to hammer and saw and put together a pile of boards so they resemble a building. With his knowledge and your bulk, I'd say we'll have this place looking the way it should in no time."

Some of the twinkle left Boone's dark brown eyes when he settled his gaze on the newest convict to join the force. He couldn't explain why, but something about Christian Page bothered him. Although he'd be the first to argue that he never judged a man by his looks, Boone couldn't help noticing the quiet assuredness to the man's stance, his sense of presence, how he commanded respect just by the way he held himself erect. Despite the clothes he wore, Page appeared to be in full control of the situation and of himself. To Boone, he conveyed a message that no matter what happened, he would always land on his feet, and at no cost to himself. Thus, until he got to know the man better, Boone decided this stranger warranted close scrutiny. He liked Wallis Pembrooke, and Pembrooke had been very fair with him when there was no need. In return Boone had made a secret pledge that whatever it took, he would protect the man and what belonged to him.

"Page." A stiff, unfriendly nod of Boone's head accompanied the solemnly spoken greeting.

Whether her father felt it or not, Alexandra was sure she sensed hostility oozing out of every pore in Lynn Boone's body. As for Christian, she had no way of knowing if he'd been affected in the same manner, since as usual the expression on his face was unreadable. And even if he had, she decided, he wouldn't care. Christian was used to people detesting him. In this instance, however, he *should* care. Alexandra had found an ally.

·☙❧ *Chapter Eleven* ☙❧·

BECAUSE THE PREVIOUS OWNERS HAD DIED AND LEFT NO KIN, the house where Alexandra, her father, and Felice planned to reside contained the furnishings of two old men, brothers who had lived quite elegantly until their desire for spirits became more important than seeing to the repairs and cleaning of the place. It was rumored that they had fired the cook and housekeeper in a drunken rage and laughed when the rest of their staff ran off in the middle of the night fearing for their lives. Until their bodies had been discovered two months later, the brothers lived like hermits, and although everyone assumed they had succumbed to their passion for liquor, just how they died was never decided, since a pack of wild dogs had devoured most of the remains.

The sight of the disarray had, at first, sorely tempted Alexandra to scream her displeasure in colorful language unbefitting a lady of her upbringing, until she had realized the task before her would provide the distraction she needed to forget about the man who would be working closely with her father from dawn to dusk. Thus, for the past two days, she had deliberately busied herself with turning a hovel into a palace.

Enlisting Felice's help, they had taken down all the curtains, washed them, patched up their tears and loose hems, and rehung as many of them as they could. Those that were beyond repair were folded and stacked away for some other use, and the lengths of fabric needed to replace them were put on Alexandra's roster of required supplies, a list she intended to give to her father the next time someone was planning a trip into town. The floors were scrubbed, rugs were taken outside to air and to have the dirt beaten from them, the hearths cleaned, and walls painted to cover cracks and smudges that wouldn't wash clean. Pictures, books, and other trinkets belonging to the dead brothers were carted to the attic for storage, since Alexandra didn't feel she had the right to throw them away and because she didn't know what else to do with them. Then, once the basics were readied, she employed the help of one of the workers in rearranging the furniture and carrying out anything she felt was too dilapidated to be of any use or value.

Since the small house had only two bedrooms, a parlor, and a dining room, through which a covered walkway led to the kitchen out back, finding a private place for Felice became their next objective. Alexandra hadn't minded sharing her room and her bed with the girl the first night, since it meant she wouldn't be alone after everyone was asleep, but she had also realized how uncomfortable it had made Felice. Thus, when her maid suggested they partition off a section of the attic, Alexandra hadn't argued too strongly, knowing that the arrangement wouldn't last forever and that Felice, being right above her, would hear Alexandra if she screamed.

The work had been exhausting, yet for the second night in a row, after she had bathed and retired, she found herself lying on her back staring up at the ceiling above her bed. She felt good about herself, and how she'd actually gotten her hands dirty rather than stand around and issue orders while others did the work. The results of her labors had pleased her, and aside from taking pride in what she saw, her father's compliment on how clean everything looked made her feel useful for the first time in her life.

But none of that helped her sleep. She simply couldn't stop Christian from stealing into her thoughts. What disturbed her more than anything was her constant fear that despite the population of the place, he would somehow come upon the chance to catch her alone, and that he'd have no qualms about killing her. It would be quite simple for him to sneak into her room, grab a pillow, and hold it over her face while she struggled and squirmed for her last breath of life.

Frightened by the vision, she threw off the covers and sprang from the soft, warm haven of her four-poster bed to stand by the window, absently studying a grassy hillside bathed in the silvery glow of the moon. She had considered sleeping with a lantern so that she might see him in time to defend herself as he raised the sash and hoisted himself over the sill. But that would only result in her father questioning the need, and she certainly couldn't tell him that she was afraid of the dark . . . or, more precisely, of what lurked there.

Over dinner that night, she had subtly prodded her father into telling her about the men who worked for him, where they came from, what their crimes had been, and how long it would be before they had served their time and were emancipated. She had sat there quietly listening to his lengthy account of each and every man's situation, though she was truly interested in only one.

Lynn Boone, a loyal, hardworking military man, had sacrificed his future when he allowed his temper free rein and struck an admiral for the disparaging remarks made about the young woman Boone had been seeing at the time. According to Boone, he had loved the girl and had planned to marry her. The admiral, it seemed, claimed to have been intimate with the young lady on several occasions, and that in his opinion she would continue such behavior even after the nuptials had been celebrated. Boone had confessed to Alexandra's father that he would have killed the man had someone not intervened. He also admitted quite remorsefully that while he awaited trial and sentencing, reports came back to him that the young girl had been seen in the company of not just one fellow officer, but many. Although he regretted having lost his commission in the navy, and that he had been too starry-eyed to realize the truth about the girl, he never once felt inclined to apologize for his actions. In his opinion the admiral had deserved what he'd gotten. As far as Alexandra's father was concerned, Lynn Boone didn't deserve to be imprisoned for being an honorable man.

The recital had explained a lot of things to Alexandra, the most important being why her father so obviously trusted and admired Lynn Boone. When she'd asked him how he could be so positive that Boone was telling the truth about the incident, her father had smiled softly and admitted that although he'd never learned the details of the court-martial that had ended

Lieutenant Boone's career, he had personally known the admiral involved and of the man's need to brag about each and every female conquest he'd made, including Boone's lost love. The best part of the whole story, she later decided, was realizing how much her father valued the man's opinion. Now all she had to do was win Boone's friendship and allow him to discover her dislike and fear of Christian. Out of loyalty to her father, Boone would probably tell the elder Pembrooke about it or take care of it himself. In either case, Alexandra would be rid of Christian Page.

As she stood staring out the window and thinking back to their conversation, she realized now that her father had never mentioned Christian and what he had done to land himself in Australia, and she wondered why. Perhaps he hadn't taken the time to ask or maybe he honestly didn't want to know for fear Christian's crime would be so heinous it would spoil his opinion of him.

Little chance of that, she mused sarcastically, certain that no matter what he asked, Christian would lie to him.

The distant howl of wild dogs drew her attention to the stand of moonlit trees silhouetted against a clear, black sky on the horizon. A yawn caught her unexpectedly and she raised her hand to cover her mouth, her gaze drifting to the left. At first glance she hardly noticed the movement at the side of the building where the men were housed. Then she saw it again. She straightened, frowned, and leaned closer to the windowpane for a better look. Caught half in shadow, half in an ashen light, whoever was standing there appeared to be acting out his displeasure over something, for a second study confirmed he was alone. His gestures were graceful, sleek, and perfectly balanced, reminding her somewhat of a ballet dancer. He was barefoot, without a shirt, and the cuffs of his trousers had been rolled up to just above the ankle.

"How odd," she whispered, completely mystified by the man's antics. She couldn't decide if he was mimicking a past argument or batting at insects buzzing around his head.

Wondering if perhaps her father had failed to tell her that one of the laborers was prone to fits of insanity, she glanced back at the rocker and her robe draped over its back. She'd stay far enough away for him not to know she was there, and to give herself plenty of time to run if he should spot her, but her curiosity, as well as her adventurous spirit, begged her to leave the house and stand close enough to hear him if he spoke. She just had to know what possessed him to dance around in the dark half-dressed and oblivious of the possibility that he might be seen.

It took Alexandra only a moment or two to sneak down the hall, through the dining room, and out the back door without a sound. On slippered feet she tiptoed across the yard to the side of the tool shed, where she paused to decide on a hiding place and to allow herself the chance to collect her composure. The mental image she still had of the prancing fool provoked the inclination to laugh out loud, and she knew if she gave in to it, he'd hear her and her fun would be ruined. Fighting the urge to giggle, she tried thinking of something unpleasant to squelch her rising mirth, and was suddenly hit with the vision of Christian. The laughter died and a scowl replaced it.

"Damned rogue," she hissed beneath her breath as she leaned and looked out past the edge of the shed.

Her ill humor deepened all the more once her gaze swept the arena where her entertainment had played only seconds earlier. Had she known the scene was nearing an end, she would have continued her appraisal of it from the window in her room rather than venture out into the chilly night. Thinking that perhaps he had simply chosen a different stage, she clasped the lapels of her robe together in one hand, raised her hem in the other, and hurriedly scampered across the thick, dewy grass to the spot where she had last seen him. Discouraged by his disappearance, and alarmed by the loud snoring that seemed to be cutting right through the wall of the convicts' quarters, she decided to return to the warmth and safety of the house.

Christian had spotted Alexandra the moment her scantily clad body disturbed the light shining out through the window in her room. Her face was in shadow, so he had no way of knowing where her gaze had fallen, if she had seen him, or what her reaction was if she had. He'd assumed her guilt had kept her from enjoying a peaceful night's sleep as he'd noticed it had the previous night, and since they had not had the chance to speak privately as yet, he had wondered how long it would be before she sought him out. She had to be worried that sooner or later he'd try something, although in his mind just watching her squirm and knowing that his mere presence had to be grating on her nerves was enough to satisfy him. Torn between returning to his quarters and confronting her on her way back to the house, he stealthily clung to the shadows as he rounded the far side of the tool shed.

The yelping of the dingos seemed to grow louder. Nervous, Alexandra shot a glance over her shoulder in their direction, wondering how close the pack of wild dogs would venture in and if they would attack her should they cross her path before she had reached the house. Her father had told her that the canines were the biggest threat in raising sheep, since their main choice of food was the slower-running jumbuck, and that ordinarily they were frightened of man and his weapons. That didn't guarantee, however, that hunger wouldn't change their habits, and he warned his daughter to be wary of them. Realizing what a foolish idea it had been to come outside in the middle of the night, she hurried her step, the barking and shrill cries of the pack bouncing off each vertebra in her spine.

Christian, too, heard the frenzied call of the dingos as he stood with his back pressed against the wall of the shed, his arms folded over his bare chest, a dark look in his eyes. Their sounds merely confirmed the decision he'd already made about suggesting to Pembrooke that he purchase a sheep dog to tend the flock and protect the animals from hungry predators. Until the sheep arrived, he didn't regard the wild dogs as being much of a problem.

He returned his attention to the young woman hurrying nervously past his hiding place. Moonlight bathed her slim figure and drew his gaze down the slender curve of her back and buttocks, along the imagined willowy length of shapely legs to trim ankles and slippered feet peeking out from beneath a raised hem of white satin. Dark brown hair flowed over her shoulders and fell in a torrent of soft curls to the middle of her back. A slight breeze molded the shiny fabric of her robe against her waist and hip, and stirred no small amount of curiosity in Christian's mind as to the tempting treasure that lay beneath it. If one could overlook her spiteful, vindictive nature, he concluded, a man might find himself eager to explore the hidden passion he was sure burned beneath her icy surface. But not he! Alexandra wasn't just an alluring woman. She was a cold-hearted, conniving vixen who silently conveyed a clear message that all men were fools and she had been put on this earth to prove it.

Christian wasn't sure just what it was that warned the young woman of his presence—she might have accidentally noticed him or she could have felt the heat of his regard—but in any case he suddenly found himself staring into round, fearful green eyes. She had swung around to face him, and in so doing had traded her grip on the front of her robe for two handfuls of its skirts, thus allowing the garment to fall open and expose the lacy, tight-fitting bodice of her nightgown. In the bright glow of the moon he could see the full swell of her bosom and how her breasts strained against the satiny fabric each time she took a labored breath. The silvery light caressed the long length of her creamy neck, sparkled in her tousled hair falling over one shoulder, and added a hint of madness to the jade-green color of her eyes. She was a fetching, bewildering vision, one that caught him unawares for a moment, until he remembered the last time they had faced each other alone and why.

Alexandra entertained the idea of spinning on her heels and running as fast as she could, but she wasn't sure her feet would move if she commanded it. She wanted to scream and alarm her father or Boone, but her mouth was so dry, she doubted any sound would escape her lips. She wished the ground would open up and swallow her or that a huge bird would swoop down, catch her up in its sharp talons, and carry her away. Anything! Just as long as she didn't have to stand there, frozen like an ice sculpture, while he had his fun. It wasn't fair! All of this was *his* doing, not hers. *And how dare he look at her like that!*

Chip by icy chip her fear of him fell away and melted into a pool of simmering rage. In her adventures with Hardin, she had faced much tougher adversaries than this blond-haired man standing before her now, and none of them had ever raised even a shred of worry. So what made Christian Page any different?

And didn't he know that a single word from her would bring the wrath of Wallis Pembrooke down upon his head? Was he willing to die by her father's hand in exchange for his revenge? She immediately shook off the absurdity of the notion. No man was that addlebrained.

Seeing where his gaze fell and how he appeared unable to pull it away, she tightened her robe securely around her and squared her shoulders. It didn't, however, end the burning sensation she felt searing the flesh along the low neckline of her gown. "What is it you hope to prove by being here?" she said through tightly clenched teeth. "Better still, how did you manage to get assigned to my father?"

Her acid tongue and the fire in those flashing green eyes failed to incite any emotion whatsoever in Christian. He blinked and shifted his gaze away from her as though he stood alone in the yard.

Alexandra's temper flared even higher. "I asked you a question, Mr. Page," she seethed, foolishly forgetting herself as she took several steps toward him. "Are you deaf as well as stupid? You must realize that if you lay one hand to me, my father will kill you."

Cold blue eyes moved toward hers, and she felt a chill course down her back. In that same moment she realized how close they stood and that her silent tormentor was stripped to the waist. Bright, silvery moonlight played along the crests of thick muscles and shadowed the taut furrows beneath them, while drawing attention to his wide shoulders and the rock-hard strength of the arms folded over his naked chest. His jaw was set, his lips tight, and his eyes held no warmth as they bore into her. His short-cropped hair fell softly against his brow, and Alexandra found herself wondering if to touch him would be like touching stone.

Christian could sense the emotions that were racing through this woman, and how Alexandra was struggling to keep her brave, undaunted façade. He frightened her . . . down deep . . . beyond the surface of words. He could understand her worry that he might reveal the whole sordid experience of their first meeting to her father, but that wasn't what truly disturbed her. At this point he surmised that dealing with her father's anger over what she had done was of little consequence. Something else had her shaking in her satin slippers. Surely she wasn't in fear of her life?

The sequence of events, from the moment she and her foolhardy friend had entered the inn to their conversation later in the gaol, flashed through his mind. He had been ordered by Ambrose to kill her, and the last thing Christian had said to her before the trial was a promise that someday they would meet again, a vague remark with several meanings. It appeared to him that Alexandra assumed he'd meant he would finish the task he'd been assigned, that he would kill her. *He* knew the absurdity of the notion, but she obviously didn't, and although the idea, at times, hadn't been all that unappealing, the truth of the matter was he'd chosen something less severe. Because she had interfered where she had no business being, Ambrose had been arrested *before* Christian had gathered the evidence he needed to see Ambrose hang. Therefore, her payment for meddling would be having to answer to her father, for that was all Christian had planned for her. He would expose her part in all of it and how her hindrance had unintentionally saved Garrett Ambrose from the executioner.

Amazed that the little fool still hadn't figured out how his actions had actually saved her life, he dropped his gaze away from her with a shake of his head. "I'm not the one afraid of your father, Miss Pembrooke." He met her worried look with a quiet confidence. "You are. Otherwise he'd know all about you and me, and he wouldn't be calling me by my given name." He stared at her again even though he didn't expect her to respond. "And yes, he probably would kill me if I laid a hand to you. That's why I've dismissed the idea of murdering you in your sleep."

Pushing away from the wall, he dropped his arms to his sides and casually stepped nearer to her. He could feel her entire body shaking, and its discovery gave him an idea. With slow deliberation, he entwined a dark brown, silky curl around his finger, purposely allowing one knuckle to touch her trembling breast. "I must admit that for a time I could think of nothing else, while I ate, slept, and worked in chains without being offered a bath or change of clothes or a single breath of fresh air. It seemed only fitting in return for what you forced on me."

Christian let his gaze move to her quivering chin, the creamy smooth length of her throat, and finally the quick rise and fall of her breasts as she fought with each breath she took. If she had made up her mind to admit everything to her father, she wouldn't be yielding to his bold advance, and that piece of knowledge spurred him on. Although he doubted he would ever carry through with his threat, simply knowing that she feared him promised a greater satisfaction than anything else he could have pledged.

"I don't intend to kill you, Miss Pembrooke," he whispered as he slid one arm around her waist and slowly pulled her delicate form against his body. "All I want is to finish what we started back there in my room at the inn."

Alexandra could feel every inch of his powerful frame molded against her, how the steely strength of his arm held her imprisoned, and wherever her body touched his, it seemed a thousand tiny needles pierced her flesh. She also sensed by the way he was lowering his head that he was about to kiss her, and that if she let him, he wouldn't stop there. He'd take what he felt she owed him right on the very spot where they stood! Terrified by the thought that she would be unable to stop him, and numbed by the fiery closeness of him, she summoned the courage to scream just as his warm breath fell against her lips.

"But not now," he murmured, a coldness frosting the edges of his words and turning the paleness of his eyes a dark, flinty blue. "Not here."

He let go of her rather abruptly, watched her stumble backward without any attempt to aid her, and then raked her shivering form with a dispassionate look that frightened her more than anything else he could have done before he turned and walked away.

··◦| *Chapter Twelve* |◦··

THE EVENTS OF THE NIGHT BEFORE HAD ROBBED ALEXANDRA of any ability to sleep. Fleeing back to her room—once she had been able to get her feet to move—she had not only locked the door behind her, but jammed the back of a chair under the knob as a safety precaution. The window created a problem for her, however. Once she had closed the shutters with the intention of locking them, she found that the latch was broken, a discovery that meant the only obstacle between Christian and her was a fragile pane of glass. She had considered moving the armoire in front of the opening, but the piece of furniture proved to be too heavy to budge. Left with no other alternative, she had armed herself with the poker from the fireplace, a letter opener, and the wood-handled brass bed warmer, all of which she carried to bed with her. If she fell asleep and he managed to gain access to her room without her knowledge, she would, at least, have something with which to defend herself.

The following morning found her curled up in a ball on top of the covers, the bed warmer clutched to her bosom, the poker on the floor, and the letter opener lost beneath the pillows. Warm sunshine seeped in between the half-closed shutters, spilling a steady stream of light against the ceiling and wall above the bed. As the sun climbed higher in the sky, the bright beam of light slowly moved downward until it fell across her sleeping face. Groaning, she rolled away from the source, her arms still wrapped around the brass pan.

She had nearly fallen asleep again, when a frown flitted across her brow. A second later she opened her eyes and pulled back to look at the item she held in her arms. The sight of it instantly brought a rush of alarming memories, and with a gasp, she sat up and jerked around to look worriedly at the window. The shutters were ajar, and she wasn't sure whether she'd left them that way. But she saw that the clasp on the frame was still locked securely, and only then did her heart slow its rapid beat. If Christian had tried to get in, he'd failed.

Her gaze shifted to the chair propped against the door as she swung her feet over the side of the bed. If she hadn't been so scared last night and so shocked by what Christian had said, she might have realized the absurdity in thinking he would come to her room to make good on his pledge. Her father's bedroom was right next to hers, and even if Christian didn't know that, he certainly wouldn't try something within earshot of the man. Her screams—and she did intend to scream very loud—would bring not only her father and Felice rushing to her aid, but Lynn Boone as well. No, being a coward, Christian would choose a secluded spot to have his revenge. And after breakfast, Alexandra would have someone fix the lock on the shutters just in case she was wrong.

Rising, she grabbed the bed warmer, scooped up the poker from the floor, and put them both away, a troubled expression on her face. She and her father were just beginning to relax around each other, and she didn't want anything to spoil it. And her problem with Christian most definitely would, if her father ever found out about it. Before he shot Christian, he'd demand to know what right he thought he had in making such a threat. Then father and daughter would be right back where they started, not speaking to each other and pretending that they didn't care.

Sitting on the bench in front of her dressing table, her elbows resting amid the pins and combs, Alexandra supported her chin with her hands and stared back at the solemn reflection she saw in the mirror. If she could have seen where her behavior would take her, she would have started trying long ago to come to grips with her mother's suicide. Instead she had allowed her fear and frustration to blind her. She had attacked the only other person in her life who meant something to her. She remem-

ered Aimee telling her one time that she should stop shoving
he responsibility of that tragic affair on her father, that in his
own way he was suffering more than his daughter. Alexandra
hadn't agreed. As a fourteen-year-old who had just lost her
mother, Alexandra had accused her father of not loving his wife
and believed that his callousness toward Jocelyn had driven the
woman to ending her miserable life.

Alexandra had blamed herself, too. She had always thought
that if she had done more for her mother, if she had been a
better daughter and had tried to make up for the love Jocelyn
never received from her husband, she could have prevented
the horrible tragedy. She had never told anyone how she felt,
and because she hadn't, her sorrow and erroneous guilt had
hardened her heart toward the one man who could have comforted her. Several times Aimee had tried telling her that, but
Alexandra had refused to listen, and the result had brought her
to this end.

"And sitting here feeling sorry for yourself isn't going to
make any of it go away," she quietly scolded as she picked
up her hairbrush and attacked the tangle of dark, shiny curls.
"You're going to have to deal with it on your own, Alexandra
Pembrooke. You're going to have to grow up and take responsibility for your actions. You're going to have to tell your father
the truth."

Determined to see it through and to bring peace between her
and her father, she drew in a deep breath, raised her chin, and
pushed herself up from the bench. She'd wait until later to get
dressed, since what she had to say was important and her father
was in the habit of leaving the house right after he ate breakfast.
If she didn't talk to him within the next few minutes, she might
lose her nerve, and if that happened, she wasn't sure how long
it would be before she would find her courage again.

The door to Alexandra's room was at the end of the hall and
at the base of the steps to the attic. Ten feet down the narrow
corridor was the entrance to the dining room, beside which
stood the grandfather clock that had belonged to Virgil and
Evart Rauscher. It was the only valuable piece of furniture left
in the house by the two brothers. Even though the dark walnut
cabinet needed to be stripped, sanded down, and restained,

its subtle elegance warmed the place each time it struck the hour and chimed a musical tune. It had become Alexandra's custom now that whenever she walked by the clock, she would stop for a moment to watch the huge brass pendulum sway back and forth while she listened to its soft, rhythmical ticking and allowed the hypnotic sound to soothe her nerves. This time was different, however, for it wasn't the clock that won her attention, but the sound of her father's voice coming from the dining room. Since he'd never been in the habit of talking to himself, she could only assume he had company and that because of the topic of his conversation, his companion had to be one of the workers. Felice certainly didn't know whether or not they should build fences, and Alexandra doubted the cook cared one way or the other. Could her father have invited Mr. Boone to share his table that morning? He had, after all, made it quite apparent that he didn't look upon the man as a convict, but as an equal, someone he trusted. It only made good sense then that he would save valuable time by discussing business while he ate breakfast. Why, then, was she feeling a prickly sensation crawling up her back?

She had just decided to return to her room to get dressed, when she heard her father tell his companion that the needed document could be found lying on the table in the parlor. A chair creaked, followed by the sound of footsteps coming to the door, and instinct made Alexandra duck into the shadow of the grandfather clock. She didn't have to look to know who had stepped into the hallway, but the temptation to verify her suspicion made her careless. She peered out around the edge of the clock, her face flushed, her heart pounding so loudly in her chest that she snapped her mouth shut thinking the intruder would certainly hear it otherwise.

Silhouetted in the early-morning sunlight shining in through the opened front door at the opposite end of the hallway, the broad-shouldered physique, the way he walked and held himself, and the aura of invulnerability all confirmed his identity. Alexandra knew the insanity of thinking Christian Page had somehow grown taller and broader, with thicker muscles and leaner hips, and all in a matter of a few hours, but she had no other explanation for the staggering effect he was having on her. She could feel her face flame, and her breasts, stomach, and the full length of her thighs tingled with the memory of the contact their bodies had made. Even now her lips burned from the near touch of his kiss. With only a few words, a look, the closeness of him, he had reduced her from a strong-willed woman to a trembling ninny too afraid to come out of her room. Was this the way she'd have to live the rest of her life?

Falling back against the wall, Alexandra closed her eyes and gasped for breath. Something had to be done about Christian Page. He just couldn't be allowed to walk around freely as if he weren't guilty of a single crime. The man had threatened her, for God's sake! And if she didn't tell her father about it while there was still a chance he'd believe her, Christian would be that much closer to having his way with her. Why, she might as well pick the time and place for him, rather than lose sleep waiting for him to decide.

All right, so do it! she silently shouted as she pushed away from the wall and jerked the sash of her robe around her waist. *March in there and tell your father what a spoiled, foolish girl he has for a daughter. Tell him you wouldn't blame him if he never spoke to you again . . . or if he shipped you off somewhere . . . or . . .*

Suddenly the air around her seemed too thin to breathe. Wondering if she were about to faint, she lifted her attention from the bow she was trying to tie and spotted a man's shadow slanting across the floor in front of her. Had he sensed she was hiding beside the grandfather clock? Nervous, she glanced down at her toes and quickly pulled them back. Or had he seen her feet? Had the hem of her nightgown caught a draft and floated out long enough for him to notice? Could he feel her fear? Or had he some magic power that enabled him to look right through a piece of furniture?

Biting her lower lip, she squeezed her eyes shut and laid her head back against the wall. *You're being silly!* she told herself. *You're letting him get to you. He's a man, that's all. He's flesh and blood, not an apparition.*

The click of a door latch shattered the silence that had engulfed her and presented Alexandra with a new problem as she listened to the sound of her maid's footsteps on the stairs.

Within the next few seconds Felice would see her hiding in the hallway, and if Alexandra's luck were such that the girl wouldn't call out to her right away, the puzzled look that would surely crimp her face would undoubtedly signal her presence to Christian. It would also force an explanation from her to her maid, for what earthly reason could she have for behaving in such a ridiculous manner?

Glancing first at the stairs and the flow of skirts descending them, to the floor in front of her, a soft, barely audible whine escaped her lips when she saw the shadow grow larger, change direction, and then disappear as Christian stepped back into the dining room. Joyful tears sprang into her eyes, but Alexandra quickly blinked them away, knowing that she had little time to bask in her good fortune. Squaring her shoulders, she turned toward her room, ready to recite her story that since she hadn't been aware her father had company, she must change out of her nightclothes before joining him at the breakfast table. She had taken only a step or two, when she looked up and saw the two-drawer chest at the end of the corridor, and the sight of it caused her to stumble, for above it hung the accent mirror reflecting not only her image, but that of the spot where she had hidden from Christian. He had known all along she was there, and rather than end her misery with a single word, he had deliberately let her cower in terror.

"The wily beggar," she hissed, starting off again. "Two can play your game, and when I'm through with you, you'll sit back on your heels and wonder why you ever dared me." Ignoring the confused look on her maid's face, Alexandra angrily grabbed the brass doorknob, swung the portal wide, and motioned the bewildered girl to follow her into the bedroom. Christian Page was about to find out what it was like to step on the tail of a sleeping lioness.

"Tell me, Christian," Pembrooke urged as he leaned back in his chair and smiled over at the young man sitting opposite him. "How is it you know so much about raising sheep? I thought you were a carpenter."

Christian would have liked telling the man the whole story, starting with the death of his parents and how Marion Troy had taken him in, all the way to how Lewis Rhomberg had helped him infiltrate Garrett Ambrose's gang and why. Someday he would, but not now. The time wasn't right. If he told Wallis Pembrooke the truth *before* he had won the man's respect and trust, it would do more harm than good. Even to him it would sound as if he were merely trying to get on Pembrooke's good side in order to make his life there a little more tolerable.

"There was a time, when I was younger," he replied as discreetly as possible, "that I gave in to my rebellious nature, and thought being a sailor would satisfy my need for adventure. To spare you the boring details, I'll tell you that I wound up in China, too sick to board the merchant ship that had taken me there and too unimportant for the captain to wait until I felt better." The vision of Min Le appeared in his head, and he quickly masked the sorrow he felt by picking up his teacup and taking a swallow. "A farmer and his granddaughter took me in, cared for me, and taught me a lot about the Chinese culture." Not wanting Pembrooke to know any more than that, he added, "Raising sheep was a part of it. I learned carpentry from my uncle."

Pembrooke couldn't honestly say he was surprised by what he'd heard. He had already judged Christian Page to be special, though he didn't know why except that the man was a hard worker who never complained or said much of anything, and to learn that Page had lived a part of his life in such an exotic place as the Orient only heightened his opinion of him. What puzzled him was why Page had turned to crime. Lifting his pipe from the ashtray, he began filling it with tobacco.

"Is there anything else I should know about you?" he asked, his gaze settled on the task he performed so that he missed the slight frown that raced across the other's brow and quickly vanished.

"Such as?"

The corners of Pembrooke's green eyes crinkled with his smile. "Oh, I don't know. I guess I was just wondering why someone as educated as you would allow yourself to fall to the temptation of a lazy man's life-style."

Christian couldn't stop a grin. "Not everyone shipped here

to Australia can be accused of that, Sir Wallis. Just as many of them were given no choice."

Exhaling a puff of smoke, Pembrooke eyed his companion through the haze while he considered the man's reply. "And which are you?"

Christian weighed his answer for a moment. "A little of both, I would say."

A rather ambiguous statement, Pembrooke observed. Had the man chosen to keep his personal matters private? Or might he have something to hide? Whether his curiosity would have driven him to inquire further, Pembrooke would only have to guess, for in that moment of deliberation he saw Page's attention shift to something near the doorway of the dining room. He also wondered at the fleeting expressions he saw cross Page's suntanned face, before his carefully guarded emotions were once again veiled behind a look of total indifference.

Alexandra thought she had seen a hint of surprise and possibly even approval change the color of Christian's eyes in those short seconds when he first noticed her in the doorway. But they had come and gone so quickly, she had to be content with assuming she had had some sort of effect on him, small though it may have been.

It's a start, she mused, silently reaffirming her ability to have him squirming in his chair before very long.

She had finally figured out that he was counting on her fear of her father's retaliation should she tell the man how she and someone like Christian Page had come to know one another. He had to be thinking that a woman, raised as she had been, would take such a secret to her grave rather than admit she had placed herself in such a compromising position. Well, he was wrong. If it came to that—and she was sure it would—she'd tell her father everything. But for now, she'd make him sweat. After all, he had it coming.

"Good morning, Papa," she sang, drawing a surprised look from her father as he turned and, along with Christian, rose from his chair to greet her.

"Alexandra! You're up early this morning." He smiled and added teasingly, "Nothing like good, clean air to change one's habits."

The air has nothing to do with it, she mused. But rather than state the truth, she agreed with him and asked sweetly, "May I join you?"

"Of course," he replied happily. "We were almost finished anyway."

"Oh, there's no need for Mr. Page to leave," she insisted as she slipped into the chair her father held out for her and met Christian's guarded look. "If you're discussing business matters, I'd like to hear them. Please. Don't let me interrupt." The smile she gave Christian on the surface appeared to be warm and genuine, but the slight curl to one corner of her mouth added a menacing twist to its sincerity.

"I doubt you'll find any of it interesting, Alexandra," her father said. "But there is one more topic Christian and I should examine." He motioned for the carpenter to sit down again as he moved for the door leading to the kitchen. "I'll tell Thomas to bring you a plate. I won't be a second."

If Christian had learned anything about Alexandra Pembrooke, it had to be that he should always be on the alert. She wasn't really interested in hearing what plans were being scheduled for the day. She was here because of him. And all he had to do was sit back and wait to find out what was on her mind. But before he'd allow her the assumption that she was in full control, he'd give her something to think about. With deliberate purpose, he let his gaze slowly travel the fine lines of her cheek and jaw, the elegant length of her neck, and the flowing dark brown curls spilling over one shoulder before he settled his admiring appraisal on the full swell of her bosom covered in a soft shade of blue cotton.

Alexandra could feel a little of her composure slipping the moment she saw where his gaze had fallen, and a hot blush rose in her cheeks. She had never before met a man who could strip her naked with one scalding look, and she hated him for it. Instead of realizing which of them had the power to cause the other the most grief, he sat there as bold as any man. Well, she was about to knock him down a peg or two. Glancing once more at the empty doorway to make sure her father wouldn't hear, she drew in a deep breath, folded her arms in front of her, and relaxed back in her chair.

"I did a lot of thinking about last night," she began, her chin raised in a condescending manner, "about your threats, and I've come to a decision. Before I'll let you frighten me, I'll tell my father everything. I'll tell him that I insisted Hardin take me to meet Garrett Ambrose, of his plan to have me murdered, that *you* were the one assigned the task, that you tried to force yourself on me, and how by my own courage I managed to escape before you succeeded. I might even tell him that *I* was the one who sent him the message that ultimately resulted in your arrest."

She gave him a hard look, expecting to see a flicker of worry in those alluring blue eyes. He returned the stare with mild interest softening the straight line of his mouth, and nothing more. She tried again.

"When he asks me why I waited until now to confess, I'll tell him you coerced me, that out of some demented idea you had, you thought you deserved revenge. I'll tell him you plan to rape me."

She gritted her teeth and waited for him to beg for mercy. Instead, he reached for his teacup and took a leisurely drink as if to savor the delicious blend. He set the cup back in its saucer and straightened the fold in his rolled-up shirt sleeves. Then he turned his head slightly toward the door as if listening for Pembrooke's return before he settled his gaze on Alexandra again. The look he gave her told her that the ploy hadn't worked. There was no fear, no worry, not even a spark of anger in those pale blue eyes, only a chilling expression of calm passivity.

Surprised by his reaction, she gave a breathy sigh and hissed, "Have you no idea what my father will do to you once he learns the truth about you? Are you aware that he doesn't even know you were a part of the gang he saw imprisoned?" She leaned sharply forward and dropped her hands on the table. "You'll be eating your meals with the rest of the convicts, providing he doesn't kill you instead. How can you sit there and be so . . . so . . . blasé about it when you know I hold your life in my hands?"

His gaze held hers for a moment before he drawled, "As I held yours in mine?"

Alexandra stiffened in her chair, her hands falling to her lap. " 'Twas not the same," she declared, aghast.

Christian leaned forward, his arms crossed and resting on the table's edge. "Wasn't it? I could have put a bullet to your head and no one would have tried to stop me."

"Why would they?" she rasped. "Every man there saw me as the enemy."

"Not all of them," he stated matter-of-factly as he picked up his cup and took another sip.

"Only Hardin," she countered hotly. "And you'd have shot *him* if he had tried to interfere." Realizing she had raised her voice, she glanced at the empty doorway, then back at Christian as she continued in a hushed tone. "You're making it sound as though you expect me to believe you'd have turned me loose after . . . after you'd had your 'fun' with me." She stressed the word he'd used for what had gone on in his room. "Well, I don't." Her green eyes darkened as she waited for him to deny her charge.

"Where's my ring?" he asked suddenly.

The question surprised her and several seconds passed while she struggled to understand its importance when they had been discussing his future . . . or the lack of it. "Your . . . your ring?"

"Yes. The one you took from the gaoler. I'd like it back. It's the only thing I have of value now."

A series of vague memories raced through her head. She had carried the gold band out of the courthouse that day in her purse. Later, when she'd been alone in her room, she had tossed it in the black-lacquered box along with the rest of her jewelry. As far as she knew the ring was still there—in the box sitting on her dresser in the other room. She honestly hadn't meant to keep it. She'd simply forgotten she still had it.

"It's . . . " She absently raised a hand to point back over her shoulder, when the insignificance of its whereabouts hit her. She clenched her fist and angrily rapped her knuckles on the table to emphasize the gravity of her words. "You don't seem to understand, Mr. Page. We're not talking about the weather. We're deciding how long you have to live, and as I see it, your only choice is a trade."

Christian cocked his head to one side, "A trade?"

"Yes!" she exclaimed. "I won't tell my father about you in exchange for your pledge never to come within ten feet of me. *More* if it's not too obvious."

A soft smile moved his lips and disappeared as he turned his head to look out the window at the bright sunshine. He appeared to be giving her offer some consideration before he answered, though Alexandra didn't know why he even bothered. There really was nothing to consider. If he planned to see his threat through, he'd be forfeiting his life in return. How could he even compare the two? Growing irritated by his delay, she sat back in the chair with her arms crossed over her chest and one toe tapping on the floor. He had a cocky, self-assured manner about himself that grated on her nerves, and she wondered if his handsomeness had anything to do with it . . . the way Garrett Ambrose used his good looks with the ladies to have whatever he wanted.

Unaware, Alexandra's gaze softened as she studied his profile. There was a rugged calm about his looks, as if he took one day at a time and always came out on top. He had a high forehead with sandy-colored brows adding a hint of mystery to his expression. His nose was straight and not too long; his lips full, the jaw lean, and she could see the pulse in his throat move with each beat of his heart. Thick dark lashes framed the exquisite shade of his eyes, and his hair. . . .

Alexandra tilted her head to one side as she imagined what it would feel like to run her fingers through that soft texture. Aside from his clothes, a convict's short hair set him apart from the other men in the colony. It was meant as a way to degrade them. But with Christian it heightened his manliness. In a subtle way it marked his defiance, and it occurred to Alexandra that defiance was a trait they shared.

Bemused by the idea that she and this criminal might actually have something in common, she unknowingly allowed her gaze to fall on the wide expanse of his chest, and she noticed for the first time that he wasn't wearing the clothes issued him upon his arrival to the prisoners' barracks. And now that she thought about it, she couldn't remember having seen any of the men assigned to her father wearing the customary garments of someone in their rank. At first glance a stranger would have no way of knowing that Christian or Mr. Boone or any of the others were convicts, and she wondered at her father's reasoning, for it had to have been his coin that paid for the new clothes. She understood that part of the reason the prisoners were given a limited amount of freedom under close supervision was to reform them and to help them blend into society again once they were emancipated, but wasn't her father carrying it a bit too far? What was to stop any of them from running off in the middle of the night?

A new worry beset her, and she frowned, her gaze distant and her hands falling into her lap. If the restrictions on Christian had been lifted to such a degree, it could mean Garrett Ambrose was being treated in the same manner. And if that were the case, all he'd have to do was walk away. *All* of his original gang could walk away. The vision of the giant who had opposed Christian that night in the hallway, and the others, rough-looking men who had leered at her when she and Hardin entered the commons, stirred around inside her head. She could see them all waiting on the top of a knoll, Ambrose walking toward them. She could almost hear them voice their plans to have Christian join them and then, once they'd linked up with all the other escaped criminals roaming the bush, they'd attack the house where she and her father lived. They'd want revenge and there would be no stopping them!

A curious frown played across Christian's brow and an amused smile parted his lips as he watched the varied expressions on Alexandra's lovely face. He couldn't imagine what she was thinking, but whatever it was, it worried her, and he wondered if it had anything to do with their conversation. Whether she knew it or not, her threat to tell her father about their first meeting gave her the edge. He knew it was too soon for Pembrooke to hear the story—or at least Alexandra's version of it—which meant he couldn't take the chance that she'd find the courage to follow through with her threat. He'd only been in the company of father and daughter for a few days now, but their behavior toward each other thus far contradicted the stories he'd been told about a strained relationship between the two. Perhaps they were on the path to mending their differences and Alexandra had just realized the serious repercussion her admission might create. Was that what had her fretting? Liking the idea, he looked away from her when the sound of someone entering the house through the front door broke the quiet. A second later Pembrooke guided a stranger through the archway and into the dining room.

"Alexandra, Christian," he began as he led the man to the empty chair on the far side of the table. "This is Harvey Smith. He was employed by the Rauscher brothers. Harvey, this is Christian Page, my carpenter." He waited until the two men shook hands before turning to Alexandra. "And this is my daughter, Alexandra."

Tall and lanky, and somewhat shy, the newcomer smiled weakly at her and nodded his head rather than say anything. Although his clothes were neat and pressed, Alexandra could see by their quality that the man didn't have much wealth. His brown hair, in need of a trim, had strands of gray in it, while his eyebrows were almost black, as were the long sideburns that ran all the way to his jaw. He had a thin, birdlike nose and brown eyes, very high cheekbones and a pointed chin, and it was obvious to Alexandra that he felt out of place by the way he kept wringing his cloth hat without being aware that he was.

"I . . . I really didn't mean to intrude, Sir Wallis," he objected when his host motioned for him to sit down. "We can talk later."

"No time like the present," Pembrooke replied. "You've traveled a long ways to get here, and since I've already told the cook to bring an extra plate, we can talk while you eat. You are hungry, aren't you?"

Smith smiled nervously, wrung his hat again, and shrugged. "Yes, I guess I am."

"Then sit down, Mr. Smith," Pembrooke encouraged as he took his own place beside Alexandra.

As if on cue, Thomas entered the room carrying a tray, and while he served both Alexandra and their guest, her father refilled his teacup.

"I hadn't planned to be gone this long," he explained with a smile at his daughter. "But I heard Mr. Smith ride up and I went out front to greet him. I hope you and Christian had time to get to know each other a little better." He glanced away just then to pick up the pipe he'd left in the ashtray and relit it, missing the cold look his daughter gave the man sitting across from her.

"A little," she replied before dropping her gaze to the plate in front of her. She was too upset to be hungry at the moment and would have preferred being excused from the table, but Christian hadn't given her an answer, and she wasn't going to leave until she had one. She spread her napkin across her lap and picked up her fork, hoping to fool her father into thinking that nothing out of the ordinary was bothering her.

"I've heard a lot of rumors about the Rauscher brothers," her father commented as he added a couple of drops of honey to his tea and stirred it around. "I guess you'd know if any of them were true."

Smith ate quickly, as if this had been the only decent meal he'd had in weeks. "Yes, sir," he replied as he wiped his mouth and reached for his cup. "And some of them are and some aren't." He took a swallow of the hot tea and winced when it burned his tongue. "They were strange blokes," he continued, setting the cup in its saucer again. "Hard to get along with, but I liked them. They were always good to me. I guess you could say we were friends." A frown gathered his dark brows together as if what he was about to reveal was hard for him to admit. "That's probably not the right word. Virgil and Evart never got married, and the rest of their family was dead. As a result they sort of adopted me as a son or a nephew, I suppose you would say."

Obviously uncomfortable, Smith averted his eyes and toyed with the edge of the tablecloth touching his thigh. A few moments passed while he collected his thoughts and decided on just how he would state his reason for being there. He was a stranger to these people, which meant they didn't have to believe a word he said, and if Pembrooke was half as smart as everyone thought he was, the man would check out the claim before agreeing to anything. That was what Smith expected. He knew it wasn't going to be easy, but he also knew it was well worth the risk.

Pembrooke could sense Harvey Smith's apprehension and that it had something to do with his having worked for the Rauscher brothers. His hesitation indicated the possibility that Pembrooke wasn't going to like what he was about to hear. Wondering if he was alone in his feelings, Pembrooke glanced over at Christian and gave him a questioning look. Christian, in turn, raised his brows as if to say he, too, sensed trouble brewing. Returning his attention to Smith, Pembrooke puffed on his pipe and tried to fathom why the man was so nervous.

"You didn't ride all this way to have breakfast, Mr. Smith," Pembrooke accused. "Suppose you tell me what it is that has you fidgeting in your chair."

Realizing the time had come for him to make a confession, Smith's worried gaze moved along the faces staring back at him before coming to rest on the one who asked the question. He gulped, straightened his spine, and drew in a trembling breath. "Virgil and I were closer than Evart and me. Can't say why, really, but we were. Anyway, Virgil told me that he'd decided he wanted me to have his share of the property after he was gone. He said he was going to write it in his will. I don't know if he actually did or just told his brother about it, but when Evart found out, he accused me of trying to worm my way in where I didn't belong and then hauled me off to the prisoners' barracks in Sydney to serve out the rest of my time. The brothers died shortly thereafter, and before I was released, I'd heard the property had been given to you." He swallowed hard and added, "I'm here, Sir Wallis, to ask if you found a will among their things. I'm not a greedy man, sir, and I'd never ask you to leave or insist that I be allowed to live here, but I feel I do have a right to what's mine. I'd be more than willing to let you buy me out."

"Providing a will can be produced to verify your claim," Pembrooke calmly pointed out.

"Oh, of course," Smith quickly agreed. "I didn't expect you to take the word of a man you've never met. Why, just anybody could walk in here and tell you the same story I've told you, and that wouldn't make it the truth. You have to be careful. I know that."

As commissioner to Sir Robert Peel, Pembrooke had listened

to his share of swindlers spin tales they were sure just about anybody would believe. He'd heard them all. Some were better than others, while some were downright pathetic. In Harvey Smith's case his allegation wasn't much different from a few already tried, but his admission that he understood how weak it all sounded and that Pembrooke should be careful didn't quite fit into place. Was there a chance he was telling the truth? Curious as to whether or not Christian had doubts, Pembrooke reached for his teacup and glanced up at the young man while he settled back in his chair. The vague half smile he saw hinted that he should, indeed, be careful.

"You'll have to ask my daughter, Mr. Smith," he said after taking a sip of tea. "She was in charge of cleaning up the place."

Alexandra could feel Harvey Smith's hopeful expression turned her way, and she wondered why her father didn't just tell the man that he was sorry and sympathetic but that there was nothing he could do. If there had been a will, Alexandra would have been the first to acknowledge it. She would have guarded it with her life, taken any measures necessary to find the rightful owner of the property, and then suggest to her father that he leave the group of assigned workers behind, since they would have no need of them living in Sydney. And that included Christian Page!

Thinking of him, she remembered that they hadn't agreed upon a compromise as yet, and she wasn't about to let him slip away until she had one. Using Mr. Smith's predicament as an excuse to have a moment alone with Christian, she suggested that her father take Mr. Smith into the parlor where they'd be more comfortable, while she pointed out which trunk Christian should carry from the attic. Perhaps she had overlooked something, she explained when her father gave her a curious look, something that Mr. Smith would recognize and she wouldn't. Understanding her logic, Pembrooke agreed, then asked his guest to accompany him into the other room.

Alexandra's father might not have known her true reason in requiring his help, but Christian did. Masking a smile, he paused near the door and held out a hand in a polite gesture for her to lead the way. His reward was an icy scowl as Alexandra brushed past him and headed for the stairs at the end of the hall. She wanted an answer, a guarantee that she could sleep peacefully at night. Well, he'd give her that much. He'd tell her that he had no intention of collecting a debt under the same roof as her father, but that he did, indeed, intend to be repaid for her vindictiveness. What he wouldn't tell her was that simply knowing that she lived every second of the day fearing the moment he would make his demand on her was all the justice he truly wanted. That threat would hold her prisoner in her own home, for he doubted she would ever find the courage to venture out from within its protective shelter.

Caught up in a whirl of emotions, Alexandra neither saw nor heard Felice when the maid glanced up from making Alexandra's bed and called out to her as she and Christian passed by the room. Even if she had, she probably would have ignored her for the simple reason that she had other matters demanding her attention, the most upsetting being the man who accompanied her at the moment. She could almost feel Christian's gaze touching her shoulders and the curve of her spine before coming to rest on her buttocks as he followed closely behind her ascent of the staircase, and she gritted her teeth while she struggled with the sensation that his intimate perusal of her was never hampered by clothes. She would have liked nothing better than to halt in her tracks, turn around, and present him with a stinging slap across a suntanned cheek for the lecherous thoughts she was sure were running through his head. At the top of the stairs she had reached out to jerk open the door and motion Christian through it, when the sound of Felice's voice finally penetrated her angry state of mind.

"What?" she snapped, glancing around and instantly regretting the sharp edge to the question once she saw the look on Felice's face. None of this was her maid's fault.

"I was wonderin' if there's somethin' I can do for ye," Felice offered, her brow furrowed worriedly as she watched the carpenter's tall frame disappear into the shadows beyond the doorway.

Noticing where Felice's gaze rested and recognizing how it must look to her, Alexandra quickly explained. "So you see, I've asked Mr. Page to carry the trunk to the parlor for me." She smiled weakly at the young woman and added as she stepped across the threshold and started to swing the door shut behind her, "We won't be but a second."

Her smile vanished the moment Alexandra heard the latch click. She couldn't blame Felice for worrying about her, but right now her concern was a nuisance. Wishing she could say the same about Christian, she turned around to confront him.

The attic was nothing more than one long, narrow room with exposed rafters and two center support beams. The only light source during the day came from the tiny window on the wall opposite where Alexandra stood. To her left was Felice's bed, a night table, and dresser, and a trunk containing the maid's personal belongings. At the far end—beneath the window and where Christian had gone to stand—sat the only reminder of Virgil and Evart Rauscher's existence. Although she doubted it, Alexandra hoped that hidden somewhere inside one of the books or packets of letters was the will Harvey Smith sought. It would greatly disappoint her father to have to lose the property just when he was beginning to enjoy his new life-style, but with its discovery she would be rid of Christian Page.

The pale shaft of sunshine falling in through the window behind him bathed his tall, masculine physique in an alluring light. It complemented his bronze complexion, his short, sun-streaked hair, and the ruggedness of his features when he turned his profile to her and stooped to examine the trunk at his feet. His mere presence sent shivers down her spine and made her bones ache. The sight of him always seemed to cause a stir in the pit of her belly and bring a rush of warmth to her cheeks. She was never able to breathe normally when he was around, and her heart always beat in a trip-hammer rhythm each time he graced her with a look of those august blue eyes. Why she couldn't see past his physical virtues to the core of his nasty disposition was beyond her. He was ruthless and uncaring, and in her opinion unworthy of praise, whether in a look or through words. Suddenly aware of how very much alone they were and that a bed shared the space with them, she fought off the weakness in her knees and moved away from the door.

"I will hear your answer now, Mr. Page," she bravely instructed. "Do we have a trade?"

Christian realized that what he was about to say would be risky and that it might even end in disaster. But as far as he was concerned this young woman needed to be taught a lesson, a hard lesson, one that might save her life one day. Although he'd never made it his practice to interfere in other people's problems, he also knew he couldn't ignore this one. Through fate he was caught in the middle of it. Perhaps if he had the time to weigh both sides he might come to the conclusion that doing Wallis Pembrooke another favor wasn't worth dying over. After all, what had it gotten him the last time he'd played guardian angel to the man's rebellious daughter?

In an effort to stop her chin from quivering, Alexandra clamped her teeth together as she watched Christian slowly unfold his long, lean frame and turn to face her. From the look in his eye, she already knew what his answer would be. He didn't like being pushed, and no one had to tell her that she had pushed him beyond his limit. All that was left was for her to hear him say it.

"A trade," he began, his tone smooth and even despite the cold look he gave her. "You're asking me to forget you clubbed me over the head, as well as the beating I took from four of Ambrose's men for letting you escape. You want me to pretend I never spent five long weeks locked up in a foul-smelling prison or that every time I turned around one of his gang was threatening to kill me because to their way of thinking, *I* was the reason each and every one of them had been arrested."

He moved closer to her, and by so doing, he stepped into the stream of sunlight and placed his face in shadow. It didn't, however, mask the rage burning in his eyes.

"Shall I tell you what my life was like after that, Miss Pembrooke?" He didn't wait for her response. "I know a lady such as yourself should be spared the details, but since you're responsible for my having had to endure it, I think you have a right to know." He continued to advance in slow, measured steps. "The lot of us was moved to the burned-out shell of an old ship anchored near the wharf and kept there for two months while we waited for the transport to bring us here. I was shackled, never allowed a bath or a change of clothes. I slept with hundreds of others on the floor of the ship with only a thin matting of straw for a bed. I worked from sunup to sundown and was served the same swill day in and day out. If I didn't move fast enough, I was whipped." He paused for a moment to let the vision of such torture sink in. "*I* was one of the lucky ones. I managed to survive. At least I thought I was lucky. That was before I realized I had been spared to serve as someone's slave."

He stood before her now and deliberately swept her shapely form with a chilling look. Fear darkened her green eyes and her chest heaved in short, trembling breaths. He'd gotten her attention.

"For nearly six months, while the transport sailed around Africa and across the oceans to Sydney, I was chained to strangers: old men, murderers, petty thieves, and the like. Once a day we were allowed topside for ten minutes. The rest of the time we sat in the hold . . . in the dark." He leaned closer, his warm breath falling against her cheek when she dropped her gaze. "The thought of you kept me from going insane."

The nearness of him suffocated Alexandra. She took a step to move around him, but he caught her elbow and pulled her back. His touch burned her arm, and hot tears pooled in the corners of her eyes.

"I kept imagining what I'd do if I ever saw you again, how I'd pay you back for everything you made me endure. Until the day I saw your father standing in the gaol yard, I never believed there really was a God. Now I know differently."

Panic and foolishness made her pull against his firm hold, and she gasped when it tightened, and his other hand came up to trap her chin and jerk her gaze up to meet his.

"I've been condemned to live out the good years of my life taking orders from someone. I died a long time ago, Alexandra, so your threats don't scare me. If your father put a bullet in my heart, he'd be doing me a favor." His eyes dipped downward and captured the soft pink fullness of her mouth. "So, if you plan to tell him about us, I suggest you do it as soon as possible because the only way you'll stop me from having you is if I'm buried six feet down."

A small cry of pain escaped her when his fingers strengthened their claim on her jaw and forced her head back. For a

second, when his hand slipped to her throat, she feared he had
changed his mind and intended to strangle her. But an instant
later those same lean fingers had entwined themselves within
the dark curls at her nape and he was lowering his head. A
bolt of white heat charged through her body and stole her
breath away once she realized that he was going to kiss her,
and the sensation mystified her. Too numb to reason with it,
she stood stock-still and watched his parted lips descend. Warm
and moist, they moved across hers, and she closed her eyes,
savoring the feel of his rock-hard body enveloping hers, the
heat of his blistering kiss, and the rapture all of it created deep
inside her. She'd never had a man show her such delights,
and she fleetingly wondered how she could have lived this
long without experiencing it. A new and surprising warmth
had been awakened low in her belly, and instinct told her that
it would not be so easily cooled if she allowed the kiss to go
on much longer. She was already leaning heavily against the
arm wrapped around her waist, and her head was beginning
to spin. She must take control, and now!

Drawing from somewhere deep in her reserve, she found the
strength to wedge her arms in between them, but not enough to
push him away. Passion waned and anger flared. Tearing her
lips from his, she gasped for air and the breath to demand that
he stop. Before the words had formed in her mind, however,
the cradling arms that held her fell away and she stumbled
back, weak and surprised. Through a fog she watched him
casually walk back across the room to the trunk that held the
memorabilia they had come to collect. Thick muscles flexed as
he scooped up the case and swung it to a broad shoulder. Flinty
blue eyes met hers, and the shame she felt reddened her cheeks.
In the next moment he was gone, leaving Alexandra to pick
up the shattered pieces of her courage. What was she to do?
Threats had only strengthened his conviction. He would have
his way with or without her consent. Trapped and vulnerable,
she glanced at the empty doorway, wondering if, when the
time came, he would be gentle.

···❧❦ Chapter Thirteen ❧❦···

"I'M SORRY, MR. SMITH," HARVEY QUOTED SARCASTICALLY as he paced the floor of his run-down, one-room abode, "but if there's no will . . . " Furious, he grabbed the closest thing to him and hurled it across the room. Hitting the wall, the pitcher exploded in a hundred tiny pieces and rained broken fragments of porcelain in a wide area. "Of course there's no will!" he shouted. "If there had been, do you think I would have waited until now to tell someone about it?"

The vision of Evart and Virgil Rauscher penetrated the red haze of his wrath and he growled, his upper lip curled back and exposing uneven white teeth as he wished he could watch the brothers die all over again. Winning Virgil's trust had been easy. Evart proved to be another matter entirely. Evart had never liked Smith, and convincing the older brother that he only meant to help whenever he offered an opinion had been the trickiest part of it all.

The task he had set up for himself had taken close to a year to complete, and it had seemed he was close to winning when, unbeknownst to him, Virgil had told his brother that he was planning to write a will and that his share of their wealth would go to his friend, Harvey Smith. Outraged, Evart had confronted Smith, accusing him of foisting his way into private family matters. Smith had pretended that he'd had no idea what Evart was talking about, when in truth Smith had been responsible for everything that had gone on during the previous months, up to and including the systematic removal of each and every other servant working for the brothers. The finishing touch was to have been the will. Once he was named beneficiary, both

Virgil and Evart would meet with an unfortunate accident, and Harvey Smith would be a wealthy man. It hadn't quite worked out that way.

Fearing his brother truly meant to send Smith back to Sydney to serve out his time, Virgil stepped in between the quarreling men. The bigger and stronger brother hadn't realized the power behind his swing until the blow hurled Virgil across the room. His head had struck the stone fireplace, and he was dead before his frail body slumped to the floor. Grief-stricken and teetering on the brink of madness, Evart had turned on Smith, blaming him for what had happened, and in defense Smith had had to kill the man to save his own life.

In those few short minutes the work Smith had done had been destroyed. No will had been written, the brothers were dead, and Smith knew he had to flee to the bush or risk being arrested for murder, found guilty, and sentenced to hang. The better part of a year had elapsed before his dismal existence had goaded him into trying again, especially after he'd heard the property had been given away to a man ignorant of how the Rauscher brothers had lived and the circumstances leading up to the availability of the land. He'd known it would be a difficult feat, but that it was worth the effort. What he hadn't figured on was coming up against someone like Wallis Pembrooke.

"Damn!" he howled, swinging his arm and sweeping the top of the dresser clean.

He'd made a fool of himself by not having taken the time to investigate the man before he appeared on Pembrooke's doorstep. If he had, he might have decided on a different angle rather than relying on the man's generosity and guilt. If he'd known in advance about Pembrooke's daughter. . . .

Leaning against his widespread hands resting on the top of the dresser, he lifted his eyes and stared back at his reflection in the mirror. He wasn't exactly ugly, and his charm had worked on practically every young lady he'd ever come in contact with. Why, his best quality was how he could tell a lie and make a person believe it. And pampered socialites were the most receptive. A calculating smile stretched his thin lips as he stood erect and straightened the collar of his shirt, thinking that since

Alexandra Pembrooke had already heard his woeful story, he wouldn't have to waste time setting her up. He'd seen the disappointed look in her eyes when their search through the trunk produced absolutely no mention of his name. If he played it right, before long he just might have her begging her father to give him what he rightly deserved.

Smith turned for the trunk Pembrooke had insisted he take with him when he left that morning, as if he really wanted Virgil and Evart's trinkets. He'd dump out the contents, pack up his meager possessions, and pay Pembrooke a second visit. At the time, when the man had offered Smith a job rather than money in exchange for the missing will, Smith had turned him down. He hadn't traveled all the way out there looking for a job! But now, thanks to Pembrooke, Smith had the perfect opening he needed to get close to the man's daughter. He'd ride in, head bowed, a look of desperation on his face, and ask if Pembrooke's offer was still good. Then he'd set to work.

The plan seemed simple enough, yet past experience had proven that even the most uncomplicated scheme had its flaws, and his excitement ebbed momentarily. If he really wanted to become the new landowner, he'd have to have an alternative method for achieving success in case the first one failed. But that would take money and he didn't have any.

Frustrated, he knelt beside the trunk and absently began to empty it out, tossing the contents in a careless heap on the floor while his mind raced for a solution. Perhaps he should talk to Charity. She always seemed to have good ideas. Of course that meant he'd have to give her a share, but if everything went the way he hoped it would, there'd be enough to pay her off. Filled with new hope, he hurried with his task.

Several minutes ticked by while he worked, and when it seemed he'd never reach the bottom of the old trunk, his anger resurfaced. The trip back across the Blue Mountains to Pembrooke's place, *after* he had visited Charity, would take him two days, and he'd already wasted more time than he would have liked. Growing impatient, he grabbed one of the rope handles and stood, giving the trunk a forceful yank that tipped it over on its side and rolled the remaining items out onto the floor. Uninterested, since he'd already examined everything thoroughly, Smith gave the pile of discarded mementos a fleeting glance as he heaved the trunk up onto his bed.

Late-afternoon sunshine spilling into the room appeared intent on singling out one item in the pile on the floor, and had it not been for the bright shaft of light glaring off the shiny object, Smith would have given it no further notice. When Miss Pembrooke had shown him Evart Rauscher's gold watch that morning in the parlor, the idea of owning it hadn't sparked even the tiniest twinge of greed in Smith's entire body, since his notion of wealth far exceeded the value of a timepiece. But that had been before her father sent him off with his pockets just as empty as when he'd arrived.

Lured by the color of its precious metal, Smith's desire to stuff everything he owned into the trunk suddenly wasn't quite so important as he lowered himself to one knee and reached to pick up the watch. Just because he'd changed his mind about having it didn't mean he'd resigned himself to being poor. Far from it! Selling it to someone for a gold coin or two simply meant the difference between having a full belly or going hungry. Thankful that he hadn't allowed his rage to totally blind him, he smiled as he tucked the timepiece in his pocket and reached for the minutely carved wooden box in which Evart had kept the rest of his jewelry. If God would grant a nonbeliever the tiniest bit of luck, perhaps he'd find something else worth selling.

The trunk's falling to the floor had resulted in a broken lid and clasp, and a split in the wood along the front of the little box. Whatever else may have been inside it had been scattered in all directions, and with a curse, Smith flung the box away in search of more meaningful treasures. The hunt yielded one gold ring, a pearl stickpin, a pair of ruby earrings that must have belonged to Rauscher's mother, and an ivory comb of the same apparent ownership. The lot wouldn't bring him much of a reward, but at this point he realized a little was better than nothing at all. Clutching the pieces in one hand, he glanced around for something to keep them in and spied their original container. He noticed then that the velvet bottom had fallen out and lay separated from the box, yet the exterior of the small case was still relatively intact. Smith would be the first to admit that he had very little experience in how the rich stored their valuables, but instinct cried out for him to satisfy his curiosity. Stretching out one arm, he hooked a finger over the edge of the box and scooped it up to examine it more closely.

"Well, I'll be damned," he murmured, once he'd looked inside and found a folded piece of paper. "A secret compartment." His surprise turned to sarcasm. "And what's this?" he mocked as he plucked the document from its resting place. "Could it be that crafty old buggar had something worth hiding?"

Settling himself cross-legged on the floor, Smith put the jewelry between his thighs and unfolded the paper. As he began to read, the delighted sparkle in his eyes and the smile on his lips disappeared. Hatred and rage soon etched deep lines in his face and nearly set the parchment on fire as his heated gaze swept over it. Yes, Evart Rauscher had something worth hiding . . . something so important to him that he had kept it a secret from his own brother.

A quiet calm came over him then as he rose and crossed to the hearth. There he paused to look at the signature on the letter he held in his hand, and for a brief moment he wondered how an old man like that could keep such a secret, especially from the one person who had the right to know. It must have been difficult. It had to have been even harder for him to admit it, even though he'd taken the coward's way out by writing it down rather than facing up to it in person.

The red glow of the embers in the hearth reflected itself in Smith's eyes as he leaned forward, held out his hand, and observed the erratic flight of the yellowed paper as it floated toward the bed of hot coals. A second later it caught fire, and while he watched a single amber flame consume the parchment, he grinned. He was glad Evart had never found the courage to confess, and if he were the type who believed in God, he might consider it a blessing that he had found the letter instead of someone else. After all, wasn't this the answer to a prayer?

The repairs to the barn and shearing shed had gone rather smoothly over the past week, and as much as Lynn Boone hated to admit it, the work had progressed in an orderly manner solely because of the newcomer. Page's talents and his subtle leadership had stirred the rest of the men into doing whatever he asked of them without once issuing an order. Boone found the revelation puzzling, since he had been trained that subordinates were supposed to be told what to do. It had taken him several days to figure out why Page had been so successful with the motley group of loafers, and once he had, it seemed painfully obvious. Somewhere along the way, Page had covertly studied each man's personality and his abilities, and had then plied the knowledge for his own benefit. Instead of telling the man to do something, Page had asked for that one's help, knowing that even the most downtrodden had pride. He had treated them all as equals and as scholars in whatever task they undertook. By example he had silently shown them that sulking over their fate would do them little good, that setting goals for themselves would help the days pass more quickly, and that exercise would keep their bodies fit and their minds healthy.

Before Page's arrival, Pembrooke had put Lynn Boone in charge, and little by little his power had diminished to overseer or, worse, to second in command. If he were the kind of man to feel threatened by the way Page had come in and taken over, he might have been inclined to undermine the man's efforts. But he wasn't. The transformation of this group of convicts had amazed Boone, and with each passing episode his admiration for Christian Page grew. So did his curiosity.

Page was a loner and obviously liked it that way. During the day he worked and ate alongside the rest of the men, but at night his free time was spent away from everyone. If someone asked about his personal life, Page was always polite but never went into detail, and the few times he told them anything, his answers were vague. It didn't take long for his companions to realize they were intruding where they had no right being, and out of respect for Christian Page, they quit prying. Boone, however, wasn't quite so easily pacified.

"Sir Wallis tells me you've visited China," Boone commented one hot afternoon as the two of them waited their turn for a drink of water from the well. "Were you there long?"

Christian sensed Boone's real reason for asking and silent-ly applauded the man's subtlety. While the others had been content with his need for privacy, Boone obviously wasn't. Short of coming right out and telling him that it was none of his business, Christian knew he'd either have to tell the man what he wanted to know or play a verbal game of chess. "A little over two years," he replied, letting it go at that when the last man moved away from the bucket and handed Christian the dipper.

"Is that where you learned kung fu?"

The question surprised Christian, but he managed to hide it behind the ladle he'd raised to his mouth.

A half smile dimpled Boone's cheek when he saw how easi-ly his companion pretended not to be affected by his query. Glancing around to make sure no one was within earshot, he leaned an elbow on the edge of the stone well, clasped his wrist, and waited. When it became obvious that he'd have to press for an answer, he added, "That is what it's called, isn't it?"

Acting as though he were deaf, Christian refilled the dipper and poured the cool water down the back of his head before giving Boone a brief glance that told him nothing.

"I knew a fellow one time who practiced it," Boone went on to explain, "and I remember thinking how silly he looked waving his arms in the air like that." He chuckled and added, "I thought differently when I made the mistake of telling him so, and he dropped me to my knees before I knew what hit me." He cocked his head and looked intently at Christian. "I suppose you could do that if you wanted to."

Christian returned the stare but said nothing.

"Yes," Boone admitted after a moment, "I guess you could." The easy smile reappeared. "And I'll wager you're considering it right now. Am I right?"

Glancing away, Christian tossed the dipper back in the bucket.

"You know, my friend," Boone continued after concluding that a conversation with a corpse would be more productive than one with Christian Page, "if you don't want anyone to know about it, you should take more care in where you practice. I've lost a lot of sleep watching you late at night. You ever kill anybody with one of those punches?"

Christian couldn't stop a smile. "Not yet," he replied, the implication unmistakable.

His meaning took a second to sink in, but once it had, Boone straightened sharply. He'd asked too many questions. Suddenly uncomfortable, he cleared his throat, shifted his weight, and looked away. He'd told Christian the truth about the man who'd given him a shot to the breastbone, and the memory of how staggering the pain had been and of how very close Boone had come to dying that day warned him not to take Christian Page as lightly as he had the other man. Lynn Boone stood over six and one half feet tall, and probably outweighed his companion by a fair amount, but he doubted he'd stand much of a chance if Christian chose to apply his skill.

A movement near the back door of the house drew Boone's attention and he appreciated the opportunity to change the subject, for he spotted Alexandra Pembrooke crossing the yard toward her maid. He watched in silence for a moment while the two women talked beside the clothesline of freshly washed laundry swaying in the breeze. The sight of Alexandra Pembrooke reminded him of something he'd observed of late, and even though he doubted he could get Christian to admit anything, letting the man know someone was aware of it was all Boone really wanted.

"Damn beautiful woman, that one," he said as he turned to pick up the ladle and quench his thirst.

Christian had seen where Boone's gaze had traveled and he suspected that the man wasn't through with him yet. "Which one?" he asked, having decided not to make it easy for him.

Boone had meant to lure Christian into discussing Alexandra Pembrooke and her nervousness whenever Christian was around, and by doing so, he'd unintentionally insulted Felice. In his opinion they were both beautiful, but for Christian's sake he had to pretend otherwise. "Why, Miss Pembrooke, of course. Don't you agree?"

Christian nodded reservedly. "They're both fine-looking ladies." He pulled a handkerchief from his pocket and wiped the moisture from his face and neck. "I've never been one to assume beauty comes only with wealth. I'm surprised you do."

"I-I . . . don't," Boone denied. This wasn't going at all the way he'd planned it. "I think Felice is a very handsome woman."

Christian hid his smile as he reached out to pat Boone on the shoulder. "I know you do. I've seen the look in your eyes every time she's around. You're smitten by her." He glanced in the direction of the women, then added, "And you know what, friend? I think she likes you, too."

"You do?" the other asked, a pleased grin crinkling his face as he shifted his attention to the young woman.

"Yes, indeed," Christian replied. "And do you know what else I think?"

Boone looked at Christian again, curious.

"I think you should do something about it."

"You do?"

"Of course! There's no law that says a convict can't fall in love and get married, is there?"

Boone shook his head, completely unaware that Christian had gained control of their conversation.

"Then why not start right now?" Christian coaxed. "Go over there and ask if you can carry in the basket of laundry for her. She'll know you're interested in her that way, not to mention how impressed she'll be with your good manners."

Boone's eyes sparkled and his cheeks had taken on a rosy hue. "You really think so?"

"Yes, I really think so." Christian's own eyes danced with humor. He would have liked having this former navy lieutenant as a friend and perhaps one day that would happen, but for now Christian had to be careful who he involved in his personal life. As long as the matter of Garrett Ambrose was still unfinished, he preferred keeping to himself.

"Yes, I think you're right," Boone finally agreed. Pulling himself up, he straightened his shirt collar and the rolled-up sleeves, and raked his fingers through the sides of his hair. He smiled at Christian one more time, wiggled his brows, and set off across the yard.

While Christian watched the man's lumbering gait carry him

toward the house, he thought of how courtship could turn even the toughest of men into little boys. He doubted there was a cowardly bone in the man's entire body, yet the mention of an amorous pursuit had set Boone's knees to trembling. If women only knew the power they had over a man once he'd fallen in love, they'd show no mercy, and Christian hoped for Boone's sake that Felice would never figure that out. Then, on the other hand, after he'd seen Felice's shy reaction to Boone's presence, he concluded that women were probably just as vulnerable.

Christian's gaze slipped past the twosome and fell upon the third member in their party. Warm golden sunshine bathed the slender figure in an alluring light and glistened in the mass of thick dark hair. The pink cotton dress Alexandra had chosen to wear nearly matched the color in her cheeks as she moved a few steps away from the couple, eyes averted. There was a timidness in the way she continually changed the direction of her gaze as though she might be uncomfortable with what was going on around her or because she felt she was intruding on something meant to be private. Her actions surprised Christian, for until that very moment, he had judged her to be rather selfish.

Alexandra couldn't understand the feelings rushing around inside her. It wasn't the first time she'd seen a man pay attention to a woman who interested him. Yet the display embarrassed her, and she wasn't quite sure why. Perhaps it was because she sensed Lynn Boone wasn't just flirting or playing the part of rutting knave. There had been a tenderness in his manner, in his words, and in the way he looked at Felice. The man honestly liked the shy, reserved young woman, and what Alexandra had unintentionally witnessed was the prelude to courtship, something she, herself, had never experienced. Was that what had her dancing around as if the ground were a bed of coals and she was without shoes? Could she possibly be envious?

Without realizing she had, Alexandra turned her head, hoping to steal a glimpse of the young woman's face. She wanted to see the happiness she was sure glowed in Felice's eyes. To her disappointment the couple had already turned their backs to her as they walked leisurely toward the house, Felice's hands clasped behind her and Boone carrying the basket of laundry. A pang of loneliness hit her then, and she sighed, wondering if she would ever be fortunate enough to find someone who cared about her.

A new sensation assailed her, and before she had given it any consideration, she felt compelled to look up. There, in the shadow of a huge tree, stood Christian, his eyes watching her, his expression reticent, his mouth unsmiling. Diffused light played against his handsome features—the strong curve of his broad shoulders, his muscular frame, his sun-lightened hair and darkly tanned skin—while marking the magnitude of his presence. The mere sight of him made her heart pound, her knees weak, and a tingling shoot through every fiber in her body. She'd been very careful for the past week in keeping track of him. There wasn't a moment when she didn't know exactly where he was. Then, when she'd let down her guard, he'd stepped in and taken the advantage.

Frightened not only by his stealth but by the response he never failed to incite in her, she pulled her gaze away from him and hurried off toward the house . . . or so she thought. The instant she looked up and saw that her steps were leading her toward the barn, she stopped so abruptly that the hem of her skirts swayed out in front of her and showed a goodly portion of trim ankles and stockinged calves. The thick layers of cloth had hardly returned to their proper place before they were jerked around with the sudden about-face that sent Alexandra off in the opposite direction. Certain Christian was enjoying the performance at her expense, she fixed her eyes on the entrance to the back of the house and never once satisfied him with a glance. If she had, she would have discovered that his interest had already been drawn away from her as two men on horseback rode into the yard and approached Pembrooke.

"Good afternoon, Wallis," Davis Pleasanton greeted cheerily as he and his son reined their horses to a halt and dismounted near the veranda. "It's been a while. How have you and your lovely daughter been adapting to your new way of life?"

"I can't speak for Alexandra, but I'm enjoying every minute of it," Pembrooke replied with a broad smile as he came to shake Davis's outstretched hand. His gaze shifted to the man's son, but when the young man made no move to greet him, Pembrooke merely nodded. "Wayne."

"I must say, Wallis, the place is really beginning to take shape," Davis continued, unaware of the cool reception his offspring had given their neighbor and that Wayne's attention had fallen on a man who stood watching them from several yards away.

"It is now," Pembrooke admitted proudly. "A couple of weeks ago I wouldn't have held much hope of it ever looking better than it did right then."

"And why is that?"

Spying Christian, Pembrooke waved him near. "Because I didn't have this man working for me. Davis, I'd like you to meet Christian Page, my carpenter," he introduced. "Christian, this is Davis Pleasanton, our neighbor, and his son, Wayne."

Christian exchanged a warm handshake with the father, but when he turned to the second man, he was treated as rudely as his employer had been. The affront neither bothered nor provoked him since he had spent the last few moments evaluating the young man and how he had reacted to Pembrooke. It had been quite obvious that Wayne Pleasanton held himself in high esteem over those in the group, and if he didn't respect a former commissioner to the Crown, he certainly wouldn't waste his time on a convict.

So be it, Christian mused. A man had a right to his opinions . . . although in Wayne's case, his opinions were totally unwarranted.

"A carpenter, you say," Davis continued. "We could all use a good carpenter. I realize there's a lot of work to be done here, young man, but perhaps when things slow down and you find yourself with time on your hands, you'll consider working for me." He glanced at Pembrooke. "That is, of course, if it's all right with Wallis."

Pembrooke took a breath to tell Davis that whatever one of his laborers did with his spare time was his business, when Wayne interrupted.

"Really, Father. There are plenty of good carpenters around," he said, haughtily examining the nails of his perfectly manicured left hand. "Honest men who came by the trade using the sweat of their brow, not by stealing what they needed. I would think with all the valuables you have in the house, you'd be more selective in whom you hire." His brown eyes moved to look at Christian. "Once a thief, always a thief. Or are you a murderer, Mr. Page?"

Knowing Christian could take care of himself, Pembrooke elected not to interfere, even though the urge to speak on his behalf was strong. Instead, he held back and fought the smile that tugged at the edges of his mouth, while he imagined Christian's answer.

Not in the least annoyed by the remark, Christian coolly returned the man's stare without blinking. "I've been tempted a time or two," came his simple but meaningful reply.

Recognizing the implication, Wayne's nose came up slightly as he slowly appraised his adversary from head to toe. "I'm sure you have," he countered after a moment of hostile silence. "I'm sure you have." He turned away then while he pulled a lace kerchief from the cuff of his white linen shirt and dabbed it beneath his nose as though some offensive odor had assailed him. "If we're to reach Sydney in time to meet the ship, Father, we really should be going."

Stunned by the exchange and a bit embarrassed as he always was whenever his son played the arrogant fool, Davis ran a finger along the edge of his shirt collar while he cleared his throat. "Yes, I suppose we should."

"Are you sure you haven't time for a glass of brandy?" Pembrooke offered, taking hold of the horse's bridle to steady the animal while Davis mounted.

"Thank you, but no," Davis declined. "We only meant to stop long enough to wish you well and insist that you and Alexandra come for dinner one night soon."

"We shall," Pembrooke assured him. "Have a safe journey."

The two men had disappeared from view before Pembrooke faced his companion. "Someday someone will put that young man in his proper place," he said, draping his arm across Christian's shoulders and guiding him toward the barn. "I just hope I'm around to see it." He chuckled and added, "For his sake, it had better not be you. He'll never know what hit him."

Christian didn't think he and Wayne Pleasanton would ever have the occasion to match wits again, but just in case he was wrong, Christian decided to learn a little more about the man.

"He's probably one of the most arrogant sops God ever put on this earth," Boone told him later that night as they sat outside under a tree where it was cool. "He thinks he's better than everybody else and only because he was born here and none of the rest of us were. As if that makes any difference."

"Is that the only reason he dislikes Sir Wallis?"

Boone shrugged. "Could be, I guess. That and because Pembrooke was given his land, where the Pleasantons had to buy theirs. Wayne doesn't feel that's fair, especially since he tried to buy this property after the previous owners died, and he was denied the chance because it had already been given to Pembrooke."

Amazed, Christian smiled and asked, "How do you know all this, Lynn? Have you been listening to gossip?"

"Nope," Boone quickly denied. "Sir Wallis told me. I guess he and Wayne had a run-in the first night they met." Stretching out, Boone lay on his back in the grass and folded his arms behind his head. "If you're asking because you're worried about him, don't be. Wayne Pleasanton is afraid of his own shadow. Besides, what good would it do him now to cause trouble?"

Boone's observation was a valid one. About all that was left Wayne Pleasanton was to sulk. Yet there had been something cold and menacing behind those brown eyes that Christian sensed shouldn't be ignored.

As long as the sun was up Alexandra felt relatively safe, especially if she stayed in clear sight of everyone. After the evening meal, however, she began to fret. With the day's work completed, the laborers were allowed their own free time, a plan her father had heard about from some of the other landowners. By allowing the crew this small compensation for the heavy, back-breaking work they'd done, the men were healthier, both physically and mentally. Fewer complaints were voiced, and for the most part they worked in harmony. Alexandra could understand the reason behind her father's actions, but her own situation had her wishing that one laborer in particular would have to work each day until he dropped. That way he'd be too tired to think about anything other than getting a good night's sleep.

The faint melody of a harmonica, mixed with the sound of laughter coming from the crew's quarters, greeted Alexandra as she closed the window and secured its lock. It had become her practice every night after dinner to sit with her father in the parlor while he went over his accounts and she worked on the lap blanket she was darning. But until she had barred the only entrance into her room, every little sound coming from the back of the house would have her nerves on edge, and she didn't want her father to notice and question why. She had learned through Mr. Boone that most of the men played cards, told stories, or spent their spare time writing letters to the loved ones they'd been forced to leave behind in England. Only Christian, it seemed, chose to keep to himself, and that worried Alexandra since Mr. Boone couldn't say where the man went each night after leaving the crew's quarters.

Gathering up the bag that held her supply of yarn, needles, and the lap blanket, she glanced around the room one last time. She just had to be sure that her precautions hadn't been in vain and that Christian wasn't already lurking in the shadows before she could sit comfortably in the parlor for the remainder of the evening. Satisfied with the knowledge that she had done everything she could to insure her safety, she exhaled the breath she hadn't realized she'd been holding, and turned to make her exit.

The indistinct conversation of her maid and the cook, while they cleared the dishes from the dining room table, drifted out to greet her as she moved down the hallway, and she smiled, knowing that in a few short minutes Felice and Mr. Boone would be enjoying each other's company. In the past few months she had come to know Felice as a young woman rather than just her servant, and it pleased Alexandra to see the girl's eyes light up every time Mr. Boone came around. Of course Felice's feelings for him were much stronger than Alexandra's, but just the same Alexandra had to admit that the tall, soft-spoken man had won her approval as well. In her opinion, Felice and Lynn Boone were the perfect couple, and if there was anything Alexandra could do to hurry the relationship along, she would. Thus, each night after dinner, she made it a point never to ask anything of the girl that would delay her from meeting her beau outside on the front porch.

Even though the days had been warm enough to make everyone a little uncomfortable while he worked, the nights always turned chilly, and Alexandra could smell the aroma of the fire her father had started in the hearth long before she reached the door to the parlor. Pausing at the threshold, once she saw that he was too engrossed in his work to notice her presence, she was struck with a twinge of regret. There had been many times in the past, in their home in England, when she had found her father in the study laboring over the papers on his desk much as he was doing now. But back then the sight of him shuffling through documents would infuriate her, for it seemed he always put his work ahead of his family. She felt differently now as she watched him, and even though she wanted to blame her past resentment on the *kind* of work he chose to do, she knew that that had nothing to do with it. What difference did it truly make if he was paid to chase criminals or raise sheep? No matter what the job, he would devote his full attention to it simply because that was the kind of man he was. She could see that now. It didn't mean he loved his family any less.

Suddenly and with no forewarning, the same old hurt reared up and knocked her off-balance. Without a sound, she crossed to the high-backed chair near the hearth and sat down. If that were true, then why had her father taken a mistress? Bitter and angry, she spread the half-finished blanket across her knees, seized her needles and yarn, and silently set to work. His affair had driven her mother to suicide, and in the six years since that time, Alexandra had never found it in her heart to forgive him. Quite honestly, she doubted that she ever would.

Lost in thought, both Alexandra and her father failed to hear the sound of someone opening the front door to the house or the footfalls that carried the visitor down the hall. Silence filled the house again when their guest paused at the entrance to the parlor, obviously wishing not to disturb its occupants before they were ready. A minute ticked by in which time the intruder sensed a coldness in the air, despite the warm fire blazing in the hearth and the fact that neither father nor daughter appeared conscious of the other's presence.

A rustling of papers drew the observer's full attention to the man seated at the huge oak desk in the far corner. A second later, Pembrooke glanced up from his work, saw his guest, and smiled as he rose and waved the visitor into the room.

"I'm sure Alexandra would tell you that my worst trait is being able to shut everything out when I'm working. You weren't standing there long, were you?" Pembrooke asked as he grabbed the chair by his desk and moved it close to where his daughter sat.

"Only a minute or two," Christian replied, his gaze slipping to the young woman who had yet to look up or to acknowledge that she wasn't alone in the room.

Flagging Christian down into the chair while he took his own place next to Alexandra, Pembrooke nodded at the rolled-up parchments Christian held in one hand. "Were you able to finish them?"

"As far as I could go without final approval." Slipping his fingers under the flap on the cylinder, Christian unwrapped his work for Pembrooke to examine. While he watched and waited for the man's opinion on the sketches he'd drawn, Christian became acutely aware of the eyes boring holes into him, and he smiled secretively, certain Alexandra had finally allowed her outside world to penetrate her thoughts. Without moving his head, his gaze left Pembrooke for his daughter.

Alexandra could feel her entire body tremble. A thunderous pounding drummed in her ears, and she was sure she was about to faint. She had given in to the painful memories of her past and closed out everything else around her, and Christian Page had walked right in, pulled up a chair, and sat down next to her without her even being aware of it. If he managed to get this close to her with her eyes wide open, slipping into her room while she slept would pose no problem for him at all!

"These are good, Christian," she heard her father say, and when the pale blue eyes fell away from her, Alexandra sucked in a breath.

Christian nodded his appreciation of the compliment. "Without knowing your specific tastes, I had to leave out some of the detailing. But on the whole, I think you'll find each drawing pretty much the way you wanted it. And it's never too late to change something."

"Well, as far as I'm concerned, they're perfect," Pembrooke admitted, grinning. "Of course, I suppose I shouldn't say anything until after Alexandra has a look at them."

She had been sitting there silently thanking her father for having turned Christian's attention away from her, and while they talked, she had been deciding how she could quietly sneak away without either of them noticing her. Now it appeared her exit would be delayed, and even worse, she'd have to join in on their conversation.

"Look at what, Papa?" she asked nervously.

Shifting in his chair, Pembrooke held out the parchments. "I asked Christian to draw up some plans for the house. I told him what our place back in Plymouth was like—its good points and bad—and that if he wanted, he could expand on it or come up with a style of his own. What do you think? Do any of them appeal to you?"

Alexandra had learned in the course of recent weeks that there was a lot more to Christian Page than any of them had assumed. She'd repeatedly overheard her father talking with Lynn Boone about him, and both men seemed awestruck by his many talents. What she held in her hands right now was just another sampling. Bold lines and delicate curves had been etched on the paper with the skill and flair of an artist. He'd not only penned the layout of the three varied styles of houses floor by floor, but he'd drawn the finished look of the mansions as one would see them while riding up to their front door. He'd claimed to have left out details, but as Alexandra studied the renderings, she couldn't understand what he meant, for each window had shutters, the wood siding was shaded, and the front door not only had a knob, but a simulated brass name plate with *Pembrooke* scrolled across it. Amazed by the workmanship and the amount of time he must have put into the project, Alexandra was unaware that she was smiling.

"Tell me something, Mr. Page," she murmured, her eyes still affixed to the sketches she held. "With all this talent, how did you wind up on a convict transport sailing for Australia?"

A lopsided grin slowly tugged at Christian's mouth, and he waited until she had looked up at him before he answered. The blush he saw starting to spread over her face told him she had realized, too late, just what she had asked, and although his reply would be vague enough for her father not to understand, his meaning would be quite clear to the one who mattered. " 'Tis simple enough," he stated, folding his arms over his chest as he slid slightly forward in the chair and leaned against its back with his long legs stretched out in front of him. "I fell victim to revenge."

"Revenge?" she blurted out before she realized who listened. "You make it sound as though you were the one wronged."

The smile left his face but shone clearly in his pale blue eyes. "If one knows only half the story, it would appear I deserved it. The truth would shed a different light."

"And gain your pardon?" she challenged. Conscious of her father's interest in their exchange, she began rolling up the parchments. "You'll have to excuse me, Mr. Page, but I doubt a single criminal would willingly admit his guilt. If the occasion arose and bending the truth was his only alternative, he'd go to any extreme to clear his name." With a flick of her wrist, she held out the drawings for him to take. "It's been done before, Mr. Page, but in the end, the guilty always get what they deserve." She met his sparkling eyes with firm determination, until long, brown fingers briefly touched her hand and retrieved the work she held out to him. The intent behind the soft caress was lost to her father, but its effects sent a scorching heat to Alexandra's face.

"Oh, I have to agree, Miss Pembrooke," Christian replied, an unspoken promise glowing in his eyes. "Though suffering the consequences of one's foolishness might be slow in coming, it will indeed happen."

Noting the puzzled frown on her father's face, Alexandra came to her feet, uttered her excuse of a headache, and stalked from the room.

"I'm telling ya, those two are nothing but trouble," Henry Abbott angrily proclaimed as he handed his empty mug to the barmaid for a refill. Leaning, he rested his folded arms on the edge of the table and centered his attention on the men sitting across from him. "I don't understand why they weren't assigned to the chain gang instead of to someone like me. I just know they're gonna bolt and run the first chance they get. Not that I wouldn't be glad to be rid of them, but I'll be out two laborers, and there's a lot of work to do."

"Maybe you should try talking to the superintendent at the prison barracks," one of his companions suggested. "He might agree with you and exchange these two for two others less interested in causing trouble."

"Why do you think I'm here?" Abbott jeered, then fell back in his chair with a disheartened sigh. "In the past two weeks Ambrose and his henchman have managed to ruin what it took me ten years to build. He's got all of my laborers thinking I'm a cruel and stingy man, that since they do the work, they should have a share. It's absurd! They know that as soon as they've served their time, they're free to go and that the money they've already earned working in their spare time elsewhere is theirs to keep. Why, most of them will have enough to buy a parcel of land once they're emancipated. I'd say they've had an easy time considering they could have spent the length of their sentence locked up in a prison or on a chain gang. Ambrose is just trying to get them angry enough so that they'll revolt and look to him as their leader. Once that happens, he and his cohort will hightail it for the bush. And I guarantee you, he won't be taking anybody else with him." Abbott shook his head and muttered, "The fools."

"So talk to the superintendent," the same man insisted.

"I already have," Abbott moaned. "He said there's nothing he can do until *after* Ambrose has actually tried to escape. Can you imagine? I can see it coming, I know it's going to happen, and I can't get any help. I'm damn tempted to turn the two of them loose myself just to save what's left of my place."

"Why don't you use the whip?" another of his companions asked.

"Are you serious?" Abbott exclaimed, his face paling noticeably. "Don't you know who Garrett Ambrose is?"

The group exchanged glances, then shook their heads, while

Abbott thanked the barmaid for the fresh mug of ale and took a long draft, oblivious of the attention someone else in the tavern was giving their conversation.

"I didn't know it the day he and Wall were assigned to me or I might have declined," he began, once he'd wiped his mouth with the back of his hand and had set the mug down in front of him. "But apparently Ambrose was one of the most notorious and sought-after criminals in all of England with forty men in his gang. Why, they even assigned a special group of agents to capture him, and you know who headed the committee?" He gave each man a look. When none could say he did, Abbott drew himself up as if having the answer had been an honor bestowed only to him. "Sir Wallis Pembrooke, that's who." Their collective blank response wasn't what he had expected, and it riled him. "Well, you've heard of Sir Robert Peel, haven't you?" He rolled his eyes when the others quickly nodded their heads. "Sir Wallis Pembrooke was the man's right hand, while he lived in England. He had almost as much power as Peel."

"Well, if this Ambrose was such a dangerous criminal that they'd go to such an extreme to catch him, why isn't he serving his time behind bars?"

"That's the part that makes me nervous," Abbott admitted, reaching for his mug. "There wasn't enough proof. I mean there weren't any witnesses to testify that he'd murdered anybody. So all they could get him for was smuggling. Couldn't even get him for treason against the Crown. He's a cold-blooded killer, that one—and now he's living on my property."

"Did you tell all this to the supervisor?"

"Tell *him*?" Abbott parroted with a sarcastic snort. "He's the one who told *me*! He said I wasn't to worry, though, that he'd have some of his men ride out to my place every so often to check up on things. Like that would do a lot of good after I'm already dead."

"So what are you going to do, Henry?"

Abbott shook his head wearily. "Either I'm just going to turn him loose, like I said, or I'm going to have to find some brave soul willing to trade him and Wall for two of his."

"Or shoot him," one of the men suggested.

Abbott managed a weak smile. "Or shoot him."

"Lovey! Lovey, wake up!" the dark-haired girl urged as she rushed into the room and swung the door shut behind her. "I've got a bit o' good news for ye, I do. 'Eard it meself downstairs just a minute ago." Hurrying to the side of the bed, she bent and roughly shook the man lying in it. "Come on, lovey. Ye've been prayin' for somethin' like this to come along. Don't go sleepin' through it now, ye 'ear?"

Buried deeply under the mound of covers, her victim groaned his displeasure at being so rudely awakened. "It had better be the best piece of news I'll ever hear, Charity," he warned, peering up at her bleary-eyed from under the edge of the quilt. "You know I didn't get much sleep last night, and right now I doubt anything else could be as important."

"Even Sir Wallis Pembrooke?" she cooed.

His brown eyes instantly focused as he lowered the covers to his bare chest. "What about him?"

"Well, it might be nothin' and then again it could be everything." Grinning, Charity sank down on the mattress beside him, pleased that for once she could prove to him how smart she was. "I 'eard ol' 'Enry Abbott talkin' to some of 'is friends and—"

"Abbott?" came the crisp retort. "What has he to do with Pembrooke?"

"Nothin'," Charity snapped. "Not the way you're thinkin', I mean. Now, will ye be quiet and let me finish?" She frowned back at the impatient look he gave her, thinking that if he wasn't the best lover she'd ever had, she'd find someone else to spend her time and money on. "I 'eard Abbott tellin' 'is friends that one of 'is convicts is a man named Garrett Ambrose."

"So?"

Her eyes narrowed. "Don't ye pay attention ta anything?" She really didn't expect him to answer and rushed on. "Accordin' ta Abbott, this Ambrose got 'imself arrested because of Sir Wallis Pembrooke. Now, don't ye suppose 'e'll 'ave it out for the man?"

A heavy, wearisome sigh answered the question. "What man wouldn't, Charity?" He brushed her aside and rose from the bed, his long, naked frame catching the pale light of late morning shining in through the window as he crossed to the washstand. "So he hates Pembrooke. What good is that to me?"

"If 'e were an ordinary bloke, nothing. But 'e ain't ordinary, lovey." Rising, she crossed to where he stood, watching as he splashed water on his face. "Garrett Ambrose was the most notorious criminal in all of England," she told him, quoting what she'd heard earlier in the commons. " 'E's a murderer, and 'e should 'ave been put on the chain gang. Abbott is afraid of 'im, 'e is, afraid 'e'll run off just so 'e can 'ave 'is revenge."

Her companion still couldn't understand the connection. "And what if he does, Charity? What good will that do me?" He shook his head when she started to cut in. "He'd have to kill Pembrooke's daughter, too, in order to clear up the title of the land." He grabbed a towel and wiped his face, silent for a minute, before he looked her in the eye again. "I'm not saying the idea doesn't appeal to me, but unless I'm guaranteed Pembrooke would leave no heirs, what Ambrose does or doesn't do is of no consequence." He walked to the chair where he'd tossed his clothes the night before and stepped into his trousers.

"But that's me point, lovey," Charity exclaimed, hurrying to his side and handing him his shirt. "The two of ye both want practically the same thing. Maybe ye can work out a deal that would give ye both what ye need."

He took a breath to explain the difference, saw the excitement in her eyes, and changed his mind about saying anything. He liked Charity a lot, and he knew she was only trying to help. But what she proposed wouldn't work. If Pembrooke and his daughter were killed, the authorities were bound to ask questions, especially after they realized that it seemed whoever owned the Rauscher property wound up dead. And the first person they'd interrogate would be the one who purchased the land, unless. . . .

A slow dawning began to roll around inside his head, a tiny inkling that held the promise of success. Charity might not have figured out the details for him, but she had most definitely given him the material with which to work. Smiling enthusiastically, he reached out, caught the girl by the back of her head, and pulled her close.

"Charity," he murmured against her lips, "someday you and I ought to get married."

···⊰[*Chapter Fourteen*]⊱···

ALEXANDRA WASN'T SURE JUST WHEN THE REVELATION HAD hit her, but while she stood on the front porch watching Christian, her father, Lynn Boone, and the other men working side by side, the feeling of being all alone in the world swirled around her and tickled the hair on the back of her neck. Unconsciously she shrugged one shoulder in an effort to chase away the chill, while she considered what course of action to take. In the few weeks they had lived on the property, Christian had somehow managed to win the respect and admiration of every single person there, including, Alexandra suspected, that of her own maid. Such an achievement meant she'd have to deal with Christian on her own, since any story she might tell about him would be viewed with skepticism. She would get no help from her father, Felice, or Lynn Boone, even though at one time the last had been the best possibility. Perhaps if she talked to Christian . . .

"And said what?" she muttered aloud as she watched him instruct one of the men loading lumber into a wagon.

Since the repairs to the barn, shearing shed, livery, and all other outbuildings had been completed the previous week, and the split-rail fences along the boundary of the place had been erected, all that was left to build were the line shacks, one-room abodes where the pair of men tending the flock could get in out of the weather. They would also serve as places for them to sleep and cook their meals rather than ride all the way back to the main house every night. When Alexandra had heard about the purpose of the small cabins, she had hoped Christian would be one of those who lived in them and that she wouldn't have to see him except for once a month when he rode in for supplies. Then she remembered who was in charge of building the new house, and she gave up thinking she'd ever be rid of him. With a forlorn sigh, she wondered if perhaps she should just shoot him and be done with it.

A shout from one of the men in the yard drew everyone's attention to the silhouette of a lone rider cutting across the grassy knoll toward the house. As curious as the rest, Alexandra left the porch and walked the distance to where her father stood, a puzzled frown darkening her green eyes.

"Do you know who he is, Papa?" she asked, her gaze slipping from the stranger's tall shape to the four-legged animal running alongside the horse.

"His name is Welch, Adam Welch," Pembrooke said as he wiped the sweat from his brow with the back of his hand. "And I believe his friend's name is Patches."

Alexandra had no trouble understanding why the dog had been so dubbed. His entire coat was a crazy quilt of colors, ranging from black to white, and deep brown to pale beige. Each paw was a different shade, as were his ears, which Alexandra thought odd enough until the animal loped to within three yards of her and she could see that he had one brown eye and one blue one. His left ear stood sharply tall while the right drooped forward, and his tail nearly made a complete circle as it curled up and over his back. A wet pink tongue hung limply from the corner of his mouth and pointed white teeth glistened in the sun as he kept an even pace with the horse, and when the canine seemed to have spotted Alexandra, she could have sworn she saw him smile. She had never much cared for animals of any kind, and he seemed to have sensed it.

"Is something wrong?" her father asked when he noticed her disapproving frown.

"He needs a bath," she replied, wrinkling up her nose when an errant breeze brought the scent of him to her.

Pembrooke laughed. "The dog's not the only one, child. We could all use one."

Alexandra raised a brow and took a tentative step backward when it appeared the trio was about to run her down. A sharp tug on the reins brought the horse to a jittery stop in the middle of the yard, but the dog continued on . . . and headed right for her.

"You'll have to excuse him, miss," Adam Welch called out as he swung a leg over the saddle and stepped to the ground. "Patches doesn't get to see many women, and he's like the rest of us, I suppose. He's just curious. He won't hurt ya none." The look on Alexandra's face told Welch that she doubted his promise, and he decided that perhaps he should intervene. "Patches! Come here, boy!" Either deaf or just simply defiant, the dog ignored the command. "Patches!"

A short distance of five feet separated Alexandra from the smelly, odd-looking mongrel, and panic was setting in, since her father had already left her side to greet their visitor with a handshake, thus inadvertently abandoning her to fend for herself. She was about to cry out her terror, when a tall figure moved in from the left and blocked the dog's path.

"No!" came the sharp retort, and to everyone's surprise, the animal halted instantly, clapped his mouth shut, and sat down on his haunches, alert and awaiting his next command.

"Well, I'll be damned," Welch muttered, awestruck. "If I hadn't seen it with my own eyes, I never would have believed it. Do you know that up until now there wasn't a human around who could make that dog behave? What's your secret, young man?"

"It's all in the tone of your voice," Christian admitted, stooping down to pat the dog's head. "No secret." He cast Alexandra a brief look over his shoulder, then added, "It's not so much *what* a person says that gets a reaction, but *how* it's said."

"Well, I guess you just proved that as fact, son," Welch yielded. "I've had that dog since he was a pup, and about all he's good for is making a nuisance of himself. And that's the strange thing. His ma is the best sheep dog I've ever owned."

"He just needs a little work," Christian replied.

"You think so?" Welch challenged with a smile. "I'll tell you what. Since he's really of no value to me, and because you're going to need a dog, I'll leave him here with you. If he works out, he won't cost you a shilling. If not . . . " He turned to Pembrooke. "Maybe you and I can settle on a price for one of the other dogs I've got. Sound good to you?"

Looking to Christian for his opinion, Pembrooke smiled
and held out his hand once he saw Christian's nod. "Since
I'm new at this, I'm going to have to trust someone," he
said, exchanging a firm handshake with Welch. "If Mr. Page
believes he can make a good sheep dog out of Patches, then
I'll have to go along with his judgment. If he's wrong, I'll be
paying you a visit. Now . . . what about my sheep?"

"I left them on the other side of the knoll. If you want to
mount up, we can ride out and take a look at them."

"I do," he answered, turning to Christian. "Can you spare
a minute? You know better than I what to look for."

"Of course," Christian replied. Ruffling the fur behind the
dog's ears one more time, Christian stood up and headed
toward the barn, Patches following right on his heels.

I don't believe it, Alexandra fumed, her jade-green eyes narrowed and focused on man and dog. *He's even won that stupid
mutt over to his side.* With a disgusted shake of her head, she
grabbed the fullness of her skirts, swung around, and marched
back into the house.

With the delivery of the sheep her father had purchased, a
routine was soon established and life took on a slow, easy pace.
Everyone had a job to do, including Alexandra, and while the
others appeared content, she faced a daily struggle with her
nerves.

Now that Christian had started work on the new house, it
had become more difficult for her to avoid him. Even though he
never mentioned his promise to her, the look in his eye, whenever she caught him staring at her, assured her that he hadn't
changed his mind about collecting and that he was merely waiting for the right moment to come along. Her father's short
absences to ride out to inspect the flock periodically didn't
help calm her apprehension either, since she had concluded
that a crowd or bright sunshine would not hinder him once
he'd decided it was time she settled her debt.

Nights were especially trying for her. While everyone else
had gone to bed, Christian would stay up to work the dog,
and it seemed he deliberately chose to do so in a spot where

Alexandra was sure to see him from her bedroom window. The pair would prance around until well past midnight, and then disappear from sight. But even then Alexandra couldn't fall asleep. Every creak or moan or rustle of leaves had her sitting up in bed and staring at the locked window, expecting at any second to see Christian's silhouette block the moonlight. Exhaustion would finally tumble her into a restless sleep, and by morning, she was more worn-out than when she had retired. Whether he knew it or not, he had won a very important victory in that Alexandra thought of nothing else from sunup to sundown.

Felice was the first to notice the dark circles under her mistress's eyes, and how thin and drawn Alexandra looked. Concerned, Felice asked her mistress if she was feeling all right and suggested that Alexandra should see a doctor. A firm guarantee that her mistress was just overly tired appeased the maid's worry to some degree, but only after Alexandra promised to nap later that morning.

Next came Thomas's inquiry as to Alexandra's health, once he saw how she played with her food rather than eat it. He, too, offered his opinion that she should slow down a bit, once she'd explained that she'd been working too hard. What she didn't tell him was how thankful she was that her father had risen early and left the house long before she made her appearance in the dining room. Convincing *him* wouldn't be so easy.

It was Lynn Boone's look of alarm when she met him on her way outside that persuaded her something had to be done before her father was made aware of her condition. Just what that would be was a puzzle, but it certainly meant she would have to confront Christian, since he was the root of her problem. But when? And where? Hadn't she already tried to talk him out of it, and with no success? What assurance did she have that this time he'd listen? Would an apology be enough?

"Ha!" she sneered as she rounded the corner of the house for the vegetable garden she was growing out back. An apology would never satisfy him, and she honestly didn't think she owed him one. Yet if that was what it would take. . . .

A weary sigh escaped her as she tucked her skirts tight against the backs of her knees and stooped down to pluck the weeds growing near the potato plants. Lost in concentration she failed to notice the pair of small brown eyes watching her from within the bushes some twenty feet away or how the creature seemed to lick his lips at the sight of her. He took a guarded step forward, then paused, eyeing his prey in meásured degrees. A moment passed, muscles tightened, and in a flash, the dingo sprang from his hiding place.

The sudden movement caught Alexandra's eye. She glanced up, saw the animal's rapid advance, and screamed. In leaps and bounds the wild dog was closing the distance between them, and in a frantic effort to save herself, Alexandra bolted toward the house, only to stumble and fall. She screamed again, tears burning her eyes as she rolled onto one hip, ready to kick out with the heel of her shoe. If only she'd brought a gardening tool with her she might have had a better chance at defending herself! Terror filled her heart, and she was just about to scream again, when a blur of color shot across in front of her and attacked her assailant. A mixture of snarls, yelps, and growls rose above the cloud of the dust she saw, and only the loud crack of rifle fire separated the two dogs.

"Patches, stay!" Christian commanded when the mongrel caught his balance and started to chase after the departing intruder. Reluctant but obedient, he slid to a halt, swung around, and strutted back across the yard, his mouth hanging open and blond fur stuck to his tongue as it bounced up and down with each step he took.

A second burst of gunfire exploded, ending the dingo's exodus, and only then did Christian turn to the young woman huddled on the ground.

"Are you all right?" he asked, resting the barrel of his weapon back against his shoulder.

Before she could answer, Felice and Thomas came running from the house in one direction, Lynn Boone appearing from another, and all three asking what had happened and if anyone was hurt. Christian explained, and Felice quickly ushered her shaking mistress into the house, leaving the three men to assess the situation further.

"It's not very often a wild dog will wander in this close, but I have heard of it happening," Thomas told his companions.

"If a dingo gets hungry enough, he'll try anything, I suppose. From here on out, I think I'll leave a loaded gun by the back door."

"A wise idea, Thomas," Boone agreed. "And if you have any scraps left over from dinner tonight, I'd suggest you give our furry little friend here a reward. What do you think, Patches?" The dog barked, bringing a round of laughter from the men.

Later that night, as usual, Alexandra stood by the window in her room watching Christian and his dog. After the excitement over the dingo had faded, everyone had gone back to work, while Alexandra had cloistered herself in the parlor, afraid to go outside again. She hadn't realized until now that she hadn't taken the time to thank Christian for rescuing her, even though he probably would have told her that Patches was the one she should thank. She could only remember one other time in her life when she had been as scared and as close to death as she had been that morning, and oddly enough it had been because of Christian. He had gone from villain to hero, and the irony of it confused her. He had plenty of reasons to want to see her dead, and yet when his chance came to just stand back and watch it happen, he had stepped in. Why?

Unable to explain it herself, she grabbed her shawl from the back of the rocker and headed for the door. There was only one person who knew the answer to that, and while they were talking, perhaps she could get him to agree to a truce.

To Christian's way of thinking, Patches had proven to be a very intelligent dog. A kind word, a pat on the head, and a firm hand had been all it had taken to get the animal to respond favorably to a simple command. Since he'd already shown Christian that he had the instinct to attack a flock's most threatening enemy, all that was left was to see how he worked with the sheep. That test came tomorrow. After breakfast, Christian and Pembrooke planned to ride out to the pasture and watch Patches perform.

A faint twinkle brightened the color of Christian's eyes as he observed how easily he could get the dog to obey him. By snapping his fingers, he could make Patches sit. A soft whistle would bring him to Christian's side. A sharp tone of voice halted him, and whenever Christian scratched the dog behind the ears, the canine's wagging tail nearly knocked the animal off his feet. What a shame it was that similar methods of training couldn't be applied to Alexandra Pembrooke, and that her father couldn't have used the knowledge on her long before she planned her visit to the inn. They never would have met, he wouldn't be here in Australia now, and Garrett Ambrose would have been introduced to the hangman.

A smile brushed his lips as he eased himself down on the ground cross-legged and tucked his bare feet under him. Even though the months before his arrival to this country had tested his resolve, the result hadn't been all that upsetting. He was doing the kind of work he enjoyed, and Pembrooke's fairness and honesty made it easy for Christian to respect him. Lynn Boone had become a good friend, and once he'd seen to it that Garrett Ambrose paid for his mistakes, Christian would probably be content to spend the rest of his life here.

Issuing a silent command for Patches to lie down beside him, Christian waited until the dog had curled himself up into a ball and lowered his head on his paws before he closed his eyes, raised his chin, and laid the backs of his hands on his knees, a half smile on his lips. Of course, Alexandra wouldn't be too pleased if he were to tell her of his decision to stay. She'd assume it was because he simply wanted to continue tormenting her. He had to admit that the idea wasn't all that unappealing to him. She deserved a life of constant unrest for what she'd done.

Thinking to block out the sounds around him, the smile disappeared as he concentrated on finding the center of his being. A soft breeze tickled the bare flesh along his ribs, chest, and shoulders, and brought with it the fragrant smell of the meadow. The chill in the air exhilarated him, and just as he was about to slip into deep meditation, the feeling that he wasn't alone stirred in his mind. The presence held no threat, only curiosity and possibly apprehension, and he chose not to demonstrate his awareness of the intrusion. Instead, he listened and opened up his senses to the sounds and redolence of the one who ventured close.

"Stay, Patches," he quietly ordered when he felt the dog's head come up and heard his tail thump the ground in quick, friendly strokes. No one else other than Alexandra could evoke such a response from the animal, and Christian relaxed his guard.

"You're up rather late, aren't you, Miss Pembrooke?" he asked without opening his eyes.

A frown briefly crinkled Alexandra's brow. How had he known anyone was there? She'd been so quiet in her approach that even Patches hadn't heard her until she was nearly on top of them. And what made him think it wasn't Lynn Boone or her father who had come to talk? She wondered if there would ever be a time when Christian wouldn't amaze her.

"I couldn't sleep," she answered quietly, pulling her gaze away from the bronzed muscles gleaming in the ashen moonlight. "Aren't you cold?"

Christian suspected the underlying reason she asked and that she really didn't want an answer. "And you thought going for a walk would help?" He loosened his rigid stance as he opened his eyes and looked at her. She was still wearing the pretty pink cotton dress with the lace trim she'd had on all day, and for a second he allowed himself the thought that he preferred her in green.

"Not really," she replied, forcing herself to stare at Patches rather than meet Christian's hypnotizing blue eyes. "When I noticed you out here a minute ago, I realized that . . . that I'd never thanked you for . . . for saving my life."

A bright smile flashed across his face and disappeared. Shifting his weight, he rolled onto one hip, bent his knee, and draped one wrist across it, his upper body braced against his elbow as he rested back in the cool grass. "Which time?"

The perfectly arched brows drew together. "Which time?" she repeated, frowning at him. "I haven't the slightest idea what you mean." She hugged the shawl more tightly around her when she noticed how his gaze had slipped from her face to her bosom. "And would you kindly not look at me like that?"

His eyes returned to study her face for several long moments. "Have you ever given any *real* thought to what happened that night in the inn?"

Alexandra tossed her head, dark, luxuriant curls bouncing with the movement. "I've thought of nothing else since! How could I not? I live in constant fear of unfounded retaliation."

"Oh?" he said, amused. "Is that the real purpose of your being here right now? To talk me out of having what I deserve?"

Realizing the foolishness in thinking he might listen to reason, she glared at him for a second, then spun on her heels and headed back toward the house.

Christian knew he should let her go, but he was tired of taking the blame for something that wasn't his fault. Jumping to his feet, he shot off after her. He was on her in a flash, catching her arm and yanking her around.

"I think it's time you and I had this out, Alexandra." He ignored the fear he saw in her eyes and glanced past her toward the dark house. "But not here." Turning, he spied the livery, the only building in the lot that was set away from the others. Choosing it for the privacy it offered, he tightened his grip on her wrist and hauled her along with him.

"Are you insane?" she shrieked, tearing at the fingers bruising her flesh. "Papa will kill you! Mr. Boone will kill you! Stop this! Right now! If you don't, I'll . . . I'll scream!"

"Go right ahead," he ground out. "Your father has a right to know how his daughter behaves when he isn't around." He gave her a hard shake when she continued to pry her sharp nails under his thumb, fighting for her release. "And it will be my pleasure to tell him every detail." Flexing his arm, he jerked her off-balance and allowed her to fall to one knee before he yanked her back up and practically dragged her the rest of the way to the livery.

Inside the darkened building, Christian pulled her with him to the spot where he knew he'd find a lantern and matches. Touching the sulfurous flame to the lamp's wick, he filled the small space with a bright glow, and only then did he release his prisoner and walk back to the door to swing it shut.

The anger that had driven him lessened a small measure once he had turned back around and saw how badly Alexandra trembled. Not completely insensitive to the knowledge that *he* was the reason for her fear, he took a moment to calm the strong desire that tempted him to add to her distress. Nothing he could do to her would ever equal the misery she had condemned him to experience, and seeking justice would serve no purpose, especially since the only hatred he held in his heart was aimed at Garrett Ambrose, not at this foolish woman. As far as he was concerned she had suffered enough to satisfy him into thinking she would never act as recklessly as she had that night there at the inn.

"How much do you truly know about the work your father did while the two of you lived in England?" he asked, unaware of the effect crossing his arms over his bare chest had on his companion.

Golden light enhanced the coppery ripples across the wide shoulders and naked muscles of a well-proportioned upper torso. Lean hips, covered in simple beige cotton, mocked the plainness of the attire by drawing attention to the snug fit and leaving little to the imagination. The handsome face, liquid blue eyes, and his short-cropped, sun-streaked blond hair, feathered softly back from his brow, stole Alexandra's breath away, but the firm set to his mouth had her shivering all the way down to her toes. The time had come for their showdown, and Alexandra wasn't quite prepared. But then, would she ever be? Deciding that perhaps she could stall him off long enough for Mr. Boone or one of the others to miss him and come looking for him, she concentrated on the question he'd asked. Just keep him talking, she told herself.

"He . . . he worked for Sir Robert Peel," she answered, knowing that it wasn't detailed enough to suit him.

"Doing what?"

Alexandra gulped down the knot in her throat and looked away. The mere sight of him was more than she could handle. "He was . . . in charge of a special force of police dealing in the . . . tracking of certain criminals."

"What kind of criminals?"

"The most severe."

"Men like Garrett Ambrose," he supplied, and she nodded. "Did you know ahead of time that one of your father's most important cases involved Ambrose? Is that what lured you into meeting him?" When she didn't appear to want to answer him, he added, "That's the part I don't understand. If you were so bent on getting back at your father for whatever it was he'd done to you, why did you keep your success a secret from him?" He could see the flush of anger rise in the fair complexion of her face, and he knew he had guessed correctly. "Come on, Alexandra. You certainly don't expect me to believe you were actually there to buy some of his smuggled goods. If that was all you'd wanted, your friend Mr. Wittemore could have saved you a lot of trouble." He shrugged off the desire for an explanation when he saw the stubborn lift of her chin.

"It's really not important," he continued dryly. "Nor am I interested in your childish reasons."

"Childish!" she exploded, dropping her clenched fists to her sides. "You don't know enough about me, Mr. Page, to make such a statement."

"And you know nothing about *me* whatsoever, Miss Pembrooke," he snarled. "If you had, you would have considered yourself very fortunate that Ambrose elected *me* to carry out his bidding that night."

"Fortunate?" she half laughed, half sneered in response. "I apologize for being so stupid, but I'm afraid you're going to have to explain how you arrived at such a conclusion."

Christian glared back at her for a moment, thinking that she was indeed stupid and how very much he'd like to tell her so. He was also wondering why he was wasting his time talking to her. She wasn't going to believe a word he said, and even if she did, what did it really matter to him one way or the other? Exhaling quietly, he braced his opened hands low on his hips and glanced away from her, while he fought to remember why he had decided to tell her the truth.

"Well, Sir Lancelot?" she jeered. "Aren't you going to explain it to me? I'd really like to know why I should have thanked you instead of clubbing you over the head."

Cold, flinty eyes captured hers. "You really haven't figured it out, have you? All the clues were there right in front of you." He snorted derisively and shook his head. "Of course you haven't. How could you? You've been too busy feeling sorry for yourself."

Alexandra bristled with the insults. "Feeling sorry for myself?" she hissed, forgetting to whom it was she talked as she walked several steps closer to him. "Is that what you think I've been doing? Are you implying nothing happened in my life that I should even consider regretting? Well, there is, Mr. Page. I truly regret ever having met you!" She glared at him for a long moment, then jutted her nose in the air, flung her head with an aristocratic mien, and started to brush past him on her way out.

"That's exactly what I mean," he barked, catching her elbow and pulling her back. He ignored her protests and the sharp nails she dug into his hand. "You can't see past the end of your pretty little nose. If you'd bother for once in your life, you might be surprised by what you see. You might even like yourself for a change."

Alexandra's mouth dropped open. "I beg your pardon!"

"You should," he rallied. "You should come down off that pedestal you've made for yourself and look at the world the way it really is."

Alexandra could feel her face flame with red-hot anger. "You have a lot of nerve, Christian Page. In case you've forgotten, I came out here to thank you for saving me from harm. If I thought you beneath me, I wouldn't have bothered." She tried to jerk free of him again. "Unhand me, sir, before you regret having been so bold."

His blue eyes darkened, and his nostrils flared as he snarled, "It wouldn't be the first time I regretted coming to your aid."

Alexandra's shoulders dropped in annoyed resignation and she ceased trying to get loose of him. "I'm sorry you feel that way," she mocked. "And if you'll let go of me, I'll promise never to put you in that kind of position again."

"Nice idea, Alexandra," he jeered, "but I know better."

She took a sharp breath, but before she could express her opinion on the matter, he pulled her toward the lantern where it hung from a peg and set her down on the three-legged stool beneath it.

"Since meeting you, there have been plenty of times I've cursed my luck," he began, one hand resting on the top rail of the stall next to him, the other curled into a fist and perched on his hip as he glared down at her. "And I'll probably do so

again tonight . . . after I've told you what it is I've brought
you here to hear and I've realized my mistake." He fell quiet for a moment, watching the fear and apprehension in her
beautiful face turn to curiosity. One of Sang Soo's first and
most important lessons had been the teaching of silence.

"A secret is no longer a secret the instant you tell someone,"
he had preached. "Guard them well, Christian. Trust no one.
Only then can you be the master of your fate."

"Not even Min Le?" he remembered asking. "She is my
wife, my love, my life."

"Even the mighty oak succumbs to the flame, Christian,"
Sang Soo had warned.

At the time he hadn't understood completely, and even now
he wondered. If he had shared his secret with Pembrooke from
the very beginning, he wouldn't be here now. The letter naming
Hardin Wittemore's association with Ambrose wouldn't have
spurred Pembrooke into doing what he had. Christian would
have been left to his own means in gathering the evidence
they needed to convict Ambrose of murder. Instead, he'd
been hauled off with the rest of Ambrose's gang and sentenced
into exile. He would hardly call this being the master of his
own fate.

The whirl of visions that had clouded his sight cleared, and
his focus returned to the young woman before him. Trust no
one, Sang Soo had told him repeatedly, and yet here he was
about to confide in the one person who hated him most. Where
was the logic in it? He mentally shook off the irony that assailed
him and reached to overturn the wooden bucket nearby. Settling
himself down, he stared at Alexandra's questioning look for
another minute, while he tried to justify his want to tell her
when he knew what her reaction would be even before he said
anything.

"I wasn't there at the inn by accident, Alexandra," he began,
ignoring the sensation that perhaps he cared what she thought
of him and figured this was the way of changing her mind.
"Nor was I one of Ambrose's gang."

The urge to laugh came strong, but it disappeared just as
quickly when other things he had said repeated themselves in
her mind and forced a conclusion. He had asked how much

she knew about her father's work for Peel, and once she had told him that it included tracking criminals, he had specifically named Garrett Ambrose. Why? What was his purpose in asking? Those questions led her thoughts to the rumors she had heard that her father's desperation had driven him to ask a risky and possibly life-threatening task of his men.

"You're not saying. . . . You don't mean . . ." She shook her head and bolted off the stool to pace back and forth in front of him. Unable to think of any other explanation, she stopped suddenly and whirled to face him. "Do you really expect me to believe you were one of my father's agents?" Laughing sarcastically, she spun away and began her aimless trek again. "You really do think I'm stupid, don't you?" she dared, her eyes affixed to his as she moved right and left of him. "I'm not denying my father didn't have agents disguising themselves as smugglers and thieves just to win a place in Ambrose's elite group, but why, pray tell—if you were one of them—would he have allowed you to stand trial, be sentenced, and then be shipped off here?" She came to an abrupt halt before him, the hem of her skirts swishing around her ankles as she raised a hand and challenged, "No, don't tell me. Let me guess. He thought so much of you and because he knew he would be coming to Australia to live, he wanted you to come along with him. Cheaper passage on a convict transport, right?"

"He didn't know about me."

"Oh," she scoffed, sitting down again. "That explains it." Her green eyes darkened as she scowled at him.

"I have a personal interest in Garrett Ambrose, one I don't intend to share with you," he began again. "Because of it, I would have taken the man's execution out of your father's hands and ended Ambrose's life without the benefit of a trial. I still might, if I'm given the opportunity again." He could see the doubt in her eyes and wondered once more why he bothered with her.

"So what changed your mind?" she taunted. "I would imagine you had plenty of chances before you were arrested."

"A friend showed me the error in my thinking."

"A friend," she repeated skeptically.

"Yes. Lewis Rhomberg."

Bounding off the stool, she started for the exit again. "Good night, Mr. Page. I need sleep more than I need to stay here and listen to this."

"Dammit, woman!" he raged, springing off after her. Sprinting half the distance to the door, he grabbed her wrist and spun her around, his anger and impatience dulling his perception long enough for Alexandra to swing the palm of her opened hand around to slap his face. The explosive crack of the blow resounded throughout the limited confines of the building, and even though it stung, the idea that she had actually hit him stirred more of a reaction than any pain she might have inflicted. Without moving for what seemed to Alexandra to be hours, Christian inwardly calmed the strong desire to return the favor, thinking that if her father had curbed his daughter's rebellious spirit years ago, the two of them wouldn't be standing there right now. At last, he raised cold blue eyes to stare back at her.

"I could have killed you that night in the inn," he growled. "I could have aimed the pistol at your head and pulled the trigger, and saved myself a lot of trouble. I didn't because I knew who you were. I also knew that if I didn't kill you, one of the other men there would . . . just before Ambrose turned his gun on me and shot me because I refused. You might be a very beautiful woman, Alexandra Pembrooke, but I don't know a single man—except for your father, perhaps—who would give up his life for yours. You're not *that* beautiful." Angry, he roughly shoved her away and turned to extinguish the lantern.

Fear, regret, then outrage whirled around inside Alexandra's head, and she struggled for the breath to voice her thoughts as she watched him turn his back on her and walk away. A second later the room was plunged into darkness, and she strained her eyes to see him in the shadows, a jumble of words stilling her tongue. She gasped when he appeared suddenly at her side.

"Good night, Miss Pembrooke," he snarled as he moved past her to open the door and step outside.

The light from the campfire flickered brightly in the star-studded night and cast long, eerie shadows against the rock canyon walls. A group of five convicts huddled around the flames to warm their hands and await the arrival of the stranger who had arranged their escape. Three were eager to thank the man. One saw his freedom as merely a chance to get away from the grueling work that had been imposed upon him, while the last wondered why he had been singled out. Curiosity was all that held Garrett Ambrose to the spot where the meeting would take place. Then, if the answers weren't interesting enough to suit him, he'd have Benton Wall kill the fool.

"Are you hungry, Mr. Ambrose?" his huge companion asked.

Ambrose glanced up from the rock on which he sat and watched Wall limp toward him. Every time he saw the giant's clumsy gait, he was reminded of how the man came to have a stiff knee and who had been responsible for it. He still hadn't figured out why Christian Page had been hauled off with the rest of them and sentenced to live out his good years in a penal colony, for Ambrose was positive the man had been one of Pembrooke's agents. And someday soon, Page would pay for his part in the trickery that had condemned Ambrose to this godforsaken land.

"Sit, Wall," he instructed, nodding at the ground beside him. "We need to talk."

"What about, sir?"

Ambrose eyed their three companions while Wall awkwardly eased himself down, making sure the trio was far enough away not to hear what he had to say. But before he had a chance to open his mouth, gunfire rang out in the darkness. In a blur he saw first one, then the second of the group near the fire fall, and finally the third when that man tried to run. It happened so fast that neither Ambrose nor Wall had time to react. Certain their lives would end just as quickly no matter what they did or didn't do, they sat frozen to their spots, waiting for the assassin to step from the shadows. Seconds ticked by while Ambrose wondered how many men were hiding in the bush, if they were the police or other bushrangers who didn't like strangers, and just how long he had to live.

"Don't look so scared, friend," a voice finally called out. "I didn't go to all the trouble of freeing you just to shoot you down. In case you haven't figured it out yet, I need you."

Ambrose could see the muscles in Wall's huge frame relax with the announcement, but he wasn't as convinced as his cohort. Just because this man said he needed him didn't mean he was trustworthy.

"To do what?" he asked as he started to twist around.

The stranger grunted menacingly. "Stay just the way you are. I think you can understand why I'd prefer to keep my identity a secret. You and I are two of a kind, Mr. Ambrose. We don't trust anybody."

Ambrose covertly studied the shadows around him without moving his head. The man surely hadn't come alone. "Fair enough," he said. "So what is it you'd like me to do?" A twig snapped in back of him, marking the movements of the stranger.

"It's more what I want you *not* to do."

Ambrose glanced at Wall who was staring straight ahead. "I don't mean to sound snide, but I don't follow you."

The voice came from a new direction. "I've heard about your dislike of Sir Wallis Pembrooke. I'm not fond of him either. But he has something I want, something he cheated me out of having, and the only way I can get it is for him to stay alive. I'm willing to pay you and your friend a handsome sum not to kill him."

Ambrose's mouth curled into a snarl. "There isn't enough money in the world for that."

"Ah, but there is. You see, there's a time limit on my request *and* a stipulation to the right of payment."

"Go on," Ambrose urged, confused.

"I want Pembrooke's property, but I want it free and clear—without suspicion aimed my way. If you were to kill him and I showed up to claim the land, *I* might be accused of having hired someone to eliminate him. So, I'm willing to pay you to wait until *after* I own the property. That way we'll both have something we want."

Ambrose could hardly believe what he was hearing. This fool was actually offering him money to do something he'd have done for nothing.

"That aspect is simple," the voice proclaimed with a touch

of laughter. "The hard part is that in order for me to buy Pembrooke out, he'll have to *want* to sell."

"And that's where I come in," Ambrose guessed, but he could go no further.

The man moved again, carefully staying at Ambrose's back and in the shadows. "Yes, Mr. Ambrose, the stipulation. I need for you to cause Pembrooke some problems."

"Such as?"

"I'll leave that to your imagination. But whatever it is, it must cost him money, so much money that he's forced to give up raising sheep. I don't care if you let him know you're the one sabotaging his efforts . . . in fact, I'd prefer it. It will leave me looking like an innocent bystander who came to help out a man in trouble." Cynical laughter floated out of the thick stand of scrubs, and several moments passed before he asked, "Are there any questions?"

"Just one," Ambrose said. "If you only wanted my friend and me, why did you free all of us?" He motioned toward the dead men.

"You were never alone, and I couldn't risk your running off before we had a chance to talk. They were expendable. So, do we have a deal?"

Ambrose liked the man's callousness. "I'd be a fool to say no," he replied.

"Good. Then you can get started right away."

A cloth bag sailed through the air and landed with a thump at Ambrose's feet.

"That's a little something to show my good faith. We'll meet here again in one week. You can report your progress and we can discuss any problems that might have come up."

Moving slowly, Ambrose reached for the bag. It jingled when he lifted it, and from its weight, Ambrose had little doubt as to the man's "good faith." He smiled at Wall, then said, " 'Twould seem you have a lot of faith, friend. I wonder what limit it will reach." He waited for a moment, and when the other failed to reply, he repeated the statement. Another measure of time elapsed without comment and only then did Ambrose realize the man had stolen away as quietly as he had come.

·∘⟧ Chapter Fifteen ⟦∘·

IF SOMEONE WERE TO ASK HIM, SAMUEL HUNTER WASN'T SURE he could say which part of his job he hated most. As Sydney's Commissioner of Police, he'd been privy to just about every crime imaginable, and over the years he'd learned to harden his emotions against them. However, every now and then one would slip past his rough exterior and turn his stomach. The report he'd been given that morning was one of those few, and the more he read, the angrier he became. The body of a young man not more than twenty-three years old had been found at the edge of town lying facedown in a shallow stream, the apparent victim of some distorted mind. The investigator who had examined the scene and the body could find no evidence that the young man had been beaten or stabbed, and from all appearances his death had resulted from drowning. Yet signs of a struggle were unmistakable, and it had been the conclusion of the investigator that the victim's head had been forcibly held underwater until he could no longer hold his breath. It was a cruel way for someone to die. What made it even harder for Samuel Hunter was learning the identity of the deceased and that the young man had the mind of a boy one third his age. Florence Pickering had given birth to her one and only child out of wedlock, and even though she had never revealed the name of the father, many assumed it was Virgil Rauscher, the only man whose company Florence had kept.

"Excuse me, sir," someone at the office door interrupted.

"What is it, Daniel?" Hunter replied as he laid aside the report, grateful that for a moment he could think about something else.

"Mr. Abbott's here to see you."

"Abbott? Henry Abbott?"

"Yes, sir."

Hunter frowned. "What's it about?"

"He wishes to report that five of his laborers have run off."

"Did you tell him that matters of that kind should be reported to the prison superintendent and not to me?"

"Yes, sir. But he said two of them aren't just ordinary laborers and that perhaps you should speak with Governor Darling about it."

Hunter waved a hand. "Send him in," he instructed before leaning back in his chair, his gaze falling on the report he'd just finished reading. "Sorry, son, but it looks like you'll have to wait."

Morning came too soon to suit Alexandra. Tired and wondering if she would make it through the day without falling asleep on her feet, she debated between pretending to be ill so that she could stay in bed and hurrying to the breakfast table to catch her father before he rode out to check the sheep. *He* was the only one who could answer her questions. Deciding on the latter, she threw off the covers and left her warm haven.

She had lain awake most of the night rethinking everything Christian had said to her before he left her alone in the livery, and she still hadn't been able to make any sense of it. He had claimed he hadn't killed her because she was a Pembrooke and that he was one of her father's agents. If she bowed to that, it nonetheless failed to explain why he had tried to force himself on her. If he had truly cared what happened to her, he wouldn't have behaved in such a deplorable manner.

While standing at the washbowl and splashing cold water on her face, the conversation she'd had with Aimee those many months ago came to mind. Aimee had seen the predicament in a different light than had her friend. She had posed the possibility that Christian had done exactly as he had claimed last night, that he had actually saved her life by taking her to his room. Alexandra hardly agreed. Yes, she was still alive because of his decision, but only because of her own strong will and quick thinking. What Aimee couldn't guarantee her was what he would have done if Alexandra *hadn't* managed to get away from him. Yet none of that disturbed Alexandra as much as her curiosity over why Christian had, all of a sudden, decided to explain his actions.

Toweling her face dry, she shed her nightgown on her way to the dresser for fresh undergarments, sliding into them as quickly as she could when a cool draft of air made her shiver. And what about his promise to finish what they had started that night? Had he changed his mind? He certainly had the perfect opportunity for it a few hours ago, and yet he hadn't made any kind of threatening move toward her. Why? Feeling oddly insulted, she crossed to the armoire and selected a dress to wear. She wouldn't be able to come right out and ask her father if there was a chance he had agents working for him whose identities were unknown to him, but if she worded it right, he might answer her without knowing it.

Returning to the dresser while she fumbled with the buttons up the front of her gown, she grabbed a brush and ran it through her hair until the dark mane crackled and shone in the early-morning sunlight shining in through the window. A moment later she had stepped into her shoes and left the room.

"Felice, has Papa left already?" she asked once she found the maid clearing breakfast dishes from the dining room table.

"Aye, mum," the girl replied with a nod of her head. "Mr. Page told 'im Patches was ready to work the sheep, and I guess 'e went out to give the dog a run." She smiled brightly and added, " 'E's excited about it, 'e is. Like a boy with a new toy, I'd say." Depositing the last dish on her tray, she glanced up questioningly at her mistress. "Shall I bring in your breakfast now, mum?"

Alexandra frowned. If she'd known her father had already set about his daily routine, she wouldn't have bothered getting out of bed. "Yes, please," she answered with a scowl as she crossed to the buffet to fix herself a cup of tea. "But tell Thomas to make it light. I'm not really that hungry."

"Aye, mum," Felice acknowledged, bending one knee in a slight curtsy before she turned and left the room.

The frown deepened on Alexandra's brow as she set the tea-cup on the table and pulled out a chair to sit down. It was her father's custom to spend most of the morning away from the house. Around noon, he'd return long enough to have something to eat while he sat at his desk and made entries in his journal. After that, he'd inspect Christian's progress on the new house, talk with Mr. Boone, offer his suggestion to Thomas on what he'd like for dinner, and then ride out again. If Alexandra wanted to talk to him before sundown, she'd have to interrupt him while he worked on his books or have one of the men saddle a horse for her.

She smiled softly as she raised the cup to her lips, thinking how surprised her father would be to see her galloping up to meet him. She'd never been on the back of a horse in her life, and although she'd heard others talk about how one must be taught to ride, she had always assumed they had made more out it than was necessary. Her father had never taken lessons, and he could ride as well as anyone else she'd ever seen. Besides, what more was there to it than climbing on, kicking one's heels in the horse's sides, and steering?

Her thoughts about her new adventure were distracted for the time being when Felice returned to the room carrying a breakfast tray. Alexandra ate in a hurry, drank one more cup of tea, and rose from the table with the intention of asking Mr. Boone to saddle a horse for her. She'd started toward the kitchen to inform Felice of her plans, when the sound of horses' hooves cutting across the front yard stopped her. Since her father was away at the moment, she realized it was her place to greet their visitor. Changing direction, she followed the veranda around the side of the house and paused once she had reached the front steps.

"Mr. Smith," she said, some surprise evident in her words. "I didn't think we'd be seeing you again."

Careful not to let her see how much the sight of her truly bothered him, Smith lowered his gaze and laughed nervously as he swung a leg over the horse's rump and stepped to the ground. "Until a couple of days ago I didn't think I'd be coming here either," he admitted, the horse's reins held in his clasped hands and his head bowed as though he were a bashful suitor come to call. "Is your father here, Miss Pembrooke? I'd like to speak with him."

"He's out checking on the sheep at the moment, and I doubt he'll be back much before noon." She frowned, curious and a little apprehensive. "Is there something I can do for you?"

He glanced up and smiled weakly. "I don't know," he confessed. "Perhaps."

"Then why don't you tell me what it is that brought you here," she suggested.

The smile remained, but in his thoughts Smith concluded that telling her the real reason he had come was something that would have her staying awake at nights . . . that was, of course, if they didn't believe his whole story and tore up the floorboards in her room before he could get to it. "Your father offered me work, Miss Pembrooke, and I declined without giving myself a chance to think it through. I'm here because I've changed my mind." He dropped his gaze away from her for a second as he cleared his throat, then added, "If the offer is still open, of course."

Alexandra couldn't think of a reason why her father wouldn't honor the proposal, except that perhaps they didn't need the extra help. But her father hadn't suggested Mr. Smith come to work for them because he needed one more hand. He'd offered because he felt sorry for the man. "I'm sure it's still open, Mr. Smith," she said, stepping off the veranda and holding out her hand in the direction of the barn. "If you'll bring your horse and come with me, I'll introduce you to Lynn Boone. He's the one who's in charge of the men. He'll show you where to bed down and what work he'd like for you to do."

"Thank you, Miss Pembrooke," Smith replied, falling in step behind her. The humble expression on his face changed the instant his gaze slipped to the sway of her hips as she led the way for them. There were few young women living in Australia, and of those even fewer were what a man like Smith would call pretty. In Smith's mind Alexandra Pembrooke was beautiful. Perhaps, after he'd finished what he was determined to do and this lovely creature was homeless and he was rich, he'd call on her. A woman like Alexandra Pembrooke was used to having whatever money could buy, and if she played it right, he'd be willing to spend a little of his wealth on her. Why, he might even be willing to marry her.

* * *

By the time Alexandra had ridden out of sight of the house, she was beginning to doubt the sanity of her notion. Richard Dolter, a cobbler before his sentencing placed him in her father's care as a blacksmith, had tried his level best to talk her into waiting for her father to come home instead of riding out to meet him. Not only was he worried she wouldn't be able to handle the mare should something spook the animal, but the storm clouds racing in from the east promised a good downpour before the morning was out. Alexandra had laughed and guaranteed the blacksmith that nothing would happen to her or the horse, then she had awkwardly pulled herself up into the saddle, sawed on the reins, jabbed her heels into the animal's flanks, and set off at a rather teeth-jarring pace. If Dolter had objected, Mr. Boone would, too. Christian Page simply wouldn't have allowed her to go, and that had been the reason she had waited in the livery while Dolter saddled up the mare. She didn't want him running off to ask someone else's opinion on whether or not she should be allowed to leave, and by the time Boone or Christian was made aware of it, she'd be long gone.

Now, however, she was beginning to wish she hadn't been so cunning. She couldn't get the stubborn-headed mare to move any faster than a trot, and whenever she pulled back on the reins, the animal obliged by turning around and heading back toward the barn. An angry shout and a sharp tug would set them in the right direction again, but at the same bone-bruising, teeth-rattling gait. She was already sore from the abuse, and they'd hardly traveled more than a quarter of a mile. That alone had her temper stewing. The dark clouds and the smell of rain quickly added fuel to the fire. Her anger exploded once she realized she had no idea where she would find her father, for once the mare had crested the knoll, neither he nor the flock of sheep were anywhere to be seen.

"Well, ol' girl," she grumbled to the horse, "I guess it's up to you to decide which way we go. Just make sure you're right. I don't want to wind up so far from home that we can't outrun the storm. Remember, if I get wet, so do you." She nudged the mare a little harder this time, but the result was the same.

They traveled across a wide, grassy meadow of rolling hills with an occasional stand of trees and scrubs. Although the scenery was beautiful, Alexandra paid it little mind as the discomfort to her derrière and the width she had to spread her knees to sit astride the beast spoiled the pleasure of other things. The wind picked up and the sweet aroma of rain in the air grew heavy. The black, swirling clouds were nearly upon her, and off in the distance to her right she could see the heavy curtain of rain sweeping across the pasture toward her. She was about to admit defeat and swing the mare around, when up ahead just beyond a dense growth of bushes, she thought she spotted a patch of white.

"There!" she shouted to her companion. "Do you see it?"

With all the strength she could muster, she kicked the horse and snapped the reins at the same time, surprised and slightly miffed that it had taken her this long to figure out how to get the mare to respond. The defiant beast bolted and galloped off toward the grazing flock. What she was about to learn, however, was that sheep didn't always stay in one group, and that her father was off in another field at that moment. She made the discovery a few minutes later as the mare raced across the meadow and scattered the woolly little creatures in four directions.

"Stop!" she shouted when the mare threatened to thunder on by. "Do you hear me? I said stop!" Out of desperation, she yanked back on the reins, a mistake that spun the animal sharply to the right when she inadvertently tugged a little harder on one of the leather straps. Jerked off-balance since she didn't know how to hang on with her knees, Alexandra was thrown from the saddle and dumped painfully to the ground. "You miserable, louse-ridden old nag!" she screamed at the rapidly departing horse. "I hope you step in a hole and break your neck!"

Tail held high, her ears back and nostrils flared, the mare galloped off with an air that proclaimed her satisfaction at having rid herself of an ungrateful passenger.

"Thomas will be serving you up for dinner!" Alexandra shouted. "And I'll use your hide for a rug, so help me God!"

Furious with herself and more pointedly with the horse, she

roughly gathered a handful of her skirts and pulled herself to her feet. The instant she put her full weight on her left ankle, however, pain shot up her leg and she collapsed back down in the grass, tears rushing to her eyes.

"Oh, damn," she moaned as she rubbed the tender limb. "Now what shall I do?"

The need to make a decision intensified when she heard a rustling noise not far from where she sat. Concerned, she glanced up and noticed that she had been callously deposited near the only growth of scrubs for several hundred feet in all directions, a thick haven that could hide just about anything. She quickly dismissed the idea that a crocodile might be lurking in the underbrush once she realized those creatures preferred a watery resort, but just the same, her fear of what was hiding there grew by leaps and bounds. Knowing the mare would be of no help, since the animal had already hightailed it over the crest of the first hill, she looked around for some other form of protection or escape. To her relief she espied one of the line cabins Christian had built nestled in a grove of trees some distance off to her left. Her problem was getting to it . . . before the storm hit and before whatever was eyeing her from within the bushes decided it was time to eat.

Concentrating on the dark shadows crowded around the base of the leafy foliage before her, she struggled to rise, ignoring the tremors of pain that cramped her leg muscles. Half walking, half hobbling, she inched her way backward, watching for the danger that emanated from the undergrowth. Thunder rumbled close overhead. A searing flash of light temporarily blinded her, followed by an even louder crack of thunder that shook the ground. Then she saw them . . . two, no four pairs of brown eyes staring back at her, and she hurried her labored steps to get away.

"Damn you, you old nag," she cursed again, fighting to control the panic rising in her. "This is all your fault. And when I get home, I'll personally hold the gun to your head and pull the trigger." Her tears burned her throat. "And I will get home again."

Another volley of white light and clamorous thunder tore through the skies, heralding the urgency for both hunter and prey to seek shelter and pick up the fight at a different time. The dingos, however, were too hungry to surrender. Alexandra was too frightened to consider the possibility of an alternative.

One by one the yellow-furred dogs moved out from their hiding place, eyes alert, their teeth bared in a fierce snarl. Alexandra assumed that with only one to fend off, she might have stood a chance. But four. . . . Glancing away from them for only a moment, she saw a pile of dried debris from an earlier storm that had uprooted several small trees. Thinking that if she were armed she might even the odds a little, she changed her immediate destination and moved toward the mound of sticks, hoping one was heavy enough to suit her purpose.

The pack seemed to sense her intention and hurried their approach, the largest of the dogs taking the lead. He was the one Alexandra watched more closely than the others, guessing that the animal world wasn't much different from their human equivalent. The weaker members always looked to their leader for guidance, which meant there might be a chance for Alexandra if she could take out the most aggressive of the group. The rest just might turn tail and run.

Seizing the thickest and most promising of the tree branches in the pile, Alexandra turned on the pack, her chest heaving, her chin lowered, and a firm determination glowing in her eyes.

"All right," she bravely challenged, balancing herself on her good ankle, "which one of you wants it first?"

As if the leader understood the dare, his snarl deepened into a growl and the fur along his spine stood up on end. While the others held back, he advanced, and Alexandra doubted the wisdom in showing an open display of courage. It seemed only to have provoked him.

"One more step, you mangy cur, and I'm going to bash in your brains," she promised, hearing the fear in her voice. "But if that's what you want—" The last exploded into a chilling scream when the dingo lunged for her.

Somehow Alexandra managed to maintain some semblance of control, timing the blow at the last minute. With all the strength she had in her, she swung the club downward in a sidewinder method, striking the animal across the left side of his head. The upward motion of her swing sent him sailing through the air before he landed with a thud and plowed a furrow in the grass with his nose. Dazed and in pain, he was slow to get up, allowing Alexandra a second or two to appraise the other beasts. Not in the least convinced that the two-legged creature they faced was of any real threat to their health, and too hungry to yield, the remaining three burst into a gallop, ready to attack as one unit.

Determined to cause the dingos as much pain as she could before their number dragged her down, Alexandra gripped her weapon and fought the panic that shook her body and filled her eyes with tears. She swung blindly, hitting the first of the dogs to reach her in the shoulder. He let out a yelp and fell. With a backhand blow, she clubbed a second across the nose, which forced him to temporarily retreat and lick his wound as blood squirted from both nostrils. The third advanced and while Alexandra took aim, their leader circled in back of her, ready to pounce. In that same moment and before any of them noticed, a fifth dog, one whose coat was longer and multicolored, suddenly appeared from out of nowhere.

As if he had taken flight, the intruder sailed through the air and attacked the largest of the dingos just as that one moved to lunge for Alexandra's legs, slamming up against the other's chest with his own and knocking them both to the ground. They fought viciously, rolling over and over as they bit and snapped and growled, tearing up tufts of grass with their hind claws. The others, having acknowledged a more worthy opponent, aborted their offensive and attacked the newcomer, and only then did Alexandra recognize her savior.

"Patches!" she screamed, tears streaming down her face. "God, no!"

Finding renewed strength and a calm that told her the scruffy little mongrel wouldn't survive without her help, her quest changed from protecting herself to aiding a friend who needed her. With the club held high, she stormed the pack of warring animals. Incensed, she neither saw the approaching horse and rider nor heard the racing hoofbeats thundering toward her as she swung the heavy stick and smashed it against the spine of one of the dingos. A painful yelp followed, and a second staggering blow hurled the dog up in the air.

"Leave him alone!" she screamed, tears choking her words and blurring her vision of Patches as she raised her weapon again. "Dammit, you're killing him!"

She clubbed a second dog, which sent him crashing into a third and left only the largest of the group remaining when it appeared the others were hesitant to rejoin the skirmish.

"Didn't you hear me?" she raged. "I said to leave him alone!" But before she could lift the thick wooden cudgel again, a shot rang out and the dingo was struck by a bullet just below his right ear. The force behind it jerked him away from his foe and threw his lifeless body to the ground several feet away.

Too numb to realize what had happened and that the gunfire had scattered the rest of the wild dogs, Alexandra stood motionless with her eyes affixed to the struggling ball of dirty fur as Patches tried to rise and failed. Dark red blood stained his coat from head to tail, and no one had to tell her that the funny-looking little dog, who had taken an immediate liking to her, was dying.

"Oh, Patches," she wept, dropping to her knees. "Oh, Patches." Scooping up his head in her arms, she hugged him close. "You silly little dog. Why did you do it? I was never even nice to you."

A clap of thunder boomed overhead, bringing with it a gentle rain that soon mixed with the tears streaming down her face as she rocked back and forth, the dog held tightly in her arms and his blood darkening the plum-colored fabric of her dress. Tormented by the knowledge that the result of her foolishness would be the demise of a loving creature who had never asked anything of her, she was blind to the figure who had dismounted from his horse and had come to kneel beside her, until a hand softly touched her shoulder.

"He's dying, Christian," she said, once she had looked up and saw him. "It's my fault. This wouldn't have happened, if . . . " She bit her lower lip to still the sob that threatened to burst from her body at any second.

"It's not your fault, Alexandra," he said gently as he stripped out of his shirt, wrapped the garment around Patches, and took the dog from her arms to lay him tenderly on the ground. "Dingos are a part of Australia and a part of a sheep dog's life. It's what he was trained to do." Taking her elbow, he drew her to her feet where he swept her up in his arms and deposited her across the saddle of his horse. Bending back down for Patches, he handed the limp form to Alexandra, then swung himself up behind the pair and reached for the reins. "Dogs are like people," he added, slipping an arm around her waist to hold her steady as he kicked the stallion and set them off toward the line cabin at a rapid pace. "They'd gladly lay down their lives for someone they care about."

Alexandra tried a second time to take the blame. "But if I hadn't come—"

"The dingos would have attacked the sheep, and Patches would have done the same thing," Christian cut in. "The difference would have been that he would have been doing his job rather than showing his loyalty to you."

Her tears flowed harder as she cradled the dog in her arms and studied his face. He was still breathing, but she noticed that the color on the inside of his ears had turned from pink to blue, and that blood continued to seep from his wounds. His eyes were closed and despite the warm rain that had soaked all three of them, Patches's body was cool to the touch.

"Hurry, Christian," she begged, even though she knew it was already too late.

Nearing the front door of the cabin, Christian pulled back on the reins and brought the horse to a rough halt. He slid from the saddle, reached up for Patches, and started to help Alexandra dismount when she waved him off with instructions to get the dog in out of the rain and to tend his wounds. Patches needed Christian's help more than she did right then, and while he elbowed his way through the half-closed door, Alexandra grabbed the pommel in both hands and slipped from the horse's back. The instant her feet touched the ground, pain shot up her leg and she unwillingly crumpled to the ground, too riddled with guilt and sadness to rise.

The tiny cabin offered a fireplace, a table and two chairs, a cot, and a minimum of supplies. Christian and Pembrooke had left the house shortly after sunrise to work with Patches for a while and to discuss expanding the business if the wool crop was anything like they hoped it would be. Pembrooke had brought his journal and a stack of notes with him, and the two of them had planned to sit at the table and go over his entries after Patches had proved himself. Things hadn't worked out that way. Shortly before they were ready to retreat to the privacy of the cabin, one of the men had ridden up with news that one of the line cabins on the north side had been ransacked during the night and that perhaps Pembrooke would want to see it for himself before it was cleaned up. Christian had volunteered to go along, but Pembrooke had assured him that there wasn't really a need and that while he was gone, Christian could look over his papers. He had just sat down to do that very thing, when he heard Patches bark. Now, it appeared, as he laid the dog on the floor in front of the hearth's crackling blaze, that the mutt would never have the opportunity to interrupt Christian again. He wished it could be otherwise . . . for Alexandra's sake. She would probably always blame herself for Patches's death no matter how hard Christian tried to convince her that it hadn't been her fault.

An ear-splitting boom of thunder rattled the windowpane and vibrated off Christian's chest and shoulders. Ordinarily, the noise would have startled the animal he comforted, and when he saw that Patches didn't move or even tremble at the sound, Christian knew the dog was dead. Placing his fingers against Patches's rib cage, he pressed them close, hoping for a sign that he was wrong. When he couldn't feel a heartbeat, and pinching the tip of the dog's nose failed to get a response, he reached for the woodbox to dump out the kindling. As soon as it stopped raining, they would bury him.

"I'm sorry, Alexandra," he said solemnly as he laid the dog inside the box and covered his body with the bloodied shirt. "He was too badly—" The sentence was never completed, for once he had turned to face her with words of consolation, he discovered that she hadn't followed him into the cabin. With a concerned frown, he jerked to his feet and raced for the door. What he saw once he'd reached the entrance was the most pathetic sight he'd ever seen, and all the adverse feelings he'd had about her vanished. Huddled on the ground and soaking wet, Alexandra sat with her knees drawn up, her arms wrapped around them, and her face buried in her skirts, sobbing. Hesi-

tating for only a moment, he rushed to her side and scooped
her up in his arms.

The door swung shut with a thud after Christian had kicked
it with the heel of his shoe. He carried her to the cot and gently
sat her down, before he knelt by the hearth and tossed in the rest
of the wood. Once the fire caught and flared high, he returned
to her side and began unbuttoning the front of her dress, lifting
the heavy strands of her hair out of the way.

"We've got to dry you off, Alexandra," he stated, even
though she had voiced no complaint. "Sacrificing yourself
won't bring him back. Stand up." Once she had, she leaned
heavily against him for support, and only then did he realize she
was hurt. He helped her out of her dress and petticoats, yanked
the blanket from the cot and tossed it around her shoulders,
then guided her to the chair before the fire where he gingerly
removed her shoes and stockings.

"Let me look at your ankle," he softly instructed when she
tried to pull away.

Still weeping, she reluctantly did as bade, wincing when
he got too rough. "I was looking for Papa," she said through
breathy sobs, her lower lip quivering. "Felice told me he had
taken Patches out to run with the sheep. I should have waited
for him . . . " She glanced past him at the woodbox, saw the
bloodstained shirt, and starting crying again. "Mr. Dolter told
me I shouldn't go, that I didn't know how to ride, but I wouldn't
listen. I never listen to what anyone tells me." Holding back
a sob, she clumsily wiped the tears from her face as she
settled her gaze on Christian again. "I'm a spoiled child,"
she admitted. "You've known that all along, haven't you? You
knew it the minute you saw me with Hardin." She exhaled a
trembling sigh and closed her eyes. "Hardin," she murmured.
"I could have gotten him killed, too, but I didn't care. All I
wanted was to hurt my father." Troubled green eyes looked at
Christian. "I was angry with him, you know. He's the reason
my mother took her own life. He'd been having an affair and
she couldn't stand the humiliation of it. What makes a man
be unfaithful to his wife, Christian?"

He knew the shock of what had happened to her a few minutes ago was forcing her to say things she probably would have

kept secret otherwise. He was honored she had chosen him as her confessor, but at the same time he doubted she realized what she was saying and to whom. "I don't know, Alexandra," he answered softly.

"Do you think he fell out of love with her? Could that be the reason he looked to someone else?"

There were many reasons why a man would choose to have a relationship with someone other than his wife, but Christian decided not to voice them. He had no way of knowing if any or all of them could apply to her father. More than that, it was none of his business. He shrugged instead.

A crack of thunder shook the ground and startled Alexandra right out of her chair. Falling to her knees, she flung her arms around Christian's neck and held on, her body shaking violently and her tears starting anew.

"I never meant for Patches to get hurt," she sobbed. "You've got to believe me, Christian."

"I do," he pledged, distracted and alarmed not only by her vulnerability at that moment, but by his own. He wanted to comfort her, but he wanted more as well, and that confused him. Since Min Le, no other woman had ever stirred the kind of sensations in him that he was feeling now. The softness of her pressed against his chest warmed his blood. The scent of her flesh excited his imagination. Alexandra was like a beautiful black leopard in the wild. She moved with as much grace and skill as the huge cat, and her claws were just as sharp. She could strike without warning and with no provocation. Her spirit begged to be tamed, and the deep green shade of her eyes could hypnotize an unsuspecting prey. Everything about her cried out for Christian to beware, and yet he was on the verge of ignoring the warning. Sucking air into his lungs in the hope of silencing the strong desires racking his body, he reached up and gently tried to pull her arms from around his neck.

"No, Christian, please," she begged, tightening her hold. "Don't push me away. I know it's what I deserve—to be hated by you—but I need you right now. I need to know there's one person in this world who cares about me despite my faults."

"I don't hate you, Alexandra," he replied. "I've never hated you. I was angry with you, yes, but only because you got in the way and put us both in danger."

"I didn't mean to," she whispered. "I didn't know about you."

He leaned back and looked in her eyes. "Would it have made a difference if you had known one of your father's agents was there?"

A strange expression softened the shade of her eyes, one that puzzled him, and his troubled frown turned to one of caution.

"If I had known how I would come to feel about you, yes, it would have made a difference." Her gaze dropped to his mouth, then back up to stare into his eyes. "You're not the man I first thought you to be, Christian."

A tingling raced through every nerve in his body. "Oh?" was all he could say.

"You're kind, patient, strong, and gentle." She smiled softly and reached up to brush a wet strand of blond hair from his brow. "You don't let past differences stand in the way when someone needs your help. You're unselfish, and . . ." A slight blush rose in her cheeks. "And you're handsome. Why hasn't someone snatched you up by now?"

The image of Min Le struggled to come to mind. Uncomfortable, Christian shifted around and raised up on his knees, thinking to break Alexandra's hold on him. Her grip tightened and the blanket draped over her shoulders slipped to the floor. He clamped his teeth shut out of fear she would hear the thunderous beating of his heart, while he tried not to notice her scantily clad body or how his blood had warmed all the more.

"Alexandra," he began, reaching for her hands again, "I don't think—"

Misinterpreting his feelings, the pink blush in her cheeks turned scarlet and she jerked her hands away. "I-I'm sorry," she mumbled, grabbing for the blanket and awkwardly pulling it back up over her shoulders. "I didn't mean to . . ." She laughed nervously and settled herself back in the chair, unable to look at him again.

Several long, agonizing minutes passed as Alexandra felt his movements around the cabin while he gathered her wet clothes and hung them near the fireplace to dry. She hadn't planned on being so bold with him. In fact, she hadn't truly realized what she was doing until he had subtly drawn her attention to it. What must he think of her? she wondered, fresh tears beading her lashes. He thinks the worst, she silently proclaimed. What else could he think? She had gone from plotting a way to see him hanged, to practically throwing herself at him. She had deceived him one minute, and then told him secrets she hadn't even shared with her best friend. Why? What was it about Christian Page that had her flying from one extreme to the other? And why, after all she'd done to him, hadn't his feelings for her changed one bit?

"You really should hate me, Christian," she said before she realized the words had even formed in her mind. "It's my fault you're here, and even if we were to tell my father the truth about you, there's nothing he could do to clear your name . . . not now. He no longer works for the Crown." Feeling as though the tiny room had grown even smaller during those past two minutes, she blurted out, "Are my things dry yet?"

"Not even close," Christian replied. "Why do you ask?"

She exhaled a quick breath, her eyes downcast. "I think it's time I went home."

"But it's raining," he advised, motioning toward the window and the steady stream of water smearing the glass. "I'll take you back as soon as it's fit to travel."

She added a second reason for her not to wait. "My father will be worried about me."

"Your father went to inspect one of the other line cabins. He's probably doing exactly what you're doing . . . waiting until it stops raining before he heads back to the house. I doubt he even knows you're not there."

She shrugged a shoulder, continuing to avert her eyes. "Mr. Boone will worry. Or Felice."

"Do you think they'd feel better seeing you ride up drenched from head to toe?" Her insistence nettled him. "We'll wait."

As if to emphasize his disapproval, a clap of thunder resounded across the heavens and pounded against the rooftop, drawing Alexandra's gaze to the low ceiling above her.

"I hate storms," she proclaimed, her lower lip quivering.

"They scare me. They always make me think God's angry."
She looked at the window and shivered once she saw how violently the rain slashed at the pane of glass.

"Maybe He is," Christian agreed, smiling softly when she looked at him. "But not at you."

Her gaze shifted past him to the woodbox. "Maybe," she reluctantly yielded. "Maybe not. It rained the day we buried my mother, and that night, too. I think it rained for a week. And it wasn't just a shower. It stormed. Now every time I hear thunder . . . " She smiled tightly at him and looked away.

"How old were you when your mother died?" he pressed, sorry he'd allowed his own desires to interfere. She needed someone to listen.

"Fourteen," she answered, swiping at a tear.

Crossing to the table, he swung the extra chair around and straddled the seat, his arms folded along the back rail. "A wise old man told me one time that each of us are the masters of our own fate . . . if we choose to be. Your mother chose her destiny, Alexandra, not her fourteen-year-old daughter. You mustn't blame yourself for what happened."

"I don't!" she snapped. "I blame Papa."

"In part," he agreed. "But it's only natural for a child to blame himself when someone he loves no longer wants to live. If only you'd told her how much you loved her. . . . If only you'd been a better daughter. . . . If only . . . " He cocked his head and looked at the dark strands of wet hair still plastered to her face as she stared down at her lap. "How many times have you said that, Alexandra? Only once? Twice? A hundred times? Have you ever found the answer? Probably not, because there is no answer. Your mother would have loved you no matter what. *She* was the one who was weak, the one who couldn't face her problems any longer. You had nothing to do with it. But you're allowing her sorrow, her failure to run your life. Do you honestly believe she'd approve of what you're doing? Would it please her to know how unhappy she's made you? I doubt it."

A delicate chin raised and her body grew rigid. "Are you saying that I should just forget about her? About what happened? About how miserable she was?"

"No. But you've got to come to terms with the fact that there's nothing you can do to correct it. You can't bring her back by hating your father and reminding him every day that she died because of something he'd done. I'm sure he's been living with that awful truth without any help from you."

"So I'm supposed to forgive and forget."

"Forgive, yes. You'll never forget."

Her chin quivered, and when she looked stubbornly at him, her green eyes were brimming with tears. "It's so easy for you to give advice. You don't know the pain."

He thought of Li-Chen and the hatred he'd felt toward the man for killing his wife and newborn son, even though it had been an accident. He remembered having similar words with Sang Soo and how his own reaction, at first, hadn't been much different from Alexandra's. It had taken him a while to come to grips with the truth, just as it would take time for her to fully understand.

"We all have our own kind of pain, Alexandra," he quietly told her. "How we deal with it is what sets us apart from one another."

"And you feel I'm not dealing with it the way I should," she said.

"I didn't say that."

She tossed her head and stared into the fire. "You didn't have to." A roll of thunder and hammering of rain against the walls of the cabin shook everything inside, and her burst of anger changed to fright. She clutched the blanket around her and struggled with her tears.

Christian watched her for several moments in silence. He knew he'd upset her even though he hadn't meant to, and that anything more he might say would only aggravate her mood. Thinking that perhaps she should elevate her foot, he pushed off the chair, caught the back rail, and swung it around in front of her. Taking the pillow from the cot, he dropped it on the chair seat and stooped to reach for her leg.

"It won't swell as much if you put it up," he explained, a bit short-tempered, when she scowled at him and drew her foot back. He held out his hand and waited for her to decide.

Alexandra had to admit that her ankle was throbbing and

that anything was better than the discomfort she felt right then. She would have preferred, however, that the idea had been her own rather than Christian's, since at the moment she was hating him for being right. Returning his look with a stubborn one of her own, her silence forced him to retreat. Once he had, she raised her foot and gingerly laid it on the pillow.

"What?" she asked suspiciously, when she heard him mumble something and turn away, the muscles across his bare shoulders rigid with his irritation.

"I said," he repeated with a quick look back at her, once he'd squatted in front of the hearth to stoke the fire, "that it's no wonder you're not married by now."

Alexandra's chin dropped. "Excuse me?" she demanded.

Christian jabbed the poker at the burning logs three or four times before he carelessly dropped the tool back in its rack and stood. "You've got a mean spirit, Alexandra. It would take a special kind of man with a lot of patience to ever fall in love with you."

"Oh, really?" she countered. "Well, I'll have you know I've had a lot of interested suitors."

He looked at her for a moment, then crossed to the cupboard where he took down a tin of tea leaves and two cups, filled a kettle with water, and moved back to the hearth to hang it over the fire. "I'm sure you have," he agreed, "but I'd guess none of them stayed around very long once they got a sampling of your true nature."

"That's not true!" she exploded.

"Oh?" He turned a cold, challenging look on her. "Name one."

"Hardin!"

Christian's expression relaxed, but there was a cynical gleam in his blue eyes. "Uh-huh," he yielded. "And look what it got him."

"Damn you!" she howled, clumsily pushing herself up on one foot. "That's not fair. Hardin asked for what he got."

"Did he? Did he ask to get caught in the middle of your vendetta aimed at me? Did he volunteer to take the witness stand? Was it his idea you send that note to your father? And where is he now? Running for his life?" He leaned a shoulder against the mantel and folded his arms over his chest, waiting for her to deny his charges.

Alexandra glared at him, her face blazing her wrath and her chest heaving with each outraged breath she took. She considered reminding him that Hardin had agreed to take her to meet Garrett Ambrose out of purely selfish reasons and not because of anything she had asked of him. He had had a debt to pay and he had used her to do it. He had nearly gotten her killed, but this pompous ass couldn't see it that way.

"The truth of the matter is the only one who really cared enough about what happened to you is lying in that woodbox," Christian continued with a callous nod of his head in that direction. "Blind loyalty, Alexandra. That's what killed Patches, and it very nearly killed Hardin."

The insults cut deep. Refusing to allow him the chance to add to them, she hobbled toward the spot where he'd hung her clothes and angrily snatched them up in her arms.

"I don't have to listen to this," she snarled, turning for the cot, fresh tears of hurt and rage stinging her eyes.

"Of course you don't. Not when it's easier to run away than to admit to your shortcomings. You're a very unhappy woman, Alex, and it's all your own doing." He jerked away from the mantel and caught her in his arms when she stumbled and nearly fell.

"Let go of me," she hotly demanded, swinging an elbow at him.

His grip tightened as he roughly yanked the dress and petticoats from her hands and tossed them on the floor. Then, without a thought to what he was doing and driven by an inner force, he seized the hair at her nape and pulled, lifting her face to his, while he clamped one arm around her waist and lowered his head. He kissed her hard and long, his mouth moving hungrily over hers as if he were starved for the sweet taste of her. He ignored her struggle of protest and failed to realize the refusal lasted no more than a brief moment or two before her arms came around his chest and she was kissing him back with as much fervor as the storm beating against the tiny cabin.

An excitement, an insatiable need suddenly burst upon them both, and while they tore at each other's clothes, their passion soared beyond control. His kisses moved along her jaw to the tender flesh beneath her ear, down her silky throat, and under her chin before his mouth captured hers again. Their breathing grew hot and labored, and with their lips still clinging to the honeyed nectar of the kiss, they stripped away the last remnants of modesty.

The instant bare flesh touched, Alexandra moaned, delirious from the branding fire that exploded inside her and held her close to the edge of rapture. She could feel the well-defined shape of his chest and ribs, the warmth of his belly and thighs, the steel hardness of his masculinity, and although the new sensation frightened her, it also piqued her womanly instincts and a curiosity and passion to explore the full measure of delight. Her heart began to pound and her flesh seemed to melt under his touch as he ran an opened hand down her spine to her buttocks then up to gently caress her breast.

"Oh, Christian," she whispered. "We really shouldn't."

"I know," he answered huskily as his lips found the hollow at the base of her throat and he breathed in the perfumed scent of her. Without further words of guilt or conscience, he bent slightly and drew her up into his embrace, his mouth claiming hers again as she wrapped her arms around his neck and savored the fierceness of the kiss.

With gentle sureness he carried her the short distance to the cot and laid her down, his gaze boldly sweeping the velvety flesh of her body from head to toe. He'd never seen such an exquisite form with its perfectly shaped hips and thighs, long, willowy legs, flat belly and full, ripe, pink-tipped breasts. Her dark brown hair lay in a silken torrent of damp curls around her face and over her shoulders. Jade-green eyes stared back at him without a trace of hatred or regret. Slightly parted lips awaited his kiss, and her cheeks were flushed with desire. The vision of another barely surfaced to cloud his want or raise the possibility that his loneliness drove him on so recklessly. With a tenderness long forgotten, he stroked her breasts, his own desire flaring high once he saw the lust rise and burn brightly in those magnificent eyes watching him. Closing his own eyes, he leaned over her and trailed light kisses down her throat and between the creamy mounds of flesh before his mouth eagerly captured one rosy peak. A warm, moist tongue drew circles around it, then moved to conquer the second taut crest while his hand fell bold against her inner thigh.

Alexandra had experienced her share of stolen kisses. She had allowed her imagination free rein. She had envisioned such splendor beneath the manly touch of the one who would one day claim her as his wife, but she had never guessed to what exulted extreme it would take her. Giddy secrets and whispered speculation with Aimee hadn't even come close. But what truly surprised her was her seemingly knowledgeable responses, and while his fingers explored the moist crevice of her womanhood and nearly took her breath away, she focused on pleasing him in a similar way. Tickling the flesh along his ribs with her fingertips, she followed the rippling muscles of his waist and hip, down one thigh and up again, pausing to draw on her courage before she daringly curled her fingers around the throbbing staff of his manliness. She heard him gasp and felt her own heart skip a beat. A second later his kiss was smothering her, and when he raised above her and parted her knees with his own, a delicious fear raced through every inch of her. She wanted him as much as he wanted her, but she wondered— briefly—at the differences. The uncertainty vanished in the next instant when the pain of penetration changed the course of her thoughts. Yet she endured it in silence once the subtle agony ebbed and a strange, budding eagerness singed the tips of every nerve in her body. A whispered word of instruction guided her and within moments she was matching the sleek thrust of hips with her own. Pleasure curled her insides. A warmth spread upward from her toes to her loins and finally consumed her whole being as they challenged the fury of the storm outside the cabin with a tempest of their own. She clawed his back with her nails. She called his name. She kissed him hard and reveled in the glorious consummation of the passion that possessed them. At last it ended but not before every ounce of strength was drained from them in their quest to reach the summit of their desires.

Breathless and sated, Christian fell to her side, his darkly tanned body gleaming in the light of the fire, his eyes closed, and the muscles across his chest and belly tightening, then relaxing as he drew air into his lungs and calmed his racing heartbeat. Unashamed of her nudity or the private moments they had shared, Alexandra shifted over on her side and openly studied the majestic profile he unknowingly presented her. He was indeed handsome, and the most alluring man she had ever met. His quiet presence never failed to arouse her, and the mystery that surrounded his very existence enhanced his male prowess and drew her closer, though reluctantly. She knew very little about him, and despite the fact, she had given herself to him with no words of love or of the future. Had that been a part of the excitement that had so fully lured her into his arms? Was he merely another pawn in the game she played with her father? Did she really feel something for him or had this been a mistake? Confused, a frown softly played across her brow, while in her heart she wondered how easily she would watch him walk away.

··⊰❏ *Chapter Sixteen* ❏⊱··

WALLIS PEMBROOKE WAS ANGRY AND TROUBLED AS HE RODE back to the house. The damage to the line cabin hadn't been enough to warrant demolishing it and rebuilding from the ground up, but it would most definitely be out of use for several days. Whoever had looted the place had done a thorough job of it, and aside from a few provisions, Pembrooke couldn't understand what the pillager had wanted except for the possibility that he took some kind of joy in vandalizing other people's property.

The storm had passed some time ago but rather than return home right away, Pembrooke had checked on the remaining cabins before heading back. He couldn't explain the feeling he had, but he'd sensed this hadn't been an isolated incident. Once he'd found that the rest of the buildings had been left untouched, he had relaxed a little, telling himself that he was overreacting and that he'd have to learn to leave his suspicious nature back in England with his former job. That had been before he'd ridden close enough to the house to see Lynn Boone and another man waiting on the veranda for him.

"Good morning, Sir Wallis," Howard Beary greeted with a nod as Boone stepped down and took hold of the horse's bridle.

"Howard," Pembrooke returned, swinging out of the saddle. "I'd like to say I'm surprised to see you, but I'm not. I would imagine you have some news that couldn't wait until I came into Sydney next week."

"Yes, sir," Beary replied, reaching out to shake Pembrooke's hand. "How did you know?"

"Instinct," Pembrooke answered without further explanation. "I assume you introduced yourself to Boone."

"Only my name, sir. The governor instructed me to share the information with no one other than you."

"I understand," Pembrooke said. He turned to Boone. "Mr. Boone, if you'll excuse us, I'll hear what Howard has to say, then meet with you later."

"That's fine, sir, but if I may delay you for a moment, I think you should know that your daughter rode out to meet you—"

"On horseback?" Pembrooke cut in.

"Yes, sir. That's why we're concerned. The mare came back without her just before the storm hit. We were hoping she was with you. But . . ."

A mixture of anger and alarm came over Pembrooke's face as he muttered, "Damn fool girl." If she had taken the time to learn to ride when he'd offered to teach her years ago, she would have known how to control the animal. All he could do now was pray only her pride had been injured and that Christian had already found her and had taken her to shelter. Masking his worry, he gave a quick jerk of his head. "Take a couple of men with you and go look for her. And when you find her, tell her I said she'd better have a damn good excuse for what she did."

"Yes, sir," Boone replied with a nod, turning Pembrooke's stallion toward the barn.

Pembrooke stood silent a moment as he watched Boone walk away. He would have preferred going along, but with capable men like Christian and Lynn acting in his stead, he was sure he'd only get in the way. Besides, Alexandra probably wouldn't appreciate his concern. She never had in the past. Why would it be any different now? Perhaps one day soon he'd sit her down and make her explain what it was he'd done to warrant such a rebellious attitude from his own flesh and blood. Maybe one day . . . but not now. With a sigh he faced his companion. "I swear, Howard, if someone had told me how hard it was to raise children . . ." He let the comment hang as he laid a hand on the other man's shoulder and guided him toward the front door. "Let's get ourselves something strong to drink. I could sure use it and I imagine you'd enjoy it yourself after that long ride."

Pembrooke's mood darkened all the more once he and his guest were seated comfortably in the parlor with a glass of whiskey in their hands, and Beary had admitted his reason for traveling so far to see him. The explanation had been one Pembrooke would rather have not heard, even though he had suspected the seriousness behind it the second he'd seen Howard Beary standing there on the veranda. Garrett Ambrose, his henchman, Benton Wall, and three other convicts assigned to Henry Abbott had run off into the bush. Normally when that happened, the master would turn their names in to the prison superintendent, who would add them to a growing list of fugitives, and a reward for their capture and return would be posted. That would be the end of it. Not in Ambrose's case, however. Governor Darling knew of the hostility the outlaw harbored for Pembrooke and how unprotected he was living out so far. The former commissioner had to be warned, and the governor had ordered Howard Beary to see to it.

"I was told to offer any help you require, Sir Wallis," Beary disclosed. "I'm also supposed to tell you that Governor Darling wishes to meet with you." He chuckled and leaned back in his chair. "Of course we both know that it isn't a request."

Pembrooke nodded. "He didn't happen to say *when* he wants to see me, did he?"

Beary smiled wanly. "I'm to wait and ride back with you."

"All right," Pembrooke relented, "but it will have to be postponed until my daughter gets back. I need to talk to her about this. She's rather headstrong at times and I must make it clear to her how serious this is."

"I understand," Beary replied, a frown creasing his brow as he raised the glass to his lips, an expression that didn't go unseen by his companion.

"There's something else you haven't told me. What is it?"

Beary toyed with the cheroot he'd been smoking, then leaned to snuff it out in the ashtray on the table next to him. "We're not sure how it happened, and we didn't find out about it until after Ambrose had escaped, but it seems one of the members of his gang was unknowingly assigned to you."

Pembrooke felt a tightening in his chest. "What?"

"He was one of those arrested and brought to trial with Ambrose, the group your daughter's friend testified against. They were all given the same sentence and shipped here to Australia, and because of someone's carelessness, he was signed over to you."

Pembrooke's mind raced to figure out which of the men working for him had been among the group in the courthouse that day and why he hadn't made himself known before now. Was it that he had seen this day coming? Was it his plan to pretend loyalty until Ambrose escaped? Then what? Aid in Ambrose's revenge? The muscle in his jaw flexing, Pembrooke glared at his companion.

"Which one, Howard?" he snarled. "Tell me his name!"

Christian had seen the subtle change come over Alexandra the moment he had opened his eyes and caught her watching him. He had almost expected it. Still, the concern he saw cloud her eyes wasn't one of regret for what she had done. It seemed more akin to puzzlement, and it had nothing to do with him.

The fire in the hearth had cooled, and without comment, he rose from the cot, caught up his trousers, and stepped into them on his way to the fireplace. It was the excuse he needed to allow her a private moment to dress, and while he stirred the coals and added a log to the blaze, he deliberately kept his back to her. If she wanted to talk, then he'd listen. But somehow he didn't think discussing her feelings with him was utmost on her mind. Whatever was troubling her was something he guessed she would have to cope with on her own. And if his intuition was correct, it concerned her father.

"I think we can head back to the house now," he said, coming to his feet and turning around to find that she had donned only her chemise and stockings. She was sitting on the edge of the cot with the blanket drawn around her shoulders, and from the expression on her beautiful face, she appeared not to have heard him. "Alex?"

"Did you really mean what you said earlier? About it taking a special kind of man to fall in love with me?" Jade-green eyes glanced up at him.

Christian had known the instant he'd said it that sooner or later he'd regret offering his opinion in haste. Well, the time was upon him, and he hadn't any idea how to answer her.

"Could you ever fall in love with me?"

The tears he saw glistening in her eyes touched his heart, and he realized for the first time how truly tormented she was. Alexandra had managed all these years since her mother's death to masquerade as a strong-willed, unapproachable young woman with a heart of stone and courage unequaled by the best. The truth was much simpler than that. She was scared, alone, and lost, and all she really wanted was someone to tell her that he cared . . . and that someone was her father, not Christian.

"What is it you're really asking me, Alex?" he posed, leaning a shoulder against the mantel.

A single tear trickled down her cheek and she quickly brushed it away. "I'm asking if you could ever find the patience to love me."

"No, you're not," he said softly.

She blinked in surprise. "I'm not?"

He shook his head. "No. You're not."

"Then what is it I'm asking?"

He wondered how she would react to the truth and decided it was worth finding out. In her own way she was petitioning his help. "You're asking me if I think your father still loves you." She started to contradict the claim, and he rushed on before she could. "You're afraid he'll abandon you if he ever learns what happened here between us. I guarantee you he'll never hear of it from me. But more than that, I suspect you're wondering why you allowed it to go that far. You're asking yourself if it was something you really wanted or if, in some strange way, it was an act of rebellion, of revenge for what he did to your mother."

She started to shake her head and flatly discredit the notion, when he raised a hand and silenced her.

"Alex, you can't even begin to question someone else's feelings until you're sure of your own. Nor can you damn someone else's actions without knowing the whole story. You owe your father that much."

The years of hurt she'd embraced as her only excuse for

her behavior flared up again. "I owe it to him to stand still
while he tells me why he was unfaithful to his wife? Why?
To ease his own conscience and confirm what I've suspected
all along?" Angry, she pushed herself up, balanced her weight
on her good ankle, and reached for her petticoats.

"Suspected?" he repeated, surprised that he hadn't questioned the origin of her proof the first time she'd mentioned
it. "You mean you have no facts to back it up?"

She awkwardly pulled on the yards of gathered white lace
and cotton and secured the waist. "Of course I have proof.
If we ever return to England, I'll show it to you. It's clearly
marked with a gray headstone."

"You mean your mother told you."

"Of course not!" she snapped, grabbing for her dress. "That
wasn't the sort of thing a mother tells her fourteen-year-old
daughter."

"Alex," he sighed, pushing away from the hearth. "Are you
telling me you've spent these past years hating and blaming
your father for something you *think* he did?"

Alexandra could almost hear the rest of his thoughts and she
didn't approve of how he'd obviously taken sides . . . and not
with her. Men! she fumed. They were all the same . . . always
sticking up for each other. Well, let him. She didn't care. She
finished buttoning her dress and stepped into her right shoe,
certain it would be too painful to wear the other one. With her
left shoe held in her hand, she started toward the door.

"Why won't you answer my question?"

The query brought her to an awkward halt. Hopping on one
foot, she pressed a hand against the wall for support and turned
back to look at him. "Why should I?" she demanded. "I know
what you'll say if I do. You'll tell me I'm not being fair. Then
I'll have to ask you how you could possibly know one way or
the other. I'll ask you to explain what other reason my mother
would have to kill herself. Why my father was never home,
and what it was I heard them arguing about night after night.
So until you have all the facts, Mr. Page, don't you *dare* tell
me I'm not being fair."

"You're not," he shot back, closing the distance between
them in a few long strides. "You're not being fair to *your-*

self. What if you've been wrong all this time? You've already admitted your mother wouldn't discuss her problems with you. Maybe she didn't kill herself. Maybe it was an accident. You said they fought. Perhaps she only wanted to get away, to be by herself for a while, and—"

"Then why did she leave a note?"

"A note?" he echoed, frowning. "What kind of note?"

"A farewell."

"Did you read it?"

She laughed harshly. "Of course not. It was for Father."

"Then—"

"I heard him telling a friend about it. I heard him say how she'd still be alive if it weren't for him. He blamed himself, Christian, and so do I." In a rage, she seized the door latch and swung the portal open, only to have him stop its full arc midway when he caught the edge against his opened palm. "I'm through talking about it, Christian."

"With me, yes. But until you've said all this to your father, you'll never be at peace. You'll never find it in your heart to trust and you'll spend your days alone. Talk to him, Alex. Scream at him if you must, but have it out . . . now, before another day of your life slips away."

The sound of racing hoofbeats cut short her reply. Glancing out through the half-opened door, she saw Lynn Boone and two others riding toward the cabin.

"I'd appreciate it if you'd finish getting dressed. Mr. Boone's coming, and I'd rather he not guess by looking at you what just went on here." The color of her eyes had turned hard and flinty when she looked back at him, a silent announcement that their conversation was over.

Yielding to her wish, Christian stepped back and donned his stockings and shoes, and retrieved a fresh shirt from the drawer where others were stored. Slipping into it, he turned to escort Alexandra from the cabin and to instruct Lynn Boone to take Miss Pembrooke home while he buried Patches under a eucalyptus tree nearby. Once he had placed her on the back of the horse behind Boone, he stood in the doorway of the cabin watching the group ride away, amazed at how the passion the two of them had shared only a short while before had

faded so completely . . . as if it had never even existed. Per
haps it hadn't for Alexandra, he silently concluded, and per
haps she would never again speak of what they had shared
but for him. . . .

"Yes, Alexandra," he whispered, his gaze locked on the
shapely figure moving away from him, her long dark hair
flowing out behind her, "I could easily fall in love with
you."

There were times when Christian cursed his ability to sense
trouble or that something was amiss. So often it came to in
terrupt pleasant thoughts and spoil his mood. This was jus
such a time as he reined his horse to a trot and studied the
faces of the men watching his arrival from the veranda. Lynn
Boone seemed to be having difficulty with his emotions as he
frowned back at Christian with a look of disbelief. Franklin
Reber and Arthur Weiland, two men Christian had taught
how to use carpentry tools and to use them well, appeared
dismayed and somewhat reluctant to be included in the group
who waited for him. Yet their presence wasn't what triggered
an alarm in him as much as the one who stood ahead of
them. The expression in Wallis Pembrooke's eyes was dark
and filled with rage, and had he been alone, Christian would
have guessed the man had drawn his own conclusions once
he'd learned where his daughter had waited out the storm and
with whom. Christian couldn't blame him for that, if that were
the case. His instincts warned him that it wasn't. Something
else bothered Pembrooke, something of such magnitude that
Christian could only guess it had to do with the stranger at
Pembrooke's side. Realizing that he was about to ride into the
middle of it without any protection, he focused his attention
on the one man who posed the largest threat.

"Christian," Pembrooke stiffly greeted him, his nostrils
flared slightly and his jaw tight. "I'd like you to meet a friend
of mine. His name is Howard Beary and he's brought a rather
frightening bit of news."

Christian hesitated a moment before dismounting. Once he
had, Lynn Boone and Franklin Reber stepped off the porch
and moved to the side and in back of him.

"He tells me that Garrett Ambrose and his cohort, Benton Wall, have decided on a change of scenery." He cocked a brow at Christian and asked, "Those names aren't familiar to you, are they?"

Christian knew the instant Pembrooke posed the question that Beary had also included the names of the rest of Ambrose's gang shipped to Australia. There was no sense in denying it. He simply would have preferred telling the man on his own rather than having been forced into it. What made it worse was how contrived the story would sound if he were to tell Pembrooke the truth just then. Instead, he remained silent, certain he would have to allow Pembrooke the time to calm down before he dared explain.

"Why, Christian?" Pembrooke asked, a hint of disappointment etching his tone. "I thought you and I . . . " He paused a moment to harden his feelings again. "It was all a ruse, wasn't it? You knew from the start what Ambrose was planning. All you had to do was wait." He looked at Boone and jerked his head. "He's to be shackled and locked in the tool shed until I can decide what to do with him. And post a guard. If Ambrose is out there somewhere, he'll have one less man to help him in his scheme."

A steely grip tightened around Christian's right arm as Reber took hold of him and shoved him away from the house. Boone was a little more hesitant to comply . . . for a couple of reasons. He knew that even two men against one was no match for Christian Page if that one decided he didn't want to go somewhere. But more importantly, Boone was having trouble believing Pembrooke's accusations against the man. Maybe Christian *had* been associated with Ambrose at one time. But that didn't mean he couldn't change. Boone liked and respected Christian Page, and he couldn't ignore those feelings. He'd do as Pembrooke ordered, but once everything had settled down, Boone planned to ask Christian himself.

Locked in her room, Alexandra sat in the rocker by the hearth absently watching the flickering fire. The chill that embraced her had little to do with the temperature of the room; its cause was the whirlwind of emotions that coursed through her. Her lower lip would quiver and she could feel tears forming in her eyes, when at the same instant a smile would touch her mouth and a rosy blush would warm her face. Close behind came anger and the strong desire to smash something against the floor; then would appear the image of Christian, her father, and finally the bloodied body of a little dog whose friendship had been unconditional. Perhaps she was only feeling sorry for herself—just as Christian had once told her—but now that she'd had time to consider her life, it seemed she was forever pushing things away. Was it possible she did so unknowingly, that it was her way of building a wall around her to keep out the hurt? And was that same wall closing in on her? Was it cutting off her very breath?

A knock on her door interrupted her musings. Before she could call out for the visitor to identify himself, her father's voice asked permission to speak with her before he left for Sydney. He had a matter to discuss with her, he said, one that couldn't wait until he returned. It concerned her safety and he wouldn't feel good about leaving until he was assured she understood its importance. Gingerly stepping on her sore ankle, she hobbled to the door and freed the latch.

"Lynn told me about Patches and what nearly happened to you, child," he softly confessed. "I thank God you're all right."

Tears tightened the muscles in her throat, and rather than tell him that God had nothing to do with it, she turned away from him and limped back to the rocker. If God had really been there, He would have let her die instead of Patches.

Assuming her silence concerned her feelings about the terrifying run-in she'd had with the dingos, Pembrooke decided it was best to drop the subject. What he had to say was more important. Soothing her jangled nerves would have to wait.

"You remember Howard Beary, don't you, child?"

She didn't, but she nodded anyway, hoping he'd leave her alone that much sooner.

"The governor sent him here with some distressing news." He moved to sit down on the foot of her bed. He wasn't sure how she'd react once he told her about Ambrose, and he wanted to be close by should she panic. "I assure you we're all perfectly safe as long as we stay close to the house. And I've asked Lynn to keep an eye on you. He'll be given a gun—"

"A gun?" she repeated, a puzzled frown on her face. "Whatever for?"

Pembrooke took a deep breath and exhaled slowly, not quite sure how to put it without being blunt. "Garrett Ambrose and one of his men have run off. The police are out looking for them, but Australia's a big country with lots of places to hide."

"And?" she nervously pressed, already sensing the rest of his story.

"Governor Darling's afraid Ambrose will come after me."

And me! she inwardly screamed. Afraid he'd see more in her expression than concern for him, she forced herself to study the fire again while she recalled the conversation she'd had with Christian about the outlaw. He'd claimed that Ambrose wanted to kill him for his part in Garrett's arrest. Ambrose would want to kill her because she had been the one to tell the authorities where to find him, and he'd want revenge against her father for being the man who arrested him. They were all in danger, and a single gun wouldn't do anyone any good.

"I honestly don't think Garrett Ambrose is that stupid," she heard her father calmly declare. "Or that interested in revenge. If I learned one thing about the man, it's that he enjoys his freedom, fine clothes, and all the money he can steal. He isn't about to go traipsing around the bush eating wild game and sleeping on the cold ground, not if he can help it. And he certainly won't get his hands dirty by killing me. He'll order his men to do it. And that's where he has a problem." He rambled on as if he were thinking out loud rather than discussing the issue with his daughter. "Every member of the gang shipped here to Australia can be accounted for. All of them except for his cohort Wall are under close guard. They've been taken off the work detail and locked up. They'll be of no help to him."

"*All* of them?" she asked weakly without looking at him. Did that mean he wasn't aware of Christian? But how could that be? She knew he hadn't recognized Christian from the start, but if Governor Darling had a list, then—

"Alexandra."

There was a tenseness in his tone, one that drew her gaze. The look on his handsome face, the frown that distorted his brow and shadowed his green eyes, spoke a million words, and Alexandra's worry turned away from herself.

"What is it, Papa?" she asked guardedly, praying her instincts were wrong.

The frown deepened, and when it appeared he was having difficulty in speaking his mind, Alexandra urged him to reply with a second query. Still he chose not to answer right away. Instead, he rose and went to the window to look outside. Several moments passed.

"It's hard for me to accept how wrong I was about him," he began, his voice low. "I've always taken pride in being able to guess a man's character just by the way he moves or speaks, by the look in his eyes. Christian had me totally fooled."

"Christian?" she whispered, wondering if her father could hear the thunderous pounding of her heart.

"He's one of them."

Alexandra gulped down the knot that was beginning to strangle her and forced air into her lungs. "Them?" she hesitantly repeated.

"One of Ambrose's gang," he replied, glancing briefly at her before studying the scenery beyond the window again. "Howard says no one knows for sure how it happened, but instead of being assigned to government labor, Christian was given to me. I should have suspected something at the time, I suppose, but I was desperate to have a carpenter." He sighed deeply and finished, "It doesn't matter now, anyway. And luckily he was found out before he could do anything. He won't be causing us any problems."

Alexandra felt the icy fingers of an imaginary hand running down her spine. "Why not, Papa?" she asked, dreading his response.

"I had Mr. Boone shackle him and lock him up in the tool shed. Reber's keeping an eye on him until I can decide what to do next." Plagued by his disappointment in a man he'd come to respect, Pembrooke failed to see how his answer had affected Alexandra. He might have questioned the soft smile on her lips, the look of relief in her eyes, and how the stiffness left her tense frame if he had. "I hate to see a man bound in irons day and night—it's a cruel punishment—but I need him. At least until he finishes the house. Then . . . " His voice trailed off.

"Papa," his daughter called to him and he turned to see her gingerly coming to her feet. "I don't think I have the right to question your judgment, since you know more about criminals than I do, but why do you think you have to 'do' anything with Chris—Mr. Page? I don't believe he's a threat. After all, he just saved my life. And look at all he's done for you. Without him—"

"I know," he cut in with one hand raised. "I've been reminding myself of that ever since Howard told me who Christian was. And I agree he's been more than helpful. That's what bothers me. I just can't take the chance." He squared his shoulders as if he'd made a decision and was pleased with it, and moved to make his exit. At the door he paused. "I'm going to Sydney to meet with the governor about this. When I get back, I'll have a long talk with Christian. Until then, he's to stay where he is." He gave her a stern look. "And so are you. As long as you stay close to the house and to Lynn, I won't worry about your safety as I would if I took you along. We'd be open targets on the road. So no more riding out alone. You hear?"

"Yes, Papa."

He turned to leave.

"Papa?"

"Yes, child?" he replied, his hand on the knob and his tall figure framed in the doorway.

"I think you're wrong about Christian Page."

He stared at her for a long moment, noticing a change in her that he hadn't seen before, but not certain what it was. "I hope I am, daughter," he confessed. "I really hope I am."

By nightfall the swelling in Alexandra's ankle had gone down and it bothered her only a little to step on it. Her father, Howard Beary, and two of the laborers armed with muskets and pistols had left shortly after noon, and the work around the place had resumed as usual . . . with one very visible difference. No one said anything more than was necessary and Alexandra guessed it was for two reasons. Though none of the men there knew Garrett Ambrose, they feared his coming and wondered if his revenge would extend to them. Their silence resulted in the heavily felt absence of the man they had all grown to admire and look to as their leader. Though criminals themselves, none of them could believe Christian Page wished Pembrooke any harm, Lynn Boone most of all. If Christian had wanted the man dead, all he would have had to do was point a finger at him.

"What do you mean?" Harvey Smith asked as Boone related his opinion over the dinner table.

"Like this," Boone explained as he raised his hand near Smith's face. With a quick jab, Boone's index finger came within a hair's breadth of Smith's right eye.

"Hey!" Smith objected, jerking back. "You nearly put my eye out!"

"Christian would have done more than that," Boone guaranteed with a sly smile as he reached for his cup and raised it to his mouth. "He would have shoved it in so far, it would have penetrated your brain and killed you like *that*." A sharp snap of his fingers made everyone jump.

"Kung fu," Francis Taylor supplied. "A Chinese form of fighting. The dance of death, I've heard some call it."

"You mean *that's* what Christian was doin' every night after we'd turn in?" Richard Dolter asked. "Practicin' kung fu?"

Lynn Boone nodded.

"He ever kill anybody?" Smith asked timidly.

Boone shrugged. "I asked him one time, and he gave me a vague answer. It's not something the Chinese brag about."

"He's not Chinese," Smith jeered.

"He's as close as any of us will ever come. And I'll tell ya something else," Boone warned, leaning in on his elbows. "If Christian Page was out to harm ol' man Pembrooke, he wouldn't have waited this long. He would have started by eliminating us . . . one at a time."

"Us?" three of the men sitting at the table chorused.

"He'd kill you with one blow, then cart you off and bury the body. To Pembrooke it would look like you ran off. Pretty soon there'd be no one left but Pembrooke and his daughter. Now, there's what? Ten, twelve of us?"

"Eleven countin' Smith here," Dolter provided with a jerk of his thumb Harvey Smith's way.

"Thirteen, if ya count the cook and Miss Pembrooke's maid," Taylor added.

"All right, thirteen. One a night . . . " Boone squinted his eyes as he calculated the figures. "Two weeks, that's all the time it would have taken him."

"Not necessarily," Taylor corrected.

All eyes turned his way.

"Before the sheep came, every one of us slept right here under the same roof. If Mr. Page had wanted us dead, he would have killed us in our sleep . . . all at the same time."

"Sweet Mother of God," Merlin Hull, a short, stocky little man, proclaimed. "I'm glad he's locked up now. Otherwise I wouldn't sleep a wink."

"That's the point Lynn's tryin' to make, you fool," Dolter spoke up. "Christian doesn't mean us any harm. None of us! Not even Sir Wallis."

The others seemed to agree, but Harvey Smith deduced it wouldn't include him. If *any* of them knew his reason for being there, they'd all turn on him. He was the outsider in this group, and their loyalty obviously belonged to Christian Page. Smith would have to be extra careful around the men from now on, and especially where Mr. Page was concerned.

"So what are we to do, Lynn?" Taylor asked. "Sit by and let Sir Wallis go on thinking Christian's the enemy?"

"If you're asking if we can change his mind, no, we can't. Christian will have to do that. But we can let Sir Wallis know that we don't agree with him. At least, I don't."

"I think we all feel as you do, Lynn," Dolter guessed. "I also happen to think we *can* change Pembrooke's mind if we put our heads together and come up with a plan. Of course we'll have to talk it over with Christian first."

"How do you figure that?" Taylor queried.

"Well, it's rather obvious Pembrooke has his own doubts about his decision that Christian is still working with this Ambrose fellow or he would have taken him back to Sydney with him."

"Yeah," Merlin Hull agreed. "I never thought of it 'til you

mentioned it, but that's true. If Pembrooke was really afraid of Christian, he would have hauled him back to the prison instead of leaving him here. But where does that leave us?"

"Well, we've heard one side of the story," Dolter advised. "I suggest we hear Christian's side of it."

"Side of what?" Hull questioned. "I don't understand."

"We hear his reason for joining Ambrose's gang, and how he feels about the man."

"That's easy," Taylor snorted. "He's a thief by trade, and joining up offered him an excellent way to practice his skills."

"No, he isn't," Boone cut in. "Christian's a carpenter . . . or he was at one time. And how do you explain his knowledge of raising sheep? He certainly didn't learn that by hanging around Garrett Ambrose."

"That's why you have to talk to him, Lynn," Dolter instructed.

"Me?" It wasn't that he disagreed. It just surprised him to hear Dolter take such a positive stand.

"Yes, you. You're the only one he'll talk to. 'Course that doesn't guarantee he'll open up about this, but I think if you remind him that he could be sent back to prison. . . "

Boone pushed away from the table and stood. "I'll tell him. But there's something else about Christian Page you should know. If he doesn't want to talk, he won't . . . no matter how hard I press him."

"Thomas?" Alexandra called once she had stepped into the kitchen and saw the man about to leave by the back door, a tray balanced in his hands. "Would that be for Mr. Page?"

"Yes, Miss Alexandra, it is."

Limping slightly, she hurried across the room to him. "If you don't mind, I'd like to take it to him."

"But Miss Alexandra—" he objected.

She waved off his concern and took the tray from him. "I'll be all right. He's locked up in the shed and his ankles are shackled. Besides, Mr. Reber is standing guard, isn't he? It won't be as if I'll be alone with him," she assured him, though she knew that was exactly what she had planned. She smiled sweetly at him and slid out the door as she called back over her shoulder, "And don't worry about Papa. If he finds out I did this, I'll take full responsibility."

The sun was just beginning to disappear over the horizon as Alexandra made her way toward the tool shed. Long shadows laced the path she took, and although the evening was quite warm, the sense that danger lurked somewhere close by made her shiver. She ignored the sensation by telling herself that she would continue to feel that way—even if Ambrose were a hundred miles north—until the bandit was apprehended again . . . or until Christian had killed him. The latter notion hurried her step. It was something she needed to discuss with him.

She had made up her mind shortly after talking with her father that the only solution to their problem was Christian. She knew her father wouldn't understand her reasoning nor would the other men if she were to confide in them. How could they, when she wasn't totally convinced the story he'd told her was true? It was logical. But then he'd had a long time to fit the pieces together before trying them out on her. Common sense begged her to reconsider her idea, while instinct told her she was right in trusting Christian. She had to be, otherwise she wouldn't have let him make love to her.

The silent battle that raged inside her head dulled her awareness to the sounds and movements going on around her. She had set her focus on the dark outline of the tool shed some thirty feet ahead of her and missed both the rustle of leaves and the swaying branches of a nearby scrub. By the time she felt the presence of someone behind her, a huge hand had come around, grabbed her mouth, and stifled any chance she might have had to scream. The tray she was carrying clattered against the ground, and a second later the shadows swallowed up the large figure of a man and the struggling captive he held imprisoned in his arms.

·❧| *Chapter Seventeen* |❧·

"FRANKLIN," LYNN BOONE SAID ONCE REBER HEARD HIM COMing and glanced up with the musket pointed in his direction. "I'm here to relieve you before your supper gets cold."

"Thanks," the other replied as he propped the long-barreled weapon against the wall of the tool shed. "I was beginning to wonder if you'd forgotten me." He jerked his head to the right, indicating the prisoner he guarded. "What about him? He gonna get fed?"

Boone glanced back toward the house and shrugged. "I would imagine Thomas will bring him something to eat sooner or later."

Reber nodded. "You got the night watch?"

"I suppose," Boone admitted, "since nobody volunteered." He grinned lazily at his companion. "Or did you want it?"

Reber quickly declined. "Not me, friend, but thanks just the same." Smiling, he reached up and squeezed Boone's shoulder. "Maybe next time. But for now, he's all yours."

The good-natured façade Lynn Boone had presented faded the instant Reber turned and walked away. "I was hoping you'd say that," he whispered, waiting until the man had moved out of sight before he turned and lifted the bar that held the door of the tool shed tightly closed.

"Christian?" he called, squinting his eyes in an effort to see through the darkness that filled the entire space. "You still in there or did you use some of that fancy stuff of yours and slip out through a crack in the wall?" He only joked, but when Christian didn't answer him, Boone fleetingly wondered if perhaps he'd underestimated his friend.

"Christian?" he called again, reaching for the lantern he saw sitting on the ground near him. Touching a match to its wick, he held the lamp high and moved into the doorway. Flickering amber light filled the small square and instantly revealed the broken shackles lying in the middle of the dirt floor. "Ah, Christian," he moaned, taking a step forward.

Lamplight gleamed in the pale blue eyes of the man watching his foe enter the shed from beneath him. With his arms and legs spread wide against the rafters of the small building, Christian held himself easily in place, waiting for Boone to clear the doorway enough for him to drop down silently behind him. Christian had feared at first that Boone, too, had turned against him. The disappointment he'd heard in the man's voice just now proved that he hadn't; Boone had merely needed some time to sort out his thoughts before making a decision. Christian was glad Lynn Boone had chosen logic over what to others seemed the obvious choice. If Garrett Ambrose was to be stopped, Christian would need all the help he could get.

Hanging suspended from the ceiling, Christian waited until his friend had stepped out from under him and further into the room before he stealthily lowered himself down, landing noiselessly at Boone's back. Wishing him no harm yet knowing he would have to hold Boone at a disadvantage for a few minutes while they talked, he shot out a hand, slid it to the inside of Boone's arm, and grabbed the man's thumb. Pulling back, he bent Boone's wrist and fingers in a paralyzing grip that weakened the big man's knees, brought tears to his eyes, and nearly sent the lantern crashing to the floor before Christian could stop its descent.

"Good God, Christian," Boone rasped. "You don't have to break my hand. I came here to talk, that's all. Please—let go!"

"Only if you give your word not to try anything," Christian offered.

"Try anything?" Boone echoed, grimacing in pain. "What do you think I am? Crazy? I've told you before that I'd learned my lesson when it comes to kung fu. If I had a musket and I was standing twenty feet away, I *might* stand a chance of winning. But even that's doubtful. Please, Christian, let go.

I think I heard something snap."

A soft smile tugged at the corners of Christian's mouth. If he'd wanted to break one of the bones in Boone's hand, he would have done it by now, and he was sure his friend knew it. Releasing his grip, he stepped away and set the lantern on the workbench beside him.

"Damn," Boone snorted as he rubbed his sore hand. "Did ya have to get so physical? You could have just threatened me. I'm not stupid, you know." He scowled at the shackles near his feet. "And how, pray tell, did you get out of those?"

Christian grinned. "Remind me later and I'll show you. Right now, I have to be going."

"Going?" Boone repeated as he opened and closed his fingers to make sure they still worked. "Where?"

"Despite what Pembrooke thinks, I'm going after Ambrose. He's got to be stopped before he does someone harm."

"Yeah, well, Pembrooke's alone in his thinking. None of the rest of us feel you should be locked up in here." He glanced at the shackles again and laughed. "As if it would make a difference what anyone thought." Serious again, he turned his gaze back on his companion. "What I need to know is why: why you were involved with Ambrose in the first place; why you never said anything to anybody, most of all to Pembrooke; and why you think you have to go after him all alone . . . or at all. The police are looking for him, and they'll catch him sooner or later. You'd be doing Pembrooke more good by staying here and keeping an eye on him and his daughter."

Christian knew it was time he trusted someone. And who better to trust than Lynn Boone? Nodding at the stool behind his friend, Christian silently invited the man to sit down, while Christian crossed his ankles and lowered himself to the floor. Time wouldn't allow him to reveal every detail of his past, only those facts that were important to the telling of his story. He included the particulars concerning his uncle and nephew and where he'd been at the time it all took place. He told Boone about Lewis Rhomberg, how Rhomberg had helped Christian infiltrate the Ambrose gang, and that because of the risk Christian was taking, only the two of them would know that he

was actually working for the Crown or, more specifically, Sir
Wallis Pembrooke. He would have preferred leaving out the
part about Alexandra, but he also knew the tale wouldn't make
much sense without it. When he had finished telling it all, he
concluded by stating that it was his opinion Garrett Ambrose
was more interested in Christian than he was in Pembrooke or
his daughter.

"So, by escaping, you're hoping to draw him away from
here?" Boone surmised.

Christian nodded.

"What if he kills you? Then what? Don't you suppose he'll
just come after Miss Pembrooke and then her father purely out
of spite? Christian, if I could choose anybody to stand beside
in a fight, it would be you. You've got more talent in one
hand than Ambrose could possibly have in his whole body,
but it won't do you an ounce of good if you're outnumbered.
A man can only do so much."

Laughter, a rare pleasure for Christian, rumbled in his chest.
"I've never been given a compliment and had it taken away so
quickly in my whole life. But thank you anyway." He pushed
himself to his feet. "I don't intend to get myself killed, Lynn.
Nor do I plan on allowing Ambrose the chance to see me, let
alone know I'm anywhere around. If you and ten others had
come into this shed a few minutes ago, I would have stayed
where I was and the lot of you would have thought I'd already
escaped. Numbers mean nothing, Lynn, if you're patient and
know what to do. Surprise is the key. Garrett Ambrose won't
even hear me coming."

"I don't like it, Christian," Boone admitted, coming to his
feet. "I think you're asking for more than you can handle. I
want to go along."

Christian shook his head. "You can do me more good
by staying here and watching out for Alexandra. Once I've
finished with Ambrose, I'll come back and have a talk with
Pembrooke. Only then will he be willing to listen."

The mention of the daughter's name provoked Boone. "I
hope I'm allowed to be present. I truly want to hear Miss
Alexandra's explanation for keeping all of this a secret."

"She had her reasons, Lynn. We should respect them."

Boone snorted. "You're a bigger man than I, Christian Page, if you really believe that."

Christian was about to confess that at one time he had been angry enough with her that he'd considered grabbing her by the hair and dragging her to her father, when his thoughts were interrupted by Thomas's frantic cry for assistance.

"Mr. Boone! Anybody! Come quick!" the cook shouted, causing both men to bolt through the door of the tool shed at practically the same time.

"What is it, Thomas?" Boone called out as he and Christian raced toward him.

"Oh, God . . . oh, God," he moaned, his small frame shaking as he wrung his hands and stared down at the ground in front of him. "I never should have let her go. I knew something would happen."

"Who?" Boone demanded. "Go where?"

His questions were answered the moment he spotted the silver tray and spilled food lying in the grass at Thomas's feet. He stumbled to a halt, his body rigid and his heart pounding in his chest. Thomas didn't have to explain. The evidence was quite clear. Garrett Ambrose had made his first move.

"What do we do, Christian?" Boone asked as he watched his friend kneel and examine the imprints in the dewy grass.

"You're to do nothing," Christian instructed, stripping his feet of the shoes and stockings he wore. "Whoever took her will be expecting you to come after her. He'll be counting on it, and he'll be counting on your making a lot of noise in the process. That's why I have to go alone. By the time he realizes I'm there, it will be too late."

"All right," Boone called after him when Christian jumped to his feet and sprinted off across the moonlit meadow. "But only an hour. I'm giving you an hour, Christian, and then the rest of us are coming. You hear me?"

Christian ran until his lungs burned. Near a cluster of scrubs he paused to catch his breath and study the tracks he followed. Whoever had Alexandra was obviously having trouble with her. The footprints showed where she had to be dragged most of the way, and that at one point she had nearly escaped her captor when the smaller set of indentations made a turn and started back the way they had come. Her freedom hadn't lasted long, however, and from the absence of the delicate imprints, Christian guessed the man was carrying her. He forced himself not to consider the possibility that Alexandra hung draped over the man's shoulder unconscious, since worrying about her welfare at the moment would only distract him, and distractions result in mistakes. This was one time he couldn't afford to make a mistake.

The flat plane of the meadow disappeared over the moon-lit horizon. Once Christian had leaped the fence that marked the end of Pembrooke's property and the beginning of Davis Pleasanton's and he stood on the knoll overlooking the grass-lands stretching out in front of him, he paused long enough to evaluate the situation. Several hundred yards ahead of him, he spotted the dark shape of a man carrying someone over his shoulder, and his heart tightened with the vision. They were alone, but the lack of greenery between him and his goal presented a problem. All the man would have to do was turn and look back just once, and Alexandra's life would be in more danger than it already was.

The sharp pain where Benton Wall's shoulder pressed against Alexandra's stomach made her head spin. She wanted to cry out and beg him to put her down, but the gag in her mouth prevented it. She would have liked clubbing her fists against his broad back, but he had tied her hands behind her. Other than kicking her feet, there was little else she could do to save herself . . . except to pray that Thomas hadn't waited very long to come looking for her, and that Lynn Boone was smart enough to send Christian after her.

Christian.

The name, the very thought of him made her heart ache. None of this would be happening if it weren't for her. It was her fault she was at the inn that night. It was her doing that got Ambrose and his men captured. She was the reason why Christian had been shipped to Australia, and why Garrett Ambrose wanted revenge. Christian had been shackled and locked up in the tool shed because of her, and now the chances were very strong that he'd have to risk his life to save her . . . again.

Tears welled in her eyes. Squeezing them shut, she tried to force herself to think on the matter at hand. Benton Wall might be big and strong, but his bulk would only slow him down if she were given enough of a head start. Even with her sore ankle, she was sure she could outrun him. The difficulty came in obtaining the chance before he'd taken her to the place she guessed he was to meet with Garrett Ambrose. How far away was that? A league? Two? A whole night's journey? Or just over the next hill?

Using all the strength she had in her upper body, she pulled herself up high enough to look back in the direction they had come. It was too long a distance for her to run without stopping to rest for a moment, and with no trees or scrubs to hide in along the way, she'd have to rely on her endurance to see her home safely again. At the moment, however, that wasn't her greatest concern. If Wall continued to carry her, worrying about how long she could run without a break wouldn't matter. Maybe . . . if she wriggled around enough. . . .

"You promised him you'd wait an hour, Lynn," Dolter reminded his friend as the group of them saddled horses and prepared to take up the chase. "It's hardly been half that time."

"So I've changed my mind," Boone snarled, yanking hard on the cinch. "You seem to forget that Sir Wallis left *me* in charge, and I not only allowed his daughter to be kidnapped, but I turned Christian loose. If anything goes wrong, I'll be the one he blames." His frown deepened. "Besides, standing around doing nothing is grating on my nerves." He flipped the stirrup down, slid his foot into it, and grabbed the saddle horn. "Wait here if you think you should, but I'm going after them." He swung a long leg over the saddle, gripped the reins in one hand, and reached for the musket Thomas held up to him. "In fact, it's probably wise someone does stay behind . . . in case drawing us away from the house was a part of the plan." His gaze scanned the crowd of men around him. "Smith. You know how to handle a gun?"

"Yes, sir," Harvey Smith quickly assured him. This was the chance he'd been waiting for, and he wasn't about to let it slip by. "I can take the eye out of a rabbit at—"

"Fine. You stay with Thomas and make sure nothing happens to Felice," Boone ordered. "As for the rest of you, do what you think is right, but let me remind you that if this Ambrose character succeeds in doing whatever it is he has in mind for Sir Wallis and his daughter, we'll be sent back to Sydney and assigned to another master. I don't think I have to tell you that we might not be so lucky next time. Working for Pembrooke has been fairly easy. But you decide." Jerking on the reins, he spun the horse around and kicked his heels in the animal's flanks, not bothering to wait for the rest of the men as they scrambled to follow after him.

"Which way do you think they're headed?" Dolter asked a few minutes later as the group of them waited for Boone to remount. "You know this area better than any of us."

Boone frowned. Perhaps he did know the area better than any of the other men, but he'd had no experience whatsoever in tracking someone. The proof of it was right there in front of him. He didn't want to say anything out loud, but it appeared to him that there were only two sets of prints, and while one moved straight ahead, the other jutted off to the left. Could it mean Miss Pembrooke had gotten free of her captor? He mentally shook off that notion. If she had, she would have run for home and they would have met up with her before now. That left the only other alternative: she was being carried for some reason—and Boone chose not to speculate on why.

His second observation bothered him even more than the first. Why had Christian chosen to veer away from the trail? Was it possible that this was the chance he'd been waiting for? Had the story he told been a lie, a way to win Boone's trust long enough for him to get away before it was discovered? Boone didn't want to believe that, and a gnawing in his gut told him that he shouldn't. Yet. . . .

"Lynn? What's wrong?" Dolter pressed, sensing the man was hiding something.

"We'll have to split up," he announced as he came to his feet and swung back up into the saddle. "You take four of the men and head north toward the woods. And don't waste any time. You'll lose them if they get there first."

"But what about you?" Dolter asked.

"I'll take the rest of the men and go this way." He nodded to his left. "For some reason Christian isn't following them anymore, and since I can't tell whose tracks are whose, we won't know who we're chasing until we catch up to them. And remember, all of you, you're not to kill the man who took Miss Pembrooke if you can help it. He's got some explaining to do and he can't do it if he's dead. Understand?"

Everyone agreed, and without further comment the two groups parted.

With the stealth and cunning of a panther Christian stalked his prey, keeping low to the ground and its tall grasses as he made his way forward. Up ahead a few hundred yards stood a cluster of cabbage-tree palms and blackboy trees, just the kind of cover he needed to work in closer to Alexandra and her abductor without being discovered. Although Christian hadn't yet seen the man's face, he was fairly certain of his identity. His size alone gave it away. And his limp confirmed it. Who other than Benton Wall would be loyal enough to Ambrose to risk his life for the sake of revenge?

In the ashen glow of the moon, Christian could see that Alexandra was bound and gagged. It would be a lot simpler for him if her hands were free and she walked alongside the man. One kick to the back of Wall's knees would separate him from his captive, and put her out of harm's way in case Wall was carrying a pistol. But she was draped over his shoulder and that created a problem.

Well, we'll just have to fix that, Christian thought with a devilish smile as he slipped, unnoticed, into the shadow of the trees.

Benton Wall may never have verbally questioned Garrett Ambrose's orders, but there were plenty of times he wondered about them. This was one of those times. He'd been told to steal into the Pembrooke home and kidnap Miss Pembrooke only if he was sure no one would see him. Then he was to

bring her to their prearranged meeting place. He had wanted
to ask his partner's reason for such a venture, since they had
been paid not to cause either father or daughter any harm, but
as always he'd simply done as he'd been told without saying
a word. After all, Ambrose had to know what he was doing.
Yet the further he traveled, the more he doubted Ambrose's
judgment.

Ever since his run-in with Christian Page those many months
ago, Wall's knee had bothered him. It ached constantly, and
there were some mornings when it was too stiff to move. The
extra weight he was carrying over his shoulder certainly didn't
help, and even though Ambrose had told him not to waste any
time in getting back to camp, he figured a short break would
do more good than harm. Limping to an awkward halt, he balanced himself on his left foot and deposited Alexandra on the
ground. He was about to warn her not to try anything, when the
distant pounding of horses' hooves behind them drew his attention. A half-dozen men, riding at full gallop, had crested the
last knoll and were bearing down on them at breakneck speed.

Cursing, he grabbed for Alexandra. If they wanted him,
they'd have to go through the woman to do it!

Then, before he could turn and focus his eyes, a sudden
movement to his right pricked all of his senses. The others
had only been a decoy. The real danger was close at hand.
Whirling, he pulled his captive toward him, but not in time to
shield himself as the full force of the blow struck him squarely
in the shoulder and hurled him backward to the ground.

Christian had planted the heels of both feet against Wall's
huge torso after he had catapulted himself through the air. The
abrupt contact dropped them both, and while Wall struggled
to rise, Christian rolled and came back up on his feet. Reaching for Alexandra, he pulled her behind him for protection.
Then, once he'd balanced his weight evenly on both legs with
his knees flexed slightly, he held his half-closed fists close to
his body, ready to attack again should Benton Wall be foolish
enough to think he stood a chance.

In obvious pain, the giant clutched his arm tightly as he
rocked back and forth and tried to sit up. The arrival of the men
on horseback and the sight of a second group cutting across

the meadow toward him, however, changed his mind about defending himself, since he was already having trouble holding his own against a single adversary. With a surrendering shake of his head, he fell back on his elbow and stared up at the one and only man Benton Wall had come to respect.

"You win, Page," he yielded with a mocking smirk. "As if there was ever any doubt." He shifted his gaze to the last party of men to join the ruckus, and added, "Apparently your friends had their doubts or they wouldn't have felt it was necessary to come along. Haven't they ever seen you in action?"

A brief smile parted Christian's lips as he relaxed his stance and turned to untie the gag from around Alexandra's mouth. "Oh, they had their doubts," he replied, glancing over at Boone, "but not about which of us would win."

"So this is Garrett Ambrose," Dolter exclaimed.

"No," Christian corrected, pulling the ropes from around Alexandra's wrists. "His name is Benton Wall. He works for Ambrose."

"You mean he used to," Dolter chuckled. "Once the superintendent hears about this, Mr. Wall will probably spend the rest of his sentence working on the chain gang." He slid from the saddle and took the ropes Christian handed him. "That is if Sir Wallis doesn't shoot him first." He jerked his head, silently instructing Wall to get up, and while he bound the man's hands behind him, Christian drew Alexandra away from the group of men.

"Did he hurt you?"

She shook her head. "Just scared me. I was worried you wouldn't find us in time."

His attention was drawn past her for a moment while he watched Dolter aid his prisoner onto his horse and then climb up behind him. "You can thank Thomas for that. He was the one who came looking for you." His blue eyes softened as he studied the beautiful face shadowed by silvery moonlight. "Alex," he beckoned, looking into her eyes. "Thomas said you insisted on bringing me my supper. Why? You weren't planning to poison me, were you?"

She suppressed the urge to giggle and could feel a light blush rise in her cheeks. "No. I wanted to talk to you . . . alone."

"What about?"

She glanced surreptitiously over her shoulder at the others to make sure no one would hear what she had to say. "I did a lot of thinking this afternoon . . . about you . . . and Papa, the things you said to me . . . " She lowered her eyes. "About us. I've behaved horribly ever since my mother died. I guess you could say I was punishing myself for something I couldn't have stopped from happening. Why should I be happy when my mother had been so miserable that she killed herself? Then you came along . . . a total stranger who cared more about my well-being than I did." Tears had gathered in the corners of her eyes and she laughed as she wiped them away. "I came to apologize, and to ask you to help one last time. Rather presumptuous of me, wouldn't you say? Considering what my father had done to you . . . what *I* had done to you." The smile faded from her lips as she stared into his pale blue eyes. "You're an unusual man, Christian Page. You're a guardian angel I don't deserve."

The thought of Min Le crossed his mind and the warmth he'd felt disappeared. He was no guardian angel. If he were, Min Le and their own son would still be alive. Knowing Alexandra was watching him and not wanting to have to explain the sudden change in him, he forced a smile and gently took her elbow.

"Mr. Boone," he called. "Would you be kind enough to escort Miss Pembrooke home? I have some unfinished business to attend to." Without waiting for an answer, he scooped her up in his arms and placed her on the horse behind Boone.

"I'd be more than honored, Mr. Page," Boone replied as he slowly lowered the muzzle of his rifle and pointed it at Christian. "But the only business you have is waiting back at the house." He nodded at Merlin Hull. "You don't mind riding double, do you?"

Hull shook his head, confused by his companion's remarks. "Is there a problem, Lynn?"

"There won't be as long as Mr. Page does as he's told."

The challenge sparkled very clearly in Boone's eyes, and even though disarming him would be a relatively easy task for him to accomplish, Christian yielded. "You still don't trust me, do you?"

Boone shrugged a beefy shoulder. "I'll admit I was a little skeptical back there when you took off in a different direction, but that was only because I couldn't second-guess you. It won't happen again. In fact, if you must know, I'd trust you with my life. But trust has nothing to do with this." He laughed at the confused look he saw on Christian's face. "You don't have any idea what's waiting for you out there, friend, and yet you're willing to take the chance just to spare Sir Wallis and Miss Alexandra. Well, I can't let you do that, and if I have to, I'll shackle both your arms and legs and drop you down a well to keep you from confronting Garrett Ambrose."

Christian drew a breath to argue when Alexandra interrupted.

"What are you talking about, Mr. Boone?"

He nodded at the man standing close to them. "His business is Ambrose, and he thinks to take him on all by himself. Now, I've seen how good he is at defending himself, and maybe he could outmaneuver a dozen or so men, but I, for one, don't care to find out. You see, Miss Alexandra, Christian admitted to me that *he's* the one Ambrose is after, not your father or you."

"If that's true, then why was I kidnapped?"

"To draw Christian out. You were the bait, Miss Alexandra." He turned to Benton Wall. "Isn't that right?"

Wall shrugged. "Can't really say."

Boone's mouth curled. "I'll bet you could if I shoved the barrel of this musket up your nose."

Alexandra shuddered at the image Boone's threat evoked. "So what are you suggesting?" she asked, deliberately changing Boone's train of thought.

"That we take our escaped prisoner back to the house and wait for your father. Tracking criminals was his specialty, wasn't it? If he caught Ambrose once, he can do it again."

Alexandra could feel Christian staring at her. The two of them knew why her father had been so successful in capturing Garrett Ambrose and his gang, and it had nothing to do with his skill as an investigator. Her father was talented, but Ambrose wasn't an ordinary criminal. Without the kind of help her father had had the first time, she doubted the results would be the same this time around. Christian was the only one who could

stop the man. She knew it. Christian knew it, and her father
probably did too.

Her intentions earlier had been to ask Christian's help. She
had planned to set him free on the condition that he stop
Ambrose before any harm came to her father. She honestly
didn't care about herself, but as far as she was concerned,
her father shouldn't have to pay for her stupidity. She'd been
remiss in thinking the assignment would be anything less than
simple for Christian, and now that Lynn Boone had pointed
out the dangers, she was ashamed of her selfishness.

"Yes, Mr. Boone," she announced. "You're right. We
should let Papa decide. Mr. Hull . . . " She settled her attention on the stocky little man. "If I may suggest, I think
it wise that Mr. Page *walk* back home. It'll be easier for you
to keep an eye on him. I'm sure there isn't a one of us who
would want to have to explain to my father how a man he
had left shackled and locked in the tool shed had managed to
escape. Am I right?"

No one responded, but their downcast eyes answered her
question.

"I thought so," she replied. "Mr. Boone? Shall we go?"

She knew Christian was staring at her, but she forced herself
to look straight ahead. He was probably having trouble understanding her change of mind right then, and well he should,
since even she was having a hard time figuring it out. She
wanted to believe it merely had to do with her desire not to
see anyone killed because of her. Yet deep inside she knew
that that was only a part of it. She didn't want *Christian* to
get killed, whether it was of her doing or not, and that was
what confused her.

·∘⟨ *Chapter Eighteen* ⟩∘·

"YOU EVEN TWITCH, SMITH," THOMAS WARNED, "AND I'LL raise a lump on your head so big it'll take a month to go away."

Harvey Smith prayed the trembling that shook his body wouldn't confuse the man who held a musket pointed at his head. He didn't want to die . . . not this way. "If you'd just let me explain . . . " he pleaded, looking from Thomas to Felice as the pair stood glaring down at him.

"Oh, you're going to explain," Thomas guaranteed him, when he heard the sound of an approaching group of men on horseback and concluded without looking that the others were about to join them. "Just as soon as Mr. Boone's here to listen, you can do all the explaining you want."

The vision of the broad-shouldered former navy man sent a chill down the back of Smith's neck. Lynn Boone stood a full head taller than himself with fists the size of cannonballs. Since Smith had gone through life avoiding fistfights, he was neither practiced in the art nor did he have the inclination to change that rather cherished side of his nature. He'd run before he'd stand and defend himself, and Boone didn't seem to be the sort who'd listen before using his fists. Once Thomas told the man that he'd found Smith tearing up the floorboards in Alexandra's bedroom, Boone would lay him out with one solid punch to his nose. Then, if Smith survived the attack, Boone would more than likely hit him again once Smith started to explain . . . whether he told the truth or not. No, it was best Smith made a quick exit before it was too late. He could always come back later . . . after Garrett Ambrose had finished with Pembrooke and his daughter, and the house was empty again.

"Please, Thomas, you don't understand," Smith begged, burying his face in his hands, his fingers spread apart just enough for him to steal a look . . . first at Thomas to judge how close he stood to where Smith knelt on the veranda, and then at the riders coming in across the field. If he made his move now, there would still be time for him to get away. "Boone doesn't like me," he moaned. "He'll never believe a word I say. He'll just hit me. Please, lock me up and wait for Sir Wallis to come home. Please, Thomas?"

A slight frown pulled Thomas's brows together as if he might be considering the notion. Everyone living there knew Boone had a hot temper, and since Thomas, an emancipated convict, had more to lose than all of the others put together, he couldn't afford to make a wrong decision. At least that was what Smith was hoping the cook would think. Working for Sir Wallis Pembrooke was a blessing, and a man would have to be crazy or a fool to jeopardize that. And then, of course, there was always the maid. Smith could play on the woman's sympathy if it appeared Thomas wasn't going to bend. Either way, however, it would have to be quick, since Boone and his companions were rapidly closing the distance between them.

"All right," Thomas suddenly announced, waving Smith to his feet with the end of the musket. "I'll put you in the tool shed until Sir Wallis returns. But let me warn you: you try something, and I won't hesitate to let Mr. Boone have you. Is that clear?"

Smith nodded quickly. "Very," he assured the man as he stumbled off the porch and headed toward the shed. Now all he had to do was wait for the right moment, when he had a musket *and* his freedom.

Christian had allowed himself to be taken back to the house only out of curiosity. Alexandra had done a complete reversal in her thinking and he wanted to know why. One minute she had decided that he should be the one to go after Ambrose, and in the next she had ordered him locked up with Benton Wall. Her moods were as varied as cotton and silk, and although he had come to expect it, this time he wanted to know what was behind it.

Drawing up near the barn, the group dismounted while Boone rode on to the house with Alexandra. At gunpoint, Christian and Wall were escorted inside the crew's quarters where Boone had instructed they be taken, and while the larger of the two men had his legs bound in shackles, Christian was allowed to sit down at the long trestle table free of restraints. No one spoke, and because none of the men would look at him, Christian guessed they were having trouble understanding Boone's motives. He couldn't blame them. They didn't know the whole story the way Boone did, and Christian was relatively certain all Boone wanted was to be included in whatever Christian had planned. His first responsibility, however, had been to seeing Alexandra safely home and that Wall was locked up where he couldn't cause anyone a problem. Then, once that was taken care of, Christian guessed Boone would make his proposal: he would turn Christian loose on the condition that he would be allowed to go along with him. Christian appreciated the man's need to be a part of capturing Garrett Ambrose, but he'd only be in the way, and Christian wouldn't put the man in that kind of danger if it could be avoided.

Several minutes passed while everyone in the room busied himself with idle work. Christian sat quietly thinking about how he'd convince Boone to stay behind while he went after Ambrose, and once he'd decided on an idea, he suddenly became aware of the amused stare he was receiving. Glancing up, he spied Benton Wall sitting on the floor on the opposite side of the room from him, his knees drawn up and his arms locked around them. The instant their eyes met, Wall grinned broadly.

"Tell me something, Page," he urged, not caring who was listening. "If you were working for Pembrooke the whole time, why is it he let you stand trial?"

Christian could feel how each man in the room stopped what he was doing to turn his full attention on his answer. "What makes you think I was?"

Laughter rumbled from Wall's chest. "Are you saying you weren't?" He waited for a reply and when none came, he posed a second possibility. "It's always been my nature to be suspicious of strangers. I was suspicious of you from the very beginning. You confirmed my feelings when you let Pembrooke's daughter escape."

Christian cringed inwardly. He would have preferred Wall not bring up the incident . . . for Alexandra's sake. But the damage was done, and from the way Richard Dolter stepped closer to the table, Christian guessed he was about to have to explain the meaning behind the statement.

"What's he talking about, Mr. Page?"

Laughter filled the room again. "You mean you haven't told them?" Wall asked. "I would think you'd have bragged about how you carried her kicking and screaming to your room." He shook his head in a sudden change of mind. "Maybe not. After all, what man would want another to know that a piece of fluff had bested him?"

Franklin Reber came to stand beside Dolter. "Is he saying you tried to rape her?" he snarled, his eyes blazing with rage.

"Oh, that's what he wanted everyone to think," Wall cut in. "After all, he was trying to impress Garrett Ambrose. Have some fun with her first and then kill her."

"Kill her?" Merlin Hull exploded, bolting from his chair to join Dolter and Reber. "I think you had better tell us what he's talking about, Page, before one of us loses his temper and beats the living hell out of you."

"Nice idea," Wall chuckled. "But highly unlikely. I ought to know. I tried once and all I got for the effort was a crippled knee. But I would like to hear his explanation myself." He cocked a brow at Christian. "No sense in keeping it a secret anymore, Page. If you were one of Pembrooke's agents, and you deliberately let his daughter escape to save her life, why did the old man reward you by shipping you off to Australia?" He could tell by the stern look he received in return that Christian wasn't going to say a word. "I got it!" he blurted. "You really did have your way with her, and she told her father. This is your punishment." He laughed loud and long. "I'll be damned. You got the best of both, you son of a bitch."

Raymond Kirpes, the most withdrawn of the group, had heard enough. "Well, I don't agree," he spoke up. "I'll admit I'm not making a whole lot of sense out of this conversation, but I know one thing: Christian Page isn't that kind of

man. I'd stake my life on it. Besides"—he turned to face
Dolter and the rest—"if that were true and Pembrooke knew
about it, do you honestly think he'd allow Mr. Page anywhere near his daughter?" He glared back at Wall. "You're
a liar."

"Am I?" Wall challenged. "Why don't you ask Page, then,
if you don't believe me?"

The entire group settled their attention on Christian, but
before he was forced to answer the charges, Lynn Boone's tall
frame stood silhouetted in the doorway and drew Christian's
gaze. The others quickly turned to look, and from the dark
expression on the man's face, they realized Boone didn't
approve of what he'd obviously overheard.

"Not that it's any of your business," he growled, moving
further into the room with Thomas close on his heels. "And I
don't think I have to tell you how upset Sir Wallis would be
if he learned you were gossiping about his daughter, but for
Christian's sake, I'll tell you this much: Sir Wallis wasn't
aware that Christian was one of his agents or we wouldn't be
standing here right now. He still doesn't know, and it's up to
Christian to correct that, if and when the time comes. As for
the rest of it, I suggest you forget everything you heard."

Shamefaced, the men glanced apologetically at Christian and
then moved away.

"That's better," Boone proclaimed before directing Thomas
to where Christian sat. Once the two of them had slid down
on the bench opposite him, Boone folded his arms and leaned
against the tabletop. "I could be all wrong about this," he
began, taking a quick glance over his shoulder at Wall before
continuing, "or maybe I'm just a little edgy, but I'm getting the
feeling there's more to this than what meets the eye, ol' boy."
He nudged the man sitting next to him. "Go ahead, Thomas.
Tell him."

Frowning, the cook rubbed his chin. "If I had known he
was going to pull a stunt like that, I would have made him
explain when I had the chance," Thomas related.

"Don't apologize," Boone ordered. "Just tell him."

"Well, I'm feeling guilty, Lynn. You can understand that."
Boone nodded. "Yes, but feeling guilty isn't going to change

anything. Just explain what happened, and let Christian figure it out."

Thomas took a deep breath, heaved a sigh, and focused his attention on the man patiently waiting to hear his story. "Just after everyone left, I noticed Smith acting a bit peculiar. You know, pretending to be nonchalant when he really wasn't. I had seen him through the kitchen window, and since he wasn't aware I was watching him, I figured I'd stay put and see what he was up to. Well, he went to the tool shed and got a crowbar, which in itself isn't much, but when he took it with him into the house, that really raised my curiosity. I can't say why, but I took my musket with me, and I'm glad I did, because I'm sure he would have tried to clobber me if I hadn't been armed."

"What was he doing in the house, Thomas?" Christian urged when it seemed the man was rambling.

"He was starting to tear up some of the floorboards in Miss Alexandra's room."

Scowling, Christian shifted his gaze to Boone, who shrugged in return. "Where is he now?"

Thomas lowered his eyes. "He got away."

"Got away?"

"Yes sir," Thomas quietly admitted. "I was taking him to the tool shed to lock him up and he jumped me."

"I found both Thomas and Felice in the shed just now after I took Alexandra to the house," Boone added. "He couldn't have that much of a head start, if you think we should go after him."

"I'll admit his behavior was odd, but was it enough to warrant the effort to catch him?" Christian posed. "Why not just finish what he started? Perhaps what's under the floorboards will be enough of an answer."

"We did," Thomas said. "There wasn't anything there."

Quiet for a moment while he considered all the clues, Christian rubbed his thumb along his upper lip, then looked up at Boone. "And you're not comfortable with that."

Boone shook his head.

"Why not?"

"Because I keep remembering why Harvey Smith was here in the first place."

"The will he said the Rauscher brothers had written naming him as an heir."

"I'd like to believe that's what he was looking for, but there's just something about the little viper that has me thinking otherwise," Boone confessed.

Christian looked at Thomas, silently asking for his opinion.

Thomas nodded. "Me, too, Mr. Page. In fact, I doubt there ever was a will. I think he made the story up as an excuse to win Sir Wallis's sympathy."

"To do what?"

"To get a job here . . . to be close to whatever it was he was looking for," Thomas finished.

"Then maybe you should send someone after him," Christian suggested. "You'll never know the answers without him."

Hearing an underlying tone to Christian's invitation, Boone deduced, "But as far as you're concerned, you don't see a need."

"I don't see him as a threat," Christian admitted.

"Well, you should."

The fact that Benton Wall had been listening to everything they'd said and that he had an opinion on the matter surprised everyone in the room. Christian, however, had learned long ago never to trust someone of Wall's character, and while the rest of the men waited anxiously for his explanation, Christian leaned back in his chair, willing to hear what he had to say but intending to weigh each word carefully.

"And why is that?" Christian asked.

"You're a smart man, Page," Wall mocked, a faint smile on his face. "Can't you figure it out?"

The only conclusion Christian could draw from the comment was that for some reason Benton Wall thought he knew Harvey Smith or at least he thought he knew what Smith had been looking for. And without that bit of information, Christian was at a loss to make the connection.

"Can you?" Boone asked hopefully.

Christian smiled. "I would if there was something to figure out."

"I don't understand."

Christian's eyes never left the face of his adversary. "I'm saying that Benton Wall likes to hear himself talk."

Wall burst into laughter. "Is that what you think? Well, you're a bigger fool than Garrett ever thought you were, friend."

Christian cocked his head. "Oh, so we're friends now, are we? Funny how being shackled can change a man's loyalty."

"Loyalty comes with wisdom, Page. In the last few months I've gotten very wise." He winced as he stretched the muscles in his back. "And I've gotten very tired."

"Meaning?"

Shifting his huge bulk around to a more comfortable position, Wall lifted his gaze to Christian and stared back at him for a minute. "I joined up with Garrett a few years back because he promised wealth and a relatively easy way of life. And that's what I got . . . for a while. But as his reputation grew, so did his greed, and he started taking more chances. He seemed to thrive on them. I don't think I'd sound too bold if I said the reason he did was because of me. Whatever he got himself into, he figured I would get him out. And I did . . . until you came along." He smiled lazily at Christian.

"I know what everyone thinks of me, that I'm all muscle and not too smart. That's what I wanted everyone to think. The truth is I'm an educated man. I used to be a solicitor before I fell on hard times and turned to Garrett's way of life." He shook his head. "Anyway, it doesn't take a smart man to know that Garrett Ambrose isn't going to do a thing to help me out of the fix I'm in right now. I'm on my own. So, I'm willing to make a trade."

"You're not serious," Boone snorted. "Do you really expect us to believe a word you've said? And what have you got to trade that would be of the slightest bit of interest to us?"

Wall's eyes moved from Christian to Boone. "I know where Garrett is. Do you? Do you know how many men he's acquired in his new gang since we were let loose?"

"Let loose," Boone repeated mockingly. "Don't you mean escaped?"

Wall turned his attention back on Christian again. "Like I said, a trade."

"Christian—" Boone began, stopping short when Christian raised a hand. "What? You're not proposing we even listen to him, are you? He kidnapped Alexandra, for God's sake! He would have killed her if we hadn't gotten to her in time. Have you forgotten that?"

"No, I haven't forgotten," Christian calmly replied. "But where's the harm in listening to what he has to trade? I'm sitting here right now because you didn't want me chasing after Ambrose all alone. If what he has to say will make it easier for us, then—"

"Easier," Boone retorted, shaking his head. "Are you saying you'll trust anything he tells you?"

"It depends," Christian answered.

"On what?"

"On what he says." Raising his brows, Christian stared at Boone, waiting for the man to yield.

Boone waved a hand as he left his place at the table and crossed to stand near the door, looking out. He obviously wasn't convinced, but he was willing to let his friend have his way . . . for the time being.

Christian appreciated Boone's concern, and he wanted to tell him that he agreed. But he'd heard Wall's near slip of the tongue a moment ago when he'd implied that he and Ambrose had had help in escaping, and he wanted to know more. He nodded at the man bound in leg irons, silently giving permission for him to plead his case.

"If I lead you to where Garrett is camped, if I even help you catch him, all I ask in return is that you look the other way long enough for me to take off. I have no intention of spending the next twenty years on a chain gang. I'd rather be dead."

"We can fix that for you," Boone promised with a look over his shoulder at the man.

Wall's eyes darkened. "Then go ahead and shoot me right now. But I think you should know something first. Garrett isn't working alone. He has help, and the plan is to break Pembrooke, to run him off his land. He's been paid not to kill him until that's done. Then, if he wants—and let me assure you, he does—he can use whatever method he wants in having his revenge . . . against Pembrooke, his daughter, and"—his gaze shifted to Christian—"and you."

"What do you mean he has help?" Boone demanded, turning around.

"Henry Abbott, the man Garrett and I were assigned to, never trusted us, especially once Garrett started harassing him and stirring up the other convicts. After a while, he kept us in shackles because he was afraid we'd run off and take the others with us. At night we were locked in our cabin. Explain to me how we could have escaped under conditions like that." When Boone refused to speculate simply because he couldn't, Wall supplied the answer. "In the middle of the night we were awakened by the sound of someone unlocking the door. We didn't know the man who freed our shackles, and I don't think it's even important."

"Why not?" Boone asked.

"Because he told us he'd been paid to do it *and* to give us directions where to meet the man who'd hired it done."

"And you did," Boone finished.

Wall nodded. "Except we never got a look at him." Remembering the incident, Wall chuckled. "The son of a bitch ambushed us. He killed everybody but Garrett and me, and he hid in the shadows while we talked."

"About what? And why did he kill the others?"

"Because he didn't need them, and I think to prove to us that he wasn't someone to toy with. He could have killed us just as easily."

"And you think Harvey Smith is that man," Christian deduced.

"Smith?" Boone and Thomas echoed at the same time. "He hasn't the backbone for something like that," Thomas added.

"And why would he go to the trouble of asking Sir Wallis for a job?" Boone further reasoned. "He could have just sat back and waited."

"True," Wall agreed. "But it's a hellava coincidence, now, isn't it? I'm not saying this Smith is the man we met in the bush, and I'm not saying that he isn't. But both men appear to be after the same thing: something that belongs to Pembrooke."

Boone wasn't quite ready to concede. "So what? That doesn't mean Smith's a cold-blooded murderer. I don't like him much, but I can't see him shooting someone from ambush."

Several of the other men who had listened in silence to the conversation spoke up in agreement. "What makes you think so?" one of them asked Wall.

"A comment. We were told that Pembrooke had something this man wanted, something Pembrooke had cheated him out of having. Now, correct me if I'm wrong, but I just got the impression that Smith thought there was a will leaving him the property and that Pembrooke denied it. Whether it's true or not, Smith thinks he was cheated, doesn't he?"

Boone didn't want to have to admit that what Wall was saying made sense, but it was. "Christian?" he asked. "Do we go after him?"

Resting his arms on the table, Christian idly traced the circular graining of a knot in the surface while he considered his answer. If what Benton Wall proposed were true, grabbing Smith now would be foolish. He'd simply disavow all knowledge of Wall's claim. But if they could catch him with Garrett Ambrose, then. . . .

"As much as I hate to have to do it, I'm going to have to trust you, Wall," he announced. "But there'll be more to the trade than what you offered."

"Such as?" Wall asked hesitantly.

"Your freedom will cost you both Ambrose and the man who set this up. Right now he's more dangerous than your partner. Have we a deal?"

A slow grin spread across Wall's face. "I don't really have much of choice, do I?"

"Let's just say it's the only way you have to prove you're telling the truth." He cocked his head, waiting for Wall to confess he'd made the whole thing up. "Do we send someone to follow Smith or not?"

Wall shrugged. "You could, I suppose, but it isn't really necessary. Garrett's to meet with him in five days. You can have them both at the same time, if you wait."

"Where?" Boone spoke up. "Where are they to meet?"

Wall shook his head. "Like I said before, Boone, I'm not stupid. The only way you'll know that is if I take you there. Then, while you're having your fun with Garrett, I'll make my exit." He glanced at Christian. "Right?"

Returning the man's stare, Christian quietly considered the alternatives. He still had his doubts about Harvey Smith, and he knew he probably shouldn't trust Benton Wall, but at the moment he had nothing else from which to choose. "Right," he finally replied, thinking that a lot could happen in the next five days.

Staring at her reflection in the mirror above her dressing table while she languidly brushed the tangles from her hair, Alexandra struggled with her thoughts. A warm breeze, drifting into her room through the opened window, tugged at the hem of the curtains and carried with it the sweet fragrant night smells, but Alexandra didn't notice. She had changed into her nightgown with the intention of retiring, but the events of the day had her mind whirling.

All the while she had been Benton Wall's prisoner she hadn't feared for her life, for something in the back of her mind had guaranteed her that Christian would come to save her. Why she felt so certain was a mystery, yet she had. Now that it was over, and Christian *had* actually come for her, the realization that she had taken too much for granted made her tremble. The idea that he could have been killed in the attempt tightened icy fingers around her heart.

Laying aside her hairbrush, she smiled dreamily into the mirror while she enjoyed the sudden warmth that spread through her body and touched her face. She remembered hearing the rain against the windowpanes, the smell of the fire in the hearth, and the feel of Christian's strong arms wrapping her in his embrace. She recalled how angry she had been, and how that rage had melted the instant his lips found hers. A delicious shiver raced along her spine and set her nerves atingle with the memory of his body pressed against her own. They had made love there in the cabin without restraint or timidness or doubt, and the knowledge amazed her. For weeks she had feared its happening, and when the time had come, she had welcomed him with open arms. Why? Had he cast a spell on her? Had he taken advantage of her in a weak moment?

The smile lingered as she closed her eyes and inhaled deeply. No, there had been no sorcery, no playing of games or one-sided desires. The fire in him had burned just as brightly in her, and even now she had no regrets. But what about him? she wondered. Was he sorry it had happened?

Troubled by the thought, she blew out the candle and rose from the velvet-covered bench, her head lowered as she watched her fingers untie the sash of her robe. Turning, she pulled the garment from her shoulders, crossed to the foot of her bed and paused, her mind racing with the possibility that *she* had somehow practiced witchcraft and that in the light of day he had come to his senses. After all, he had more reasons to hate her than to care about her.

All at once she felt sick inside. Twisting around, she sat down on the edge of the bed, the robe knotted in her hands. She thought of the agony he must have suffered in the prison back in England and on the convict transport coming to Australia. His life had to have been in constant peril the entire time, and it had all been because of her. How, then, could he possibly feel anything for her other than hatred? Tears moistened her lashes and she squeezed her eyes shut to halt their flow as she silently considered why any of it really mattered to her. Hadn't her argument been that he had deserved it for what he'd done to her? And what, exactly, had he done?

The claim that he had planned to kill her after he'd had his way with her sounded weak in her mind. Too much had happened since then for her to hang on to such a notion, and her revenge afterward tasted bitter in her mouth. The idea that an apology would mend the wrongs she'd done him was ludicrous. It might make her feel better, but it wouldn't erase the fact that he had suffered because of her foolishness. Her lower lip trembled. Yet it was a start. To ask his forgiveness might ease the memory of his pain.

Squaring her shoulders, she raised her chin and stood, firm determination showing on her face. She'd do it tonight, right now. She'd explain why she hadn't let him go after Garrett Ambrose, why she reacted the way she had, and most of all, she'd tell him that she loved him. Tears suddenly filled her eyes, and she smiled through them, shocked by the revelation.

"I do," she whispered. "I really do."

Turning, she started for the door when a shadowed figure near the opened window moved and made her gasp. A second later he stepped into the moonlight shining into the room.

"Christian," she breathed, the robe she still held in her hands dropping to the floor.

In silence he crossed the distance to her and slid his arms around her narrow waist, pulling her close and lowering his head. Warm lips covered hers, the masculine scent of him sent her mind reeling, the warmth of his nearness ignited a fire, and without hesitation, she kissed him back. A hunger burned inside her and raged out of control as she slipped her arms around her neck and entwined her fingers in the thick mass of short-cropped hair at his nape. Pressing her mouth to his, she tasted his lips with her tongue while she molded her delicate frame against the sinewy strength of his body. She fought to draw him closer, to feel his heartbeat, to share each breath he took.

"Oh, Christian," she whispered when his kisses moved along her throat. "Christian, I love you."

Surprised to hear the words, he pulled back and stared into her eyes, his own dark with desire. Alexandra misread the look on his handsome face for doubt, and her heart ached suddenly. If anything, she had never lied to him, and to think that he could misjudge her so tore at the very essence of her being. She had fashioned herself in love with Hardin, but now that she experienced the true meaning of the word, she knew how silly that had been. Love was more than just enjoying one's company or sharing the same adventures. It went much deeper than that. Love meant the blending of two souls as one, devotion, selflessness, giving without expecting anything in return, and it meant blind trust. And she truly felt all that for Christian. Without him, there would be an emptiness in her life.

Moving away from him, she went to stand beside the bed, hoping with all her heart that he wouldn't deny her the chance to prove her declaration of love. Bathed in the silvery glow of the moon, she watched him while her fingers tugged at the crisscross lacing of her nightgown. A moment later the silky cloth shimmered to pool at her feet.

"I want you, Christian Page," she murmured, her hand held out to him. "Now and for always."

He closed the distance between them in three long, hurried strides, enveloping her slender form in his arms the moment he reached her. He kissed her parted lips, her chin, the long column of her neck, and the hollow at its base where her pulse beat wildly. He buried his face in the dark tresses of her hair and breathed in the sweet scent of it. His hands roamed the full length of her spine, and while one pulled her hips close against him, the other traveled across her narrow waist, then up to cup one breast. Staring deep into her eyes, his thumb stroked a rosy peak before his mouth, warm and demanding, claimed the treasure he had found.

Impatient to fall with him upon the feathery softness of her bed, Alexandra's hands moved to the buttons on his shirt. Next came the fastening on his trousers and while he shed his clothes, she turned down the covers. A sultry smile darkened the shade of her jade-green eyes, and moonlight traced the perfect profile of her cheek when she lifted her face to look at him.

"Be it only for this night, my love," she vowed, "I will be yours completely as you shall be mine."

Their lips met again, this time with a fierceness and hunger that rocked them from the summit of their restraint. Clinging to each other, he slowly lowered her down upon the crisp white sheets, their bodies glowing in an ashen light. They moved against each other, then as one, when he rose above her, parted her trembling thighs with his knee, and answered her desire with his own. Rapture exploded within them until at last they fell exhausted in each other's arms, their passion sated and their naked flesh warm with the afterglow of their lovemaking.

"Alex," Christian murmured after a long while of blissful silence, "have you thought about what you said to me?"

Rolling onto her side, she laid her cheek against the hardened ripples of his chest and snuggled close. "Yes. Why do you ask? Is it so hard to believe?"

He smiled, but the shadowy darkness that surrounded them hid the expression from her. "Only that I question the timeliness of it. A lot has happened to you, and sometimes we tend to confuse love with gratitude."

Pushing herself up, she folded her arms and propped herself against his chest, her face inches from his. "Is that what made you hesitate? Were you afraid I had misconstrued my emotions? And if so, why did you yield?" Her eyes sparkled with mirth. "Choose your answer carefully, Christian Page, lest I think you deliberately took advantage of me."

Laughter spoiled the seriousness of his charge. "Could you possibly name one man who, standing in my place at that moment, wouldn't have yielded? I am, after all, of flesh and blood, and not some mythical hero void of prurience." Folding an arm behind his head, he laid his other hand on the small of her back, enjoying the warmth of her naked body touching his. "But perhaps I should put the burden on you and say that you took advantage of me."

"Hmmm," she murmured. "I did, didn't I?" She laughed, kissed the tip of his nose, and then settled down beside him once again, content enough to be cradled in the crook of his arm for the time being. "Yet if you still doubt my honest feelings, consider why I stopped you from going after Garrett Ambrose. Or have you already figured it out?"

Christian had drawn his own conclusions on that long before now, and he had come to her room to hear her admit it. However, he had expected a denial, not an open confession. "And have you considered what you shall tell your father? He left here thinking the worst of me, and I doubt his opinion will have changed any by the time he returns. If you tell him that you've fallen in love with the man he thinks wants to kill him . . . " He chuckled at the image he saw. "Well, let's just say I don't believe he'll approve." He kissed her brow and reached for the quilt to cover them.

"I'm sure he wouldn't," she agreed, drawing little circles over the smooth, hard surface of his chest with the tip of her finger. "That's why I'll have to tell him the truth . . . about everything."

Christian sighed. "Telling him how we met won't convince

him of my innocence, Alex. I need Lewis Rhomberg for that. And he's in England."

Twisting, she looked up into his eyes. "But surely there's something you could say that would prove you were working for Papa and not Garrett Ambrose."

Christian shrugged one shoulder. "Wall never believed I was who I pretended to be, but he's hardly the type whose word your father would take." He hugged her close. "We have one thing on our side, however."

"What's that?" she asked hopefully. She had just discovered her feelings for Christian, and she wasn't about to give in without a fight . . . even if the opponent was her own kin.

"If your father had been dead set against me, he would have hauled me back to Sydney with him. He has his doubts, and that's what might save me. For a while, anyway. If he'll allow me a moment to plead my case, he might consent to send a message to Lewis asking his side of the story."

"Why wait?" she posed. "I can send a letter just as easily. Do you know where he can be reached?"

The vision of a scruffy, ill-tempered lad came to mind. "Not exactly. But I have someone working on it."

"Who?"

He told her about T. J. Savage, how they met, and why the boy hadn't wound up in Australia with the rest of the prisoners. He admitted that he wasn't sure just how hard and how long T. J. would search for Lewis, but that at the time he hadn't had a lot of other alternatives. Then he laughed and said how much the youngster had reminded him of himself when he'd been T. J.'s age. From there he told her about his uncle and Russel, a boy who'd been taken in by Garrett Ambrose's promises, and how Christian wanted revenge for his cousin's death. He told her about Min Le and their infant son, and how a jealous beau had accidentally killed them when he set the house on fire, thinking Christian was alone inside. He told her about Sang Soo, his wife's grandfather, and everything else that had happened to him up until the night they had met at the inn. Until now, Christian had never felt the desire to share his secrets, his past, or his feelings with anyone. Even Min Le hadn't been aware of them all, and for him to have opened up so easily with

Alexandra not only surprised him, but confused him as well.

"Christian?" Alexandra whispered when it seemed a long silence had passed between them. Pushing up on one elbow, she studied his handsome face for a moment, noticing how he'd seemed to have drifted off in thought somewhere. "You're not sorry you told me all of this, are you?"

He smiled suddenly and ran his hand along her bare shoulder and arm. "No," he confessed. "I'm just trying to figure out why I did. I've never confided in anyone before."

"Not even Min Le?" she asked without a trace of jealousy.

"Not even Min Le," he replied. "Why do you suppose that is?"

She wanted to say that she hoped it was because he loved her, but she preferred he make that declaration on his own. "Maybe it's because you feel comfortable with me. Sometimes a good friend knows more about a person than his own family does."

"A friend?" he repeated, grinning. "Is that how you think I feel about you, Alex? That we're good friends?" His hand slipped beneath the covers and traced the gentle curve of her spine to her buttocks. "How many friends have you allowed in your bed?"

"None!" she responded vehemently. Shocked and a little hurt that he would even suggest such a thing, she pushed away, thinking to get dressed, but a strong hand caught her wrist and pulled her back.

"I didn't think so," he teased, drawing her close, his lips brushing hers before settling on the tender flesh beneath her ear. "So what other reason could there be, do you suppose? Is there a chance I might actually have fallen in love with you?"

Tears of joy sparkled in her eyes. "I don't know. Is there?"

He trailed hot kisses down her throat. "Maybe," he replied, turning with her in his arms to pin her beneath him. "It certainly doesn't make any sense, but I guess it's true." His eyes darkened lustfully, and he lowered his head. "I love you, Alexandra Pembrooke," he whispered against her parted lips, the flame of passion soaring high once more.

·∘⟨ *Chapter Nineteen* ⟩∘·

SINCE THE DECISION HAD BEEN MADE TO WAIT FOR THE AP-
pointed meeting time between Garrett Ambrose and his newest
partner, tension ran high among the men and for Alexandra,
even though she tried to put her mind on other things. Christian
busied himself with finishing up the new house and pretending
that he wasn't worried about Pembrooke's return. At night after
everyone else had gone to bed, he would steal into Alexandra's
room and into her waiting arms. They would make love, talk,
sleep awhile, and then make love again. In the morning when
she awoke, she'd always find him gone, and although she knew
he wasn't far away, an emptiness never failed to assail her and
push her out of bed. She'd dress, eat a hurried, light breakfast,
and go looking for him, unaware that nearly everyone around
her had noticed the change in her. Her face glowed with love
each time she looked at Christian, and while some speculated on
the happiness they would share once her father gave his blessing, the rest worried the couple would never have the chance
to explore the full realm of their feelings for each other.

By the morning of the third day, with Wall safely locked
away in the crew's quarters and under guard, even Lynn Boone
was having trouble coping with the pressure. It heightened when
one of the men came racing in from the pasture on horseback.

"Mr. Boone!" Clarence Feipel shouted, sawing cruelly on
the reins to pull his animal to a halt near where Boone stood
talking with Christian. "Mr. Boone, we got trouble."

"What kind of trouble?" he asked, dreading the man's reply.
He knew it had to concern Garrett Ambrose and that whatever
answer Feipel gave, Boone wasn't going to like it.

"We found some of the sheep dead this morning." He jerked his thumb back in the direction from which he had come. "Along the boundary of Pleasanton's property. Their throats had been cut so they'd bleed to death."

"How many?" Christian asked.

"About a fourth of the flock, we figure."

"Damn!" Boone raged. "I should have expected this. And I suppose the ram was one of them?"

Feipel nodded.

"Where was Hull? He was supposed to be keeping an eye on them."

"Whoever did it hit him over the head. We found him tied up and lying unconscious in the line cabin."

"Is he all right?" Christian asked.

"Yes, sir. He's got a pretty good headache and a bump the size you could hang your hat on, but I think his pride hurts more. I asked him if he got a look at the guy what hit him, but he said no, that he didn't even hear anything." He hesitated, then added, "Dolter and me think . . . well, if Mr. Page would take a look, he'd probably know for sure, but we think there was more than one man."

"And you can bet your supper Ambrose gave the order," Boone bitterly surmised. He shook his head and sighed, frustrated. "Round up the rest of the crew and herd the sheep in closer. We'll have to set up groups of three to watch them day and night. We certainly can't afford to lose any more."

"Yes, sir," Feipel replied, yanking back on the reins and swinging his horse around.

"Christian," Boone grumbled as he watched the man on horseback ride away, "I'm not sure we can wait two more days. And I'm beginning to think we shouldn't have let Smith walk off so easily. I say we go after Ambrose now, this very second."

"We could," Christian agreed. "But that would leave the man behind all this free to hire someone else to take up where Ambrose left off." He turned and picked up the toolbox he had constructed out of wood. "I really don't see where we have much of a choice."

"Of course we do," Boone argued, following his companion across the veranda of the new house. "All Pembrooke would have to do is offer a reward for Harvey Smith's capture. Bushrangers are poor men who'd turn in their own brother for the right price."

"Maybe," Christian yielded as he opened the door and went inside. "But can you honestly say you'd sleep well at night purely on the assumption that Harvey Smith is the man we're after?" He crossed the foyer and started up the long staircase.

"What do you mean assumption?" Boone asked, coming to a halt at the bottom of the steps.

"You heard Wall. He said he never saw the man's face."

"But who else could it be?" Boone called after him as Christian disappeared around the landing. "Dammit, man! Can't you stand still for a minute?"

A moment of silence passed before the answer floated down. "Not when there's work to be done and no time for idle talk."

"Idle talk," Boone mumbled. "What's he think I am? A woman?"

"Is there something wrong with being a woman, Mr. Boone?" a voice from behind him asked, the tone laced with humor.

Turning abruptly, he found Alexandra standing just inside the opened doorway, her dark hair pulled back from her face and her eyes sparkling in the sunshine that surrounded her. He certainly didn't want to insult her, but she'd obviously overheard his comment. He cleared his throat and glanced down at the floor.

"No, ma'am," he offered, hoping she wouldn't press the issue. Deciding not to allow her the opportunity, he jerked his head in the direction Christian had gone. "He's up there, if you're looking for Christian."

Although the urge to laugh was strong, Alexandra held back. "Actually, no. I was looking for you."

"Oh?" he questioned, surprised, wondering if she could see how red his face felt.

"Yes," she said, stepping further inside. "Christian told me that the parlor and dining room are finished enough that we could move in some of the furniture from the other house today.

I was wondering if you could spare a couple of men this afternoon to help out. It would be a nice surprise for Papa, don't
you think?"

Boone wouldn't bother her with the other surprise he was sure
her father wouldn't find nice at all. "Yes, Miss Alexandra. And
I think I could spare a couple of men. Just tell me when."

She smiled her thanks, turned to leave, and stopped suddenly.
"Oh, yes, there was something else I needed to ask Christian
about." She pointed at the staircase. "You say he's up there?"

Boone nodded and moved out of her way. "If that's all you
needed from me, I've got something to take care of," he said,
knowing full well she had never intended to leave without seeing Christian first, and that she'd probably appreciate it if he
were to leave them alone.

"Yes, that was all," she said, one hand resting on the newel
post as she watched him start for the door. "Oh, and would you
be so kind as to tell Felice where I am? I left without saying
anything to her."

I rather doubt she'd have a hard time figuring it out, he
thought, while he politely bowed his head. He straightened
again and watched her shapely figure ascend the stairs. *A
person would have to be blind and stupid not to know that
wherever Christian Page is, so are you, Miss Alexandra, but
I'll tell her just the same.* Chuckling to himself, he turned and
left the house.

Alexandra found Christian working in the bedroom she had
already decided would be hers once it was livable, and without
making a sound, she entered just beyond the threshold to watch
him in silence for a moment, while his back was to her. Bright
morning sunshine, streaming into the room through the opening
where he planned to hang the French doors he was working on,
bathed his tall frame in a warm yellow light. The shirt he wore
clung to his broad shoulders while he stretched and reached in
various directions and plied his talents to the door frame he had
laid across two wooden sawhorses. Beside him on the floor was
a stack of perfectly matched pieces of glass he had cut from
a larger one as well as a bucket of putty he planned to use in
securing the panes in their framework. The amount of skill,
time, and effort it took to build a single French door amazed

Alexandra, and the knowledge it took to complete the work left her in awe of the man who accomplished it as effortlessly as others drew breath. On the day Weiland and Kirpes arrived home from Sydney with the wagonload of supplies Christian had sent them after, Alexandra wouldn't have guessed he could turn piles of boards, bags of nails, and various other inventories into a place stylish and worthy enough to suit the king of England. But he had, and she was very proud of him.

"Someday you and I will share this room," she announced matter-of-factly. When he turned an amused look her way, she ignored the doubt she saw touching the edges of his expression and walked past him. Stepping onto the small balcony, she laid her hands on the wood railing, closed her eyes, and breathed in the crisp morning air. "You don't believe me, do you?" she asked over her shoulder.

"I believe that's what you believe," he replied, dropping his putty knife in the bucket and wiping his hands on a rag. "I'm just not too sure your father would approve."

Turning, she leaned back against the banister with her hands stretched out on either side of her and resting on the railing. "You're not worried, are you? I know he's angry right now because he thought you deceived him, but once I tell him the truth—"

"It isn't going to be that simple, Alex," Christian warned her. He tossed down the rag and moved toward her. "The first thing he'll ask for is your proof, and you'll have to tell him that you don't have any, that you're simply repeating everything I told you."

"But if I swear to him that I know you're telling the truth—"

"It still won't be the proof he needs." He smiled at her and drew in close, placing his feet on the outside of hers while he gently cupped her face in his hands and kissed the tip of her nose. "Your father didn't get to be Commissioner to the Crown by listening to opinions, Alex, and even though you're his daughter, he isn't going to listen to yours any more than he would to a total stranger's."

"Then I'll ask him to explain why you allowed me to escape that night, especially when Ambrose had ordered you to kill me. If you had indeed been working for that . . . that awful man, you would have shot me right there in front of him."

Christian laughed at the angry frown wrinkling her face. "Will you listen to yourself? It wasn't that long ago that you were claiming just the opposite was true."

She started to open her mouth and clarify her reasons for changing her mind, when she realized how the explanation would sound . . . to Christian as well as to her father, should she ever tell him the events that led up to it. Blushing, she dropped her gaze away from him. "I'll just have to be careful how I word it, I guess."

Pinching her chin with his thumb and forefinger, he lifted her face and smiled back at her. "I'm afraid, dear Alex, that one look at you will give it all away."

"Then I'll put a gunny sack over my head while I talk to him," she replied irritably. "But I *will* talk to him, Christian. What else can I do? Stand by and watch him put you in chains? Or worse, haul you back to Sydney and have you thrown in prison? I won't stand for it, Christian. I won't!" Tears of frustration glistened in her eyes as she stood erect and slipped her arms around his neck. "I'm not afraid of my father, if that's what you're trying to tell me. I might have blamed him for something that wasn't his fault, but I was never afraid of him. I'm still not, and if I have to, I'll have Lynn sit on him long enough for me to explain."

Christian chuckled at the image. "I bet you would, you little hellion."

"Then bet everything you own," she advised. "You'll be a rich man." The seriousness of their conversation ebbed when he gave her a squeeze, and in its place the happiness she had come to know so well in the past couple of days returned. Smiling coquettishly at him, she invited, "Now kiss me before I change my mind."

If either of them cared for a moment that someone might be watching them, it wasn't apparent as they held each other close and shared a hungry, passionate kiss. Had it been Boone or Felice or even Thomas who observed, they would have enjoyed the scene. Harvey Smith didn't.

"Isn't that sweet?" he mocked, crouched low in the bush a safe distance away. "I wonder if Sir Wallis will approve."

At that same moment, the sound of an approaching rider on horseback cut into the stillness behind him. Diving deeper into the underbrush, Smith held his breath while he listened to the hoofbeats grow louder. A moment later they stopped, and he cautiously moved his head to get a peek at the intruder who had reined his animal to a halt only a stone's throw from him.

I guess he wouldn't, Harvey mused sardonically as he covertly stared up at the angry expression on Wallis Pembrooke's face, for he, too, had spotted the couple standing on the balcony.

"Tell me about Min Le, Christian," Alexandra urged once he had returned to his work and she stood nearby watching him.

"What do you want to know?" he asked, surprised that for the first time since her death it wasn't painful for him to think about her.

Seeing that he was ready for one of the panes of glass, she quickly handed one to him. "What was she like?"

A flood of memories washed over him, and he shrugged. "She was very tiny, almost frail, I guess you could say. But most Oriental people are. She had beautiful brown eyes and long black hair. She was soft-spoken, had an infectious laugh, and she seldom, if ever, got angry. In the years since her death, I've often wondered if I forced her into falling in love with me."

Alexandra shook her head, denying the possibility. "I doubt that, Christian. I was never forced into it."

Smiling, he glanced up at her. "Thank you for feeling that way, but you and Min Le are two very different people." He laid the glass in place and reached for his putty knife. "Chinese women are taught from birth that their sole purpose in life is to marry, have children, and serve their husband. They're rarely allowed any say in it whatsoever. In fact, Min Le had been promised to another long before I entered her life."

The confession surprised Alexandra. "Really? What happened?"

"I'm not really sure, but I have my own suspicions."

"Such as?"

"Min Le was orphaned at a young age, and her grandfather took her in, her mother's father. From some of the things he said to me, I got the impression he was never very fond of the choice he'd made for his daughter, that the man was cruel to her and at times would beat her. It's not all that uncommon a practice if their women were disrespectful, but Sang Soo wanted better for his granddaughter. He wanted her husband to love her, not to marry her simply because it was expected of him."

"And you did love her," Alexandra finished without rancor.

"Yes, I did. I loved her enough for both of us. That's why I said I wondered if I forced her to love me back."

"What about your son? What was his name?"

The happiness left his face, and he concentrated on his work, silent for a moment. "We never had the chance to pick a name for him. They were killed the day he was born."

Overcome with sympathy, Alexandra came to stand beside him. When he looked up, she smiled softly and slid her arms around him, hugging him close. "I'm sorry, Christian. I didn't mean to bring back painful memories."

"Don't apologize," he soothed, kissing her brow. "Ignoring what happened won't make it go away. And that's what I've been doing these past six years . . . trying to pretend it didn't happen." He leaned back and smiled at her. "A wise old man pointed that out to me."

"Sang Soo?"

He nodded.

"You loved him, too, didn't you?"

He pulled her back into his arms and brushed a kiss against her temple. "He was the most unselfish man I've ever known. He taught me more about life than life itself."

"It must have been very hard for you to leave him."

"Very. But if I hadn't gone, he probably would have had me bound and gagged and thrown on board the first ship sailing back to England." He laughed suddenly. "He told me that one day I'd find you."

Alexandra stared up at him.

"You will love again, he said. But he said that it would never come about if I stayed there with him. I didn't believe him, of course. I felt as if I had died right alongside Min Le and our son." His eyes sparkled with devilish warmth. "I'm glad he was right." He glanced around the room as though he were looking for something. "Meet me here tonight, after everyone's gone to bed."

"Here?" she laughed. "But there's—"

"I'll bring some blankets."

"Can't we just wait? It won't be much longer before it's—"

He shook his head. "It won't be done before your father returns."

"I don't understand."

"Just in case I'm unable to convince him that I mean him no harm and he shoots me on the spot, I want to die knowing that no matter who shares this room with you, I will have been the first."

"Oh, Christian," she giggled, "he isn't going to shoot you."

A commotion in the foyer below pricked Christian's instincts and moved him toward the door. "I believe, Alex, that we're about to find out."

"Page!" her father's voice boomed out and reverberated off every wall in the house.

Christian took another step to move out into the hallway, when the flash of Alexandra's shapely figure cut in front of him and exited first. In his entire lifetime he had never had a woman stand up for him, and the new experience stunned him. She was well down the hall before he realized it.

"I can explain," he heard Alexandra call.

"Out of the way, young lady," came the heated response. "This doesn't concern you."

"Yes, it does, Papa. Everything about Christian concerns me, and for once in your life you're going to hear what I have to say."

The silence that followed alerted Christian. As angry as her father was, to have his daughter speak to him in such a manner could very well have some alarming consequences. Christian appreciated her desire to take the blame for whatever her father was thinking, but he couldn't allow her to do it alone. The tangled concoction of lies and half-truths were as much his doing as hers, and he'd stand beside her when she confronted the man.

Alexandra was standing at the top of the stairs, her father halfway up when Christian moved into the hallway. He had planned to join her there, then suggest they take their discussion to the parlor in the other house. But the instant Pembrooke saw him, he raised the pistol he held at his side and pointed it at him, his nostrils flared, the muscle in his jaw twitching.

"Papa, no!" Alexandra screamed, horrified.

"Move aside, daughter," Pembrooke snarled. "This man has played us for fools for the last time."

"I will not move aside," she declared hotly, her arms widespread as if to block the path of her father or the bullet he might fire. "He has done nothing to deserve your wrath, and if you choose not to hear his side of it, then the only person who has played you for a fool is *you*."

Pembrooke's green eyes darkened all the more. "His side of what?" he growled, his weapon still aimed at Christian. "How he manipulated his way into my trust?" He gritted his teeth, then added, "*And* into your arms."

Remembering where they had stood while they kissed, Alexandra assumed her father had seen them as he rode up to the house. "I love him, Papa," she confessed, her tone strong and sure. "If you kill him, you might as well kill me, too." She could see the effect her comment had on him; his rage lessened a bit and fear gleamed in his eyes. "All I'm asking is that you give us the chance to explain . . . to tell you the whole story. One minute, Papa. Surely you can spare us that much."

The sound of footsteps on the veranda turned Pembrooke half around, and when Lynn Boone called out to him, Pembrooke asked that he and everyone with him wait outside for a few minutes. Boone consented and ushered his companions back onto the porch, closing the door behind them as he went. Once Pembrooke was sure they were alone again, he looked back at his daughter, then at Christian.

"One minute," he said, lowering his gun. "I'll give you one minute." Turning, he crossed the foyer and exited out a back door into the privacy of the shaded yard outside. Sensing that both his daughter and Christian had followed him, Pembrooke refused to face them, looking instead at the rolling meadows that surrounded his property. He'd listen to what they had to say, and for Alexandra's sake, he hoped it was believable.

"Papa?" Alexandra beckoned. "Won't you at least look at me? I know I've done some awful things since Mama died, and I probably don't deserve the consideration, but I want you to *see* that I'm telling you the truth." She waited, allowing the man his own time to decide, and then smiled once he'd granted her wish. He was a stubborn man about a lot of things, and Alexandra couldn't deny that that was one trait she had inherited from him.

"Christian doesn't agree with me," she began, giving the man at her side a soft smile before she looked at her father again. "At least not completely, but I feel that all of this is my fault. Christian wouldn't be here right now . . . *we* wouldn't be here right now if it weren't for me. I've been angry with you ever since Mama . . . ever since she died. I blamed you for it, and by some twisted reasoning I decided that I'd make you pay for it by defying you every chance I got. During one of those escapades, I met Christian."

The telling of it came easier for Alexandra once she got started. She told her father everything, every detail, even about the letter she had sent to him telling him where to find the Ambrose gang, and about the ring Christian had given the gaoler, the one she now had in her possession. She told Christian's story, and why he had been at the inn that night. Through it all, her father just stood there, listening, the expression on his face masking even the barest of clues to what he was thinking. When she had finished, he looked away from her. A long while passed before he spoke.

"Your uncle," he said solemnly. "What was his name?"

"Marion Troy," Christian supplied.

"And your cousin's name was Russel."

Christian frowned, surprised that he knew. "Yes, sir."

Turning back, Pembrooke looked Christian squarely in the eye. "You're the nephew Marion Troy raised after his sister died. He took you in and raised you as his own. He taught you how to be a carpenter."

Only Lewis Rhomberg knew that about Christian. He hadn't even told Alexandra. "How—"

"How do I know?" Pembrooke cut in. "How could I not know? We'd been keeping track of every move Ambrose made, every person he came in contact with in the hope that somewhere along the way one of those people would

turn against him. We knew about a young boy who had
joined his gang, and we had made plans to get to him. What
we couldn't foresee was that Russel would panic and run when
confronted by one of my deputies. He wasn't supposed to
get killed." The memories appeared to weigh heavily against
Pembrooke's shoulders as he sighed and shook his head. "All
I wanted to do was talk to him." He fell quiet for a moment
as if he were reliving that awful night all over again. "Your
uncle seemed to understand. He told the constable that he didn't
blame the deputy for what had happened, that in his opinion
Garrett Ambrose was to blame. Then a few days later I was
told that Marion Troy had been killed when he took the law
into his own hands. I should have expected that, I suppose."
He looked briefly at Christian before he turned away again.
"That sort of thing was a part of my job," he went on to
explain. "I had seen it happen many times, and I was afraid
it would happen again if Marion Troy had any kin willing to
take up where he had left off. So, I had one of my men ask
around about him. That's how I found out about the nephew
he'd raised. What I wasn't told was the young man's name,
only that he had left England years before." He snorted and
turned around to face the man watching him. "Amazing, isn't
it, how one missing piece of information could have spared a
lot of suffering?" He shook his head. "If I had only known you
were Marion Troy's nephew . . . " He shifted his attention to
his daughter. "If I had only known how much you hated me
for your mother's suicide . . . "

"I never really hated you, Papa," Alexandra denied. "I was
angry with you for having an affair, but—"

"I beg your pardon?" he cut in, his brows drawn tightly
together.

She could feel the blood rushing to her face. She hadn't meant
to blurt it out like that. It had to be embarrassing for a man
to learn that his daughter knew all about his personal matters
away from home, and doubly embarrassing to have them aired
in front of anyone other than kin.

"Alexandra?"

Ashamed, she couldn't bring herself to look at him.

"Alexandra, where did you get such a notion?"

She could hear the anger in his voice and it sparked her own. "A notion, Papa?" she challenged. "It's what Mama believed or she wouldn't have killed herself."

"Did she tell you that?"

"Of course not. I was only fourteen years old. I wouldn't have understood what she meant if she had. I figured it out for myself years later. Are you denying it?"

His eyes flashed at her before settling on the man at her side. Seeing how uncomfortable Christian was at that moment, he elected to ease the younger man's difficulty. "I'm assuming since Alexandra has declared her love for you that you must feel the same about her. Or am I taking too much for granted?"

"What has that got to do with any of it?" she demanded, and in return received a scalding look from her father.

"As always, Alexandra, you're too busy turning assumption into fact to notice how your tirades make other people uneasy," he sternly pointed out. "If he has plans to marry you, then I'll have no compunction whatsoever about sharing family secrets with my future son-in-law."

"If you must know, we haven't discussed it," she replied. "And I'd prefer he ask on his own without any prodding from you." He drew in a sharp, angry breath to argue her choice of words, but she cut him off. "Papa, I understand your reluctance, but don't you think, after all Christian's done for us, that sharing family secrets with him won't even begin to pay the debt we owe him?"

Pembrooke started to reply, glanced at the man about whom they spoke, and breathed a tired sigh. He hated to admit it, but for once in his life he actually agreed with something his daughter said. "Yes, child, you're right. Christian deserves that and a whole lot more." He moved past them on his way down the knoll toward the other house. "Come with me," he ordered, not bothering to look back to see if they were following him.

Once they had entered through the front door, he waved the couple into the parlor while he went into his bedroom. A moment later he emerged carrying a folded piece of paper, yellowed with age. He motioned for Alexandra to sit down and then took the chair next to her by the fireplace. Christian, who still felt out of place no matter what father and daughter had decided, chose to stand near the window, close enough to hear should one of them ask something of him, yet far enough away to give them a small measure of privacy.

"I know how much you loved your mother, Alexandra," he began, "and that was the only reason I've kept the truth from you. I thought I could shoulder the blame and your resentment for as long as it took, if it meant your feelings for her would never change. Now I realize how unfair that has been to you." He handed Alexandra the letter he had taken from his wife's jewelry box and studied her beautiful face while she read it, thinking how much she looked like her mother and how very much he still missed his wife. When she had finished and he could see the confusion and hurt in her eyes, he clasped her hands in his. "Promise me," he urged, "that you'll listen to everything I have to say and that you'll judge her fairly, that you'll take all things into account and weigh them as she had seen them. It's important that you understand how she felt and why the last thing on her mind that night was to ask for my forgiveness."

"I promise, Papa," she whispered, sensing how much pain he was in and that whatever he was about to tell her would be difficult for him to admit.

"I would suppose I'm not much different from most men who have a wife and family to care for," he confessed, leaning back in his chair and staring into the cold fireplace. "I wanted the best for them. And the only way I felt I could do that was to work harder. Before long I lost sight of my reasons, and my job became more important than my family. I started working late and when I came home, I went straight to bed, too tired to spend any time with my wife or my daughter." He smiled a tired kind of smile. "But I guess you know that, don't you?"

"What happened, Papa?" Alexandra asked, reaching out to touch his hand and show him that she had already forgiven him.

"Your mother dealt with it quite well . . . for several years as a matter of fact. What woman wouldn't make the sacrifice if it meant having fine clothes and jewels and being invited to all the right parties and dinners and the like? At least that's what I thought. But your mother was different from all the other women. Money wasn't important to her. Her husband was.

After a time she felt she was losing me . . . to my work, not to another woman. She began to think that she'd lost her beauty and charm or whatever it was that had attracted me to her in the first place. That wasn't true, of course. I love her as much right now as I did on the day I asked her to become my wife."

Alexandra noticed how his eyes glistened and that he had to swallow hard before he could continue.

"In a moment of weakness she let herself be swept away by another man's sweet words of adoration. It was my fault, of course. I forced her into his arms."

"Oh, Papa," Alexandra moaned, tears streaming down her face.

"It only happened that one time, but the guilt over what she'd done simply became too much for her. I noticed a change in her, but I was never able to figure out what had caused it. We began to argue . . . over stupid things, and rather than face up to the fact that I might have had something to do with it, I found excuses for being away from home more often and for long periods of time."

He angrily brushed away a tear from his cheek. "I knew she was unhappy, but I never dreamed to what extent. I swear to you, daughter, had I known . . . "

"It's over, Papa," Alexandra encouraged, slipping from her chair to kneel in front of him on the floor, her hands covering his. "It's time we both stopped blaming ourselves or each other . . . or even Mama. It just happened. We can't pretend that it didn't and we can't change it, but we can stop letting it rule our lives." She reached up and gently stroked his cheek. "Forgive me, Papa?"

Dark green eyes filled with tears looked back at her. "If you'll forgive me."

"I do," she vowed, smiling through her pain. "And I swear I will never doubt you again for as long as I live. Never."

Together, they rose and held each other in a long overdue embrace.

"Tell me something, Christian," Alexandra asked later that evening as they stood on the veranda watching her father talk with Boone and the other men near the barn. "Do all parents pay such a high price for loving their children as my father has?"

Slipping his arm around her waist, he gave her a gentle squeeze. "Sometimes," he admitted. "But if you were to ask your father that question, I'm sure he would say it was all worth it."

She gave a trembling sigh and laid her head on his shoulder. "Promise me we'll never drift apart the way Mama and Papa did, that no matter what, we'll always be able to talk to each other, openly and freely."

He smiled and kissed her brow. "I doubt your father would ever allow that to happen as long as he's alive, but if it will make you feel better, I promise."

A soft breeze rustled the treetops and drew his attention away from her, for with it came the faint odor of smoke. Dinner had been over with for some time now, which meant the smell couldn't be coming from the wood stove in the kitchen, and the night was still too warm to warrant starting a fire in the hearth in either the crew's quarters or the house. Christian wanted to pretend that he had simply imagined it, and that there was nothing to be concerned about, but he knew better. A brush fire sweeping across the meadow with just the right amount of wind. . . .

"Christian? What's wrong?" Alexandra asked, breaking into his thoughts. She had felt his body tense and knew something had distracted him.

He inhaled deeply, testing the air again. "Go and find Felice and Thomas," he instructed, stepping off the veranda. "They need to hear this too. I'll be with your father and the rest of the men."

His urgency frightened her. "Christian, what is it?"

He glanced off at the horizon, his blue eyes searching. "Not what, Alex. Who." He looked back at her and jerked his head toward the house. "Go!" he ordered, turning on his heel and sprinting off.

"I knew there was something devious about Harvey Smith the first time I laid eyes on him," Boone seethed as he stood talking with Pembrooke and the others. "The little viper couldn't pick on a man of normal intelligence. He had to go and kill a simpleton."

"It's only speculation, Lynn," Pembrooke reminded him. "We're not absolutely positive he's the one responsible."

"But you said they had a witness who saw Smith talking to the Pickering boy. An hour later they found his body."

"That's true, but talking to someone doesn't make him a murderer." Pembrooke shrugged. "Besides, the commissioner hasn't come up with a reason why Smith would kill him." He frowned, remembering the rumors he'd heard. "Except . . . "

"Except what?"

There were still a few pieces missing, but the longer Pembrooke thought about it, the more sense it made. "Gossip has it that the Pickering boy might have been the illegitimate son of one of the Rauscher brothers."

"What?" Boone exclaimed. He remembered why Smith had run off and drew his own conclusions. "Do you suppose that's what he was looking for under the floorboards in your daughter's room?" He shook his head. "That doesn't make any sense. If he knew the will named the boy as sole beneficiary, you'd think finding the will would be the last thing on his mind. Killing the only heir is logical, but . . . " He fell quiet for a moment, trying to sort it all out, when a strong breeze stirred up the scent of smoke. He cocked his head, frowned, then glanced off toward the horizon. Where the green of the meadow met the darkening clouds of an approaching storm, a gray-white haze divided the two. He was about to draw Pembrooke's attention to it, when he spotted Christian running toward them and raised a hand instead to point at the skyline.

"Take as many men as you need and herd the sheep to the stream," Christian ordered without waiting to be asked. "The rest of you grab a shovel or anything you can find. If we're to save the buildings, we'll have to dig a fire break."

Confusion ruled the moment as many were unaware of the danger sweeping across the grassy plain toward them.

"You heard the man!" Boone shouted. "Move!"

Within minutes the entire place was bustling with activity. Boone had taken five of the men with him, leaving the other four, Christian, Pembrooke, Alexandra, Felice, and Thomas to work frantically with shovels and pickaxes. No one spoke while they uprooted the lush, green grass in a path four feet wide, exposing dark soil and their only hope of stopping the fire before it spread close enough to destroy everything everyone had worked so hard to build. Thunder rumbled in the distance, and while the last rays of daylight slipped beyond the hills, black clouds raced in from the east. The wind grew stronger. The smell of smoke thickened, and it became more difficult to breathe as the gray fog inched closer. The heat intensified.

Exhaustion claimed its first victim when Felice, too tired to continue, dropped her shovel and sank to the ground.

"Thomas!" Christian directed. "Get Felice a drink of water— and bring the bucket back with you."

The man hurried off.

"And bring some rags!" Christian called after him.

He returned a moment later with the supplies and everyone paused long enough to quench his thirst and dampen the cloth he was given. With the wet cloths tied over their noses and mouths, they took up their task again.

The only thing that seemed to move quickly was the fire. The trench they had dug and the time they had spent working on it fell short of Christian's expectations, and he paused in his digging to reevaluate his thinking. Amid the smoke that stung his nostrils he could smell the sweet odor of rain. But would the downpour come soon enough? He glanced at the work they'd done thus far, and he wondered how much longer they should stand their ground. Felice had already collapsed once, and he was sure Alexandra couldn't last much longer. Within minutes the flames, which were quickly devouring everything in their path, would soon be upon them.

"Sir Wallis?" he shouted over the roar of fire and thunder. "It's not safe here for the women anymore."

"I agree," Pembrooke called back. "It's not safe for any of us." He turned to the man at his side. "Richard, you and the other men harness what horses we need and turn the rest loose. We're leaving . . . all of us."

"But, Papa," Alexandra argued, "everything you own is here. We can't just turn our backs on it."

"And if we're all dead, what good would it be to any of us?" he asked, throwing down his spade. Squinting up through the smoke circling above his head, he looked at the sky. "It's in God's hands now."

A crack of thunder boomed close by, drowning out any response any of them might have had. A gust of wind swirled the smoke downward, and while Alexandra pulled the damp cloth from around her neck and covered her mouth and nose with it once more, she and everyone with her raced for the barn. A short while later the group, including Benton Wall, galloped off just as the fire swept across the yard and ignited a pile of straw near the barn which in turn exploded in a hot, rolling ball of flame.

"Where are we going?" Alexandra shouted, her arms clutched tightly around Christian's waist as she sat behind him on the chestnut stallion.

"To one of the line cabins," he replied, glancing briefly over his shoulder at the fire. "It sits on the other side of the stream. You'll be safe there."

"What about you?"

"Once I'm sure you'll be all right, I want to check on Lynn and the sheep. I'll be careful, if that's what you're asking."

Christian waved the group north once they had crested a knoll and headed them toward a line of trees a few hundred yards further on. The dense smoke thinned out as soon as they cut down into the valley, and by the time they reached the stream, it was easier for them to breathe. The cabin stood just on the other side, and once Christian had led his party across the water and had helped Alexandra down, he swung his horse around, ready to ride out again. It was then that he discovered they were one person short.

"Dolter," he called. "Where's Sir Wallis?"

"I don't know, Christian. He was right behind me when we left the barn. You don't suppose he went back for something, do you?"

"Christian?" Alexandra whimpered, her eyes wide circles of fear. "Find him."

"I will," he promised, yanking on the reins and spinning the horse back in the direction of the house.

The violence of the storm had increased by the time Christian cleared the knoll again. To his left he could see a curtain of rain pelting the ground as it swept across the meadow, but it had come too late to save the barn, the tool shed, or the livery. While the fire further threatened the old house as it shot across the yard to the veranda, there was hope the downpour would soak the ground long before the flames reached the newly constructed building sitting high atop the hill to his right. Yet the instant Christian saw Pembrooke's horse tied to the front porch railing and how the animal was frantically trying to break free, nothing else mattered. For some reason Pembrooke had put his life in danger by going back into the house, and it was up to Christian to show him the error in his judgment. Kicking his heels in the stallion's flanks, he tightened his grip on the reins as the horse reared up, whinnied loudly, and then lunged forward, head held high, ears back and nostrils flared.

By the time Christian had cut the distance to the house in half, the fire had spread across the veranda. Long, orange flames seared the walls on the front of the house and stretched to ignite the roof. Smoke obscured the entrance and the windows facing him, and he couldn't understand how Pembrooke had failed to notice that his exit from the place was in jeopardy. Knowing the man probably wouldn't hear him calling to him, Christian did so anyway.

"Pembrooke! Get out of the house! Now!" he shouted, his words lost in the explosion of thunder overhead.

Suddenly the sky opened up and he was hit full force with the fury of the storm. Unaffected by the rain, the fire shot up the front of the house to engulf the roof, the porch, and most importantly, the opened doorway, and Christian kicked his horse again, urging the beast to run harder and faster. He shouted a warning a second time, a third, as he raced the stallion onward, the distance between him and the house seeming to multiply rather than shorten. Before his very eyes, he watched the wood-framed building turn into a wall of fire.

"*Pembrooke!*" he screamed one last time, knowing in his heart it was too late.

···❧[Chapter Twenty]❧···

"HOW'S SHE DOING, CHRISTIAN?" LYNN BOONE ASKED AS HE came to stand beside the man at the edge of the stream.

"As well as can be expected," Christian answered solemnly. "Felice is with her."

Boone glanced back at the one-room cabin, then up at the clear, moonlit sky overhead. Australian nights had a special kind of beauty that no other country's possessed, yet this particular night failed to arouse even the slightest amount of pleasure. The rain had come in time to save the new house and the crew's quarters, but not in time to spare Pembrooke, and everyone felt the loss. In Boone's opinion, whatever it was that had made the man go into the house simply wasn't worth paying for with his life. Boone couldn't help wondering what would become of him and the rest of the crew now that Pembrooke was dead. Would his daughter sell the property and return to England? And what would happen to Christian? Curious about whether the same thoughts were running through his companion's mind, he stole a peek at the man standing beside him, knowing that now was not the time to ask.

"Christian, have you any idea why Sir Wallis was so careless with his life?" he asked instead.

Closing his eyes, Christian slowly shook his head before answering. "I found a locket in his hand. I'm not positive but I would imagine it belonged to his wife, and he didn't want to part with it."

"How sad," Boone declared with a sigh. "Did you give it to Miss Alexandra?"

Christian shook his head again. "No. I buried him with it.

I decided that that was what he probably would have wanted, since he took such a lethal risk in going after it. I told Alexandra about it, and she agreed."

The pair grew quiet for a time, each with his own thoughts on the tragedy, before Boone muttered under his breath and bent to pick up a twig. "I suppose Miss Alexandra would be better off going back home to England, don't you?"

Christian shrugged. "That's up to her, but I rather doubt she will. At least not for a while, anyway."

"What will happen to you if she does?" Boone was bold enough to ask. "I know you two care a lot about each other. I wouldn't think she'd leave without you, and you're not exactly free to go. As far as the governor's concerned, you're a convict . . . like the rest of us."

The comment brought Lewis Rhomberg to mind. He had been Christian's only hope, but now that Pembrooke was dead, Christian wasn't sure Lewis's testimony would be enough to convince the governor, since Darling and Rhomberg were virtual strangers. Stooping, Christian plucked a single wildflower from the batch growing on the bank of the stream, idly twirling the stem between his thumb and forefinger while he considered what else he might do to clear his name. It wasn't so much that he cared about his own reputation, but rather that Alexandra's name not be linked with that of a convict. After all she'd been through, she deserved every kindness possible. Frowning, he tossed aside the flower and stood. And the most important kindness would be seeing that her father's killer was brought to justice.

"I'll be staying here tonight," he said, glancing at the soft light shining out through the cabin window. "You and the rest of the men can head on back. And take Wall with you. Just be sure someone's watching him all the time. He's our only chance at finding the man responsible for Pembrooke's death, and I don't want him disappearing on us."

"Don't worry, Christian. There isn't a one of us any less determined than you to see that done," Boone assured him. "If you'd like, after I see that everything's safe and sound, I could come back and relieve you for a spell."

Christian shook his head. "I'm a light sleeper." He took a

deep breath; his nostrils flared as he tried to control what little he had left of his patience. What he truly wanted to do was go looking for Garrett Ambrose. He wanted to kill the man right then and there. But Ambrose was only a part of what had transpired, and no justice would be served until both Ambrose and the man who had hired him were caught. "I'll be all right, but thanks just the same."

"See you in the morning, then," Boone replied as he waved for the group standing nearby to mount up.

Fatigue set in once Boone and the rest of the men had ridden off, and Christian settled himself down against the trunk of a tree. He was bone weary and his body ached to stretch out on a soft bed of grass, but he knew if he closed his eyes, sleep wouldn't come. He simply had too much on his mind. For the first time since Min Le's death, he'd found a reason to want to go on living, and now because of what had happened in the last few hours, he was in danger of losing it. He'd told Boone that he doubted Alexandra would return to England and he'd meant it. But there was a very real chance she would. And if she did, she would have to leave without him.

The pain of such a thought was more than he could bear, and he raised his face to the black sky above him, silently seeking a greater power to give him strength. A quiet had enveloped the land and made a mockery of all that had transpired earlier, a cynical kind of peace that brazenly reminded him of how very fragile human life really was, that no matter how much love one had in his heart, it would never be enough. Angry all of a sudden, he jerked himself to his feet and leaned heavily against the tree, willing himself the knowledge to understand its meaning. He had already suffered more than any man should have to suffer. Must he do so again?

In the distance he heard the faint rumble of thunder as the storm moved farther away, taking with it the last evidence of the fury it had reaped upon the earth, and he turned to look at it. Instead he saw the shadowy figure of someone walking toward him, and his heartbeat quickened when she stepped into the moonlight, her radiant green eyes filled with sadness. Without a word, she came to him, and he held her in his arms as though there would be no tomorrow. He kissed her lips, her brow, her cheek. He breathed in the sweet fragrance of her perfume, while he held her close and comforted her.

"I'm afraid, Christian," Alexandra wept.

"Of what, my love?" he questioned tenderly as he lifted a dark curl from her brow.

"That someday I will lose you, too." She hugged him more tightly to her. "Swear to me that it will never happen."

"I swear," he whispered, though in his heart he knew the danger of such a pledge.

The sound of racing hoofbeats against the earth jarred Christian awake. He sprang to his feet, shook off the numbing effects of his half-conscious state, and squinted in the direction from which the noise had come, one hand raised to shade his eyes from the bright sunlight of early morning. Two riders approached, and within minutes Christian recognized Lynn Boone on the lead horse. The man's arrival didn't surprise Christian, since they had agreed to meet, but the sight of the second man, the one Boone had tied facedown across the saddle and whose horse's reins Boone held in his hand, brought a puzzled frown to Christian's brow.

"Good morning, Christian," Boone called out cheerfully. "Sleep well?" He directed the pair of animals across the stream, pulled them to a halt beside his friend, and tossed the second set of reins at Christian. "Here, I brought you a present."

The gag around Harvey Smith's mouth prevented him from objecting to the treatment he'd received, but from the agitated manner in which he struggled against his bonds, Christian was sure he wasn't at all pleased.

"We found the little snake rooting around what's left of the old house this morning," Boone said as he threw a leg over his horse and jumped to the ground. "I was inclined to beat him senseless, but Dolter showed me the error in my thinking. He said that honor should be yours. So . . . " He smiled, stepped close, and slapped Smith across the back of his head. "I'm volunteering to hold him while you do."

"What was he looking for?"

Boone shrugged. "Don't know. I didn't bother to ask him." He grabbed the man by the scruff of his neck and unceremoniously dragged him off the horse. "Would you like to ask him?" He gave Smith a hard shake and glared in his face while he untied the gag. "Every word that comes out of your mouth had better be the truth," he warned. "Because if it isn't . . ." He deliberately let the rest go unsaid. "What were you looking for?"

"Gold," Smith quickly confessed. "I was looking for gold."

"In a burned-out building?" Boone roared, his eyes narrowed with rage. "What do you think we are? A couple of morons?" He doubled up his fist and held it beneath the man's nose. "Let's start again. What were you looking for?"

"It's the truth! I swear it!" Smith whined. "I found a letter Evart Rauscher had written saying he had hid a large amount of gold under the floorboards in his room . . . Miss Pembrooke's room."

"And you decided it belonged to you," Boone finished.

"Yes! Yes, it belongs to me," Smith argued. "I'm the one who took care of those foul-tempered, crazy old men. I'm the one who fed them, put them to bed, and nursed them when they were sick. Nobody else had to put up with their insanity. Me, just me!" In a rage, he tried to jerk free of the iron grip Boone had on him, only to find himself nearly lifted off his feet. "Oh, you're such a brave man as long as my hands are tied. Turn me loose, Boone, and then let's see how hard you're willing to push me around."

The rage on Boone's face turned into a cynical smile. "You'd like that, wouldn't you? It's easier to run when your arms aren't bound behind you." He shook the man again. "Well, forget it, Smith. You're not going anywhere until we've heard the whole story."

"I've told you everything!" Smith screeched.

"No, you haven't. You haven't told us who killed the Pickering boy."

Smith's face went ashen.

"You see?" Boone continued dryly. "I knew there was something you forgot tell us." The smile vanished and he pulled the man in close. "Shall I tell it for you, and you can stop me if I get something wrong?"

Smith's body began to tremble all the more, and he looked

at Christian for help, only to find a pair of cold, flinty blue eyes staring back at him.

"I don't know where you got the letter, but I'm willing to bet it told you two things: one was the location of the gold, and the second was that the Rauscher brothers had an heir. Now, in order for you to have the gold free and clear, you had to get rid of the illegitimate son. No problem, really. After all, the boy was retarded. Getting to the gold, however, turned out to be a little more difficult than you had figured on. The yarn you told Pembrooke about a will got you nowhere. So, you decided on a different approach once you'd heard about Garrett Ambrose and his obsession with the man who was living in the house where the gold was hidden."

"No!" Smith exclaimed, positive he knew what Boone was implying.

"You made him a deal. You set him loose on the promise that he run Pembrooke off the property." Boone tightened his hold on the man's shirt front, intending to strangle the breath from him. "You slimy little bastard. Sir Wallis's dead because of you."

"No!" Smith choked out. "Mr. Page, please! Get him off me! That's not . . . how it was at all. I swear—"

"Lynn, wait," Christian cut in, reaching out to seize his companion's wrist. "He's telling the truth. Let him go."

"What?" Boone exploded, his eyes black with rage. "You actually believe he's innocent?"

"Only of Pembrooke's death." He squeezed Boone's wrist a little harder. "Let go."

Boone had learned his own shortcomings years ago. A quick temper and the failure to hear a man out were two of his worst. When he believed he was right about something, nothing else mattered and no one stood in his way. The first trait had landed him here in a penal colony, and although he had vowed then to work on changing that part of his character, it had proven difficult. He was getting better at it, but he still had a long way to go, and if it had been anyone other than Christian Page asking, he probably would have ignored the demand. Gritting his teeth, he released his hold and shoved Smith away.

Christian realized how hard Boone's surrender had been

for him. The man had made no secret about his feelings for Pembrooke, and even though he wasn't alone in his determination to see someone pay, Christian was glad Boone had decided to wait for absolute proof before acting.

"I suggest, Mr. Smith," Christian began, "that you tell your version of what happened, and that you not leave out a single detail. If I think for one minute that you're lying, I won't step in the way again." He gave him a hard look. "Am I making myself perfectly clear?"

Smith nodded and nervously glanced past him at Boone. He swallowed, cleared his throat, and took a deep breath. "All my life I've avoided work. That's the reason I wound up here in Australia. I got caught stealing and was sentenced here. I was assigned to Evart and Virgil Rauscher, and the minute I met them I knew I could make them do anything I wanted . . . well, Virgil, anyway," he corrected, shifting his attention from Christian to Boone long enough to see that the man wasn't glaring threateningly at him anymore. "I pampered the two of them like they were kin until I had convinced Virgil that he should write me into his will. Evart went crazy when his brother told him what he had planned, and they wound up shoving each other around. Then Virgil fell and hit his head, and Evart blamed me for killing him!"

"Go on," Christian urged, impatient to hear the rest.

"Well, Evart attacked me and I had to shoot him to save myself. And I ended up with nothing! So I ran. Then a few months later I heard the property had been given to Sir Wallis and since I didn't have anything to lose, I decided to tell him that the previous owners had left a will and that I was named in it. All I was after was some money." He grunted and looked away. "And he gives me a job," he muttered.

"Where does the letter come in?" Christian pressed.

"Remember the trunk with the brothers' stuff Pembrooke let me have? I found it hidden in a jewelry box. It was written from Evart to his brother, and in it he told Virgil about the bastard son Virgil had fathered and that Evart was paying the boy's mother to keep quiet about it—not much, he said, because he didn't want the woman to think they were rich. He had some twisted idea that the mother would lay claim to everything the brothers had, so Evart was hiding most of their wealth under the floorboards in his room. Even Virgil didn't know how much money they actually had."

"So you killed Sir Wallis to have it all to yourself," Boone growled as he took a step forward and shot out a hand to grab Smith by the throat.

"No!" Smith screamed, jumping back. "I took Sir Wallis up on his offer of a job because I was hoping that sooner or later I'd have the chance to get at the gold without anybody knowing. I swear to you I don't know a thing about Garrett Ambrose. Think about it, Mr. Boone. What sense does it make for me to include someone in on this when all I had to do was wait for my chance? I didn't want the damned property! I wanted the gold!"

Boone scowled back at him, obviously not convinced but willing to consider the possibility. "Do you believe him, Christian?" he asked after a moment. "I'm not sure I do. He killed one man because of his greed. He could certainly kill another."

"Well, there's an easy way to find out," Christian replied.

According to Benton Wall, the gang Garrett Ambrose had assembled since his escape totaled ten, a number that concerned Christian, since of the group he was taking with him, only Lynn Boone and he knew how to handle a gun. It meant they would have to catch Ambrose and the others off guard if they were to prevent any bloodshed.

"Figured out what we're going to do once we get there?" Boone asked as he rode alongside Christian, the reins of Benton Wall's horse gripped tightly in his hand.

"It depends," Christian admitted with a glance over his shoulder at Richard Dolter and Clarence Feipel.

"On what?"

"On whether or not Ambrose is alone."

"You think he will be?"

Christian shrugged. "If I've learned anything about the man, it's that he doesn't like to share if he doesn't have to."

"You're thinking he might try to cheat the rest of his men by not telling them about the meeting?"

Christian nodded.

"That is if there's anybody to meet," Boone added sarcastically. "Personally, I think Smith's our man." When his companion failed to agree or to make any comment at all, he raised an eyebrow and smiled over at Christian. "You don't."

Christian shook his head.

"Why not?"

A slow smile worked Christian's mouth. "Just a feeling I have."

"A feeling," Boone repeated. "No wonder you wound up in Australia. I'll bet you had a feeling Miss Alexandra wouldn't turn you in."

Surprised by the remark, Christian couldn't hold back the laughter. "You know me better than I thought you did, Lynn. That's exactly the mistake I made." He laughed again and studied the path they were taking.

"Have you ever considered what the results would have been if she hadn't wanted her revenge?" Boone further teased. "You wouldn't be here, but the two of you wouldn't have gotten to know each other."

Christian thought about asking Boone if he believed in fate and decided against it, as his mood turned solemn again. Fate, in his opinion, had killed Alexandra's father. He loved Alexandra, but if he'd been given the choice, he would have continued living without her if it meant Sir Wallis wouldn't have had to die. He doubted anyone really blamed him for the accident that took Pembrooke's life, but the events leading up to it had all come about because of him.

"I'm surprised she didn't insist on coming with us," he heard Boone speculate, and he forced himself to dismiss his thoughts. What lay ahead of them was dangerous enough without his mind being muddled with regrets.

"She did," he admitted. "That's why I instructed Franklin not to listen to a word she says. It wouldn't surprise me any if she tried to trick him into thinking we needed their help."

Boone frowned. "Well, I hope you're right in that respect . . . that we don't need their help. I've played a part in a lot of fights, Christian, but this one makes me nervous."

Christian glanced at Wall who had been listening to their

entire conversation. "Just remember to keep him in front of you. If he's been lying, he'll take the first bullet."

A half smile lifted the corner of Wall's mouth, but other than that, he showed no reaction.

The meeting place, Wall had instructed, was a little over an hour away. It had been Christian's idea to arrive there ahead of the prearranged time so that he and his men could station themselves in the rocks overlooking the spot. Once Ambrose and the stranger—and any of the men Ambrose might have elected to bring with him—were in clear view, Boone was to fire off a warning shot that would hopefully convince the group not to make any sudden moves. But once Christian had explained his plan, and their destination lay only a short ride further on, Wall decided to point out a major flaw.

"You weren't listening to me, Page," Wall criticized. "I said we never got a look at the man's face because he didn't want us to be able to recognize him later. Do you really think he'll have changed his mind about that? He'll stick to the shadows or stand behind a rock while he meets with Garrett. You'll hear his voice, but you won't know where he is."

The last observation brought a chuckle from Lynn Boone. "And you don't know much about Christian Page. He doesn't have to see a man to know where he is." He pulled the pistol from his waistband as he dismounted and motioned for Wall to do the same. "And just in case *you've* had a change of mind, Dolter's gonna gag you." He nodded at Dolter who quickly obliged Boone's suggestion.

An hour passed in tense silence. The sun was beginning to slip beyond the treetops as night descended upon the land, and the air was still as if it sensed the danger lurking all around. The four men had taken up their positions where each of them had an unrestricted view of the clearing below them. They had readied their weapons and prepared themselves for battle as each had made a personal vow that this day Sir Wallis Pembrooke's death would be avenged . . . at any price. Then, in the distance, a faint sound broke the quiet.

"Wall, you do anything to warn them that we're here," Christian hissed as he crouched low before the man, "and you'll be the first to die. You understand me?"

No fear showed in the man's eyes as he inclined his head, only a hint of respect, and in that moment Christian was sure of Wall's decision to leave the Ambrose gang. They continued to stare at each other for a few moments, until the pounding of a single horse's hooves against the earth alerted Christian. Dropping to the ground, he quickly shed his stockings and shoes, and slipped noiselessly into the darkness surrounding him.

Only now did Garrett Ambrose truly miss his henchman's company, for with Benton Wall at his side, Ambrose feared very little. Even the pair of pistols he carried failed to chase away the eerie sense that he was being watched, and he shook off the chill that started down his spine as he moved to sit on a rock where a sheer bluff behind him protected his back and the location gave him full view of the meeting place. A rustling noise to his right brought him to his feet and one of the pistols to his hand. He listened and waited, then cursed the unseen rodent that had set his nerves on edge as he slowly lowered himself back down. The pounding of his heart marked off the minutes that elapsed, and just when he had about decided that no money in any amount was worth all this, the cynical laughter of a man hidden in the shadows catapulted him upright once more.

"Why, Mr. Ambrose," the voice mocked, "you seem nervous."

"What man wouldn't be when he's put at the disadvantage?" Ambrose barked in return. "The least you could have done was call out."

Silence enveloped him again, and he strained to hear the man moving about as he had done the last time they had met.

Finally, from a different direction, the voice came again. "Where's your huge friend? He's not hiding somewhere close by, is he? 'Twould be foolish, if he is."

Ambrose wondered if he should keep Wall's capture a secret. He needed the money this man promised him, and if he were to learn that there was a possibility Pembrooke might already know about their deal. . . . He mentally shook off the notion. Benton Wall would never turn on him.

"I didn't think he needed to be included," he said instead.

Laughter answered him. "I'm sure you didn't." A black bag sailed through the air and landed with a thud at Ambrose's feet. "Besides, this way he'll never know what his share really was. Clever, Mr. Ambrose. Very clever."

Perspiration dotted Ambrose's brow, but rather than allow the man to see how jumpy he made him by wiping it away, Ambrose bent and scooped up the pouch.

"The fire . . . was that your doing? Or just the cruelty of nature."

"Mine," Ambrose shot back, stuffing the bag inside his shirt. "I got tired of waiting."

"Luckily for you it turned out all right," the stranger advised.

"What do you mean?" Ambrose demanded, irked by the insinuation that it had been anything less than brilliant. A twig snapped from somewhere close by, and he jerked around in time to see the tall figure of a man move out into the fading light of the sunset. His frown deepened once he realized, too late, that the bag of gold he'd been given had only been a ploy to trick him into letting down his guard. And it had worked, for while his gun hung at his side, the stranger's pistol was aimed at his head.

"A shift in the wind and you would have destroyed everything *I* own," Wayne Pleasanton snarled, his face twisted with the contempt he felt for the man he confronted. "You're dangerous, Garrett Ambrose, because you're inept. I should have realized that from the start. Without men like Benton Wall surrounding you, you're nothing. He's the one I should have hired. He's too dumb to think on his own. You're just plain stupid."

Ambrose's body stiffened with the insult.

"You think not?" Pleasanton challenged. "Then explain to me why you let yourself get caught. Are you fond of prisons? Or did you decide you simply needed a change of scenery?"

Wayne Pleasanton's mistake came in allowing himself the pleasure of laughing at the aspersions he'd made, for when he threw back his head, Garrett Ambrose seized the moment. In one swift move, he raised his gun, cocked and fired it, striking Pleasanton in the chest and hurling him backward to the ground. Without waiting to see if he'd killed him, Ambrose turned for his horse.

Christian had listened to the conversation of the two men from a few yards away. He hadn't wanted to intervene until he'd heard enough to know that Pleasanton was working alone and that the danger would end with him. He hadn't, however, meant to wait until it was too late to stop one of them from killing the other. And he certainly wasn't about to let Ambrose get away. Like a cat, he leaped from one rocky plateau to the next until he had placed himself high above where Ambrose was about to mount his horse. Then, without a sound, he sprang.

Ambrose saw only a flash of something before Christian hit him. Together they tumbled to the ground, but while he struggled to come back up on his feet, Christian had already disarmed him and stood waiting. Knees bent, feet apart and one a little ahead of the other, his arms held close to his sides and his fingers curled into half-closed fists, Christian focused all of his energy on the death blow he would administer. He had been taught by a master, and while the temptation was strong to break every bone in his opponent's body one at a time, he couldn't ignore the words that drummed in his head.

"Be merciful, Christian," Sang Soo had preached. "Even your enemy should die with honor."

"Why?" he could remember asking. "If a man threatens your life or that of someone you love, why show mercy?"

"If hatred guides your hand, it will seize your heart as well. By his death, he will win."

Christian had always listened to the old man's beliefs, and there were times when he had questioned them. But he had never doubted the wisdom behind the words, and he didn't doubt it now.

Shifting his weight off his back foot once Ambrose lunged, Christian leaned forward and shot out his right hand with lightning speed, his forefinger extended. The blow caught his adversary in the chest, the finger thrust between the man's ribs and into his heart, killing him instantly.

"For you, Sang Soo," he whispered, staring down at Garrett Ambrose's lifeless body. "And for Alexandra."

·❈⟩ Epilogue ⟨❈·

"PATCHES! HERE, BOY!" ALEXANDRA CALLED ONCE SHE SPOT-
ted the multicolored puppy bounding for the clothesline and the
sheets billowing in the breeze. "Oh, Patches, Felice is going to
take a broom to you if you muddy the laundry with those big
paws of yours. Patches!"

A shrill whistle from in back of her rent the air and brought
the dog to a clumsy halt in midstride. He stumbled, fell forward, and rolled three times before he could catch his balance,
come up on his feet, and head back in Alexandra's direction,
his pink tongue bouncing with each lumbering step he took.

"Oh, Christian," she laughed when she felt his arms encircle
her and pull her back against his chest. "Do you really think
there's any hope for him?"

"Nobody thought his namesake would amount to much
either, but he turned out all right," Christian assured her.
"It'll take time, but yes, there's hope. After all, he's still just
a puppy. But on the outside chance he doesn't, Mr. Welch told
me to let him know, that we can have the pick of his bitch's
next litter."

"Too late," she told him with a smile. "This one's already
won my heart."

"I know what you mean," he agreed.

A month had passed since the fire, and with the exception
of the tool shed that had yet to be torn down and rebuilt, there
was hardly any evidence of the destruction Garrett Ambrose
had caused. The completion of the new house had taken prece-
dence, and although it was sparsely furnished, Alexandra and
her maid had been able to move in within the first few days.

The kitchen, barn, and shearing shed were next, and Christian predicted that by the end of the week, the livery would be ready for use.

Governor Darling and a party of four other dignitaries had paid them a visit within days after the news of Pembrooke's death had reached him. He had expressed his sympathy to Alexandra for her loss, stating that her father would be missed by a great number of people as well as by him. He had voiced his gratitude to Christian for his help in stopping Garrett Ambrose, and his dismay at learning how greedy Wayne Pleasanton had been. He thanked him on behalf of Florence Pickering for capturing her son's murderer, and once he'd heard Christian's story, he guaranteed him that he would write a letter to the king asking for a pardon, but that he couldn't promise it would be enough.

As for Alexandra, she had told Christian that it didn't matter to her, that she'd marry him whether he was a free man or not. Love had no boundaries, she had claimed, and she would prove it to the world if given half a chance. But Christian had insisted they wait until word came back from the king.

"You know who I really feel sorry for?" she asked as they walked arm in arm toward the house. "I feel sorry for Davis Pleasanton. He had no idea how bitter his son was or to what lengths he would go just to prove he was better than any of us. I think Wayne had it in mind to rule Australia one day."

"He probably did," Christian agreed. "But then, so did Garrett Ambrose. Greed has a way of clouding a man's vision."

"Christian," she said suddenly, stopping in the middle of the yard. "Do you think Sang Soo would want to come here to live? I know how much you—"

Christian shook his head. "I could ask him, but I doubt he'd accept. He's never lived anywhere but China. He'd be out of place."

"Then perhaps he'd come to visit," she suggested. "I'm sure he'd love to see how things turned out for you."

He smiled and kissed her temple. "And I'm sure he'd love you. I do."

"Only half as much as I love you," she declared, her eyes sparkling.

The moment was interrupted when Lynn Boone called out to them. "Someone's coming," he shouted, pointing to the road that wound its way toward the house and circled past the fenced-in plot of land where Wallis Pembrooke was buried.

There were two of them, and it took Christian only a second to realize that one of the riders was a young boy, the other a man. They were too far away yet for him to see their faces, but instinct told him who they were.

"Well, I'll be damned," he murmured.

"Do you know them?" Alexandra asked as he took her hand in his and led her toward their guests.

"The ragamuffin's name is T. J. Savage."

"From the prison ship?"

Christian smiled. "Yes. I didn't think I'd ever see him again."

"Who's that with him?"

"An old friend," Christian admitted. "A *good* friend for him to have traveled this far."

"Good afternoon, Mr. Page," Lewis Rhomberg joked as he reined his horse in close and dismounted. "Lovely day for a visit, wouldn't you say?"

"A damn lovely day," Christian returned, smiling broadly as he extended his hand and gripped Lewis's in a warm expression of brotherhood. "And what brings you here?"

Sucking in a deep breath, Lewis glanced up at the sky. "I'd heard Australia was a beautiful country, so I decided to see for myself." His gaze shifted to the woman at Christian's side. "*Very* beautiful. Good afternoon, Miss Pembrooke. I'm Lewis Rhomberg. I don't believe we've ever met, I'm sorry to say."

Alexandra smiled nervously in return. Lewis Rhomberg didn't appear to be upset with her for all she had put Christian through. But then, maybe he wasn't aware of the details.

"And this is T. J. Savage," he continued, turning with his hand held out toward the young man who hadn't bothered to dismount.

"Hello, T. J.," Alexandra said warmly. "Christian's told me all about you. He was hoping that someday the two of you would meet again."

The start of a smile flickered across the young boy's face and disappeared. "He was?" he asked, his voice full of doubt.

"Still afraid to trust, aren't you, T. J.?" Christian challenged as he moved to stand beside the boy's horse. "As I recall, I made you a promise. Well, I'm not one to go back on my word. It might have taken some time, but I would have come for you." He reached up and patted the youth's thigh. "I'm glad you couldn't wait."

Tears glistened in T. J.'s eyes and he blinked them away, too stubborn to allow himself the weakness. "I had to come, Mr. Page," he said, fumbling inside his shirt for the folded piece of parchment he carried there. "I had to give you this myself, so I'd be sure it didn't get lost." He handed it over.

"What is it?" Christian asked.

"It's from King George, himself," T. J. proudly proclaimed. "It's your pardon." He nodded at Lewis. "Mr. Rhomberg got it for you. You're free, Mr. Page. You can go home now."

Alexandra's heart skipped a beat. Until this very moment she hadn't realized just what Christian's freedom could mean. If he wanted, he could return to England now and no one could stop him . . . not even her.

"I'm already home, T. J.," he said, sending a smile Alexandra's way. "And if you want, you can make this your home too."

The boy's lower lip trembled. "You mean it?" he asked. "You want me to stay?"

"Of course I do," Christian assured him, glancing at Alexandra. "We both do." He turned back to the boy, expecting to have to wait for T. J.'s answer, when suddenly the youngster threw himself off the horse and into Christian's arms. "Does this mean you accept?" Christian teased, tousling the boy's dark hair.

"You're damn right," T. J. answered, beaming, then realizing how his language might have offended Miss Pembrooke, he looked up sheepishly and apologized.

"I've heard worse, T. J.," she said with a smile, then held out her hand. "Why don't you and I go find the cook. I would imagine you're hungry after your long ride."

"Yeah, I am, kinda," he answered, his cheeks a bright red.

"Good. Then let's go and get something to eat while these two get reacquainted. All right?"

"Sure," he agreed, allowing Alexandra to lay her arm across his shoulders.

"You'll be staying awhile too, won't you?" she asked Lewis.

"Until I wear out my welcome," he replied, grinning. Then, becoming serious, he added, "My sympathies, Miss Pembrooke, on the death of your father. He was a great man, and his presence will be missed."

She nodded her appreciation and started to turn away, when Lewis remembered the letter he had brought with him and stopped her departure by calling out her name.

"I nearly forgot. A friend of yours asked me to give this to you," he said, handing over the parchment he had taken from his pocket.

"A friend?" she asked before she had broken the seal.

"Yes. A Miss Aimee Welu. Rumors spread fast when the king's involved in pardoning a convicted man, and once she'd heard that that man was Christian Page, she paid me a visit, asking if I'd also deliver this to you." He smiled devilishly. "It seems she had this all figured out before any of the rest of us."

Alexandra smiled and hugged the unopened letter to her bosom. "Yes, she did, and she told me so the day of Christian's trial. I should have listened to her. Well," she sighed happily, "I guess what I have to tell her when I answer this won't come as much of a surprise, will it?"

"No, miss, it won't," Lewis said, his gaze dropping to the gentle sway of Alexandra's skirts as she and T. J. walked away. "You know, old friend," he said to his companion after he'd enjoyed the view for a moment, "it's not hard to understand how a man could fall in love with a beauty like that. What I don't understand is how she could fall in love with you."

Christian laughed. "Am I that unlovable?"

Lewis looked him up and down as if he might be trying to decide. "I guess not," he finally replied. "But you have to admit you are a little strange. And speaking of strange, would you mind filling me in? I had a nice long conversation with Governor Darling before we rode out here, so I know most of what happened. What I don't know is when you fell in love."

A soft smile curled Christian's mouth as he turned his head and watched Alexandra disappear into the house. He wouldn't have guessed it then, but now he knew that he had fallen in love with her the very first time he saw her. He also knew he would love her for the rest of his life.

HISTORICAL ROMANCE —

—send in the coupon below—

To get your FREE historical romance and start saving, fill out the coupon below and mail it today. As soon as we receive it we'll send you your FREE book along with your first month's selections.

Mail to:
True Value Home Subscription Services, Inc.
10489-B

P.O. Box 5235
120 Brighton Road
Clifton, New Jersey 07015-5235

YES! I want to start previewing the very best historical romances being published today. Send me my FREE book along with the first month's selections. I understand that I may look them over FREE for 10 days. If I'm not absolutely delighted I may return them and owe nothing. Otherwise I will pay the low price of just $3.50 each; a total of $14.00 (at least a $15.80 value) and save at least $1.80. Then each month I will receive four brand new novels to preview as soon as they are published for the same low price. I can always return a shipment and I may cancel this subscription at any time with no obligation to buy even a single book. In any event the FREE book is mine to keep regardless.

Name _____

Address _____ Apt. _____

City _____ State _____ Zip _____

Signature _____
                (if under 18 parent or guardian must sign)
Terms and prices subject to change.